D0054302

PAYBACK

PAYBACK

A NOVEL BY

Thomas Kelly

Alfred A. Knopf NEW YORK 1997

THIS IS A BORZOI BOOK
PUBLISHED BY ALFRED A. KNOPF, INC.

http://www.randomhouse.com/

Grateful acknowledgment is made to Farrar, Straus & Giroux, Inc., and Faber and Faber Limited for permission to reprint an excerpt from *The Cure at Troy* by Seamus Heaney, copyright © 1992 by Seamus Heaney. Rights outside the United States administered by Faber and Faber Limited, London. Reprinted by permission.

Library of Congress Cataloging-in-Publication Data
Kelly, Thomas, [date]
Payback : a novel / by Thomas Kelly. — 1st ed.
p. cm.
ISBN 0-679-45051-3
I. Title
PS3561.E39717P3 1997
813′.54—dc20 96-36674
CIP

Manufactured in the United States of America

First Edition

This book is dedicated to the memory of Thomas G. Kelly,
1929–1982

and the twenty-three men who have died
building New York City Water Tunnel Number Three

Human beings suffer,
They torture one another,
They get hurt and get hard.
No poem or play or song
Can fully right a wrong
Inflicted and endured.

—SEAMUS HEANEY

PAYBACK

No one could remember a time when so many cranes worked the New York City skyline. Wherever you looked, the huge metal frames swung over the city like prehistoric beasts, hoisting steel and wood, concrete and brick. It seemed only a matter of days before buildings rose beneath them to cast new shadows over chaotic streets. The bellow and clank of construction was everywhere. New York City was once again a boom town.

Paddy Adare loved the cranes in his neighborhood. He sat in a dusty gin mill on Ninth Avenue and watched as one of them loomed over the row of tenements across the street, lifted a bundle of heavy rebar, then lowered it out of sight. The building craze had finally reached Hell's Kitchen, and the wrecking ball was swinging with a vengeance. Hundred-year-old walk-ups were being razed to make way for yuppie palaces. Speculators who had waited decades for this occurrence were being rewarded for their patience with gold.

For Paddy Adare and his boss, Jack Tierney, the construction boom also brought rewards. Ten years before, when Paddy gave up boxing and went to work for him, Jack Tierney's empire consisted of a decent neighborhood gambling operation and nickel-and-dime shakedowns of local merchants and drug dealers. Now, through creative use of threat and force, they ran the lucrative construction rackets on the West Side.

Paddy turned on his barstool and closed the *Daily News* that lay on the bar in front of him. He looked at his reflection in the smoky mirror and saw the sharpness coming back to his face. He'd lost ten pounds since Easter. Ten pounds, and it was only May. With another ten shed, he'd be back down to his fighting weight.

He thought about Easter at Rosa's father's apartment. How Rosa had kidded him about the weight as he was stuffing his face and how it had bothered him. Bothered him because she was probably the only person who could get to him on any level, and bothered him because he realized he was getting soft. That was not something he could afford in his business. He had put his third helping of turkey and mashed potatoes in the trash and that night went to the gym, pounding the heavy bag until his arms felt like they were filled with wet sand. He'd been at it religiously ever since, even laying off the fried food and the alcohol. He felt good, strong, and alert.

The phone rang behind the bar. Paddy looked down past the half-dozen old juiceheads, perched silently over cheap booze, to the bartender, who moved quickly to turn down the television. Paddy picked up the phone and listened as a voice said simply, "He's alone."

Paddy hung up and turned to Mickey Lawless, who was watching from the pinball machine. "Let's do it."

Two blocks away, they walked onto a construction site that was enclosed by a chain-link fence backed by plywood so passersby couldn't stop and gawk. Signs by the gate told them they needed hard hats and warned that blasting was going on. The air was heavy with the smell of wet earth. The site was still just a hole in the ground, the workers getting ready to pour the foundation. Three wagon-wheel rock drills stood idle on one side of the lot, and the handful of hard hats who had remained on-site for lunch sat on upturned buckets, eating sandwiches with dirty hands.

Paddy was careful not to make eye contact with the man who had made the phone call. Walking toward the superintendent's trailer, he felt his heart pick up a few beats, that jolt he always got going on a job, his senses heightening. He expected this to be routine stuff, but it was important to be aware, prepared for anything.

They walked around a brand-new Jeep Cherokee with Jersey plates and climbed the trailer's three wooden steps. Mickey Lawless bent down and worked the lock quickly with a slim metal bar, brushing his blond hair from his eyes. The door clicked open, and Mickey turned to Paddy, smiling. "Age before beauty."

Paddy entered the trailer, turning left. He headed for a partially open door at the end of the hallway. A voice called from behind the door. "Mary Ellen, that you?"

5

Paddy pushed the door with his right hand. It opened away from him. A man sat with a phone pressed to his ear, looking up at Paddy, who said, "It ain't Mary Ellen."

The man looked surprised, then annoyed. He said, "Lemme get back to you," and hung up the phone. Standing, he came around the desk toward Paddy. He was tall and thick, his face weathered from dozens of construction sites. His hair seemed newly white, like virgin snow. He wore gray slacks that touched the tops of black, spit-shined work boots, and a navy windbreaker over a white shirt and blue tie.

In a voice accustomed to ordering men around, he said, "I told you the last time, I got no business with you." He punctuated his sentence with a thick forefinger in Paddy's chest.

Paddy nodded and held up his right hand, palm toward the contractor, as if to say, No problem, then came around hard with the left hook, catching the guy with a nice kidney shot, driving through four inches of love handle to land it. The punch brought the contractor to his knees, his face going green and scared.

Paddy leaned over him. "I got your fuckin' attention?"

The guy looked up, pain showing like years on his face.

"This is the second time I come talk to you. That's all I was here for. But you gotta play the tough guy." Paddy shook his head, then bent down and helped the guy up. He held him and pulled a chair over with his foot and sat the man down gently. The contractor seemed grateful. It no longer amazed Paddy how quickly most of them came around once you gave them a taste of hurt.

Paddy ran a hand through his thick dark hair. He spotted a small refrigerator and pulled the door open and grabbed a soda. He called to Mickey, who was up front, watching the door. "Hey, you want a soda?" Letting the guy know they were not alone. Paddy opened the door and tossed a can to Mickey. He turned back to the contractor, took a long drink of Coke, then said, "Last time I was trying to tell you, You crossed that river, it's a whole new world. Like maybe that's America over there, but this here is the West Side. Things happen different here. Now, some might say better, some say worse. I just say different. You understand?"

Paddy paused and looked around the office. The place was clean and well organized. Besides the desk, there was a long wood cabinet running under the windows that looked out over the site. On top of the cabinet was a horizontal row of codebooks and construction-equipment catalogs in order of size. A computer glowed with blue light on a table adjacent to the desk. The wall by the door was lined with tall metal filing cabinets. The room was spare and efficient. The guy looked like he belonged there.

"I know you're thinking fuck this guy; I can tell. Because it's obvious you're someone that works hard for what he's got. We respect that." Paddy throwing in the ominous "we," as if it was some higher power, impossible for any individual to fight against.

"I told you we don't expect things to be a one-way street here. It's more like you help us, we help you. A mutual thing. We provide each other with opportunities. You see what I'm saying?"

The guy nodded, his color coming back to where it should be.

"This is a tough business we're in. You got your Italians, we'll keep them off your back. They can be very greedy people. The unions, same thing, awfully hard on a businessman at times. But it ain't just that—that shit's old hat. The times are changing. You ever get a visit from one of these coalitions? A couple hundred fuckin' water buffaloes show up, half of them with picket signs, the other half with machine guns, screaming about how you the blue-eyed devil, how you violatin' their civil rights?" Paddy softened his tone. "Yeah, what you got here in the 1980s in the Big Apple is choices. And I'm just trying to tell you we're the best choice you got."

The man sat silently. Paddy looked in his eyes and could see behind the pain that there was still fight left. He walked over to the man's desk and picked up the picture of his wife and daughter. They looked so clean and blond, like they were glowing with some holy golden light. Paddy walked around and looked at the picture while he spoke in a neutral tone, using the information Charles Eliot had given him.

"You live in Upper Saddle River, Maple Lane. Two, three blocks from Nixon. Nice place. I been there once—nice lawns, I remember. You married into the company, little bit of luck there, eh? You run another couple of these jobs right, you're gonna end up with the company, is what they tell me. The old man's getting ready to head south, enjoy his last coupla years. They also tell me you were a good carpenter in your day, worked on the World Trade Center job before you became a boss."

Paddy got down on his haunches in front of the guy and dropped the picture on his lap, faceup. The man looked down at it, then back up at Paddy, a certain resolve coming into his eyes. "The daughter goes to Columbia—that's really a great place, Ray." Using his name for the first time. "Sophomore. Likes to toss back a few with the football players at Gannons'."

Paddy stood up. He really did not like bringing a guy's family into it, but that usually worked best. Gave people, might be hard guys, a different perspective. His voice was almost sad. "Ray, unless you come around, decide you're gonna do business with us, this is the last time you're gonna see me. I'm the nice guy of the bunch. Trust me on this. My boss has guys working for him, I mean guys I grew up with, they scare the fuck outta me, like they're right out of some Hollywood horror movie. Eat your insides outta you, keep you awake the whole time they're working on you. Only, these guys are real, Ray. It's up to you."

Paddy turned and walked toward the door. He felt a movement behind him, a rush of air, and swung his body to the right, flattening himself against the wall of the narrow hallway. He heard a grunt and saw a flash of steel. Grabbing the lunging contractor by the hair and the back of his shirt and using his momentum against him, Paddy slammed him facefirst into the metal door. The contractor dropped the knife, and his knees buckled. Paddy spun and propelled his attacker, like a bouncer evicting a drunk, down the hallway into the office. He rammed his face into the computer screen. There was a loud pop and the shattering of glass. Paddy threw him to the ground. Slivers of glass protruded from the contractor's face. Rivulets of blood began to run off him and pool on the floor.

Paddy, driven by rage and adrenaline, lifted a half-empty five-gallon bottle from the water cooler and smashed it on the man's rib cage. He kicked him once, a deft, savage blow to the testicles. Satisfied, he turned to leave. His breath was short, and he began to sweat.

Mickey stood grimacing. "Ouch. He's gonna feel like crap, he wakes up."

"Tough shit. Wants to be a fucking hero. Let's get out of here."

Paddy pushed past Mickey. He was pissed off for underestimating the contractor. It was sloppy, and sloppy led to problems. The contractor would do them no good in the hospital. He hoped he hadn't hit him too hard. As he reached for the door, Paddy noticed wetness on his side. He reached under his shirt and pulled his fingers out. Blood. The guy had grazed him. He tucked the shirt in and opened the door.

Paddy and Mickey walked past the workers filing onto the site after lunch. On the way back to the bar, Paddy stopped at a pay phone, dropped in a quarter, and dialed a number in Brownsville, Brooklyn. It was time to rain a little hell on the job site.

"New City Empowerment." The voice was hard, young, and black.

"Gimme the King," Paddy said.

After a pause, a sleepy voice came on the line. "Yeah."

Paddy envisioned the cloud of reefer following Julius King, president of New City Empowerment, to the phone. Paddy figured the guy had been stoned ever since they met in the joint, but it did not seem to slow King down one bit. He had seen what happened to the few people who thought old King Julie was too stoned to react.

"King, I just seen something that really and truly is a pity. There's this construction site over on Ninth Avenue, right in my own neighborhood. I counted forty, fifty men on the job, there was one black man, another guy Puerto Rican, maybe Italian. In this day and age."

"Sounds like a situation in need of rectifying." King Julie was perking up, like he always did when cash was about to flow his way.

"I think some pressure should be brought to bear. I mean, it's goddamn 1987, for chrissake."

"What type of pressure you suggest?"

Paddy did some quick calculations in his head. The King would charge them fifty bucks a day per man, plus you had to double it when you factored in the King's cut. And that was violence-free. Mayhem was extra.

"Fifty guys, no muscle, just picket signs and noise, coupla them bullhorns. Two days should do it." Paddy gave him the job site and hung up, feeling he had just invested ten grand very wisely.

Billy Adare, son and grandson of sandhogs, was dying to go to work. He sat on the shapers' bench in the hoghouse and watched as a steady stream of men came in, changed into work gear, and headed for a shift in the tunnel. While he waited, three other shapers—men not on steady gangs—had been told to change their clothes for a night of work. Billy glanced at the clock: 10:45 P.M. He still had time.

The shapers' bench was just inside the door to the hoghouse—a room filled with rows of dented metal lockers and wooden benches. Cheap cigar smoke floated up and hung around the bare bulbs that lit the room. The smell of old sweat stung his nose. He sat alongside a half-dozen other shapers. They ranged in age from late teens to a man who appeared to be well into his sixties, and all did their best to project earnestness and the ability to toil mightily. They were there to sell muscle for a day's pay. They tried to look hungry.

The man to Billy's right, his long legs stretched out before him, bragged about his exploits in the construction industry. His shoulders and neck had the thickness of a professional wrestler's. His brow and knuckles were scarred. According to his oral résumé, he'd been there for the building of the Alaska pipeline, some dam in a western desert, the Javits Center, skyscrapers too numerous to list. Billy ignored him, focusing all his attention on the shifters, or foremen. He made eye contact with each one as he passed the bench. *Pick me.*

The door opened, and he turned to see Frankie Ryan, his friend since kindergarten, pointing him out to one of the foremen, Mule McIntyre. The Mule, a large man with the grayed skin and broken features of a lifelong miner, walked over to Billy and said, "Change your clothes," in a thick brogue.

Billy grabbed his bag and ran to the supply shed for rubber boots, rain gear, hard hat, flashlight, and earplugs. The equipment man, cigarette dangling from his mouth, put his paperback down and raised his eyebrows. "Adare's kid?" Billy nodded, and the man handed him what he needed. Back in the hoghouse, Billy found an empty locker, changed quickly, and headed for the elevator shaft.

He waited for the cage with the handful of graveyard-shift workers who had not already gone down. The night air was soft and held the promise of summer. A metal gate stood in front of the shaft, and a steel support frame rose forty feet above the surface. At the top of the frame was a large wheel for the elevator cable which raised and lowered the platform that brought men and materials into and out of the hole.

Standing by the shaft, Billy felt the damp, familiar air of the tunnel. He read the sign, rusted with age, that hung by the gate. "MAY GOD BE WITH ALL YE WHO ENTER HERE, THAT THE EARTH SHALL RETURN YE SAFELY. Saint Barbara, Patron Saint of Miners." It had been burned into the metal with an acetylene torch.

He watched as the wheel, silhouetted against the night sky, started to turn. The platform rose, picking up speed, and the wheel gave out a loud, metallic whine. When the platform was level with the surface, the bellman pulled the gate open for the forty men who were crowded onto the cage. The men, filthy from the evening's work, walked off, joking with the night shift. Many coughed up bad air. Billy acknowledged the men he knew, laughing with them, feeling the warmth of old friends.

Billy and the others stepped onto the cage, and the bellman shut them in and rang the bell, three short for men on board and two long for down. Billy watched the walls of the shaft go by as they picked up speed. An uneasiness settled over him. His heart gained a few beats as they plunged away from the night. It was something he often felt, dropping into the earth knowing his father had once made the same trip and had never seen the sky again. He went to work one night and was buried beneath tons of bedrock, his body crushed beyond recognition. Billy always thought the little slap of fear was his father's way of urging him to get out of the business, get an education. He knew the feeling would pass once he reached bottom and started work.

His father had been the first of twenty-three men killed building Water Tunnel Three, a body count that made it the most dangerous job in America. Billy was three at the time. His father came to him as a vague recollection, a warm presence. The rest was filled out by pictures and stories told by friends and family, coworkers. The old-timers, when they saw Billy, would pull back slightly, as if startled by a ghost. Billy's face, turning from boy to man, had become his father's. Even he was made uncomfortable by the resemblance he saw in family pictures and the yellowed newspaper accounts of the accident twenty years before.

The shaft darkened as they descended, leaving the surface lights behind. The air grew damp and flat and tasted like chalk. As the cage neared the tunnel, lights from beneath them reached up and Billy could see the outline of the other men. The cage reached the bottom of the shaft and stopped. Billy stood for a minute and looked out at the tunnel blasted through the ancient bedrock of Manhattan. He was eight hundred feet beneath the city.

Arc lamps near the shaft cast dead white light. Strings of incandescent bulbs lined both sides of the tunnel, fading into the mist. The wet air was a garrote of diesel fumes and rock dust. The tunnel bellowed with sound. Water pumps sucked and spat. Diesel motors, some new and finely tuned, others old and struggling, rumbled and coughed. High-voltage lines buzzed, and air compressors hissed. Hoses and wires and pipes ran through the tunnel, a tangle of conveyances. Chaos, noise like the scream of a construction site jammed into a subway station. Billy winced and paused to put his earplugs in.

He noticed the metal stretchers, complete with body bags, propped up against the tunnel wall next to the bell shack. They perched like vultures waiting for carrion. A first-aid kit emblazoned with a red cross hung on a nail. Someone had painted SAFETY FIRST on the wall around it.

A small train, two passenger cars and a locomotive, was filled with men and parked fifty feet from the cage. The cars, metal boxes with open sides, looked like run-down trolley cars. Billy made his way to the train, sloshing through the ankle-deep muck on the tunnel floor. Like bad air, it was a constant in the tunnel. He pulled himself onto one of the cars, each of which held about twenty men. Sandhogs sat or stood, joking with each other, enjoying the last few minutes before work. Billy found Frankie and stood next to him.

He turned back to the shaft, and there, still on the cage, stood the man who had bragged about his wealth of experience, his ruggedness. The man gawked in stunned disbelief at the scene before him. He was now the blowhard silenced. The bellman gestured for him to step off the cage, to get to work. But the shaper merely pointed up, unspeaking, toward the city air and release. He looked like a man trapped at the bottom of a dead lake.

Frankie said, "Another one bites the dust." The train pulled away, heading deeper into the earth. Frankie smiled. "Billy, man, is it good to be back or what?"

"Yeah." Billy turned away from the embarrassing sight of the man on the cage. "I might be crazy, but it is."

"Good. We'll see how much that pansy-ass college life took outta you—get you on a rock drill."

Billy laughed. Back in the Bronx. Back to work as a sandhog. He, too, wondered how much college had taken out of him. That very day, he had finished his B.A. He dropped his last paper in a professor's mailbox and rode the train home from upstate. He was headed for law school in the fall. He'd been accepted by several good schools and waitlisted at Columbia, his first choice. The plan was simple. Spend one more summer working in the tunnel, and at the end come up with enough money to get through the first year of law school. After that he would spend his school vacations in air-conditioned offices, a long way from the toil and noise of mining.

Billy and Frankie rode on in silence. Billy watched the scarred and beaten gray rock of the tunnel walls. He listened to the chatter around him. He sometimes wondered how the old-timers, men who had been at it since before he was born, could bring themselves to work each day. It was the kind of labor that wore a man down, made him old before his time. Billy was happy that this was his last stint in the tunnels.

They passed one mile into the earth, then two miles, and three. Overhead, life went on, oblivious to their endeavors eighty stories beneath the streets and living rooms of the city. Four miles in, the train stopped. Billy and the men stepped off. The man car started back toward the shaft. As they prepared for work, the sound of the train receded and the gang was alone, as remote as anyone would ever be in New York City.

The Mule barked instructions. Billy and the gang climbed up on the jumbo drilling platform, with its three levels, three drills to a level. The drills were run by compressed air, weighed over a hundred pounds each. Billy wrestled his drill into position. By the time he was set up, he was slathered in grease. The light was dim, the air worse than usual. Billy felt like he was breathing through wet wool. He stood a hair under six feet tall, and his hard hat scraped the raw rock ceiling above his head. He hunched slightly and, with Frankie holding his drill bit to the rock face, let rip. The other sandhogs started drilling, taking up where the swing shift had left off. The howl engulfed them.

Billy worked, feeling the burn in his back and arms, down his legs. He knew he'd be sore for a week, but it didn't matter. He had to pull his weight. The other men would rain abuse on him if they thought he couldn't handle the night's work. Unwilling to let that happen, he drilled with abandon. The drill spit water and rock chips into his face; his hands began to go numb. He used his weight to steady the drill. The vibrations rattled through every bone in his body. Between holes, he bent to touch his toes, trying to keep his back loose. The tunnel was dim and dreary, the only color evident the dirty yellow rain slickers and green and blue hard hats the men wore. All else was drabness.

They drilled for four hours, stopping only for a ten-minute coffee break. Billy was finishing a hole when Frankie tapped him on the shoulder. Lunchtime. Billy straightened up, and all the muscles in his back came together in a ball of fire. He climbed carefully off the jumbo. Each rung of the ladder was coated with grease.

He took out his sandwich and sat on a makeshift bench between Frankie and Lenny Coyle. Ground-table water dripped down on them. Lenny took off his hard hat. His hair was the color of old silver. A man of average height and build, Lenny had a pleasant face, the skin smooth from decades underground. Only his nose, scarred and bent, distinguished him from a middle-aged accountant.

"So you're done?" Lenny asked.

"Yeah. You believe it?"

"I knew you would make it. Congratulations, kid." Lenny extended his hand, and Billy shook it.

Billy thought back to when he had just started in the tunnels, right out of high school. Although he had some desire to go to college, he had no direction. He'd never known anyone who went beyond high school. He figured he'd work a bit and see what happened. The first time they met, Lenny asked him how old he was. When Billy replied, "Eighteen," Lenny looked at him thoughtfully and said, "Eighteen. You got the world by the balls, kid. Get an education—it's the one thing they can't take away from you."

That had stuck with Billy. After a year, he took Lenny's advice. He enrolled at Lehman College, where he maintained an A– average for a year, going to class by day and work by night. He then transferred upstate to a prestigious liberal arts school. It was like going to another planet. But he came home to work when he could. Summer vacations, holidays. He did not have the luxury of family money.

Lenny's constant encouragement had been invaluable. And now, finished with the first part of his education, this flight from a life of toil, Billy felt indebted to him.

Frankie nudged him and pointed to Eamon Cudahy, who sat across from them. He was eating an onion as if it were an apple. He washed each bite down with a sip of warm Budweiser.

"Regular gourmet dining experience, eh, Eamon? This is America—you ain't gotta eat like a peasant no more."

Eamon shrugged and took another bite. He was unflappable and possessed a certain renown among sandhogs. On his first night in the hole, he had tumbled down a shaft and was buried alive in muck. They dug him out by hand over an arduous three hours. Another man was dead above him. Somehow Eamon survived. He sat before Billy this night munching his onion, a fluke incarnate.

Frankie manhandled a French bread laden with cold cuts. It was the size of a football. Billy finished his ham sandwich. He felt bone tired. Graveyards took some getting used to. He looked at his hands. They were red and swollen from running the drill.

Lenny stood.

"You got great timing, kid."

"What's up?"

"We been without a contract for four months. This contractor, took over from his dead uncle, is a real hard-on. Things could get interesting around here."

Lenny walked over to the tunnel wall and pissed with his back to the gang. Frankie dropped his dessert, a candy bar, into a puddle of muck.

"Motherf . . ." He picked it up and wiped it as clean as he could, then ate it in two large bites.

"Billy, I been busy when you was away at college. I been banging half the broads in the neighborhood and beyond. Good thing you're back, though. I need some help."

"Love to help, Francis."

"I was thinking the other day—you figure every woman on the planet has a vagina, right?"

"Yeah, most, I hope."

"How many people are there, a billion?"

"More like five billion."

"Five? No shit? Wow, I'm glad we sent you to college. That's probably about two and a half billion twats on the planet. Fuckin' amazing."

Billy laughed as the Mule walked up.

He nodded his large head at his men. "Social hour's over."

Back to the hump.

A half hour later, the lights went out. There was a stunned silence to accompany the darkness, for it was a blackness known only to the dead. Billy moved a hand in front of his face. Nothing but a breeze crawling across his skin.

"Jesus, it's blacker than the devil's own arsehole," Eamon said.

There was nervous mumbling and chuckling. Billy left his drill half buried in rock. He squatted, then sat on the metal grating of the jumbo. He was unsure of his ability to stand upright, to keep his balance without sight. He took his earplugs out, as if it might help him see. His other senses kicked into overdrive. The air had a taste and a sound to it, a weight. It was like swimming in black ink. He imagined early humans confronted with their first lunar eclipse and doubted that even in their terror they knew darkness this complete.

The men fumbled for flashlights. Billy cursed; he had left his down below by his jacket. Beams of light sliced through the blackout. The men shone the lights upward, projecting their own faces. Their heads seemed to float, severed, ghostly.

"For fuck sake," the Mule cursed, more upset about being prevented from working than by the darkness itself. Billy sat back, now secretly relieved by the unscheduled break. He massaged the knot in his lower back. Frankie lit a cigarette beside him. The coal burned like a laser, the smoke hanging in the thick air.

"What's up with this shit?" Frankie said.

"I don't know, but it don't get any darker than this."

"You ain't lying. Reminds me of being knocked the fuck out. Got a flashlight?"

"No. Down there."

"Me either. Guess we just wait."

They sat in the darkness, waiting for the lights or for the man car to come in and evacuate them. Billy wondered if maybe he should work somewhere else for the summer. He fought off a premonition. This was the one place he knew where he could make the kind of money he needed for school. Besides, he wanted to be here, wanted to be back where he started from. Wanted to prove to himself something he was not yet quite sure of.

After ten minutes, the lights came back on. The men stood like guests caught at a wedding party by an intrusive flash camera, blinking, disoriented, their faces slack and stupid while their pupils constricted violently. The mule wasted no time. "Let's hit it, lads."

They turned back to their drills and finished the holes. They blew the holes clean with compressed air. The powder monkey brought in cases of Tovex explosive, and the gang loaded the holes for the shot, connecting the sticks with blasting wire. Billy felt awkward. The other men moved with a sureness the time in school had robbed from him.

When the shot was ready, they pulled back three hundred feet from the tunnel face, trailing the blasting wire behind them.

Lenny turned to Billy. "Here, kid. Welcome home." He handed Billy the detonator. With the other gang members watching, Billy yelled, "Fire in the hole!" and slapped down on the cap. A chemical charge ran down the line, detonating the blast. The tunnel shook with the explosion, the dozens of caps going off in timed sequence, building to a crescendo. It sounded as if all the thunder they had ever heard was trapped down there with them. The air was sucked past them by the concussion. Billy stood and felt the power of the blast roll over him. It was good to be home.

Joe Harkness stood before the mirror in his office, dressed in a black tuxedo with a maroon cummerbund and matching ascot. He practiced the speech he would be giving later that evening, after accepting the Contractor of the Year award. He thrust out his chin and held his shoulders back, turning his head to catch the best light. His voice was heavy with the echo of the Virginia hill country.

"I'd like to thank you collection of dumbshits for finally coming to your senses and putting this plaque where it belongs, in my hands." He chuckled at himself in the mirror.

Contractor of the Year. It was an award his uncle and his jewboy partner had never won, with their misty-eyed concern for the workers. All that ever got them was raised eyebrows. Maybe it went over big at society cocktail parties with the liberals, but it didn't mean a damn thing to a real businessman.

Joe Harkness brushed lint from his sleeve. He knew he had come a long way. He was only forty-eight years old, and he had total control of an international construction conglomerate. Men in his employ were at work in twelve states and on three continents. On his orders, rain forests were being slashed and burned, tenements razed, swamps drained, mountains blasted to gravel, rivers diverted. All the destruction that was necessary before great works could begin. The tearing down led to progress—the inevitable lurching forward of mankind. Joe Harkness considered himself an agent of change, a captain of industry. His works would endure.

17

While tunnels were Harkness and Company's bread and butter, the corporation was also heavily involved in dams, highways, and airports, and had recently moved into high-rises and shopping malls. If it was big and turned a profit, they'd build it. But the third water tunnel was the company's prize project. The largest public works project in American history, it was a lifeline for the city. A work of epic scale and import. When finished, it would stretch for sixty miles and run as deep as eleven hundred feet through the hardest bedrock in the world. It would deliver two billion gallons of pristine mountain water a day to a metropolis surrounded by salt water. Water Tunnel Three was what had prompted Harkness's move to New York after his uncle's death.

He sat behind his large mahogany desk and poured himself a glass of bourbon. The office was richly paneled and carpeted. A series of paintings depicting Confederate victories in the Civil War hung on three walls. Off to the side was a couch, where he often took power naps. The table in front of it held a chess set, its pieces fashioned as Civil War combatants.

He pressed the intercom.

"Joanne, darlin', a Charles Eliot will be up shortly. Be a good gal and give me a holluh the minute he shows."

He walked over and hefted his putter. Dropping a golf ball, he shepherded it to the end of the putting green. He'd be flying to Pebble Beach for the weekend. A little practice never hurt.

Harkness's track record was remarkable when it came to breaking unions and putting up jobs without them. But of course that had been in places like Brazil and South Carolina, where popular support for unions was not like it was in the Northeast. New York City was the big test. You got something accomplished there, the others would be easy.

He thought about the little problem he was having. On a major construction site aboveground, you could have a dozen trades and twice that many locals. A smart manager could cut a lot of corners just by pitting the unions against each other. Divide and conquer. Get them fighting over jurisdiction. But the problem with the sandhogs was that they were the only union underground, with the exception of a few operating engineers. They were more like a tribe than a damn union. There might be a lot of casual divisions based on ethnicity, but the sandhogs tended to stick together when the situation called for it.

He sank a twelve-foot putt, then turned to look out his windows to the city skyline. He couldn't think of anything in life he hated more than New York City. But he knew it had one bright side, and that was its piles of money. The family business had made millions off public projects, and it would continue to do so as long as he could help it. Now that his weak-assed uncle was dead and buried, he planned to turn things around, cut some costs, up his profit level considerably, and put together his plan of wresting control of tunnel construction from the union. For that he'd deal with New York. Besides, he returned to his family in Virginia almost every weekend, and his house in Ossining was an easy escape whenever he required one.

Harkness was anxious to see Charles Eliot. He was a man who knew people. A man who could arrange things. A broker for illicit and unseemly business. A mostly legitimate accountant who simply brought people together, allowed things to transpire. A black market entrepreneur of sorts.

The intercom buzzed.

"Yes?"

"Mr. Eliot to see you, Mr. Harkness."

"Fantastic. Please send him in, and that will be all for tonight, Joanne. Reroute my calls."

Harkness stood at the window, his back to the door, until he heard it close behind Eliot, then he turned and strode across the thick carpet with his hand outstretched.

"Charles. Damn, a pleasure, a real pleasure. It's been far too long."

They met in the middle of the office and shook hands vigorously. Harkness motioned to a high-backed chair, then sat at his desk.

Eliot was dressed in a basic-black tuxedo. He had a sharp, pleasant face. His skin was burnished brown, setting off blond hair and blue eyes. Appearing to be a man who enjoyed much leisure time, he evoked five-star resorts and crisply played tennis games. He looked quite at ease in evening wear. Harkness thought his hair longish for his age.

Harkness touched his red beard, then brushed his padded right shoulder. He figured he would get right to the point.

"I'm damn glad you could stop by on such short notice. We both know why you're here, so let's cut to the chase. We'll start with a fifty-thousand-dollar retainer. Things go as planned, there will be a quarter-million dollars waiting for you. I like to reward excellence."

Eliot shrugged. "Things go as planned . . . That's a little vague for my taste."

Harkness looked at him closely. He stood up and walked toward the windows. "Charles. It looks like some trouble with the union is imminent. They have been working without a contract for four months now. Some of these people, they think maybe they have some cause, something for them to be excited about. Maybe they're confused about the issues. I—and you, I might venture to guess—we're not deluded by such silliness. There is a job to do, and it must get done. I also believe that since we have the expertise and are taking the risk, putting up the capital"—Harkness laid a soft hand on his shirtfront—"we should set the agenda."

He poured himself another bourbon. "Care for a drink?"

"Scotch on the rocks."

Harkness prepared the drink, handed it to Eliot.

"I have been working on this thing for a long time. In the last year I have placed men on crews. I even added a couple of gangs. My men are involved on all levels. I have a judge who will issue an injunction ten minutes after they walk off the job. I'm prepared to bus men in to work this tunnel." Harkness paused to let Eliot speak.

"I know you know that you're not the first person to attempt this. Pressuring the sandhogs." Eliot sipped his drink. He looked at Harkness intently. "I've heard stories. Accounts of swift and effective resistance."

"I know the history," Harkness said, in a manner to demonstrate he was obviously on top of the situation. He held a hand up in front of himself. "But you understand, the climate is different today. The traffic controllers' deal with Ron Reagan started it. I think the time is right. And I am a different man. The others who tried before—maybe they lacked the will to follow through. Anyway, I will handle that end. I need you to put me in touch with the right people. Your Mediterranean friends."

"You forward the retainer, I'll know you're serious," Eliot said. He stood up and shook Harkness's hand.

Harkness watched him go. Yes, he would attack the union from the outside and from the inside. And when it was over, Joe Harkness would be in command. He went back to the mirror.

"I'd just like to thank the association. I realize many of you deserve this award . . ."

Vito Romero and his boss, John Tuzio, sat in the Citizens Social Club in Bensonhurst, Brooklyn. Although the club was empty, they leaned close and spoke under the blare of the television. John Tuzio always played the television and played it loud. He was cautious to the point of paranoia, often going to extremes to avoid the scrutiny of law enforcement. He never spoke on the telephone. He avoided public places, fancy clothes, cars, and women other than his wife. He had not signed his name in thirty years. And although his crew controlled most of the construction rackets in Manhattan, he rarely visited that island.

Tuzio was sixty-six years old and chubby and he had the look of a man harboring grudges both ancient and incomprehensible. He was driven by the basest of motives—profit—despite his far from lavish lifestyle. Vito looked around the social club. With its cheap paneling and harsh lighting, its accumulation of dust, the cigarette butts ground into its worn linoleum floors, it bordered on bus-station seamy. It occurred to Vito Romero that Tuzio garnered riches not to afford himself a decorous life, but simply to deprive others of the opportunity. In his twenty-plus-year association with the man, Vito had never once seen him smile.

Tuzio was widely feared. He possessed a psychotic streak, which he struggled to control. The slightest provocation, often imaginary, could send him into a murderous rage. He had once choked the life out of an underling who he thought had laughed at him. The guy had been clear across the room, merely reacting to a funny story.

Vito was only half listening as John Tuzio instructed him regarding his meeting with Charles Eliot. His attention was equally focused on the television behind Tuzio. Oprah Winfrey, the on-again/off-again hippopotamus, was commiserating with some pimple-faced kid who could not understand why his parents didn't like the idea of his sleeping with boys. The kid was fifteen. Vito wished he could smack the kid himself.

Tuzio gestured with a thick hand. "So you see this guy Eliot. Says he's got something with—whaddaya call those guys, dig the holes, the subways? Groundhogs?"

"Sandhogs." Vito thought of his own child, his daughter, and shuddered. The kid was a problem. He could picture her up there, all palsy with that fat slob, letting the whole world know what a scumbag he was, crying on that big black shoulder. Or, worse, rubbing up against that pudgy Irishman Donahue. The guys would never let him live it down.

Tuzio shrugged. "Yeah, whatever—sandhogs. Says it might be nice. See what's in it for us."

"Yeah, John. I'm going to the city tomorrow, I'll see the guy."

Tuzio nodded, then turned his thick body to look back over his shoulder at the television. He watched Oprah and the pimple-face. He got the gist of the story and turned back to Vito. "You imagine? *Marrone.* Kid was mine, I'd leave him in a pool of blood."

Vito left the social club. Driving home to Long Island, he couldn't stop thinking about his daughter. Ever since he lost the wife to the Big C, it had been all downhill with his only child. She started with the nuns at Saint Mary's. Skipping school, fighting, pushing it to the point where they had to toss her out, which in some ways was okay. Got her out of class with Vinny No-Nose's kid. The little rat broad was constantly running home to Vinny, letting him know how fucked up Angela was. At least in public school she did not stand out so much.

Things really got bad when the story broke in *Newsday,* describing his rise in the business. The "quiet killer," the paper had called him. Written by some snot-nosed reporter, looking to make a name for himself. An Italian kid, no less. That crippled his relations with her. After that, anytime he tried to lean on her, reel her in a bit, she'd say it. "At least I'm not a murderer." Spitting it right through his heart.

Quiet killer. In a way it was almost funny. In all his years in the business, he had been involved in exactly one murder. Some punk had made the mistake of dating Tuzio's daughter. That was bad, but then the guy was stupid enough to slap the girl around, send her home to her chemically imbalanced father with a shiner right out of a heavyweight title fight. Vito went with Jimmy Baggio. Vito had simply driven up to the curb and watched as Jimmy got out and shot the guy three times in the face. Shot him dead, right in front of a bar on Queens Boulevard.

Later that night, Jimmy Baggio, the contents of a bottle of vodka clouding his judgment, drove into a light pole at eighty miles an hour. Vito was smart enough to take credit for the hit. He'd made his bones. Tuzio, grateful for the avenging of his daughter's honor, put Vito on the fast track. It quickly became evident that his talent lay in creating the flow of cash, not blood. His day-to-day existence was no more directly violent than that of the average life insurance agent. The inevitable aspect of their work—the slack-jawed corpses—was nearly as remote.

This was not something he could explain to his daughter. She was relentless, always going out of her way to spite him. It started with the earrings. First, two in each ear; then they seemed to multiply weekly, like they were contagious. He lost count at six per ear. Then the nose ring. Looking like something he used to whack off to in *National Geographic.* As bad as he wanted to smack her, slap her head so hard he'd knock the nose ring and the twelve or fifteen earrings right off her head, he just could not. That's when he wished he had had a son.

He pulled onto the Grand Central Parkway. The car radio played country music. The whiny cowboys gave him solace. Let him know he wasn't the only guy with troubles. He looked at the picture of his wife taped to his dashboard and shook his head. Poor woman, dead at forty-three. She must be turning in her grave over Angela. Vito sometimes felt the cancer and his kid's attitude were payback for the life he led. Angie, his wife, had begged him to get out. She never understood. He had had plans. He had been the only kid from the block to go beyond high school. He was a year into Brooklyn College when Angie got pregnant. He promptly dropped out, married her, and went to work on a concrete truck. When she lost the first baby, he thought about going back. But he was making money, and it seemed silly for a married man to be going to college.

A Buick in front of him braked hard. Vito swerved to the right. The near miss snapped him back into focus. He thought about what Tuzio had said. Sandhogs. A bunch of unruly Irish hard hats. He recalled a beef back in the fifties. A move was made to take some of the tunnel action from the Irishers. It did not go well, that much he knew for sure.

Vito knew Charles Eliot. The man had brought them many profitable ventures. He looked forward to seeing him, finding out what this tunnel business was all about.

Tuesday broke like a blue diamond over the city. Paddy Adare watched from his bedroom window as the first rays of sunlight from the east reflected from the Hudson River. He liked being up at this time, the quiet time in the neighborhood. The last of the late-night desperadoes had stumbled into hiding, and the working stiffs were just waking up. The only sounds were the rumbling of heavy trucks on their way downtown.

When he was fighting, this was when he did his roadwork. He'd get up, down a glass of OJ, and hit the streets. Some days he'd run down to the Battery just in time for the sun to come up and wash the Statue of Liberty in soft gold light. Other times he ran up Riverside Park to the bridge as the cars started coming over from Jersey. He always felt sharpest then, mentally and physically, before all the distractions of the day started piling up on him. He used to wish he could fight at sunrise.

He went over to the pull-up bar and started exercising. He let himself go all the way down, stretching his body, feeling the rip in his shoulders. He could smell Rosa on his skin. That soft, sweet smell. He did twenty-five pull-ups.

He showered before waking Rosa.

He dressed, went into the kitchen, and scrambled some eggs. He made toast, cut a melon in sections, then brought a tray in to Rosa.

He placed it on the nightstand and stroked the side of her face, brushing her hair back. She woke slowly. He envied the way she slept so soundly. His sleep often seemed just below the surface, like he was never fully at rest. He bent down and kissed her.

"Come on, I made breakfast for you," he said.

"I don't want any breakfast. I want you," she said.

This woman is going to kill me, he thought, then said, "Now come on, I don't usually do this."

She sat up and made a face. "You're right. What's the big occasion?"

He handed her the tray and went over to look out the window again. Watching as a tugboat pulled a barge up the river, he wondered where it was going. Albany probably.

"Paddy, this melon is great. Where'd you get it?"

"Down the Koreans."

He turned and sat on the windowsill, watching her eat. He liked how her dark hair fell over her breasts, the way the light played on her face. The morning light was no enemy to her. As he watched, he enjoyed the warmth he felt toward her. She was the one thing in life he felt comfortable about, his one refuge from all the craziness and shit he dealt with.

He remembered back to when she was working in the A & P. She was a kid really, nineteen. He was a fighter who had just missed the big time. His hand breaking worse in each fight, till he just couldn't do it anymore, retiring at 18–0. Two fights from a million-dollar payday, the old-timers said. Still, he was something of a neighborhood celebrity then. He'd go in there to shop, teasing her, flirting. She came around slowly, not like the other girls, who found him exciting and jumped into bed with him. He never thought it would amount to much. He had never let anyone close before her. It had been nine years. Christ. And now he felt like he somehow depended on her. That worried him.

He stood up and walked over to get his jacket.

"I gotta make the rounds."

"Come on, Paddy. It's my only day off." She put the tray on the night table and got up. Walking over to him, she put her arms around his neck.

"Pleassse." The fake pout, teasing him.

He buried his face in her hair, then pushed her away gently.

"I got work to do."

She stepped back and put her hand on her hip, showing off what he was passing up, rubbing it in. "Yeah, yeah. Big bad tough guy. See you later?"

"We'll get dinner, my treat."

"Wow. You're my hero."

He pushed her onto the bed again. "Don't start."

As he was leaving, she hit him in the back of the head with a pillow. Her laughter followed him out the door.

He drove over to Ninth Avenue and picked up Mickey Lawless, practically needing a blowtorch to the toes to get him out of bed. Mickey waited in the car when Paddy stopped at the half-dozen job sites to pick up packages. It was payday. They had anywhere from five to twenty no-shows on the sites. Cash from various other schemes, including gambling and loan-sharking, was brought to them at the Midnight Lounge. Jack liked to send someone to the sites on a regular basis, to reinforce the crew's presence. It was Paddy's week.

When they got back to the bar, Sully, the bartender, came over and took the packages from Paddy.

"They got one of those mutts robbed that payroll. Jack wants youse down at the warehouse."

Paddy drove to Thirty-eighth Street, knowing they were about to see something ugly. Jack Tierney needed to put his viciousness on display occasionally, keep the troops in line. Paddy looked at Mickey. "What's wrong with you?"

Mickey shook his head. "I ain't ready to see this kinda shit again, Paddy. I mean, I'm a thief. I ain't no fuckin' tough guy. I'm just not cut out for this shit. I'm more like a Gandhi kinda criminal." He shook his head again.

With his longish blond hair and big blue eyes, Mickey reminded Paddy of a kid on the way to the dentist. Though he was thirty-four, he could pass for someone barely out of his teens. He looked on the verge of tears.

"Gandhi, the Indian guy? From the movie?"

"Yeah, except I would never go around in a diaper. I mean, that's taking things a bit too far."

"Just don't stare at it. You know, look away, think about something else. Something makes you happy."

"It ain't so easy. I hope that psycho Butcher Boy ain't there."

"It's business, Mickey. Keep it in perspective."

Paddy turned up the radio and made a left onto Thirty-eighth. He, too, wished Butcher Boy, Jack's brother Terry, was not going to be there. But he knew that was too much to ask for.

Parking on a block lined with run-down warehouses, they got out and crossed the street, stepping over puddles of dirty water. A sour wind blew off the Hudson. Two homeless men pushed shopping carts filled with empty cans. The towers of midtown loomed in the near distance. Mickey followed Paddy down a rubble-strewn alley.

Paddy rapped lightly on an old steel door. It swung open, and Bobby Riordan stood there, grinning. He said, "Come on in," like he was welcoming them to a party. Stepping through the door, Paddy could taste the fear in the place.

Jack had worked up a sweat. His sleeves were rolled to his biceps, and his face was flushed. The carpenter who had robbed a payroll from one of the crew's job sites was tied to a chair. Paddy caught a glimpse of him in the bad light. His eyes were battered shut. What was left of his nose was two inches to the left of where it had started the day. His shirtfront was covered with blood. It looked like a bib.

Jack looked over his shoulder at them. "You believe this fuckin' douchebag?" He seemed to be grinning. The sheen of sweat made his face glow. Paddy thought he looked possessed. He knew to be quiet. When Jack got in a mood, it was like a bad storm. You just had to ride it out.

Jack turned his focus back to the carpenter and punched him in the face, snapping the guy's head back.

"You half-a-fag junkie fuck. What made you think you could rob my fuckin' payroll and get away with it?"

The dank room was empty except for the chair the carpenter was in. Paddy heard rats scurrying in the corners. Mickey stayed behind him, trying to shield himself from Jack's rage. The carpenter tried to speak. He spit blood and pieces of broken teeth. Paddy thought he heard him say please.

Paddy leaned toward Bobby Riordan. "He give up his partner yet?"

"Fuckin' A. The pussy gave him up before we even got here. Jack's making an example with him."

Paddy thought about some of the examples Jack had made. The dead ones were better off than the living. He had a vision of Bernie McSwiggan limping through the neighborhood. Bernie had been a tough, good-looking ironworker who had the ill fortune of running into Jack when Jack was in the mood to set an example. Jack had been partying with a guy from Belfast, who told Jack all about an IRA six-pack: a bullet to each knee, each elbow, and each ankle. Jack loved the idea of it. McSwiggan had the audacity to scream while being shot, so Jack pistol-whipped him into a coma. He was reduced to a crippled idiot, shuffling around the neighborhood sweeping out stores for nickels and dimes. But Jack never set an example without reason. McSwiggan had owed him nine hundred dollars.

Paddy watched Butcher Boy. He was rocking back and forth, from foot to foot. He looked like a steroid-crazed high-school linebacker, just dying to be sent into the game.

Jack stood up straight. He looked at Butcher Boy and nodded his head at the carpenter. Butcher Boy, his eyes bright and wild, grabbed the carpenter's hammer off his belt. Eagerly, he lifted the hammer high in the air. He looked to the other gang members, smiled, then brought it down hard, claw end into the carpenter's skull. The carpenter shook like an epileptic and shit himself. When the death rattle stopped, the room was silent. Then Mickey vomited, and Butcher Boy started to giggle. He looked at Mickey, then back to the carpenter, and said, "Live by the hammer—die by the hammer," and he burst into laughter.

Jack's breathing was coming back to normal. He turned to Butcher Boy. "Shut up. Tonight you drop him on that site. I want people to see him, they come to work. And find me his scumbag partner. . . . Paddy."

Paddy followed Jack out into the light of day. He was back, the job done. The storm passed.

"What a fuckin' day, huh?" Jack looked up at the clear sky and spread his arms. He skin was pale and flecked with blood. "How it go today?"

"Clockwork."

"Good."

"Blood." Paddy nodded at him.

"What?"

"You got blood on your face, the shirt."

Jack looked down at his shirt. He took out his handkerchief and wiped his face and shirt, looking at the blood. Paddy watched him stare at it, as if he was wondering how it got there.

Billy slept all day Saturday, and by the time he woke up, dusk was settling over the Bronx. He got out of bed and went into the living room. His grandfather, JP, sat in a worn cloth recliner, his feet up, listening to an Irish program on the radio.

"JP, you hungry? I'll fix something."

"Fine, Billy." JP stood up and went over to switch off the ancient radio. He turned on the television and reclaimed his seat.

The apartment was furnished much as it had been since Billy was a child. Besides JP's chair, there was a brown couch, threadbare in spots. On either side of it stood veneered end tables. Each table held a lamp and, although neither of them smoked, an ashtray from a long-ago visit to Atlantic City. A coffee table was covered with Irish and New York newspapers. The floors were faded hardwood. The walls were painted a faint green and except for a map of Ireland, a picture of JFK addressing an adoring throng in Dublin, and a heavy wooden crucifix, they were bare.

Billy wrapped two potatoes in foil and put them in the oven. He set two pots on the stove, emptied a can of corn into one and a can of beans into the other. He went across the street to the bodega and bought a couple of steaks. While waiting in line, he noticed that the bodega, once the center of Puerto Rican life in the neighborhood, had been acquired by Dominicans. There was a faded campaign poster for Juan Bosch, and flags of the Dominican Republic had replaced the Puerto Rican ones in the windows. A milestone had been reached, he sensed, one that was beyond him.

Back in the kitchen, he slapped the meat in the broiler. When everything was ready, he lightly fried two eggs for himself, then he filled two plates and carried them into the living room. He went back and grabbed some orange juice and milk. Dinner for JP, and breakfast for Billy.

Billy was still trying to adjust to the graveyards. He felt groggy. It was like having continuous jet lag. They ate off trays and watched the news, the routine they had followed in the years since Billy's grandmother had died.

There was a piece about the President that showed him walking toward a helicopter with his hand to his ear. He shook his head no and shrugged to indicate he was having a problem hearing.

"Your man's playing dumb again, Billy." JP indicated the screen with his steak knife and laughed.

"My man?" Billy took a mouthful of steak. "You know what gets me is how many guys in the local voted for the fool."

"Stabbing themselves in the back. Some people need to be told things they know are not true. It makes their lives a little easier."

The segment ended, and a commercial came on. Some people sang joyously about laundry, the most important thing in their lives. JP shook his head and killed the volume. "Sixty years, and I still have trouble believing what I see in this country. How's t'ings in the tunnel?"

"Good. Looks like I'll be on steady soon. Lenny's in the gang." Billy picked up the plates.

"Coyle's a good hand. Tell him hello for me." JP looked at Billy. He was about to say something else and stopped. He drank some milk. Billy stood waiting.

JP turned to the television. "Just keep your wits about you. I lost your father down there. I don't want to lose you."

"Yeah, Grandpa." Billy did not know what else to say. He thought maybe he should do more to assure him, but nothing came to mind except false bravado. That would be wasted on his grandfather.

JP nodded absently and stood up. "I'm going for my walk."

Billy watched him don his jacket and hat and leave, closing the door softly behind him.

Billy washed the dishes. He called Frankie and told him to meet him downstairs in the bar.

Pausing a minute outside the bar, Billy looked up the street. Identical five-story brick buildings lined both sides of the block, interspersed occasionally with wood-frame houses, most of which had fallen into disrepair. A few were burned out and boarded up. Graffiti spread like an infectious disease.

Billy ducked into the bar. The patrons, not one of whom was under fifty, turned in unison. They greeted him like a prodigal son returning.

"Well, if it ain't the next JFK."

"Bullshit. Stay outta politics, kid. Wall Street's where it's at. Money talks and bullshit walks."

"You look great, Billy. Just as handsome as your father."

Somebody punched a few songs into the jukebox. Tony Bennett crooned. The conversations resumed. Billy settled in at the bar. Eddie Mahan, the bartender, slapped down a coaster and placed a Bud on top of it. "Here you go, Billy. The first one's on me."

Billy sipped the beer and listened. He felt at home in the smoky rhythm of the bar. He had lived above it since he was three, and it was the one place in the neighborhood that had not changed. The only difference was that the patrons had grown grayer and more stooped, lives folding under the weight of time. Otherwise it was Briody's Bar, once and forever.

It was a gin mill like hundreds of others in marginal neighborhoods across New York. Just inside the door was a jukebox and a cigarette machine. The bar ran the length of the wall opposite the door. Along the street-side wall were four small tables, with two chairs each. A pool table was in the rear of the room. Next to the cash register, an aquarium was filled with an assortment of goldfish. Above the liquor shelf and covering the entire back wall were framed pictures from thirty years of bar life: the softball and football teams, the bar parties, the politicians and sports figures. A dozen or so yellowing front pages framed on the wall had headlines announcing assassinations, political demise, hunger strikes, labor unrest, athletic conquests, and violent death. Next to an Irish flag was Billy's acceptance letter to college, which they had hung despite his protest.

Bobby Nolan, an aging patrolman, shrugged. "I'll tell you, us Catholics, we got our signals crossed on this one. After thirty years working these streets, I ain't only pro-cherce, I'm pro-abortion. I mean, the way some of these poor kids gotta live. Sad to say, they'd be better off not being born."

"Fuck 'em," his postman brother, George, said.

Bobby waved him off as he had for half a century. "I went to see a woman about a child-abuse case, says her ex-husband is diddling her daughter. I'm trying to get a statement out of her, and the whole time I'm there, she's yelling at her fourteen-year-old daughter, who in turn is screaming at her baby. Incredible. Just what this city needs, twenty-eight-year-old grandmothers."

"Fuck 'em. Eddie, give us another."

Tony Bennett scratched to a halt. Someone kicked the jukebox.

From High Bridge to Bay Ridge,
When New York was Irish . . .

The sugary sound of loss turned the talk to the state of the neighborhood.

"Now I got Dominicans above me, below me, and on either side of me. This keeps up, I'll have to take merengue lessons," Bobby Nolan said.

"They ain't so different once you get used to them," Eileen McCoy said. "I'm the only Irish left in my building, and nobody bothers me. Besides, you're cheaper off living around here. They're gonna have to carry me out in a box before I give up my place." Everyone nodded. They knew Eileen was serious.

"Dominicans." Pappy Lopez shook his head sadly.

"You ain't Dominican?" George teased him.

"No. I am Pwuerrto Rican."

"Billy, they got Dominicans up at college?"

"They got everything. It's like Noah's Ark. Two of this, two of that. Except it's mostly Wasps."

"Yeah, and one sandhog." Frankie came in and slapped Billy on the back.

"Maybe you should go up there with him, Frankie, even things out."

"I would, 'cept they make you read. I hate reading more than anything. Give us a round." Frankie indicated the length of the bar.

"I'd go tomorrow, but the wife, she says no way," Ted Early said. Ted's jaw had been broken by a mugger, and he sipped his beer through a straw. Eddie had brought him one of those Krazy Straws for kids. The pale liquid made six circles before reaching his mouth. He was fifty-three.

"Your wife, huh? I hear maybe she hired the guy that jumped you, Early."

"Don't think I ain't thought it. I don't really wanna go to college. I just wanna get the shit outta this neighborhood."

"Where'd you go?" Bobby Nolan asked. "You want to stay in the city, what's left? Mosholu's okay, but it ain't worth the move. Woodlawn's nice, but you're talking at least six hundred for three rooms. I'm paying one seventy-eight. I can't beat that. Last time I moved was 1969. Right after the Mutts won the series, I used the money I made on them for a deposit. I started on 138th Street, moved to 161st, then to High Bridge, then here. This is the end of my Trail of Tears."

"Last time I moved was for rent concessions," Eileen said. "They were giving three months free rent. We moved six times in three years. The biggest move was two blocks."

"I never thought I'd miss the Jews. But it was that Co-Op City that started it. It's been all downhill ever since they left the Concourse for that pile of shit," George Nolan said.

"Ah, Georgie, let them leave in peace. Things are the way they are because that's how they're supposed to be. The bunch of you, hollering alla time about the neighborhood. When was the last time any a youse stooped to pick up a piece of trash? And that lousy dog of yours, always crappin' all over the sidewalk." Eileen swirled her whiskey, then continued reflectively.

"My sister-in-law left when the bingo went Spanish. I just learned the letters and numbers. What's the big deal? They teach three-year-olds letters and numbers. Spanish, English, Chinese—who cares? Bingo is bingo, for cryin' out loud."

"You're a regular humanitarian."

Billy listened with amusement. His generation of Irish Americans was the first to be the exception and not the rule in many neighborhoods in the city. In his experience, New York was never Irish. He envied the old-timers their memories but wondered how accurate they were. The city they described was beyond his conception. His whole life, the city had been changing rapidly, taken over by newer immigrants.

Frankie downed his beer and slammed the empty on the bar.

"Something similar?" Eddie asked.

"You betcha, and another for Joe College here."

Eddie handed over two beers. Frankie turned to Billy. "Let's shoot some pool."

Frankie put two quarters in the pool table and released the balls. "I got the scam of the century lined up, Billy." His eyes glowed.

Ever since they were kids, Frankie had looked for the easy score. Not that he was trying to avoid hard work; Frankie loved to work hard. He also loved to make money. During high school, he had scoured the Bronx, appropriating scrap metal for sale to salvage yards. Some of his acquisitions were less legitimate than others. The high point of his career was sawing down one of the aluminum goalposts at Lincoln High School the night before the big game.

"Well?"

"You ain't gonna believe this, Billy. It is totally legal. It could be a career move."

"Well, come on already, the suspense is gonna kill me."

Frankie racked the balls and smiled. He looked back over his shoulder to make sure he was out of earshot of the other patrons. "You are looking at the newest and—I am sure of this—the best, paid sperm donater in America."

"What?"

"Yep."

"Get outta here."

"I shit you not. I go down to this place on Park Avenue, and they pay me to whack off. They fuckin' pay me. You believe that shit?"

"No way."

"Yes way. I go in there, the nurse, receptionist, whatever she is, comes up, you fill out all these forms. Then she hands you a jar and a couple of old *Penthouses* and puts you in this room. Whackadoo, whackadoo, whackadoo. Forty bucks a pop." Frankie leaned back, a man fully satisfied with himself. "Is this a great country or what?"

Billy shook his head. "Where'd you get hooked up with this?"

"Jimmy Grogan. He found out about it from his girlfriend, the nurse."

"Jimmy the Drooler?"

"Yeah."

The thought of countless children fathered by Jimmy the Drooler Grogan running around was profoundly unsettling to Billy.

"That's scary."

"What? Jimmy? Who cares. They wanna pay me, can you imagine? Pay me to whack off. The nuns at OLR would love this one."

"Professional masturbation. That definitely ranks up there with sloppy mass homicides."

"I was hoping they wanted a reference. I was gonna put down Sister Mary Clare."

"What about your mother?"

"Jesus Christ. She's losing it. Billy, she's driving me crazy. She goes to church every morning. You believe that? Every day. She's turning into one of those crazy old ladies lives to go to mass. I mean, can't she get a hobby, take up aerobics? She's leaving religious pamphlets in my room. Tells me I'm going to end up like my old man. I'm like, Ma, what's so bad about that? You know? I mean, the guy's been with the fire department twenty-three years—ain't such a bad life."

"At least she stopped bringing his dinner down to the bar."

"God. You remember that shit? He was five minutes late, she'd march down here, rain or shine, summer or winter, out in front of the whole neighborhood, putting on a real show."

"Remember the time they videotaped her?"

"Yeah, after she seen that's when she finally stopped, I think. She ever heard about this jism thing, it would put her over the edge. Don't say nothing to my sisters."

"What's it worth to you?"

"Don't fuckin' start, Billy Boy." Frankie laughed.

"Hey, Billy." Eileen waved him over. "Comere, handsome. Do me a favor." She handed Billy some change. "Play that colored fella for me, the one with the nice voice. What's his name?"

"Nat King Cole?"

"Yeah. I love the way he sings."

Billy returned her change and played the song for her. He went back over to Frankie.

"So anyways, you want, I can hook you up. You, too, can be a professional jerk-off artist."

"I think I'll pass, Frankie. I'd probably get stage fright."

"Hey, whatever. You change your mind, lemme know."

"Sounds like the scam you were born for."

"Speaking of scams, why don't we make a run over to Rodman's Neck for old times' sake? Clean out the lead at the pistol range."

"Ain't we getting a little old for that?" Billy said.

"Too old to make money? Never."

Billy shrugged. This was exactly the kind of thing he wanted to avoid. School had given him something to lose. "All right, Frankie. Last time. I got a reputation to destroy."

They left the bar to the sounds of Nat King Cole.

Mary Moy watched from her office window as a wrecking ball crashed into a building across the street. They had been at it all day and now, in late afternoon, a row of tenements lay reduced to heaps of broken bricks, plaster, and splintered wood. She sat and rubbed her temples. The noise was driving her to distraction. Each time the ball found its mark, the items on her desk would dance from the vibrations.

She took out her pistol, emptied the cylinder onto her desk, and snapped it shut. She twirled the weapon like an old-time gunslinger and smiled. That was it! Operation Wrecking Ball. She was in charge of creating a strategy to cripple mob influence in the construction industry and needed to come up with a name for the project. Wrecking Ball was perfect.

Still in the preliminary, information-gathering stage of the investigation, she was cramming, trying to get a handle on a hundred-billion-dollar-a-year industry. It was not easy.

In her nine years as an agent, she had earned a reputation for her thoroughness. Early on, she was lucky enough to work under an older agent, Mike Del Pezzo, who took the time to show her the ropes. He warned against shoddy preparation, pointing out cases that collapsed because the agents involved were more concerned with politics or publicity than with being thorough. Mary took the lessons to heart.

She had immersed herself for three months and was just starting to understand the scope of things. She studied reports, dug through mountains of files, reviewed confidential informants' statements. She networked with a number of other investigators within the Bureau and beyond. There was so much activity, an explosion of building in New York since the early eighties. In the last half-dozen years, forty million square feet of new office space had gone up, along with nearly seventy thousand new residential units. Public projects doubled the amount of construction. Quarter-billion-dollar developments were commonplace. It was as if a midwestern city were rising amidst the vertical confines of New York.

With all this economic fury, it was amazing how few individuals it took to bring such huge jobs to a standstill. The industry was ripe for exploitation. Interest on construction loans could cost several million dollars a month. The simple fact was, it was often easier and cheaper to pay someone off. Not to mention safer. She leafed through some chilling confidential informant reports that detailed beatings and intimidation. One CI had been an enforcer for a mob crew chief. He'd talked matter-of-factly about his profession.

"I go on and tell a guy—maybe he's a shop steward, maybe he's a subcontractor, whatever—I say, 'Hey, how you doin'?' I hand him an envelope, say maybe twenty grand in there—a lot of money, right? In there with the money, say maybe six, eight names, fictitious. I tell him I'm gonna pick up paychecks for those names every week. Guys know who I am, what I represent. So it's those checks every week—or the river. His choice.

"I can arrange bogus pickets, trucks disappearing, sabotage, make sure you get watery concrete, all sorts of chaos. You don't want a problem? Pay me. 'Cause it's either kick back or I'll kick you down a flight of fucking stairs."

She cleared her desk and arranged a series of index cards before her in three colored piles. White cards bore the names of construction contractors suspected of mob influence; blue, corrupt union officials; yellow, organized-crime members involved in construction.

She thought of her father, retired now, formerly a masonry contractor in Missouri. He'd gone from replacing stoops and sidewalk slabs to building strip malls and garden apartments. She wondered if he ever had to deal with such problems. Mary was the last of four sisters born within forty months. It was no secret that her father wanted a son, but her mother had begged off after Mary was born. She became, by default, her father's surrogate son. Mary was glad to oblige. She captained three girls' sports in high school: basketball, field hockey, and softball. Her father never got his son, but he got a bigger trophy case than any other father in town.

He did, however, balk when Mary suggested that he put her to work during college summers. She remembered him sitting at the dinner table, his thick, tanned forearms surrounding his plate. He smiled when she suggested he hire her. It was the one time he had resisted her. The problem was, he had taught her the value of tenacity. She kept at him until he backed down and gave her a job as a flag person, stopping traffic for deliveries of material to the sites. But she knew the flag jobs were traditionally reserved for the old-timers and she was resented both for being a woman who took an old-timer's job and for being the boss's daughter. She protested until her father agreed to let her have a go at mixing cement for the masons. He predicted she would not last a single shift. She proved him wrong.

All one hundred thirty-five pounds of her was determined to do the job. From seven until four, with thirty minutes for lunch and two ten-minute coffee breaks, it was sixteen shovels of sand, a ninety-four-pound bag of portland cement, and water from a five-gallon bucket into a smoking cement mixer under the hot Missouri sun. Her skin burned brown, her muscles hardened. Slowly, over a span of weeks, she earned the respect of her coworkers. By the middle of July they were inviting her to go for beers on payday.

Those summers had given her respect for the kind of work that ground a person down, shortened lives. Her last month before Quantico, a mason walking along a scaffold four stories up was pitched sideways into space when a plank snapped. He was impaled on rebar sticking out of the foundation. He died slowly, calling for his wife as the rescue workers struggled to save him.

She put the cards down and went to get a diet Coke. She crushed a cockroach that scurried out from under the refrigerator. The Bureau had set them up in a dump on the West Side—broken toilets, weak air-conditioning, welfare hotel for a neighbor. She forced herself not to think that her gender had anything to do with the location. She had worked under worse conditions. She paced back and forth, trying to organize a plan, trying to find a weak link. She had to get the biggest impact for the amount of resources assigned to the task.

And she needed to work quickly. She was almost four months pregnant and had not yet told anyone at work. When she found out, she had already taken the assignment. It was a career case; she was not about to turn it down. She figured she could work hard and build enough of an operation before taking a short maternity leave. Monitor the effort from home, then come back and resume her position. She hoped.

She took the cards into the conference room and laid them out, visualizing the connections between them. No matter how she arranged them, it all led to one conclusion. John Tuzio was at the hub of most of the nefarious activity. He was like an evil octopus, with tentacles snaking through every aspect of the industry.

"Polacks."

"Polacks?" Paddy asked.

"Yeah, fuckin' Polacks. Right-off-the-boat, kielbasa-eatin' Polacks."

Jack Tierney sat on his living-room couch, counting money. He wore sweatpants, and his hair stuck up wildly, his face still heavy with sleep. Jack was in a good mood.

Paddy watched him stack hundred-dollar bills in piles of ten, treating the money gingerly. Paddy thought Jack was probably kinder to cold, hard cash than to anything or anyone in his life. Jack placed a rubber band around each pile and dropped it into a shoe box on his lap.

"You figure we're payin' those donkey Irish pricks ten, twelve bucks an hour. I got this guy from Greenpoint, a Polack himself, tells me he can provide all the illegal Polacks we need. We pay 'em six or eight bucks an hour, and we pocket the rest—benefits, everything. That can mean two C-notes a week a head more than the Irish. And besides, these Polacks don't speak English, so they can't even complain. It's perfect."

Jack's wife, Linda, walked in. "Hey, Paddy. Like my new couch?"

"Nice, Linda. Real nice. Where'd you get it?" The color reminded him of fresh pigeon shit.

"Over in Secaucus. At a specialty warehouse."

Paddy watched as she walked away, noticing how big her ass was getting. She looked like some overstuffed housewife who whiled her days away with junk food and soap operas.

Jack turned toward the bedroom and yelled, "Hey, Linda! How 'bout a coupla beers here!" He leaned closer to Paddy, all business. "Listen. I was talking to Romero. They got a little piece of work that they need us to take care of. Up in the Bronx."

Paddy's stomach started going then. It had been a good day till then. He wished he could get the bottle of Pepto-Bismol from the glove compartment of his car.

Jack went on. "They got these spics sellin' crack out of a house up near Arthur Avenue. They've been asked to leave twice." He leaned back and rubbed his belly. "Hey, the beer!"

Paddy did not like where the conversation was leading. Jack leaned in again. "We got it all worked out already. Four or five guys go in dressed as cops. Bang bang. Take out everything that moves." He smiled. "Cakewalk."

Paddy felt the fire in his stomach spread. "Why do they need us? They got more shooters than they can use."

"Come on, Paddy, use your head. Five guineas show up sayin' they're cops? That don't send out an alarm? This is where havin' an Irish mug comes in handy. Now, you're in or you're out. I got Terry and the Riordan brothers lined up. We get fifty large for the job, plus five large per dead spic crack dealer, or whatever resembles a dead spic crack dealer at the time. It's a nice score."

Paddy leaned over slightly to try to push the burn out of his belly. He looked Jack in the eye, searching for clues. Paddy's aversion to dealing with the Italians was becoming a sore point between them. "I'm out, Jack. You know that ain't my kinda job." Getting involved with Butcher Boy and the Riordans in a shootout in a crack house was about the last thing he would ever want to do.

"You sure?" Jack shook his head, disappointed. "Linda! Christ."

"All right already, King Tut. I'm coming."

"So's fuckin' New Year's. . . . You know, Paddy, this shit with the Italians—things have been working out nice for us. Everything we've done with them has been on the level. We're making a lot of money with those guys."

"Nothing's on the level, Jack."

"The fuck that supposed to mean?"

"Come on, Jack. Yeah, they're real nice guys. Hey, *paisan*, all that shit. Best friends. You help us, we'll help you, botchagalup. Next thing you know, they own you like every other Irish dummy they own." Paddy felt cold anger replacing the heat. "Then, you don't do what they want, you end up stuffed in a garbage can. The only way to deal with them is to keep them convinced the biggest mistake they could ever make is to fuck with you. What I can't understand is why I'm telling this to you when I know you know all about it."

"Christ, Paddy, it's business. We do business with all kinds. All of a sudden you got something against these people."

"They ain't neighborhood, Jack. They got no percentage in standing up for one of us—that's what I got against them." He noticed Jack stiffen and decided he'd better back off. "Terry and them want to make the money, let 'em. I'll sit this one out."

Jack was quiet for a minute. His face darkened. "Your call."

Linda came in with two beers and stood next to Paddy with a furniture catalog. She opened it and leaned over on Paddy so her heavy breasts were pushing against his biceps. "Paddy, which of these grandfather clocks you like best? I want one for the family room."

Paddy glanced at the page, then back at Tierney, who was opening his beer and not looking too happy. "They're all real nice, Linda. I'm not big on clocks, though, tell the truth."

"Linda, go pick up the kids," Tierney said.

"What, my skin darker than I think it is?"

"Shut the fuck up and go get the kids!"

Paddy knew he was serious; when he used that tone, something bad usually happened. Linda must have realized it too, because she waited till she was out of reach before yelling at him. "What about PTA, Jack? It's your turn this month. Asshole."

Jack's eighteen-year-old son, Kevin, came in and dropped his gym bag on the floor. He was the image of Jack, minus twenty years and forty pounds.

"Hey, Paddy, what's up? I been banging the heavy bag. You gonna help me train for the Gloves?"

Linda, standing by the door, yelled, "And you! Get out there and mow the goddamn lawn."

"Jesus Christ, I just got home. Gimme a minute?"

"Hey!" Jack was off the couch, his face crimson. "I hear you talk to your mother like that again, you'll be shittin' teeth for a month. Go fix the fuckin' yard." Jack turned to Linda, his voice dropping ominously. "Get a fuckin' move on."

She gave Jack the finger and slammed the front door.

He turned back to Paddy. "See the shit I put up with? I think there's only one thing they unnerstan'. Last week she had a few in her, starts yappin' about how she comes from some good family, mine's a piece a shit, all that. You'd think she popped outta Rose Kennedy's twat, the way she talks. Two, three times I ask her, Please, Linda, not now. But no, they don't wanna listen a reason. So finally I nail her with a backhand. Whap!" He demonstrated for Paddy. "She hit the kitchen floor like a shotgunned cow. Out cold. Five minutes she laid there, not moving. Finally I had some peace and quiet around here." He took a long guzzle of beer. "She wonders why I run around with young gash from the neighborhood."

"Yeah, I know what you mean," Paddy said, thinking how lucky he was with Rosa.

"So, we'll take care of that. Anything else? Let's sit on the patio. Gimme a minute to drop this in the safe, get my kid."

Paddy wandered into the family room and looked over Jack's Vietnam mementos. A glass case contained various medals and an assortment of bayonets and sidearms, plus one of those cone hats the Vietcong always wore in movies. There was a string of shriveled black objects that Paddy took to be the collection of ears Jack liked to boast about. A dozen framed photos from the war hung on the wall above the case. The one in the center caught Paddy's eye. A teenage Jack Tierney, shirtless and thickly muscled, held a detached Vietnamese head in each hand, a look of satisfaction on his face. The lifeless heads had expressions that might be described as bemused. Paddy backed out of the Tierney family room.

They sat on the patio, and Jack bounced his smiling baby on his knee. A jetliner passed silently far above them in the Westchester sky. An ancient weeping willow cast most of the large, fenced-in yard in shadow. The scene evoked tranquillity, quiet success. Jack, Paddy thought, did not fit in the picture.

Jack held up the baby, legs dangling. The infant giggled. "Look at the size of the feet on this thing, hah? Kid's gonna be a fuckin' monster. We decided we wanted another kid, I laid off the booze and went on a special protein diet. The ol' lady might be a piece a shit, but she still pops out a nice kid." Jack displayed his son as if he were a prize Rottweiler.

He pointed out over the yard. "I'm puttin' the pool right there, hah? Whaddaya think? Kidney-shaped. Maybe I'll start them Polacks out right here. Make them dig it out by hand. Welcome them to the Land of the Free."

Jack's older son came into the backyard with the mower. He started on the far side of the yard, and every time he passed behind his father he made a jerking-off motion with his fist. Paddy had to struggle not to laugh.

Jack patted his baby. "Listen. I think I wanna send the kid on a job."

"Jack, the kid's eighteen. I mean, you really want him involved in this shit?"

"Fuckin' A right he's eighteen. And living under my roof. Kid lives under my roof, he's gonna do things my way. I was eighteen, I was into my second tour in Nam. Besides, he come to me with the idea."

Paddy did not know what to say.

"So, what happened with that job over on the avenue?"

"Coalition showed up, put on a nice show. The guy called me. He's all ears now."

"Good." Paddy stood up.

"You leaving?"

"Yeah. I gotta get back to town. See a guy."

"I get the pool in, you bring your girl out. We'll barbecue." Jack stood up and tucked his baby under his arm like a sack of oranges. "I'll be in town tonight. Meet me at the bar. I might have something new."

Paddy made for his car in a hurry and opened the glove compartment. He finished off the whole bottle of Pepto-Bismol before crossing the New York City line.

On the way back to the West Side, Paddy stopped off in the Bronx, around the block from his grandfather's. He dropped a quarter in a pay phone and punched the number, hoping Billy would answer. The thought of talking to his grandfather always made him uncomfortable.

The old man had written him off long ago. It was easier when they avoided each other.

While the phone rang, two hard-eyed Puerto Rican kids started toward him, checking him out. Paddy turned and pulled his jacket open, giving them a peek of his shoulder holster with the .45. They crossed to the other side of the street, walking slow, trying to prove how big their balls were. Paddy wondered what the hell the neighborhood was coming to.

His grandfather answered. For a second, Paddy wanted to hang up, but he fought the urge. "Billy home?"

There was a cold silence. Then: "He's not."

"Is he back from college?"

"He is."

"Tell him I called?"

"I will."

Paddy hung up and jumped back in his Monte Carlo. Pulling away from the curb, he smiled at the Spanish kids. He drove down the Concourse, wondering if things would be different with the old man if Paddy had ever told him about his uncle.

Paddy had been twelve when his father died in that lousy tunnel. They sent him to live with his father's sister in Manhattan. Billy stayed in the Bronx with the grandparents. Paddy remembered the first Christmas in his new home. His father had been dead five months.

He woke early that Christmas morning. It was like a reflex, jumping out of bed to open the presents. He and his cousins Tommy and Clare ran into the living room and found a good-size pile of gifts. They were wrapped in bright-colored paper. Each present had a homemade bow. Paddy's aunt sat on an ottoman by the tree in her frayed housecoat, her hair in rollers. She smoked nervously. No one seemed to care that his uncle John was not there. The kids tore into the presents with joy. Hockey sticks for the boys, a Barbie doll for Clare, footballs, a train set.

They were almost finished when Paddy heard heavy, unsteady footsteps on the stairs. He watched his aunt stiffen, and the charge passed through the kids like static. The door opened, and Uncle John entered with a bunch of wilted flowers in one hand. He smiled, and said "Merry Christmas," and Paddy could feel the collective relief in the room. His uncle came over and ran his hand through Paddy's hair. He smelled of bar smoke and cheap whiskey, of faded Old Spice. His eyes were blood red. He sat heavily in his chair.

The kids went back to ripping open presents. His aunt resumed smoking. Paddy couldn't remember what set him off. Not that his uncle ever needed any real reason. Clare, eight years old, was holding up a doll that was in fashion that Christmas, looking for attention. Her father waved his hand across the room. "I bust my ass for this, and you ain't even got the common fuckin' decency to wait till I get home?"

Paddy remembered his aunt's eyes turning small with fright, the kids sinking into themselves, their hopes deflated. It felt as if fear was trapped in the room with them. His uncle went after his aunt then, all the disappointments and self-loathing of his failed life bubbling up inside him. Before she could move, he punched her up and off the ottoman. Her head cracked one of the windowpanes, and she landed unconscious in a sitting position, her housecoat up around her waist. Clare ran screaming to her, wiping at the thin line of blood that ran down her mother's nose. Tommy just sat with his fists clenched, making noises like a wounded puppy.

Paddy's uncle turned his rage on the presents. He did not stop until he had smashed every one of them into uselessness. His last act was to topple the Christmas tree. Then he sat down in his chair and was asleep within thirty seconds.

Paddy pulled onto the Cross Bronx Expressway and punched the accelerator. The four-barrel carburetor opened up, and he shot over into the fast lane. He never let his grandfather know what went on in that house. But Paddy had known, that Christmas morning, at twelve years old, that his life was changed forever.

He saw the sign for the last exit in New York and turned onto the Henry Hudson Parkway, wondering why his brother had not called him.

JP Adare swept the sidewalk in front of Briody's Bar. He dragged the broom back and forth across the chipped concrete. It was a daily ritual. When he was finished, he would hose it down. It was his small way of combating the creeping decay in the neighborhood. He paused to let a pair of elderly Puerto Rican women walk past. They both pulled grocery carts and greeted him with pleasant smiles.

When they passed, he resumed his work. JP felt his strength, his vitality, sinking back into the ground. He was waning; the years were taking their toll. Sometimes it took all his effort and strength to drag the broom across the sidewalk, to complete the little chores that he set for himself each day. The arthritis was nearly unbearable, and the decades of sucking rock dust were exacting a vicious toll. The silicosis robbed him of oxygen, so that the simple act of breathing was an ordeal. He worried what would happen when things got worse, when he could no longer care for himself, when the inevitable feebleness came upon him.

He did not want to burden Billy. His grandson had plans, a future. Billy was realizing the promise that had eluded JP in America. His adopted country had provided a haven from war but not from bloodshed. His son was dead these twenty years now. A grandson was involved in a life of crime. Lately, JP wondered if this was not punishment for the violent acts of his youth.

He dreamed some long nights of returning to the lakes and hills of his childhood. It was a place where a different value was put on the aging. In America, the old were shunted aside, hidden in homes and institutions, forgotten. The only reward for a long life seemed oblivion, loneliness. The thought of ending up in some cold, gray institution, abused by underpaid orderlies, did not sit well with him. He'd fight that fate to his last breath.

He finished sweeping and hooked up the hose on the side of the building. Out front again, he sprayed the sidewalk till it glistened. He thought about Paddy's phone call. Sometimes he considered relenting, reconciling with his grandson. But he just could not condone the life he lived, the violence for the sake of gain.

He watched as Bobby Nolan, Yankees cap pulled down to his eyes, a *Post* under his arm, came out of his building across the street. He made directly for Briody's.

"JP, you missed a spot."

"I'll get to it, Bobby. Time is all I have."

"Yeah, me too. I got two weeks off. Fourteen days I'll be like the idle rich. More time at the track, more time at the bar." He unrolled a pack of Marlboros from the sleeve of his faded T-shirt, knocked the pack against his fist, took the butt in his lips, and lit it with a flourish.

JP thought it strange that Americans maintained these teenage affectations past middle age.

"I'd love to be your apprentice here, JP, but there's a cold beer calling to me. See ya." Nolan ducked into Briody's.

JP turned back to his task. He had little else left to fill his days.

Vito Romero used Charles Eliot's name at the door of Martin's, and as usual, it was like uttering a magic password. He was ushered to a prime table. The maître d' fussed over him, and waiters descended upon him, ready to cater to his every whim. Vito waved them off. They made him feel like he was some kind of invalid. He sat with his back to the wall. It was a habit born not of caution but of curiosity. He liked to watch the goings-on around him. The place was old New York: dark wood, black-and-white photographs, rich cigar smoke, the crowd mostly male, all in suit and tie. Vito could feel the deals being cut. The lawyers, lobbyists, businessmen, and government types all there for the same reason. Money.

To the casual eye, Vito was indistinguishable from those around him. He dressed in expensive but conservative suits. He wore his hair in a bland executive style. He forsook the gaudy pinkie rings of Tuzio and the others. The only gold he wore was a tastefully subdued Rolex watch. And despite his underworld associations, he had legitimate business with Charles Eliot. Vito was president and general manager of Vicon Construction, a concrete-contracting firm.

He watched Eliot make his entrance. Vito admired the way the man moved through the lunchtime crowd. A nod here, a wave there, the occasional backslap and handshake. The recipients of his attention seemed pleased to glow in the moneyed presence of Charles Eliot. He belonged in a way Vito never could. No matter how well he dressed or how many expensive meals and bottles of wine he downed in places like Martin's, Vito did not fit. In the minds of his fellow diners, he'd always be a Brooklyn guinea, with all the baggage attached to that.

"Vito." Eliot was all teeth and blond confidence.

Vito stood, and they shook hands. By the time they sat down, the waiters were back, crisp white towels folded over their arms.

"Let's start with a nice bottle of wine. Give us some of the Mouton-Rothschild '82," Eliot said; then: "Vito, you're looking well."

"It's all the nice meals I eat with you, Charles, keeping me healthy." Vito patted his stomach.

"Well, what's the point of living if you don't do it right?"

"Yeah. You got something there."

The waiter came over and proffered the wine to Eliot, letting him see the label. Eliot nodded, and the waiter deftly uncorked the bottle and poured a sample into his glass. Eliot sipped the wine, swirled it around his tongue. He put the glass down and smiled. "Now that is something to write home about."

The waiter filled the glasses and took their lunch order. Eliot went with the prime rib, Vito the salmon. Over appetizers of mussels in garlic and wine, Vito listened to Eliot tell a boring story about a golf outing he'd had with a couple of state legislators and a deputy mayor. Vito hated the very idea of golf. He considered it a perfect way to fuck up a nice walk in the country.

Vito basically liked Charles Eliot. He thought him a decent guy and recognized him as a valuable business contact. But there was something that bothered him about the man. It was the way he was able to remain so aloof when it came to the violence that accompanied their dealings. Vito wondered how Eliot would feel if he realized how many deaths he was at least partly responsible for. Guys like Eliot had been above the mix for so long, Vito figured, secure behind their bloodlines and college degrees and soft jobs, that they had no conception of how things played out on the streets.

The waiter reappeared with their entrées and set them down gently.

"The gentleman in the gray suit, the bald one?" With a subtle nod of his head, Eliot indicated to Vito a man two tables over. "Newly appointed chairman of the Zoning Committee. A proclivity for the ponies. Someone to keep an eye on."

Vito made a mental note. You never knew when an opportunity might arise. He stabbed at the fish with his fork. The salmon melted in his mouth. "They sell a nice piece of fish here." He spoke while chewing.

Eliot carved his prime rib as if it were still alive and he was trying not to hurt it. He took a long, thoughtful sip of wine, then he got down to business.

"Joe Harkness is a decent fellow. His outfit is a major concern. Jobs of this magnitude—several billion dollars by the time it's complete—there are many opportunities to secure a profit."

Vito nodded. "That's a lotta zeroes."

"Certainly is."

"What's the deal with the union?"

"They are currently without a contract. The dollar amount here is significant. Just for argument's sake, say one thousand workers. Five dollars an hour differential times forty hours a week times the thousand men, that's two hundred thousand a week. The bid is set. It's now a question of to whom the cash flows." Eliot finished the last of his beef. "I really should have my cholesterol checked." He leaned closer to Vito. "If the union can be . . . persuaded to settle? Well."

"I get the picture."

After some small talk, Vito turned down Eliot's offer of dessert.

"I gotta get back to beautiful Brooklyn."

Walking out, Vito realized that he was embarrassed about himself. Somehow he always felt dirty leaving Eliot, dimmed by his glow. To make himself feel better, he thought about the pictures they had of Eliot and the big Ubangi transvestite. He knew that would knock the smile off the guy's face, shake his Ivy League confidence. Pillars of the community—and Charles Eliot was definitely that—were not supposed to wrestle in seedy motel rooms with members of the black race—and especially ones with ten-inch salamis. Vito chuckled. It was rare he got to laugh anymore. You could never have too much insurance in his line of work.

Paddy laid out the crack-house hit for Mickey Lawless over a game of pool. Mickey agreed heartily with Paddy's reservations over dealing with the Italians.

He shook his head. "This business with the greaseballs is bullshit, you ask me, Paddy." Mickey stroked a shot. He waited for the four ball to drop gently in the side pocket and said, "You know me, half the time I don't even like being hooked up with Jack."

They were in a pool hall on Thirty-seventh Street. The place was empty except for three Chinese couples playing nine ball.

Mickey chalked his cue. "The guy's got this weird math. You know? I mean, I can't figure it out. We went to the same parochial school, had the same math classes, same nuns. We do a job, though, he comes up with some figures, I tell you what—they don't make sense to me. He ends up making a lot more than I do. I sure as fuck don't wanna work for no fat Italian ain't even neighborhood. I can imagine what kinda math *they* do." Mickey missed a long corner shot and stood back to let Paddy shoot.

"The way I look at it, we lost this thing with them back in Europe a coupla thousand years ago. Nice shot. I read this book on the Romans." Mickey had not read a book from the time he was ten until he did an eighteen-month stretch in state prison for grand larceny. Since then he read constantly, always citing his discoveries to Paddy.

"The Celts kicked their asses, terrorized them. You know, they used to fight naked and attack at night. They made necklaces for their horses with people's heads. The poor guineas thought they was civilized, they couldn't figure these nuts out. The Celts, they didn't care about the gold, the artwork, and that. They just wanted to fight. Well, after this went on awhile, the Romans figured it was time to come up with a plan. I mean, these guys sacked Rome, Byzantium, fucked all the broads. How else you figure Sinatra got his blue eyes?" Mickey watched Paddy miss, stepped up, and rolled the cue ball gently down the green, sinking the six.

"It was a big battle somewhere in France. That was Roman turf then. They had this hill with three rings of defense going up it, thousands of guys. Well, here come the Celts, smelling blood. Battle went on for days. They busted through the first two rings and almost made the third but ran out of men. One on one, the Celts were unbeatable, even two or three against one of them. Their problem was they liked fighting too much to worry about strategy. Just give me something to hit, they said. After that, they pretty much just had Ireland. But you notice something—the guineas never tried to take Ireland. Old Caesar heard it was an island full of those guys and said, Fuck that. We'll settle with the English." Mickey comboed the twelve off the four.

"I'm a firm believer in history, Paddy, and those who forget it are doomed to repeat it. We stick with the West Side, they know better than to come down here. They can have the rest."

"Amen, Mickey. Amen."

Billy Adare, feeling restless, put on his running shoes and headed out into the thick Bronx evening. He ran down Fordham Road, past the workers hurrying home for dinner and the shop owners pulling down window gates for the night. He crossed the Harlem River into Inwood, picking up the pace, his legs loosening. He turned up Broadway and wove his way around cars double- and triple-parked. Music blared from a dozen boom boxes; people drank cold beer in the heat.

Over the Broadway Bridge, back into the Bronx, he ran up the hill into Riverdale, rising above the crowded streets. There the streets were lined with neat lawns, and the farther he went, the larger the houses became. Sprinklers arced gracefully in the gathering dusk. Landscaping crews, sunburned and dirty from the day's work, loaded their equipment onto trucks. Luxury cars whispered past him and braked softly for stop signs.

In his daydreams, Billy imagined someday living in a place like this. For him, education was a means to an end. He'd been running through this unattainable corner of New York for years, filled with want. This is what all the studying and the sacrifice would land him. These lawns and houses, these expensive cars, security. A life purported to be there if you went along with the system, kept your head down, worked for it. Now he felt closer to it than ever. This moneyed existence and all its trappings almost within reach. Still, a nagging doubt about his ability always lurked in his consciousness. The feeling that someone would come along and say it was all a joke and he had to stay where he belonged, that places like this were not for him.

He ran hard now, his legs pounding, his lungs on fire. He ran down past Manhattan College, crossing Broadway under the el. He sprinted across Van Cortlandt Park, past a group of Salvadorans playing soccer in the dying light. He made a right on Bainbridge and slowed down steadily to a jog.

He turned his corner. People sat on milk crates, playing dominoes. Women passed babies back and forth. Merengue blared from a boom box. Billy nodded to men who were both his neighbors and strangers. The wind picked up, warm and dirty, and trash swirled along the block. The men held on to their baseball hats and laughed. He felt a long way from the fresh lawns he had just passed.

Billy ducked into his building. He had to get ready for work.

Mucking the sump. The bottom of the elevator shaft clogs with muck, and it needs to be kept clear so the cage can go all the way down.

There is nothing to it except shoveling, pure and simple. Billy knew better than to come up with half a shovelful. The Mule stood right among them, screaming when a shovel wasn't full. The muck itself worked against them. A combination of rock, dirt, cement, oil, and water, it stuck like clay. If Billy stood in one place for too long, he had to dig himself out of the mess.

There were two large metal buckets, and as one was raised, the other was right there, waiting to be filled. Billy tried to get into the mindless rhythm: legs, ass, back, shoulders, arms, using his body to minimize the strain, always stepping back and forth to keep his feet free. Within half an hour his muscles were on fire, his skin was soaked with ice water. No quarter from the Mule.

They worked at a steady pace until first coffee. Steam rose as their sweat cooled in the cold air of the shaft.

The coffee bucket was lowered down to them by rope, and Billy dropped his muck stick to pour a cup. It was rancid but hot.

Lenny came over with his cup. "Ain't this a barrel of fun?"

"Yeah. Too bad we can't do it every night."

They stood in the wet shaft. The sound of other crews, other work, echoed from above. Billy took off his hard hat and wiped the sweat and dirt from his forehead. "What's this I hear about them canceling the safety meetings?"

Lenny took a sip of his coffee, then dumped the rest out. "This crap is not fit for human consumption. I guess the company doesn't think we need to waste their time on issues like safety. I mean, this is only the job with the highest death rate in America."

"What a bunch of bullshit," Frankie said.

"What does your brother say about it?" Billy asked.

Lenny pulled his gloves back on. "My brother's been business agent for ten years now, and we got our differences, but I don't envy his position on this one. He's got an election coming up and no contract. This guy Harkness knows what he's up to."

They sat quietly on buckets to conserve energy, like fighters between rounds. After five minutes, Lenny went for his muck stick. Back to work.

Billy wished he could just lean back and relax the rest of the night, but he went and picked up his muck stick and, to the Mule's "Asses and elbows, lads, that's all I want to see," dug with all he had.

When Billy had arrived at work, he was given a piece of welcome news. The company told McIntyre to hire another man, and Billy was placed in the gang full time, meaning no more bullshit shaping up and not knowing if he would work or not. He was lucky to land in McIntyre's gang. The Mule was one of a breed of Irishmen and West Indians in the tunnels who abhorred the slacker, the dog-fucker, the tit-job seeker. It was as if they found validation in insanely hard work. The Mule had once broken his wrist at the start of a shift, gone to the hospital for X rays and a cast, and been back at work by lunch break. The company noticed such things. When work slowed down, it was men like the Mule the company kept on. You pulled your weight, you got to stay working right alongside him. Billy figured that at twenty-three, no matter what the pace, he had no reason not to last through to the fall.

They were let out of the sump for lunch. Billy sat on a bench in the pump room and chewed on a stale ham and cheese, washing it down with warm ginger ale. Eamon Cudahy sat across from him, eating his onion. The floor of the pump room was metal grating, underneath it a ten-foot-deep pool of slimy water with cans, cups, banana peels, and other trash floating in it. Eamon was working off a two-day drunk, and his eyes were heavy with the guilt of the self-abused.

"Well, Billy, we're halfway there now."

"Eamon, where you been? I missed you at the union meeting yesterday," Billy said.

"I was in church, Billy, if you don't mind. Payin' me respects to the Lord Jaysus."

He smiled and pushed his hard hat back with a big gnarled hand. The hand looked as if it had been taken from someone else and stitched onto his wrist.

"It's gonna be a long night," Billy said.

"Yes, it's a rough business, it is. But don't worry, lad—the first ten years are the worst. After that, it's all downhill." Eamon laughed.

Billy left him with his onion and went to find Lenny. He found him in one of the drifts, small tunnels branching off the main tunnel, which led to riser shafts where the water would be pumped into water mains. Lenny was sitting on a bench doing the *Times* crossword puzzle, and Billy watched as he filled it in quickly, rarely hesitating. Without looking up, he said:

"Six letters, Greek tragedy."

"I suck at crosswords, Len."

He looked up. "You mean to tell me you went to college and you can't do the *Times* daily?"

Billy shrugged. "What do you think's going to happen, Lenny? That new super?"

"This business, you believe about ten percent of what you hear, you'll do all right for yourself. But things are gonna get rough. The way I see it, these assholes want to take a strike, for some reason. Things have been quiet for a long time. There was a lot of head-splitting going on when I broke into this racket, and guys like Harkness were the reason for most of it."

"That was a long time ago. I doubt they'd pull that today, don't you?"

Lenny raised his eyebrows. "Let me tell you something. You're stupid enough to believe that it can't happen today, tomorrow, or yesterday in this racket, you're a dumb prick like the rest of them. That's what they're counting on—that no one's hungry enough to put up a fight and we won't know what hit us. And it's you young guys that are gonna hafta pull the freight."

Billy nodded. He did not know how to respond. He took labor peace for granted.

Lenny continued: "Look around the country. I don't have to spell it out for you, do I? Fifty years ago they knew they had to give something up or they'd have a revolution on their hands, so they said, Okay, here's your unions, here's your eight-hour day, here's your unemployment. Since that time it's been slowly changing back. The labor law's full of loopholes, the companies are moving everything overseas, they convinced the public we're all Commies and crooks, and what happens? They don't need to use clubs and guns—they're beatin' us 'cause we forgot what it was like. We thought it was gonna be easy street forever, soon we'll be on the outside looking in."

"But Lenny, this is New York."

"Twenty, even ten, years ago, kid, that was all you needed to tell me. Now it don't mean shit. Look at the safety meetings. Every chance they get, they're cutting corners. With some of them it's just a matter of money. With others, like this guy Harkness, it's the money and a way of saying, Fuck you, I'm the boss.

"The sad thing is, his uncle and his partner were two of the best I ever worked for. The kinda guys that give a workingman a break. And they knew what it was all about. Both of them spent time in the hole so they would understand. This guy, I doubt he's ever once had dirty hands."

"Sounds like an asshole," Billy said.

"Not so much an asshole as a guy that is in a situation because of someone else's hard work and don't know any better. He's out to make a name for himself, and since he don't know shit from Shinola about the business, he's gonna have to do it by causing problems."

Billy followed Lenny back to the sump. Though he was a staunch defender of unionism in general and the sandhogs in particular, he somehow felt that all this no longer involved him. He picked up his muck stick, hoping things would hold till September.

Paddy Adare stepped over a fallen drunk and pushed open the door to Murray's Gym. He took the stairs three at a time, enjoying the tattoo of punches on leather, the familiar stink of exertion in the close space. A vague dread had settled over him lately. The edge that helped him stay alive and on the streets was blurring toward something more ominous. He hoped the gym would be, as ever, his respite.

Murray Block, attired in brown slacks and a soiled white T-shirt, chewed an unlit cigar as he expertly wrapped Paddy's hands. He paused and held the surgically repaired right fist, shaking his head. The frailty of that hand had cost them both a ticket to Fat City. He sighed, nothing more to be said on the matter, no dream to be resurrected. He pulled a custom-made glove, heavy with extra protection, onto the right hand, a regular glove onto the left.

"You won't believe the crap coming through here these days. This racket is dead."

Paddy nodded. As payment for Murray's loyalty over the years, he would sit and let Murray go on before he worked out. He realized he was Murray's only link to a much more promising past.

"I got this kid, twenty. Strong kid. Heavyweight. But he ain't much inna smarts department. Tells me he wants to improve his vocabulary, so I says great. That's a worthwhile thing. It ain't like he's gonna make much of a living with his hands—moves like a walrus I seen at the aquarium with my grandson. So I go by the bookstore, I drop a pound on a used Webster's for the kid." Murray kneaded Paddy's shoulders. "Week later, he tells me he learned a new word. I'm like, Fantastic, what's that? He says, 'Minuscule.' I says, 'Minuscule?' He says, 'Yeah. It means very, very small, tiny.' You believe this? I wanted to say, Yeah, like your brain. I went to the third grade, I know this word without any book. I wasted five bucks for 'minuscule.' "

A young, slender Latino fighter came over.

"Hey, Murray."

"How you feeling?"

"Good, Murray. I gotta keep my immunes up. My immunes is good, I can beat anybody." The kid did a little jig. Maybe a Hector Camacho imitation.

Murray rolled his eyes at Paddy. He looked like a man working long past retirement.

"Stay away from the junk and the pussy, kid. Your immunes will fend for themselves. Now the two of you get to work." He slapped Paddy on the back.

Paddy went for the heavy bag. The thermometer in the gym read 102. He started slowly, feeling his muscles respond. Soon he was lost in sweat and the storm of punches. Jack and his Italians, the streets, the dread, even the lake of fire in his belly, fell away. He pounded furiously, ignoring the toll of the rest bells. Swept up in fury and release, he pounded until he was new again.

Outside the bar, a large bouncer stood and said, "Three dollars."

"Three dollars? For what?" Frankie stood to his full height and looked the bouncer in the eyes.

"Live band," the bouncer said solemnly.

"Fucking highway robbery." Frankie handed him seven dollars and said, "Buy yourself some pimple cream."

As they entered, Billy felt the music pulsing through him, vibrations cutting to the bone. They parted the crowd, pushing their way past bodies. Frankie flirted with every girl they passed, screaming over the music, so it took them awhile to get to the bar.

They nudged themselves into a spot at the end and ordered drinks. Flesh pressed against them from three sides. The girls all seemed to be dressed in acid-washed jeans and bright-colored shirts. Big hair was in abundance. The guys were all trying to be tough and funny at the same time. Billy knew that by the end of the night most of them would be sullen and sloppy. He'd been there.

"Billy, man, I'm telling you, this place is hopping with slut puppies tonight. Now remember the five F's. Find 'em, feel 'em, finger 'em, fuck 'em, and forget 'em."

Billy went to the bathroom, and by the time he returned, Frankie was sitting at a table with two girls who seemed to have grown out from under outrageous hair. He wondered if he should be more worried about the ozone layer. They wore eye shadow and too much lipstick. It dawned on Billy that at college, the only people who wore eye shadow were the cafeteria ladies.

Frankie leaned over and said to Billy's ear, "I met these two here last week. Ten to one says they're good to go." Then, to the table: "Billy, I want you to meet a couple of old friends." The girls giggled in unison. "This here is Tricia." He pointed to big blond hair. "And this is Maria." He pointed to big black hair. "They're from Yonkers. Visiting the big city for an evening of adventure."

"We come here alla time." Maria looked as if she had been born smirking. She blew a bubble.

"I bet you do, girls, I bet you do. Can I buy youse a drink?"

They looked at each other, then Maria said, "I'll have a Sex on the Beach."

Frankie looked at Tricia, who said, "I'll have a White Russian. No, on second thought, make that a Fuzzy Navel. I need to change my paces."

Frankie said, "We better watch out, Billy. These girls like the hard stuff." He went to the bar. Billy smiled at them. They huddled together and whispered fervently. Frankie came back and placed neon-colored drinks in front of them.

"So what do you girls do?"

"We told you last week."

"Forgive me, girls, my favorite aunt passed away this week. It's been kinda distracting." Frankie attempted a sad face.

Billy patted him on the shoulder to ease his pain.

Maria blew a bubble. It did not seem to matter to her whether Frankie was lying or not. "I'm a colorist. She goes to business college."

"A colorist?" Billy asked.

"Yeah. Nobody never knows what that is. I color hair. I don't cut at all—I'm more of what you would call a specialist. I went to a year of school for it. Wilfred Academy of Beauty in Cross County Mall. What do you guys do?"

"We're sandhogs," Billy said.

"What the hell's a sandhog?" Maria asked.

"I told you last week," Frankie said.

"Yeah, well, my fucking favorite uncle died. It's been kinda distracting." She blew a bubble. The smirk. "So what's a sandhog?"

"I'm awfully sorry about your uncle. What's a sandhog. You believe this, Billy? Sandhogs, we build all the tunnels. Subway tunnels, water tunnels, sewer tunnels. Anytime anyone takes a drink of water, a crap, a piss, or a train in this city, we are responsible for it or them coming or going. Not to mention anyone driving or taking a train onto the island of Manhattan by means other than bridge or ferry. And don't forget the foundations for most of the biggest buildings and bridges in town."

Tricia said, "Oh, you mean like Norton on *The Honeymooners.*"

"You're asking for it."

"What I do?"

"Norton was a sewer worker. We build tunnels, he cleaned them. We're miners."

"Oh, you mean like the Lincoln Tunnel?"

"Now you're catching on."

"That must be dangerous," Tricia said.

"My boyfriend's an ironworker," Maria said. "That's really really dangerous. He works so hard."

"Get outta here. As long as you ain't stupid enough to fall, it's sissy work. Those guys pay us to hang out with them. Ain't that right, Billy? You must be really gullible."

"No I ain't. What's that supposed to mean?" The smirk melted to a pout.

Frankie changed tactics. "You got really nice hair. I never seen such nice hair."

Billy thought he'd never seen so much hair.

Maria blushed as much as she could through the makeup. "Thanks." She blew a bubble, then stood up. "I'm going to the little girls' room. You coming, Tricia?"

"Nah. I'm okay. I don't want to start now, or I won't be able to stop. I got a weak bladder," Tricia confided.

When Maria left, Tricia was quiet. Frankie had set his sights on Maria, so he tried to sell Tricia on Billy. "Billy here won't admit it, but he's a college man. Elbow patches, little Limey convertible, the whole nine yards. Just finished. He's gonna be a lawyer. You better snag him now, before he's rich and famous and moves to Scarsdale or some shit."

Tricia turned to him. She did not seem impressed. "Really? Wow." She leaned toward him, resting her breasts on the edge of the table. "Are you another asshole that goes to college and turns into a liberal?"

Billy was taken aback. "I was a liberal before I went. Now I'm a Communist. Your father must be a Republican."

Tricia snapped her gum. "Damn straight. Voted for Reagan twice."

"And you would've if you could've."

"At least he don't give everything away to welfare."

"You kids play nice now," Frankie said.

They went through a couple more drinks, and then it was Tricia's turn to use the bathroom. When she left, Frankie turned to Billy. "She's got nice eyes, hah, Billy?"

"Those are contacts she's wearing. Her eyes ain't even green, they're gray," Maria said after sitting down.

"No. You kidding me?" Frankie demonstrated mock surprise.

"I was there when she got them."

"Billy, you hear this?"

Billy shook his head. He was scanning the room. The air was thick with smoke and cheap perfume. He went to get the next round, and by the time he came back, Maria had climbed on Frankie's lap. It looked like she was trying to swallow his head. Billy sat down and smiled at Tricia. The animosity washed away in a stream of alcohol. Fuck politics. Her eyes were moist. She touched his arm, her fingers hot. The bar melted into the background. Billy was getting too drunk to concentrate on anything farther than a few feet away. He felt warm and careless and happy to be home.

"How old did you say you were?"

She smiled coyly. "I didn't. Twenty-one."

"Come on." He took in the high curve of her young breasts, the soft skin of her neck. He suddenly wanted to pounce on her and fuck her silly. Fuck her until she denounced her father, Ronald Reagan, and Republicanism. He realized it had been awhile since he had gotten laid. He started to count the weeks—the months? He pushed that out of his mind. Women can smell desperation at a thousand paces.

"Nineteen and a half."

"And a half."

Frankie was still tongue wrestling. The band started again. A bad cover of Dire Straits. The lead singer, a skinny guy in a bad seventies mustache, sang, "Down in the tunnel, trying to make it pay . . ." Ain't that the truth, Billy thought.

Frankie came up for air, and the girls went in tandem to the bathroom. "She's hot shit, Billy. I got pulled muscles in my tongue." Frankie worked his jaw.

"Watch out she doesn't put your eye out with that hair."

"Tell me about it."

When the girls came back, they all pushed their way to the dance floor. Motion was reduced to drinking and dancing. When they danced close, Billy felt himself hard against Tricia. She smelled good, fresh. A rap song came on, and they pushed their way off the dance floor.

"I hate that nigger shit," Maria said.

"A *racist* Republican."

"I'm not racist. I just don't like their music, that's all."

"Let's get out of here. Go for a ride?" Frankie said.

Smirk, gum snap, smile. "Sure."

As they were walking toward the door, a fight erupted on the dance floor and spread like a brushfire in shifting wind. When it cut off their escape route, Frankie grabbed an unwitting drunk, slapped him across the face, and tossed him to the floor as a roadblock. A half-dozen brawlers fell over him and lay on the floor like capsized turtles, groping for purchase. Frankie then used his elbows to clear a path to the door. Billy dodged a barstool. They barreled through the door into the night, leaving the sounds of breaking glass and bone behind.

"Jesus, still Saturday Night at the Fights," Billy said, laughing.

"No shit, Billy. See what I gotta put up with for a beer?"

Maria liked Frankie even more when she saw his wheels. "Oh my God! Niiice car." He had his '66 Plymouth Belvedere convertible. "Let's put the top down."

"What, are you crazy? Shut up and hop in the back," Frankie said.

"Fuck that, I'm riding shotgun." Frankie slapped Maria in the ass as she jumped in the front seat.

Driving down Mosholu Parkway, Frankie turned to Billy. "Let's park down by the zoo."

Billy smiled, the alcohol reclaiming his veins from the adrenaline.

Maria played with the radio. "What's with the zoo?"

"We go there to enjoy nature."

In the back seat, Tricia moved close to Billy.

"Here's my number. Call me anytime." She pressed a bar napkin into his hand. He took it and said, "Sure, Tricia."

Frankie pulled off the road into the zoo parking lot. He jumped out, unlocked and opened a metal gate, then jumped back in.

"My cousin works here. Cleans up gorilla shit."

They parked by the tree line. The air smelled of wet fur and animal piss. Frankie slipped in a Peter Gabriel tape. He did not care for the music but had confided to Billy that he was convinced it could get him laid.

When Billy leaned over to kiss Tricia, their heads collided. They laughed, and then he kissed her sloppily. His hands moved over her. She deftly deflected his attempts to find flesh. Every move he made was countered. It seemed she had a dozen elbows. Their tongues stayed entwined the whole time. Then he heard Frankie yell, "Hey, watch them teeth! I want head like that, I'll jump in the fuckin' crocodile cage."

Billy tried to pull Tricia's head down. She responded with a quick elbow to the point of his chin. His hand came away covered with something sticky.

"I ain't that way. Call me first." She jumped out of the car. Billy followed her, defeated. She lit a cigarette. She blew the smoke at him, then turned her head away.

Billy popped open a can of beer. "Hey, come on. You want a sip?" She shook her head.

"Ah, fuck. I didn't mean anything by it. You get carried away, you know?" Billy downed the beer. He felt woozy and embarrassed. The car started to rock. They walked over by the fence and sat on a guardrail.

There were groans, getting louder. Billy stole a glance at the car. Was that a knee, an ass?

"She's crazy," Tricia said.

Billy thought crazy wasn't so bad. A foot popped through the hole in Frankie's ragtop. The groans became shrieks. Suddenly the zoo came alive with noise. Billy and Tricia jumped up and turned to look. From the darkness came a cacophony of animal shrieks and baying. It was as if this act of bald recreational sex were being soundly denounced.

Maria jumped out of the car. Laughing, she wiped her chin and buttoned her jeans. The convertible top rose and folded back on itself. Frankie stood on the front seat, wearing only a hard hat. "That's right, it's Saturday night and I'm gettin' me some!" His pale miner's body was luminous in the June moonlight. He looked down and gave Billy a big, fat-cat grin.

"Billy Blue-balls."

"Fuck you, Frankie."

"Let's go, girls."

Billy and the girls piled into the car.

"Aren't you gonna get dressed?" Maria asked.

"In due time, ladies."

The girls shrieked with laughter.

At the gate, they were confronted by a security guard equipped with radio and flashlight. He had the no-nonsense bearing of a retired civil servant. The situation seemed grim. Tricia clung to Billy. Frankie stood and saluted the man. "Howdeedoo, Private. I am General Swinging Dick, Master of all I survey. You, son, look like you could use a little R and R." Frankie handed him a can of beer. The guard stepped back from the car and waved them through. The look on his face said, This they do not pay me enough to fuck with.

On the drive to Yonkers, Frankie shouted, "Grab the wheel," half a dozen times, then stood like a modern-day MacArthur parading up the Canyon of Heroes and saluted oncoming traffic. It was almost too much for his passengers to bear.

Per instruction, he pulled up silently in front of Tricia's, where both the girls were staying. Crickets made the only sounds.

"Slumber party, girls?"

"Shh. My father will kill me. Call us."

As the girls tiptoed toward the house, Frankie turned to Billy. "Looks Republican, don't it?"

"Sure as shit does. Get a front lawn, become a Republican. Sad what happens to our people."

Taking this as his cue, Frankie stood up and put one foot on the horn. He honked three times and bellowed, "Your daughters are consorting with trade unionists!"

The girls scurried into the hedges just as floodlights came on and large dogs started to bark. Frankie hit the gas and left a hundred feet of tire behind.

They stopped at the White Castle on Fordham Road. Billy ordered six of the small, square cheeseburgers, some onion rings, and an orange soda. Frankie, now dressed, ordered the same thing in triplicate. The counterman took their money and gave them worn pieces of cardboard with blue numbers on them. They sat and waited for their food.

Two red-faced Fordham students in baseball team T-shirts ate at the next table. They chewed slowly, so drunk it seemed they would pass out if they stopped eating. They regarded the brown people around them with an air of distaste and superiority. One of them nodded in Frankie and Billy's direction. Hail, fellow white men.

Frankie nodded back. "Fuck you, college faggots."

The students looked at Frankie, briefly considered a fight, then turned their attention back to their onion rings.

"Thanks, Frankie."

"Shit, Billy. You ain't like those assholes."

As they walked back to the car, Billy wondered what exactly he was like.

On the short drive home, Frankie said, "We're the only guys left, Billy. Me and fuckin' you. Jimmy moved to Yonkers. Gimpy moved to California; Timmy too. They both join the navy, like asshole buddies. Fuckin' Hymie, Kenny Mac—Pearl River. Sean goes and gets himself killed. Kevin and James in the program. I mean, shit, I could go on all night." Frankie ran out of steam.

Sean had been dead nearly five years. Billy was amazed at the passage of that time. Some nights it seemed that he'd been dead only a week. The three of them had been inseparable. He had been closer to Sean than to Frankie. He winced at the memory of the night he died. Billy felt depression crowding the borders of his drunkenness. Prelude to hangover.

"Ah, fucknut, them chicks were great, eh?"

"Yeah. I got to wrestle with mine in the back seat. You almost caused a stampede at the zoo."

"Yeah, well, you ain't got these good, you know, Ryan looks. Hey, remember the way they ran for cover?" They both had a laugh over that.

Frankie stopped in front of Billy's. "Billy, come by tomorrow. I got a new video—two and a half hours, nothing but hockey fights. It's great. We'll get some beers and check it out."

Billy stopped in the bar before going up to bed. A sole patron, his forehead on the bar, snored loudly.

"He's a great conversationalist, Billy." Eddie Mahan stood behind the other end of the bar, a drink in his hand. His eyes glowed eerily in the neon light. He, too, was drunk.

"Uncle Eddie, you all right?" Billy addressed the bartender as he had when he was a kid.

"All right? Hell, Billy, I'm fine and dandy. I've got a perfect audience, plenty of supplies." He indicated the liquor shelf with a majestic sweep of his hand. "What more can a man ask for?" He picked up a coaster and flung it down the bar like a Frisbee, bouncing it off the sleeper's head.

"Not much, I guess."

Eddie seemed to come a few degrees more sober. "This is it, Billy," he said somberly.

Billy looked at Eddie for a minute. He had seen him drunk many times before, but something was different about him.

"What's it, Eddie?"

"What you've got to leave behind."

Butcher Boy Tierney drove through the Lincoln Tunnel, trying to figure out how he had spent twelve thousand dollars in less than a week. It was a mystery to him. The whole week flashed back at him in images. The killing in the Bronx crack house, the trip to Atlantic City, the night in the Korean whorehouse. He distinctly remembered getting paid for the Bronx job. Thing about Jack's guineas, they paid and paid promptly. It was after that that things got hazy, like he wasn't sure what parts were real and what parts happened in a dream.

Suddenly he remembered taking the ears off the honcho who

thought he was a badass. He thought about the ears, and panic hit him like a force. Where the fuck had he put them?

He came up on the car in front of him and realized he was doing eighty. Decelerating, he looked in his rearview mirror. No cops. He pulled to the side of the road and patted his pockets as if he might find them there. Taking a deep breath—he had to be calm—he took out a Handi Wipe and vigorously wiped his face and hands. He felt all clammy, bad nervous. He fumbled with a prescription bottle filled with Valium, swallowed half a dozen, and drove on, feeling his way around the desolate side streets of Jersey City.

Seeing the motel, he pulled into the parking lot. Garden State Motor Lodge. It always struck him as funny that they called Jersey the Garden State. Place didn't even have too many trees. All he ever saw were smokestacks and shit. He parked at the end of the lot, far from the office. The motel looked like the kind of place where businessmen might go for a quick afternoon hump. The kind where people went to great lengths to mind their own business. Hourly Rates.

Carrying a gym bag, he walked up the stairs to the second floor. The Valium was kicking in nice, taking the edge off. He almost felt happy.

As he knocked on the door of room 247, he scanned the parking lot. Nothing. Cars and trucks sped by on Route 1-9. The door opened, and a young college-looking asshole stood there. The guy stepped back and waved him into the room.

"You're late, my man." He looked at his watch.

Butcher Boy nodded and grunted in response.

"That's okay. Tone says you're okay, says you're good people. He says you're good people, you're good people in my book." He extended his hand and said, "The name's Marc—Marc with a *c*."

The gym bag still in his right hand, Butcher Boy reached over with his left and grabbed the guy's hand.

Butcher Boy put the gym bag on the bed. The place smelled of mothballs and cheap sex. He made an effort not to touch anything in the room. He was conscious of germs, bacteria lurking. He watched the college asshole take a briefcase from under the bed and place it on the dresser, his back turned. He snapped it open and pulled out a bag full of white powder, turning so Butcher Boy could see him.

"This, my friend, is the finest product the fair nation of Colombia has to offer." He held the bag aloft as if he were making an offering. He placed it on the bed, opened it, and scooped some rocks and powder onto a tray.

Butcher Boy watched him chop the coke into long thick lines. The Valium was coming on a little too strong. He felt detached.

"Here." Marc with a *c* offered him the tray and a rolled-up hundred-dollar bill. Butcher Boy leaned over and inhaled.

The coke hit him like a fresh, cold breeze. He stood up straight and smiled. He was refocused, on top of the situation.

Marc with a *c* followed his lead, making a show of it. He held his head back, with his eyes shut, like he was getting a blow job.

"Yes indeed. That, my friend, is how it should be. These people I deal with are heavyweights. The big time. They take very, very good care of me. You notice the Beamer in the lot? The black one? That was a bonus, a gift. I move product, my man—that's why they take care of me. Tone says *you* are in a position to move product. Well, you do right by me, my man, I'll be sure to pass along a good word." The guy was all hand movements. Fluffing his hair, smoothing the creases in his jeans, picking at the front of his polo shirt.

"Because I, my man, am a week away from my MBA. That's right. I'm going to quit and go legit. A regular Joe Kennedy. That's me."

Butcher Boy wondered why cocaine made everyone talk so fucking much. With him, all the talking went on inside his head.

"You ever—"

"Let's take care of business, Dobie Gillis." Butcher Boy turned and opened his gym bag.

The dealer looked like his mouth was stuck in neutral, like he was having a hard time being interrupted. "Well, yes. Here is my end of the bargain." He pushed the case shut and tossed it on the bed.

Butcher Boy reached into his bag. He heard a noise from the bathroom. He stopped and looked up at the dealer. The dealer froze.

"The fuck?"

"Just a little insurance, you understand."

Butcher Boy pulled his hands out of the bag. In his right hand was a pistol, in his left, a silencer. He tried to screw the silencer onto the pistol. He dropped the silencer as the door opened. He raised the pistol to the Spanish-looking guy coming out of the bathroom and shot him in the neck. He turned to Marc with a *c*.

"I . . ." The dealer struggled to make words. He started to sob.

"You finally shut the fuck up." Butcher Boy shot him twice in the head. He sat down and snorted a couple of fat lines. Then he picked up the silencer, took the gun, the drugs, and left.

Driving back to New York, he felt good. Back in the saddle. At least now he would not have to go to Jack for money.

Vito sat quietly, watching Tuzio handle a discipline problem. The guy with the problem was young, maybe twenty-five. He stood a head taller than Tuzio.

"What, are you some kinda fuckin' retard? I gotta give you a special education, spell things out for you like some kinda dope drools all over himself?"

In response, the young guy just shrugged and bit his lip. Tuzio reached up and slapped him across the face—front of hand, then back. Tears welled in the kid's eyes. Vito hoped Tuzio kept it in control. He was in no mood to be disposing of a body.

Tuzio had been growing increasingly unpredictable as he watched the trial of Fat Tony Salerno progress. The series of betrayals unfolding in the Manhattan courtroom fed his paranoia.

"I take you in off the street, I give you a fuckin' income, separate you from the welfare office you was headed for, you fuckin' degenerate. Now you interrupt my peaceable afternoon to tell me you fuckin' lost the guy's address? What, am I suppos' to feel sorry for you? I should make a corpse outta you." He turned to Vito. "You believe this fuck?"

Vito watched as Tuzio's color went from pale to pink to crimson. Tuzio, moving with surprising swiftness for a man of his girth, turned on his underling and punched him hard in the face. The guy dropped straight down. He hit the ground and started to grope, trying to pull himself up. Tuzio kicked him square in the temple. "Stay the fuck where I put you!"

He turned back to Vito and sat down. "Now tell me about this tunnel thing, about the Irishers."

It had been Vito's idea to use the Irish gang as a kind of auxiliary crew. A few years back, they had made some brazen moves against Tuzio rackets in Manhattan. Vito had been the one to convince Tuzio that co-opting the Irish was a better move than getting involved in a sloppy shooting war with them. So far it had worked well. There was plenty of work for everyone. Vito felt the tunnel piece was perfect for the Irish.

Vito leaned close under the blare of the television.

"We let the Irish gang handle it. This union, these guys won't go easy—they got their own muscle, John. I think we let them soften it up for us, then we go in, set it up for ourselves."

Tuzio stuck a thick finger into his ear and dug around. "They did a nice job in the Bronx. Nice piece of work."

Vito thought about that. It made him queasy. The stories coming out on that one, these Irish guys were like a pack of wild Comanches, chopping people up. But he knew that appealed to Tuzio's sense of mayhem.

"All right," Tuzio continued, "but I think we send one of our people along, keep an eye on things. Maybe we'll send the fuckin' retardo here, give him a chance to redeem himself." He kicked the guy on the floor. "Hey you, get outta here." The guy scrambled to his feet. "You go home, you stay in that house, you don't do nothing or go nowheres till I send for you. You unnerstan'? Now get the fuck out.

"Where's all the smart kids nowadays? Hah, Vito? They must be runnin' off to college and screwing Wasp broads. It's a shame." Tuzio grew silent.

Vito was about to leave, when Tuzio said, "You just never know, you never fuckin' know. I seen inna paper, Vito, this guy down Florida, one of those trailer parks. He's arguing with the wife. She wants to go bowling, he don't wanna go bowling. For this I don't blame him, bowling. He gives her a smack, she calls the cops. The guy runs down the street—whack!" Tuzio slammed his hand on the table. "Lightning bolt hits him right inna ass. Dead. You just never fuckin' know."

Vito nodded at the story. As close as he was with John Tuzio, he knew it meant nothing. The second Tuzio perceived that he, Vito, was an impediment to his cash flow or his freedom, Tuzio would put a knife in his heart and smile while he was doing it. Vito stood, feeling a sudden need for fresh air. He hoped he had made the right suggestion on the tunnel job.

Billy Adare stood outside Yankee Stadium and scanned the crowd for his brother. He watched people pour off the subway, the suits from downtown mixing with the Bermuda-shorts crowd from the suburbs making a rare foray into the wilds of New York City, their one trip beyond the pale.

Billy was anxious to see Paddy. The last time they had gotten together was back in January, and that was only briefly. If there was anyplace that evoked his relationship with Paddy, it was this cavern of ghosts and heroes. He thought of those summer nights and days when he would accompany Paddy here. His grandfather the Irishman never took to baseball, so it was Paddy who took him by the hand and introduced him to this magical place. The electric crack of the bat in the hot night, the roar of the crowd, the baying of vendors. It was in this stadium that their relationship was formed.

After the games, Paddy would escort him home and then ride the subway back to Manhattan. Billy always felt secure with Paddy, who even as a young teenager had some elemental confidence that Billy felt he would never possess. When he was a kid, Billy thought Paddy was invincible, and somehow this aura extended to him, Billy. When Paddy was fighting, he was a real hero in the neighborhood, although he lived miles away. Everyone wanted to be part of Paddy's fame, and Billy basked in his early glories. Later, as Paddy rose in an altogether different way, he was, in the insane way of the streets, held in an even higher esteem.

But the glow of Paddy's celebrity stopped abruptly at his grandfather's doorstep. Since the manslaughter conviction, JP and Paddy had rarely spoken. With Billy it was different. No matter what his crimes, Billy simply could not judge his brother. The bond of their blood transcended morality or right and wrong. They were brothers, plain and simple. He wished Paddy had made it as a fighter or could leave and become something else, far from the world of mayhem and hurt. But that was not the case.

Billy felt a fear, a deep worry in the pit of his stomach about Paddy. He was smart enough to know that his belief in Paddy's invincibility was a child's illusion, like Santa Claus, or believing you could be anything you wanted to be when you grew up. Billy knew his brother's world could come crashing down on him at any time.

He saw Paddy coming through the crowd with Rosa and Mickey Lawless. Even smiling, Paddy and Mickey gave off that air of fuck-you. The crowd instinctively opened for them. The fans who wanted to gawk at Rosa's dark beauty merely stole glances. Rosa had been the first real sexual infatuation of Billy's life. She still made his knees sag and his cheeks burn.

"Hey, Einstein." Paddy gave him a bear hug.

Billy shook hands with Mickey. Rosa gave him a kiss and a hug.

"Good seats?" Billy said.

"Who the fuck you kidding? Of course."

The seats were directly behind the Red Sox dugout. Billy sat between Paddy and Rosa. Mickey started in on Wade Boggs the minute they sat down.

"Hey, you adulterer! Boggs, you pervert!" Mickey leaned over the dugout, shouting.

Billy and Paddy laughed.

"Come on, Mickey, there's kids around. Sit down." Paddy grabbed Mickey by the shirt and pulled him down.

"Fuck that, Paddy. The man is a degenerate. He deserves whatever he gets. You know Billy Bird? The guy they call Big Daddy? He works security down the hotel where the Sox stay. Tells me the guy is always bringing in strange broads. Not his wife."

Rosa said, "Mickey the saint. Billy, you hear about the time he had two wives? I think that might be worse than adultery. What do you call that, bigamy?"

"Ah, come on, Rosa, that's not fair. It wasn't my fault. And besides, this is different. I ain't no role model."

The crowd rose to their feet as Mattingly took Clemens to the wall. They sat with a collective sigh.

"Billy, you remember we used to come here, those night games, the place was practically empty. April games. May."

"Yeah. I remember freezing my ass off, chasing the foul balls down the line. I still got a few of those balls lying around."

"No shit? You could run like a fuckin' gazelle, that's for sure."

"Remember Reggie came out that time, signed that home-run ball?"

"Yeah, I also remember that prick—what was his name?"

"Jim Rice?"

"Yeah, Rice. That guy treating you like shit, a little kid waiting for him out there. Told you to get lost. I came this close to throwing him a beating."

The crowd went wild as Dan Pasqua slapped a fastball into the cheap seats. The loudspeaker blasted "We will rock you." They sat down. Mickey bought a round of beers. When the inning ended, Mickey continued his ribbing of Wade Boggs, who cast angry looks in their direction.

"That's right, you fucking degenerate!"

A bald, red-faced man leaned over from the row behind and said, "Hey, pal, I got the grandkids here. I mean, can you tone it down a bit? Please."

Mickey looked over the three blond-haired kids. "That's some good-lookin' grandkids." The kids looked at Mickey shyly. "Sure, mister, I'll clean it up a bit. But I can't let the guy off the hook. I mean, that wouldn't even be fair to the kids, you know."

The man leaned back and shrugged at his wife. He'd made the effort.

Paddy put his arm around Billy. "You need help? I hear those lawyer schools ain't cheap."

"Money's good with the hogs, you know? I should be okay. Get some more student loans if I need them."

"Get outta here. Student loans. You'll be an old toothless fuck, the time you pay back the government. You come see me, I'll give you a rate."

"Watch him, Billy," Mickey said. "He's in constant violation of the state's lending laws."

Billy laughed and let the subject trail off. He had to balance himself between Paddy and his grandfather. He'd been in the middle since Paddy went away to prison. His grandfather had made him promise not to take money from Paddy. JP did not want Billy corrupted by Paddy's illegal gains. He had the immigrant's burning belief in the benefits of hard, honest labor.

Paddy went to the men's room. Rosa put her arm around Billy.

"He's so proud of you, Billy. He's always bragging on you to everyone. You should call him, come by more often." She squeezed his thigh. He felt faint. Her smell enveloped him, and it was something wondrous.

In the seventh inning, Wade Boggs made an error that cost the Red Sox the game. Mickey was ecstatic. On the way out of the stadium, they stopped at Boss Tweed's for beers. They drove Billy home. Paddy stopped on the corner.

"Hey, Billy, I think those are drug dealers." Mickey, in the back seat, shook his head. "That's awful. Such flagrant disregard for the law."

"How's the old man?" Paddy asked.

Billy tensed. "He's good, the same."

"He tell you I called?"

"Yeah." Billy tugged at the front of his shirt.

"Tuesday?"

"Something like that."

"Yeah, right."

"Come on, Paddy, don't bust my balls. I gotta live with him. He's good to me."

"Yeah. I guess he oughta be. Here, buy yourself some pencils, Einstein. Happy graduation." Paddy put his arm around Billy and pulled him close. He stuffed something in Billy's shirt pocket. "Now get lost. Call me."

Billy stood on the corner and watched as Paddy sped away. Reaching into his pocket, he took out the money—five hundred-dollar bills, so shiny and new they glowed. He stood under the streetlight in the close Bronx night, the crisp bills calling to him like temptation.

Vito Romero strolled along the Battery Park promenade, eating an ice cream cone. He came upon an empty bench and sat down. The sky was a deep June blue, with soft clouds floating overhead. Vito took in the wide sweep of the Hudson River, the boats sailing into New York Harbor. The sun and the salt air were almost enough to make him feel young again. He considered taking a ride on the Staten Island ferry when he was finished meeting with Jack Tierney. Pay his half a buck, relax for an hour.

Tourists, sweaty and laden with cameras, gawked at Ellis Island and the Statue of Liberty. Vito watched the families—impatient fathers and tolerant mothers shepherding young kids who for the most part appeared to be still full of something like wonder. When Angela was a little girl, he would take her places like this, her big brown eyes always wide with happiness. That seemed to Vito to have been a very long time ago. Last night she had come home at 4 A.M. drunker than an off-duty Irish cop on payday, her lip pierced, her eyes heavy with the booze. Sweet Jesus. What was he gonna do with her?

He looked north along the promenade, and there came Jack Tierney, one of the most cunning and vicious men Vito had ever met in the violent business he called his own. Dragging a kid about five years old, Tierney was trying to move inconspicuously, just another pasty-faced accountant whiling away his vacation time in the Big Apple. Fat fucking chance. The guy was all thickness and menace, the linebacker going to seed.

Bringing the kid was actually a smart move. Vito admired that—the guy was watching out for himself. Not many shooters Vito knew would carry out a hit, guy had his little kid along.

"Say hi to your uncle Vito. This here is Jimmy."

The kid was towheaded and sullen. Chip off the old block.

"Hey, Jimmy, you like ice cream? Here, Jackie, let's get the kid a cone."

Vito bought Jimmy a cone, and Jack said, "Thank your uncle Vito."

The kid smiled shyly. Maybe there was hope.

"Go watch the water." Jack pushed his kid toward the fence. Jimmy sat against it, his world reduced to the ice cream cone.

"Jackie. Siddown." Vito indicated the empty bench beside him. "Have a look at the view—today the view is fucking great. You can see clear out the Narrows."

Tierney sat down heavily. He was the kind of guy who did everything with force. He pulled off his sunglasses. "Yeah, looks like a fuckin' postcard, don't it though?"

"Someday, Jackie, I'm gonna get one of them boats for myself. Take a nice long sail trip."

"Not a bad idea, long's you don't get seasick."

"This is true."

Now it was time for business. First a compliment. "Jack, your guys did nice work. The big man, he's happy. That's a good thing. He likes to be happy—makes him like most of us, I guess. Now listen. We got something new for you. We got a little union problem needs straightening out. There's a guy, a business agent with the sandhogs—the tunnel guys?"

"Yeah. Bernie Coyle. I know who he is."

"Is that right?"

"I came out of the can one time, I went to work on a tunnel job."

"No problem, doing this job?"

"Business is business. I don't owe the guy nothing. It wasn't no fucking picnic working in that hole."

"Good professional attitude. We want he should get a message. Now, of course you do it your way. But Jack, one thing I've found over the years—what works best is fear. You don't need to go in there like cowboys alla time. You never hit the principal. You hit around him, most guys get the message. Come around like gentlemen."

"Vito, not a problem."

Vito paused while a man in dark sunglasses passed too close.

"I can't stress this too much. We don't want no one getting killed don't hafta be killed. You get a guy like this, gets up there in years, thinking about retirement. He don't wanna start his golden years in a wheelchair, all busted up. Worse yet, he don't want to miss them altogether."

"Know someone that does?"

"Exactly. Now, this work is more high-profile. Crack dealers—let's be honest here—outside of their mothers, nobody gives a rat fuck. Matter a fact, most people wanna run you for mayor, you take out enough of them. A union leader, that's more of what you call a citizen. Especially one that's legit, like this guy. You get heat—newspapers, feds, the six a'clock fuckin' news for chrissake. You gotta keep it under control."

"Yeah, no problem. Straightforward like. Throw him a beating."

" 'Cause now, Jackie, you're hitting in the big leagues. And in the big leagues, you fuck up, you strike out, people notice. You got more at stake." Vito let that thought hang out there a minute, then said, "How's the kid, your brother?"

"Okay. We got a hook with his PO."

"The other guy, the boxer? *Marrone,* that fucking guy could bang, both hands." Vito made a little bob-and-weave motion.

Tierney hesitated before saying, "He's doing fine."

Vito heard something there. Trouble in paradise? Maybe, maybe not. But it was another fact or feeling to stash away in case. Vito's head was full of such information. Who liked who, who was angry with who and for what. What a guy did to relax, where he might let his guard down. Who fucked around with whose woman. Who grew up together, did time together. Grudges unsettled. A catalog useful for deception and betrayal.

"Good. He seems like a capable guy, and Jackie, this business, these days—few and far between."

"You ain't shitting."

"Here—read that." Vito handed him a piece of paper with a name and address on it. "Memorize it."

Tierney read it and handed it back to Vito, who walked over and dropped it into the Hudson. He bent over and patted Jimmy Tierney on the head, handing him a dollar bill. "Here, Jimmy, put that in your piggy bank, from Uncle Vito."

"Hey, Daddy, Uncle Vito got a beef?"

"Good-looking kid. Must look like the mother."

Jack Tierney did not laugh.

"As a favor to the big man, we're gonna send a kid along. He's all right, learning the ropes, up and coming."

"Yeah, why not."

"One more thing, Jack." They leaned on the railing. Vito looked down at the dark waters swirling along. "Out of gratitude, the big man wants you to have a piece of this drywall contractor out of Yonkers. Nice legitimate cash flow. It'll help you out, the feds start nosing around. Eliot will put it together for you."

"Thanks. That's nice of you. I appreciate it."

"You're just getting your due, Jackie. Just getting your due."

Vito, watching Jack Tierney walk away through the tourists, thought: Christ, I'm tired of tough guys. He looked at his watch. Not enough time for the ferry. He cursed softly and headed for his car.

Mary Moy unwrapped her pastrami sandwich. She smoothed the foil and regarded the pile of greasy meat between two thick slices of rye bread. She popped a diet Coke and took a sip. She put the soda down and lifted the massive sandwich to her lips. It seemed all she wanted to do lately was gorge herself on grease. She talked to her friends and her sisters about pregnancy. They told stories of morning sickness, of emotional roller coasters and irrational cravings. So far she had been assailed by a huge appetite for unhealthy foods, the greasier the better. Cheeseburgers, french fries, eggs, bacon, sausage, fried chicken, fried fish, fried everything. Last night she had devoured two orders of sweet-and-sour pork at the local Chinese dive. The other affliction visited upon her by pregnancy was a growing inclination to nap. It came upon her with the wallop of a narcotic. The day before, she had fought fiercely to stay awake during an afternoon briefing.

She drank some Coke and imagined giving birth to a giant blob of fat. Like one of those fifteen-pound slabs they held aloft to frighten housewives into buying some forty-nine-dollar piece of plastic that promised to transform them into supermodels with minimum effort. She considered tossing the sandwich away. Instead she sank her teeth into it as if it were the last meal on earth. She was halfway through the sandwich when her door slammed open.

She looked up with a start, grease dribbling down her chin. A man stood in the doorway. He was large, rumpled, and square. He looked like an old-time beat cop dressed for a wake. His head melted into a thick neck, which he stood there and scratched. "Whoa. Sorry to interrupt your meal. Looks like you're enjoying it." He looked past her, scanning the room.

Mary Moy placed her sandwich down on the foil. She wiped her chin. She bagged the remains of her lunch and dropped it in the wastebasket. She said, "You are?"

"I'm looking for Agent Moy. He around?"

She clenched her jaw. He was not the first man to presume she was a member of the secretary pool. She stood, her service revolver visible on her hip. "I'm Agent Moy. Who are you?"

Without blinking or blushing or stammering, as they usually did, he said, "Patrick Cullen. NYPD."

She shook his oversize hand. Maybe it was an honest mistake and not an ignorant presumption. He pulled out a chair and sat directly across from her. His broad face seemed to have been made from pliant, dented clay. He looked worn by time. Except his eyes. Something danced there that seemed decades younger than the face they were set into.

They exchanged guarded interagency pleasantries. She laid out the case for him in general terms, the mutual mistrust subtle but plain.

"We hear you have a lot of insight regarding the Tierney crew."

"Tierney crew. Jack would get a hard-on, he heard you say that. He fancies himself a crime boss." He had a pleasant face when he smiled.

"We have a good sense of the Italians. But this Tierney's name is turning up everywhere we look. We are considering widening the focus of our operation. I hope you can provide some insight. As we progress, you can serve as a consultant."

The detective nodded. "Patrick Cullen, consultant. Nice ring to it. You got another of them diet colas?"

Mary went to the refrigerator and brought back two cans. She handed one to Cullen. He took it and said, "Jackie Tierney. I can tell you about Jackie Tierney."

Mary Moy sensed she was about to be regaled. These old-time city cops, the ones that were beyond proving themselves, beyond cynicism even, seemed to enjoy nothing more than telling the tales of their job. He started as he might if he were down at the end of some cop bar after a tour, surrounded by young suppliants.

"It was back in the sixties. Lemme see." He held up his hand as if counting the years on his fingers. The bang-clank of a pile driver started out in the street. "Must've been '65, '66 maybe. I was working anticrime on the West Side. The city was going through a lot those days. You had your riots uptown, whites running for the suburbs like they were being chased by an invading army. Drugs. Drugs were just coming in big then. Crime was the number-one issue. Some things never change, huh? Anyways, there was a killing in the neighborhood. A local merchant was shot down in his store. Guy sold shoes. Was there forever. I used to get my school shoes there when I was a kid." Cullen paused. He pulled out a soiled handkerchief and proceeded to blow his nose furiously. Finished, he tucked it away and went on. "Excuse me there. Truth was, the guy was running numbers, tide him over when the shoes weren't moving fast enough. Doesn't make him the worst guy in the world.

"Jack Tierney was seventeen, eighteen at the time, working as muscle for a local boss. Turns out the shoemaker was skimming. They send Jack to set the record straight. Jack already had a scary reputation by that time. Now, what transpired exactly I can't say. But Tierney pops the guy, end of story. Just another half-assed wise-guy mess, right? You would think so. Problem was, the papers got ahold of it. They turn it into a symbol of the downfall of civilization, barbarism, all that. The wife and kids weeping. Wouldn't you know it but the widow's brother runs a parish up in the Bronx. So now we have the saintly victim, the martyr, the all-around good guy. Not some schlep bookie stupid enough to steal from the animals." Cullen finished the soda and crushed the can in his hand. He looked around till he located the wastebasket, then tossed the can in a smooth arc into the bucket.

"Now, everybody knows Tierney done it. But witnesses are suddenly struck dumb and blind. Which is a common occurrence in some parts of this city. Ninety-eight percent of the neighborhood people, they might be honest citizens, but why stick your neck out for a guy they all know was not on the level. This left us with nada to go with. The only hope we got is a confession. You got one more of these diet colas?"

Mary got him another soda and waited for him to continue. It was the time of day when she usually felt a great need to nap. Cullen's visit had changed that. He was a charismatic presence.

"The word comes down to find Tierney. I happened to be driving down the avenue when he comes out of a tenement. I'm from the neighborhood, people know me. I say, Hey, Jackie, let's do the smart thing here. Come for a ride. My partner opens the door for him, and he gets in without a beef. Like he knew there was no way we had a case. We don't even cuff him. We turn him over to Homicide. This was a Friday evening." He took a deep drink of soda. "I put away seven, eight of these a day since I gave up the booze.

"Now, Tierney, he knows he's gonna spend a hard weekend. This was before Miranda." Cullen said it like it was a lost epoch to be mourned. Before Miranda. The good old days. "Back then you got a hard case, you take him down the basement, handcuff him to a chair, and let the pros go to work on him. It never took long. The place was horrible. It stunk of crap and piss, there were rats, one bare bulb lit the room. It was some type of medieval torture chamber. Which was the idea. You didn't want anyone comfortable down there."

Cullen paused. He produced a cigar and twirled it in his hand. He took a breath and said, "I never got too personally involved in those things. There were enough guys then that enjoyed it. These angry guys kept coming out of the basement with blood splattered on them all weekend long. They worked on Tierney for thirty-six straight hours. It became a titanic battle of wills. These old-time cops, all from World War Two and Korea, they took it as an affront that they could not break the kid. Me and my partner, they had us take him back where we found him. There was not much left of him. But he was still cursing us. I called an ambulance as soon as we dropped him off. He was in the hospital for fourteen weeks. He got out and went to Vietnam. The rest, as they say, is history.

"I had a few beers with one of those cops about a week later. He said it was like they were beating on an I beam all weekend. He said it was the scariest thing he'd ever seen. This from a guy that went straight from high school to an infantry unit at the Bulge. Guy put in his papers the next day. Said if he had to go up against that crap, he'd rather get the house down Florida. Play with the grandkids."

Mary was surprised at Cullen's mood swing. During the course of the story he had turned reflective. There was something like remorse in his voice. "You know, I wonder sometimes what terrible lesson we taught that kid over that weekend." He ran a hand through his graying hair. He tugged at the bottom of his tie.

Mary Moy nodded. This business of basement beatings meted out by police was alien to her. The most she had seen in her time with the Bureau was the occasional surreptitious kidney punch.

"Ah, hell. What are you gonna do?" He snapped back, was all bluster and cop bravado again, his face lit by a boyish smile. "Listen. All these stories about Jack Tierney, everybody's got a favorite. You know what mine is?"

"No." She wondered if she was in the mood to hear it.

"There was this mutt in the neighborhood, awhile back. Real mad-dog desperado type named Screwdriver Belson."

"Screwdriver?"

"Yeah, Screwdriver. And he did not get that moniker because he used said instrument to pop off hubcaps. Anyway, Screwdriver feared no one. Turned out to be his biggest mistake in life. He would tell anyone that listened what he thought of Jack Tierney, and let's just say he was not very complimentary. That you can be sure of. Unfortunately for Screwdriver, Jack does not take kindly to people that insult him. Maybe he's got a sensitive side. Story goes that he lured Screwdriver somewhere and made him a pair of concrete shoes. Nice touch, right? A nod to the old days. But while Jack might be old-fashioned, a traditionalist at times, he's also a modernist. They say he put Screwdriver in those concrete shoes but before he dropped him in the river he fitted him with scuba gear. Taped the regulator over his mouth. Tied his hands behind his back, then tossed him in. Gave Screwdriver plenty of time to think what a bad idea calling Jackie Tierney names was. I wonder what was going through Screwdriver's mind, he's down there watching the carp swim by, maybe a snapping turtle or two."

"Nice guy." Mary Moy felt weariness coming on. All the mayhem she stared at each day took a toll. Outside her windows, the sun moved out from behind a bank of clouds.

"Yeah. Is it true? Matters is, people think it is."

Mary stood and thanked Patrick Cullen for coming by. When the detective left, she perused the folders she had on Jack Tierney's crew. She took out his mug shots and looked at the face that inspired such terror. He had thick Irish features that were totally devoid of pleasantness. The picture reminded Mary Moy of a portrait of a captured Indian warrior she had seen once, the unsettling power, the look that said the only way to stop me is to kill me. Well, Jack Tierney, we'll see about that.

She was a quarter Irish, on her father's side. The Irish she knew back in Missouri were soft and successful, with nice lawns; they voted Republican and were only mildly nostalgic about their heritage. A green tie on Saint Patrick's Day, maybe a plate of corned beef and cabbage. If they were really into it, they sent their kids to Notre Dame. Jack Tierney and his associates were of another stripe altogether. They seemed locked in the bloody tribalism of a former age. She considered Patrick Cullen. He had come from the same place as Jack Tierney. She was glad he was on her side.

She incorporated Tierney's folder into the Operation Wrecking Ball file. She slapped the file drawer shut and put her head on her desk. All she wanted was ten minutes' rest. Loose clothes would not conceal her condition much longer. The minute she put in for maternity leave, she knew the sharks would be circling, waiting to take credit for her work.

The muscles along Billy's back and shoulders hardened. The calluses on his hands grew in thick ridges. His body clock adjusted to working the graveyard shift. He slept deeper during the hot summer days. He banked his weekly paychecks. His only real extravagance was Saturday-night barhopping with Frankie.

He went downstairs to catch the Yankees game and wait for his ride to work. JP was filling in behind the bar. Eileen McCoy was nursing a highball. She had a racing form, a pack of Pall Malls, and a bologna sandwich on the bar in front of her.

"Comere, Billy, tell me about the girls at college. I bet they were beating down your door up there."

"It really wasn't that distracting."

"I bet you were dating Protestant girls, weren't you?"

"Whatever I could get my hands on, tell the truth."

"Have your fun, Billy, but when you're ready, marry a nice Cat'lic girl. Protestants believe too much in the divorce. JP, freshen me up. And give me a glass with some water. My gums are killing me." She placed her dentures in the glass.

"Whatever you do, Billy, enjoy life. You don't wanna be old. I'll be seventy-seven in September. I'm older than that kook we got for a President."

Billy drank a Coke and looked forward to work. The nightly toil had become enjoyable, now that it was linked with a growing bank account. As he sat in the bar, watching Eileen and his grandfather, Billy felt a strange sense that he could walk through walls and would live forever, felt inside himself a current of energy potent enough to power the city. It was as if their age and frailty had just dawned on him, and they seemed a different species altogether. He tried to imagine what such proximity to death was like. It was beyond him. He was too young and strong and alive. For him, anything was possible.

Thinking about his grandfather and death, he felt guilt wash over him. He went over to the jukebox and looked for something cheerful. Too many Irish songs, songs of despair and loss, bloodshed and betrayal. What a happy race. He punched in "Rising of the Moon," a nice song about insurrection and skull bashing.

He heard Eileen's voice. "Now promise me when you get to be Mr. Bigshot you won't forget where you come from. You'll come back and buy me a drink from time to time."

"That's if you're not banned from here by then." JP placed a fresh whiskey in front of Eileen, then retreated to the end of the bar.

"Billy, is your grandfather irregular again?"

"Beats me, Mrs. McCoy. He seems okay."

Eileen got quiet then. She sometimes would sit there lost in the fog of memory. If she had too many highballs, she would sit and cry silently, the tears muddying her makeup. The first time Billy had seen her cry was shortly after her husband died. Billy had asked her if she was thinking about Mr. McCoy. She had replied, "Yeah. I'm wondering how I spent forty-three years of my life with that bastard."

On the ride to work, Frankie was quiet, an occurrence about as frequent as a lunar eclipse. He looked stricken.

"Frankie, what's with you today?" Billy drummed his fingers on the dashboard.

Frankie attempted to speak, but only sounds came out, no syllables. He shook his head.

Billy looked over at him as they came to a stoplight. "Frankie, my whole life I've known everything about you. I know about the time you slept with Maureen O'Hare, quite possibly the ugliest girl to ever walk the streets of the Bronx. I know about the time you got the crabs, remember? You didn't know what it was, so you put one in a Dixie cup and showed it to your mother. I know you stole the chalice from the church and traded it for a Bad Company eight-track. I know you Krazy Glued the locks on the convent door six, no, seven times."

"This is different."

"Gimme a break, Frankie. Worse than fucking O'Hare? I doubt it."

Frankie drove on. "I called the clinic today, the donation place."

"Yeah, so what's wrong? Their check bounced?"

"Uh-uh."

"So?" Billy turned down the stereo.

"Low sperm count." The words escaped Frankie's lips like the last gasp of a dying man.

Billy stifled a laugh. Frankie looked devastated, his manhood laid to waste by three short words. Billy did not have it in him to bust his balls over this one.

"Shit, that doesn't mean a thing. I had a biology class at college. Sperm counts go up and down all the time. Depends on what you eat, when you last got laid, how tight your underwear is, all kinds of shit. Serious. Relax, Frankie, it's no big deal."

"Are you sure?" Frankie pleaded.

Billy had no idea. He vaguely remembered something from Biology 101. Since he started college, Frankie had deferred to him on matters of fact. Billy occasionally took advantage.

"I'm positive. Besides, do you really want to start bumping into these kids in bars twenty years from now? They might all start asking for back child support. Twenty years times four, five thousand kids, that's a lot of dough. It just ain't worth forty bucks a pop."

"Shit, maybe you're right."

"Plus you'd probably go blind."

"That would have happened by eighth grade, it was gonna."

They parked by the river and walked up the hill to the job site. A crowd had gathered outside the superintendent's trailer. The shop steward, Bobby Barrett, his red face plump from a decade of soft duty, was arguing with the super.

"It says in the fuckin' contract the company shall supply all appropriate safety equipment."

The superintendent's voice stayed even. "There's your problem, Barrett. You don't have a contract anymore."

Billy thought the super looked like a warden from back when prisons were still called prisons and seen as punishment, not rehabilitation. He could see him policing a chain gang with a bullwhip, just to prove he was a hands-on boss.

"That's bullshit. We got precedent."

"I'm going into my office to take care of business. I suggest you do the same. Whoever does not want to go to work, I'll get their money right here and now." He pushed past Barrett and climbed the stairs to his trailer. As he was opening the door, a soda can bounced off the wall. Laughter from the crowd. He turned and cast a grim look over the assembled sandhogs, then went inside and closed the door behind him.

Barrett turned back and pushed through the crowd. He was going to call Bernie Coyle, the business agent, and register another complaint.

Lenny Coyle leaned against the wall of the hoghouse. Billy went over to him, and Lenny said, "Everyone thinks these guys are joking. Watch what happens."

That night Billy drilled without a mask. He wrapped a damp T-shirt around his head to protect himself from the rock dust. The mood of the gang was sour. After the blast, they waited for the air to clear so they could return to work.

"The company can't afford masks. Bullshit." Bobby Washington trimmed his fingernails with a small folding knife.

"Scumbags." Frankie spit out rock grit he'd inhaled. "Well, maybe it's time we teach them a little manners."

The men nodded in agreement. They turned as a man car came chugging up the tunnel, out of the mist. It pulled to a stop where the gang stood, and the superintendent, Chris Devine, one of his assistants, and a city engineer stepped off. Bobby Moran, the motorman, gave the finger to their backs as they walked toward the gang. Devine looked at his watch and said, "McIntyre, what are you waiting for?"

The Mule, who rarely spoke at all unless barking orders, simply said, "Smoke time."

"I heard the shot twenty-five minutes ago. That's long enough." Devine looked glumly at the men.

"I'll not send my men in till the smoke clears." The Mule held Devine's gaze. He might not say much, but he was confident of his knowledge of mining.

"Twenty minutes is plenty of smoke time."

"Aye. Maybe if we had masks. No masks, we wait longer."

Billy watched Devine stiffen in the face of this insubordination. They were waiting for Devine's reply, but the debate ended when Frankie pointed down the tunnel and exclaimed, "Look at this! Holy shit!"

The Mule's son Danny, who had shaped with the gang, came staggering out of the poison mist like the lone survivor of a firefight. Blood trickled from both his ears. Drunk, he had crawled into a toolbox to sleep it off and was left behind for the blast. His eardrums were blown out.

The Mule, devoid of parental empathy, started for him. "You fucking narrowback cunt, ya. I'll break every bone in your fucking body."

Lenny and Frankie stepped between them.

Chris Devine said, "Get him out of my tunnel."

Jack Tierney woke to the scream of a jackhammer. He looked at his watch: 7:30 A.M. What the fuck? Sitting up quickly, he forced his brain to remember where he was and the blood started pounding through his temples. He reached for his pistol on the nightstand, then looked at the woman lying next to him. The coat-check girl. He relaxed.

Outside the hotel window, a Con Ed crew was ripping into the street. The nerve of some people. Jack was tempted to shoot the peasant on the jackhammer, put him on workers' comp for a while, teach him some common fucking decency. He walked across the thick carpet to the bathroom. The broad was snoring. Christ.

He sat on the toilet and thought about his meeting with Vito Romero. It had gone well. The gindaloons were pleased with their work, and things were opening up nicely. The piece of the contractor would come in handy, explain some of his earnings. His operation was growing so quickly, they were running into problems with too much money lying around. Imagine that—too much cash. He grabbed some toilet paper and blew his nose. Their accountant, Eliot, was doing a good job of helping them launder it, but Jack still needed better explanations for why he was able to afford his new, more lavish lifestyle.

The Italian connection had proved valuable, and he was pleased. He did not like the way Romero talked down to him, though. Like he was some amateur street punk. Telling Jack Tierney how to apply muscle. Sitting there in his fancy suit, like some movie star gangster. Someday he'd slap the smartass around a bit. Make him beg for his life.

The sandhog deal had huge potential, but he knew there was one big problem with that piece of business. And that problem was Paddy Adare.

Jack Tierney shifted around on the bowl. He was all blocked up. He planted his feet and, grimacing, leaned forward, his elbows digging into his thighs. Paddy had been a major asset for a long time, but now, with his aversion to dealing with the Italians, he was proving himself to be narrow-minded, to be a pain in the ass. Besides, Jack was getting a little tired of him and the way the other guys were taken with him. He was too popular for Jack's taste. The other guys were always eager to defer to Paddy. He was becoming a potential rival.

Jack knew for certain Paddy would never go for muscling the sandhogs. That was his family, and the guy had strong notions about things like loyalty. Jack did too, as long as it did not cost him any money. He was not about to pass up good work for anyone or anything. Business came first. Plain and fucking simple. Paddy was the only threat to Jack Tierney's absolute dominance. They had had some good times together, but if Jack Tierney started letting his feelings get in the way, he'd be dead in a week.

He had to do it smart. If he just whacked Paddy out of the blue, it might start an uprising. Same thing if he had the Italians do it. He'd take his time. Something would present itself. Something always did. In the meantime, it would be business as usual. He pressed down harder, on the balls of his feet now. He heard the broad call to him in the other room but tuned her out, focused. Finally his bowels moved, large and wonderful.

Driving across town, Jack felt better than he had any right to after all that whiskey the night before. He had jumped on the broad for another go-round, worked up a sweat. Nice box on her. He muscled his Cadillac through the crosstown traffic and parked around the corner from the club. He walked to his brother's building, acknowledging nods from the locals, the people who feared him. He enjoyed that look on their faces, the silent plea that had taken years of hard work and ruthlessness for him to achieve. He felt powerful, his walk more of a strut, his shoulders rolling forward. He was the cock of the walk, no doubt about it.

He let himself into Butcher Boy's apartment. His brother was lying naked on the couch, some young twat wrapped around him. The girl had a tattoo on her ass. Jack leaned over for a closer look. It was a winged penis. Fucking Christ. He took a pistol from his waistband and poked her in the tit, hard. Her eyes popped wide open. "Skank. Get up. Get dressed. Get out." He stroked the side of her face with the barrel, enjoyed the terror in her eyes. He considered fucking her, but no. Who knew what his brother might have contracted? "Now."

He handed her a twenty-dollar bill on her way to the door. Terry slept on. When the girl was gone, Jack took a little tour of the apartment. His baby brother never ceased to amaze him. His place was like some whacked-out teenager's. Except it was clean, meticulously clean. There were stacks of comic books and rows and rows of kung fu movies. His hundreds of CDs were divided about evenly between heavy metal and classical. Go figure. The walls were adorned with posters of Bruce Lee, Charles Bronson, Clint Eastwood. There was a water bed with silk sheets and mirrors above.

The second bedroom was converted into a sleek-looking weight room. The kid kept up his jailhouse physique, Jack had to give him that. Although he had help. In the kitchen cabinets were cans of protein powder, hundreds of vitamins, and bodybuilding crap. In the refrigerator were syringes and Terry's steroids. His brother seemed to live on steroids, Twinkies, and cocaine.

Back in the bedroom, in a dresser drawer, he found what looked like three ounces of cocaine lying next to a pile of twenties. For a long time Jack would have gone crazy, dumped the shit, smacked him around. It was too late for that now. Despite being the weirdest fuck he had ever known, Terry was his ace in the hole. He would slice a nun's throat for him without question. Jack just had to control him. He grabbed a handful of twenties—a little big-brother tax.

Pushing some of the mess from last night's party off the coffee table, Jack sat down on it, put his pistol on the tip of Butcher Boy's nose.

"Bang!" Butcher Boy jumped up, staring down the barrel of Jack's gun. "You really need to watch out for yourself better, Terry."

"Fuckin' Jack, man. This ain't funny."

Butcher Boy was bloodshot and gray. He looked to be in pain.

Jack stood up. "You really ought to watch what you fuck around with. You'll end up with the virus. You think Mommy would like that? She goes to bingo, all those church broads looking at her like she's fucked up, got a son with the virus?"

"Jack, don't even talk like that. I mean, shit, man. I'm no faggot. I ain't no junkie."

"Yeah, well, you know, I was reading the other day there are some more high-risk groups, and it's funny, you know, one of them just happens to be little cocksuckers with winged-penis tattoos on their asses. Imagine that."

Butcher Boy groaned. Jack had him in a weakened state. Terry would agree to anything in exchange for peace.

"Can I trust you with something, you won't shoot your mouth off to half the gang, half the neighborhood?"

"Jack, I'm your brother, man, your brother."

"What happened your end of that Bronx deal?"

"I got some things, spent some here and there. Still got plenty left."

Jack stood up. "Your parole officer calls me the other day, tells me he ain't seen you in a while, Terry. Wants to know maybe my brother went on a vacation somewhere, forgot to call in. You think I need to spend my time baby-sitting you?"

"Come on, Jack, I'm doing good. My shit is tight. I just lost track of the days."

"Lost track of the days." Jack shook his head. His brother was the king of weak-assed excuses. Jack thought it was too bad the kid never had any military training—might have taught him a bit of discipline. He was about to berate him but decided not to. He needed some work out of him.

"All right, here's how you make it up to me. You go see this kid from Tuzio. You and him are going to start on some work. You tell anyone—Riordan, the O'Neils, Paddy, any-fuckin'-body—I'll wash my hands of you. You'll be back in the joint in about half a hot minute. You got me?"

"Yeah, Jackie—sure, man. I got you."

Paddy sat at the bar, waiting for Rosa to cash out. He liked to watch her at work. She had been manager of the place for almost four years now. A romantic spot in the West Village, candlelight and nice linen, half the customers gay. Rosa said that was okay; they had money and behaved themselves. Paddy thought she was right; who cared who they slept with, as long as they were good for business. He popped a couple of Rolaids and washed them down with a sip of Jameson. His stomach actually felt decent the last few days.

Rosa walked by with a handful of checks. She stopped and kissed him on the cheek. "Fifteen minutes, Paddy." He nodded. He could tell by her tone it had been a bad night.

The bartender, a young guy with feathered-back hair and a year-round tan, came down the bar to refill his drink. Paddy waved him off. "No, thanks. I'm fine."

The bartender shrugged. He knew enough about Paddy to keep his distance.

When Rosa came back, she had her bag over her shoulder.

"What's wrong?" Paddy said.

"Just not the average day."

"Why not?"

"Why not? Well, first the cook comes down with something, he goes home. It's too late for me to get anyone, so me and Jesus, a dishwasher, had to cook for the night. We had a bigger rush than usual for a Tuesday. Figures. I come out to check on the bar, there's a group of yuppie assholes, and one of them says, 'Nice tits,' and grabs my chest. I hit him with an ashtray. Now he wants to sue me. I go back in the kitchen and—"

"Whoa. Back up, Rosa. What this fucking guy do to you?"

"You heard me."

"Who the fuck is this guy?"

"Paddy, please."

"Don't 'please' me, Rosa. I wanna know who the fuck this guy is, grabbed your chest."

"Paddy, what you really mean is who's this guy that grabbed your woman's chest."

Paddy pulled back. "What?"

"You're trying to protect your property. I can handle myself. You asked how my night was, what was wrong? Now, do you want to hear, or do you want to play hero?"

Paddy looked at the bartender. "Come down here." The guy came over, uncertain, looking between Paddy and Rosa. Paddy said, "You know this guy, grabbed her?"

The bartender looked at Rosa as if weighing the consequences. Piss off Paddy or Rosa. It was an easy decision. "Yeah. He's some dickhead from the Island. Comes around after work sometimes."

"Is that right? Here." Paddy pulled two hundred-dollar bills off his roll and handed them to the bartender. "He ever comes back, you tell the little pervert fuck if he ever steps on the island of Manhattan again I'll fucking bury him. You give him one of those for carfare home, you keep the other. Hear me?"

The guy nodded. Rosa stormed out the door. Paddy turned to watch her go. He followed her into the warm night. The West Village streets were crowded with revelers.

He saw her standing by his parked car. He opened the door for her, knowing he was about to put up with an earful. These days he seemed to be getting it from all sides.

In the car, Rosa said, "What I don't need from you, Paddy, is you following me around with a baseball bat, threatening to kill everyone that makes me unhappy."

"Rosa, what the fuck? I look out for my own. I'd do the same thing for Billy or Mickey, for my fucking grandfather even. It's what a man does." He was getting pissed off.

"Is that right? Does that little list include those Tierney brothers? All those psychos you run around with?"

Paddy wondered about that. There was a time when he would have said yes immediately. Now he was not sure. He made a right onto West Street.

"Paddy, every man in my life, from my retarded brothers with their macho bullshit to my father, my uncles, and my cousins, has always decided I was so helpless they would beat the shit out of anyone who came near me. Well, fuck that. That is not what I need from men in my life, Paddy. I don't need any more heroes."

"Well, what the fuck do you want?"

"I want understanding."

"What?"

"I want someone that's gonna take a minute to think about what I want, not expect me to just be a moon circling their planet. I got my own ideas about my life."

He realized this was bigger than some asshole grabbing on her.

"Rosa, what the fuck here? I ever give you a hard time about what you want to do? I ever stop you from going anywhere or doing anything?"

"Jesus, Paddy. I'm not talking about permission." She pressed her head back against the seat. "Your blessing to go on a vacation."

"I don't get it." Paddy was running out of steam. He had a hard time staying mad at her. For weeks, he'd sensed something was amiss and hoped it would pass. He knew he did not have the strength to fight with her on one level and Jack on another.

"You remember we used to have those little talks about getting out of the city, me opening a place somewhere in the country?"

He remembered. It seemed like a nice life to plan out. Too bad it was impossible. He could just picture Jack responding when he told him he was leaving to become a country gentleman. Jack would bury him.

"Well, it's been a year and seven days since we talked about it last, Paddy."

She had that tone in her voice. The one that said, I'm taking care of me first. He'd heard it before, but now it seemed to have a finality to it. "A year and seven days?"

"Yeah, my birthday."

"Things have been rough. I guess I been preoccupied."

"Well, so have I. I'm taking a manager's job next month, up near Lake Champlain, the Vermont side. Putting a down payment on a house."

Just like that. He felt something slipping away from him, a mooring snap lose.

"Where'd you get the money?"

"I saved it, Paddy. I've taken five and a half sick days off work in this decade. I guess what it boils down to is I love you, Paddy, but I'm not going to sit around waiting for your funeral. Look at yourself. You drink—what?—a case of Pepto-Bismol a month? You should own stock by now. I'm making a new life for myself. You've known that's what I wanted since we started going together."

"Rosa."

"You can move with me or you can stay behind. If I leave alone, I don't want you coming up for weekends. It's all or nothing."

He felt as if he'd been smacked with a bat. "Christ, Rosa. What am I gonna do, wash dishes for you?"

"Why not? Maybe I'll let you bartend. Paddy, someday you can be partners with me, the way we used to talk about it."

"I can't leave. It's business."

"Business. Bullshit. You've been at war your whole life, Paddy. I hate to say this, but I don't think you're going to last much longer. I got a real bad feeling about things."

"Fuck, Rosa, don't start with your mother's voodoo bullshit—you'll jinx me. I need time."

"I'm out of time. I'm through with this city."

"All of a sudden."

"Jesus, Paddy, are you deaf? Are you blind? I always thought you were different, but if you can't break away, you're no different than Bobby Riordan or that freak Butcher Boy or any of them. Life is about choices, Paddy. The choices you make in life tell what you are."

"You see that somewhere, TV?"

"Don't try to ridicule me. Drop me off at my place. You decide, you know where to find me."

He stopped in front of her building and watched her walk away. It was a hot summer night, but a coldness passed over him like shadow. He felt the sting of loss. He wanted to run after her and follow her to the end of the earth. Instead he drove recklessly over to a bar and hit the whiskey like a man trying to drown himself with fire.

"I done like thirty." Butcher Boy said it and watched the Italian guy, Vinny or Tony, whatever, pull back with a look Butcher Boy took to be awe, respect. It was 4:30 A.M. They were parked on a quiet street in Suffolk County, waiting for Martin Donelly, the sandhogs' secretary-treasurer, to go for his morning jog. Butcher Boy was not sure what type of psycho got up at five in the morning to run around in his shorts. But one thing he did know—it would be his last jog for a while.

"That makes you like some kind of serial killer?"

Butcher Boy shot him a hard look. "I ain't no fucking serial killer." Serial killers were all weird fat guys from Ohio, places like that. Perverts. "I'm a hit man."

"Fuckin' A. Thirty." Low whistle. "That's wild."

Actually, he wasn't sure. It was like screwing broads. Once he got up near twenty, he'd lost track. "Yeah, we do what we hafta do. We got the West Side sewed up. Nobody fucks with us."

"So they say. I work for my uncle, he's a made guy. Connected all over the fuckin' place. He's in tight with the big boys—shit, he *is* a big boy. They got a piece of everything. They're nationwide, these guys."

Butcher Boy wondered why the Italians always had to tell you about their connected uncles. They'd been waiting on that street—it was more like a country road—for two hours. At first Butcher Boy would get out to take a piss, snort a couple of lines quick, then he'd jump back in the car, but the Tony or Vinny said, "Hey, we're gonna work together, we might as well share."

Butcher Boy, feeling good to be working, thought, Why not? So they sat snorting lines and bragging, waiting for the nutcase in his shorts.

"We had this prick on one of our jobs, right? A fuckin' *molignon,* Terry. But he's from Jamaica, some coconut-picking place. I'm the shop steward. My uncle set me up big time. I take the numbers, get the coffee, then I go home and sleep. Anyways, this guy, he's bustin' balls about safety rules—this, that, every other fucking thing. He says, 'I have rights, mon,' like he believes the shit they teach you in immigrant schools, the asshole. I talk to him, warn him he's gonna get hurt, he keeps it up. But the mollie, he's stupid, you know? Pass me that mirror."

He snorted a line. "Yeah, baby. Wow. Good shit." He dragged his finger along the remains of the line and rubbed it on his gums. "Damn. Where was I? Oh, yeah. So my uncle comes on the job to visit him, a personal visit. I'm pissed off 'cause I ain't looking too good, I can't take care of this asshole myself."

Butcher Boy snatched the mirror back.

"Yeah, all yours. My uncle starts talking to this guy, and he's making like he don't understand. A fucking big mistake right there. Terry, my fucking uncle is crazy. You get him pissed off, forgetaboutit. So he grabs a concrete shovel and whacks the nigger on the head. Bang! You hear me now, you cocksucker? Whack, crack, fuck you! Later, they said he got brain damage from it. I says no fucking way. Guy's got no brain to start with, how can he get brain damage?"

"Reminds me of a guy owed my brother some money," Terry said. "Wanted to be a tough guy too, I know the type—dumb fucks. We grabbed him off his job site. My brother drove, me and this other guy we got the guy in the back seat, throwing him a beatin'. He put up a fight, though." Butcher Boy leaned over and snorted a line. "Till we tossed him out while we was doing seventy up the West Side Highway. Bounced along like a fucking spaldeen."

They had a good laugh.

"Our guys, we're fistfighters. My uncle likes guys that can handle themselves with their bare hands. Of course, these days you don't see much of that, but you never know. I work this club, a bouncer on Saturday nights? This guy comes in, he don't realize it's a connected club." Vinny snorted another line. "Big football player asshole. About my size. He starts going off. Me and these other two guys, we stomp him. Broke his back."

This guy was starting to get on Butcher Boy's nerves. The cocaine was beginning to shut him down, making him all tight and paranoid like it always did. "You ever fight by yourself? Or you always need a crowd, fight for you?"

"Whoa, baby. I done plenty. I know karate. Tae kwon do. I work out on the job, breaking two-by-fours and shit."

"Boards don't hit back." Butcher Boy doing his Bruce Lee imitation, feeling the edge fade slightly.

The guy came right back with, "Oooooeeeee. *Enter the Dragon.* Best fucking movie ever made, 'cept maybe *The Godfather.*"

Friends again, Butcher Boy told him about the guy who slapped his sister, got right to the point now. "I stabbed the fuck twenty-seven times and threw him off the roof."

Vinny was silent for a minute. He snorted the last of the cocaine. "That's wack, Terry. What you got for tonight?"

Butcher Boy reached over the seat and pulled out a thirty-three-ounce Louisville Slugger with three sixteen-point nails driven through the meat of the bat.

"Whoa! Fuckin' Terry, you going after big fucking game here or what?"

Butcher Boy shrugged. "It'll do the job."

"Wow. Look here. I prefer to get in close." Vinny displayed a set of brass knuckles with steel studs that sparkled like diamonds in the weak light. He made a few short uppercut motions. "Make Frankenstein outta the fuckin' guy."

A half hour passed, during which Butcher Boy did not utter a single word and Vinny never once stopped talking. The porch light went on. They slid out of the car and hid behind a large pine tree. Martin Donelly came out and ran in the other direction.

"Fuck." Vinny went to run after him. Butcher Boy grabbed his arm.

"No. We wait till he comes back."

An hour later, crashing from the cocaine high, they were still waiting. This did not make them happy. When finally they heard footsteps and breathing coming from the other direction, the sky was bright enough that they could be easily seen, so they stayed crouched behind the shrubbery.

"The guy runs in a fucking circle. What's wrong with him?"

Butcher Boy took out a pistol.

"Put that fucking thing away, Terry. We ain't supposed to kill him."

"I'll shoot him in the balls."

"Too much noise."

Butcher Boy reluctantly slid the pistol into his waistband.

Donelly stopped running a hundred feet from his house. When he headed toward the front door, covered in sweat and breathing hard, his back was to his assailants. Vinny ran up behind him. Donelly heard the steps too late. As he turned, Vinny hit him hard in the face with the brass knuckles, breaking his nose and a cheekbone. He fell to his knees. Butcher Boy ran up, swinging the bat hard, the nails in the end driving deep into Donelly. Butcher Boy swung again and again, trying to avoid the guy's head. Don't kill him, Jack had said. In between swings, Vinny danced in with roundhouse rights.

They left Donelly bloodied and broken twenty feet from his front door. Driving back to the city, chowing on Egg McMuffins, Butcher

Boy remembered what Jack had told him. "Shit. We forget to say something about the contract."

"What are you talking about?" Vinny chewed like a rabid wolf.

"We were supposed to say something like, Hey, sign the fucking contract. Like that. It's some union thing. That's why we were doing this guy. 'Cause he's like the second in command. We're sending a message to his boss with this beating."

"Nobody never said nothing to me about that." Vinny belched, and a small piece of egg hit the dashboard. He wiped it off with his shoe.

"Fuck it. We say we said it, say the guy forgot, getting hit in the head or something."

"Cool."

Billy woke up with a hard-on for the ages. He needed a woman the way a man staked to the desert floor at high noon needs water. He considered calling Donna De Feo. The previous Saturday night, crazed on beer and lust, they had copulated furiously on her kitchen table while her parents celebrated their twenty-fifth wedding anniversary at Mount Airy Lodge. The episode had ended badly. The table crashed to the floor, forcing Billy to buy off her startled younger brother with veiled threats and a twenty-dollar bill. He'd better steer clear of Donna.

He rolled over and grabbed the bar napkin with Tricia's number. So he had not called her. She'd understand. He dialed for salvation. Her father answered.

"Who is this?"

"Billy."

"You listen to me, you little punk bastard—"

"Blow me."

Billy hung up and was left to his own device.

Later, after lunch, Billy went for a run down the Grand Concourse. He'd been running five to seven miles a day. He followed the Concourse south, loping along at midday past scores of people sitting out on stoops with the dull stares of heatstroke victims. The whole city was torpid, drained by humidity. At 161st Street, he ran down the hill toward Yankee Stadium, which stood like a ghost town in midday, the Yankees playing out West. He ran north on Jerome Avenue and cut across a side street toward the Concourse. The neighborhood had gone to shit. Even in the debilitating heat, crack dealers hung on every corner, eager to ply their trade, impervious to the threat of law enforcement. In the three years Billy had been going away to school, many stable Bronx neighborhoods had fallen prey to the scourge of cheap cocaine. There were no children on the street on a summer day, no women, no elderly. Only young men with hard energy and quick eyes. Though the sky was cloudless, a pall seemed to hang over the street. Billy picked up his pace. As he neared the corner, a late-model car with Jersey plates rolled to a stop. One of the salesmen stepped forward and leaned into the car. Billy saw blond hair, a flash of hands, an exchange. The dealer stepped back, and the car pulled away.

Billy passed the Concourse, and the streets were reclaimed by playful, screaming children, by mothers, by light. In the middle of the block, kids ran laughing through the cold fountain spray of an open hydrant. Billy walked through the water slowly, enjoying the relief, letting the cascade cool him.

At the corner, he noticed a closed-down bar, its facade faded, rusted metal gates guarding it from further despoilment. He made out the name through years of neglect, SULLIVAN'S, and suddenly was transported to his childhood, remembering this place, an event. He was five or six years old. It was a christening, or maybe a first communion. Family and neighbors gathered in celebration, to mark a rite like so many from his youth. The bar was crowded; there were trays of cold cuts—ham, salami, turkey, and roast beef—yellow and orange cheese, jars of mustard with plastic knives sticking from them. The men smelled of Old Spice and beer. Their faces were red and tightly shaved. He could feel the roughness of their hands when they patted his head or shook his hand. The women wore polyester pants and blouses, lipstick, their eyebrows penciled on. Billy remembered their sunglasses, like Jackie Kennedy's, lying on the tables and the bar. The talk was of politics and war, of sports and the neighborhood.

Billy ran with other children through the legs of the adults, collected quarters, and drank Cokes till his belly was ready to break. He ate the cherries that came with them, three or four to a glass, pulled the chilled fake fruit from the stems, which he dropped into ashtrays on the bar. Cigarette smoke drifted like fog.

He remembered his grandfather, flushed from whiskey and political talk, singing the sad ballads of his youth. Someone taking up the accordion, laughter, the tinkling of glasses. He remembered all this like it was yesterday.

He stepped back to the curb, away from the ruins of Sullivan's, and thought of a line from a song: "Everything that dies someday comes back." Billy shook his head no—not this time it doesn't. A ball bounced in front of him, and he snapped back to the present. A child dressed in shorts and torn sneakers ran past him, chasing the ball. Billy turned and jogged the rest of the way home, the lost voices of the past echoing in his ear.

The tunnel was an escape from the heat. Billy actually looked forward to the nightly descent into the cool earth.

Later that night, he and Frankie moved forward cautiously with scaling bars—long poles used to pull down rock knocked loose by the blast. The swing shift had blasted before leaving, and the Mule's gang was sent to muck out.

"Shit, there's a lot of bad rock here." Billy peered at the tunnel ceiling.

"It's been getting worse all week."

Frankie wedged his pole into a crevice and jerked down. A rock the size of a coffee table crashed to the ground. They turned their heads to avoid being hit in the face with flying stones.

"Christ, a fucking meteor. I think we need some roof bolts here. Get Lenny."

Lenny Coyle came over and pointed his flashlight up to the tunnel ceiling. White streaks, indicating pockets of unstable rock, reflected the light. A sinister sight to the miner.

"You guys are right. Get the rest of this pulled down. From here back. Leave that. I'll get a platform, we'll throw up some roof bolts. Be careful."

The gang worked gingerly for an hour, clearing the rest of the rock. Billy contemplated how many million tons of rock were between him and the night sky. He pushed that thought right out of his head.

When they finished, a mucking machine came in and cleared away the fallen rock. They took lunch.

"It's nice, Mule not being here this week." Frankie switched to a brogue. "Going back to the old country, seeing to the family farm, tending to the sheep and all." He popped open a quart of Gatorade.

"Is that why things are so quiet around here?" Billy was wet and filthy from drilling. He reached underneath his sweatshirt and flannel shirt and wiped his hands on the T. Now that was dirty too. Billy looked at his sandwich. Running late, he had bought it from the site chow wagon. The ham looked green, but he was starving.

"Yeah, maybe we'll get lucky and he'll fall in love over there, stay."

"The Mule's only got one true love—American money. It's gotta kill him, to have to take a week off. Nice to have Lenny running the gang, though."

"Yeah. No shit. You do your job, he leaves you alone."

"The way it should be."

"Hey, who's the new guy?" Frankie indicated the shaper.

"It's Connie O'Noon's nephew."

"That prick?"

"Yeah. You hear they made him a walking boss in Queens?"

"The biggest ass-licking Irish asshole I have ever known," Frankie said to Billy. He looked up at the new man. "Hey, you. Come here a second."

The shaper walked over to them.

"This your first night in the hole?"

"Yeah."

"Whatsa matter? You look a little spooked."

"I'm awright. Just ain't used to working one of those fucking drills."

"It can be a bitch. I'll tell you what, give you a little chance to take a break. We need some supplies—you take a walk for us?"

The kid nodded his head, eager to put some ground between himself and the drill.

"All right, head back to the shaft. Straight back all the way. You get back there, you tell the bellman we need—what?" He turned to Billy. "About a hundred yards?"

"Make it a hundred and fifty, be safe."

"All right, one fifty. Tell the guy we need a hundred fifty yards of shoreline back here. And we need it pronto. He tries to fuck with you, bust your balls, don't let him. And while you're over there, get me a left-handed monkey wrench, all right? I'm a lefty."

The shaper looked grateful. "Shit, I'm a lefty too. That's cool." He walked eagerly back toward the shaft, fading into the mist.

"What's it—three miles to the shaft now?"

"Closer to four."

They were having a good laugh when Lenny came over.

"Let's get this done, guys. Billy, you work with Frankie. Where's the new guy?"

Billy and Frankie exchanged looks.

"Said he had to take a shit."

They pushed a platform in and started drilling sixteen-foot holes up into the roof. Since there were only two drills, the gang alternated. When a hole was drilled, a long bolt with metal plates like giant washers was screwed into the holes with torque wrenches. The hope was that this would prevent cave-ins.

It was an hour past lunch when Chris Devine came walking up with Connie O'Noon's nephew and a city inspector. Devine was grim. He pushed the kid forward and looked down at his watch.

"Where's McIntyre?" It was more a demand than a question.

"He's in Ireland. I got the gang this week," Lenny said.

"Coyle."

"That's my name."

"How come you're not drilling for the next shot yet?"

"We got bad rock here, Devine. Putting up more roof bolts. Doing the job right."

"According to who?"

Lenny looked at the superintendent. "I been a miner a long time, Devine. When was the last time you worked in a tunnel?"

Devine pointed out the roof to the city inspector. "What do you see?"

The inspector scampered up on the drilling platform with his flashlight. He made a show of checking out the rock, poking around, pulling back for a better view. "That is more than enough. I don't see a problem here."

"I got a quota to meet," Devine said.

"Yeah, well, so do we—it's going home after the shift is over."

"Get these men back to work."

"You guys ever stop and figure what a dead miner costs the company, how that fucks up your bottom line?"

"That's not something you need to be concerned with. Get these men to work, or I'll get your money."

They worked on, and Devine stayed and watched them until the next break. His presence made everyone uptight. Billy, feeling Devine's eyes on his back while he worked, thought he was being judged. As the gang broke for afternoon coffee, Devine rode the man trip away.

Lenny took a cup of coffee and said, "Kid, you got to use your head. This ain't like old times. There's no more fun and games. These guys will take any excuse to send us down the road. How you gonna pay for law school, you get laid off?"

"I'm sorry, Len. I—"

"Don't be sorry, kid. I ain't looking for an apology—I'm just looking out for you. You didn't come this far to throw it all away. 'Cause you get canned and you're looking for sympathy, the only place you're gonna find it is in the dictionary, somewhere between 'shit' and 'syphilis.' And it sure won't pay for your schoolbooks."

Chastised, Billy went back to his drill. He picked it up and spent the last two hours drilling as hard and as fast as he could. He drilled for absolution.

When they came out of the hole, they learned what had happened to Donelly.

Jack Tierney stood looking out the window of the Midnight Lounge, a feudal lord surveying his domain. He was dressed in blue trousers and a short-sleeve sport shirt, and he was mightily pissed off. Butcher Boy and the fuck that went with him had beaten the sandhog to death. It had taken the guy the better part of a day to die, but die he did. He knew this made him look bad with the Italians, and Jack Tierney did not like to look bad, because looking bad was expensive in his line of work.

He watched a little old lady, wearing a winter coat in the heat, pull a granny cart loaded with cans and crap up the avenue. She was bent nearly parallel to the ground. Jack admired her determination, her will to soldier on. She looked to be ninety.

Jack cracked his large knuckles absently. He still had not figured out what to do about Adare and was growing impatient. Now that he had begun his assault on the union, it was only a matter of time before Paddy found out. He needed to make a move, head off a showdown. Once Jack made up his mind on something, he liked to get it done quickly. Otherwise it would start to fester and end up being a major distraction. Distractions cost money too. This occasionally made him act rashly.

The bag lady was making her way across the avenue now, trying to beat the light. Silently, Jack rooted for her. A row of cars and trucks waited for the green like penned bulls before the rodeo. The light changed when she was still ten feet from the safety of the sidewalk, and the car horns blared. The woman pulled herself up and gave them the finger, then bent again and trudged on, past the fat broads sitting on their chairs in front of the buildings down the side street.

Jack wondered what the fuck they talked about all day out there. It seemed they had been there forever, since when he was a kid, sitting on their fat asses yapping away, in frayed housecoats, outdated blouses. Probably talking shit about whoever wasn't sitting there with them. The only thing that made them move was the sun dropping. Then they moved fast enough.

His focus came back to the tunnel union. He was intrigued by the possibility of taking over a local. Almost all of his action in construction was run through companies. The guineas seemed to have the right idea. Take over a local here and there, you're talking millions. Pension funds, site control . . . the money was large. Now, if it weren't for Paddy . . .

But then, out of the blue, like a gift from the gods, Bobby Riordan, who had come up behind him, said, "I wanna whack him, Jack. What the fucking guy did to me wasn't right. Besides, everybody knows about it. I look bad."

Jack smiled. There it was. It amazed Jack Tierney how things always seemed to work themselves out. He turned to face his underling. Riordan wanted to kill Ray Keegan. Just happened to have been buddies with Adare when they were kids. He'd give the hit to Adare. If he did not follow through—and Jack did not think he had it in him, killing a friend—a perfect justification to whack him. He turned to Riordan.

"You're right, Bobby. You're absolutely fucking right. The guy has got to go."

Riordan smiled. "Jack, it means a lot to me. Thanks."

Tierney looked at him. Big stupid mean Bobby Riordan. Not realizing he was the solution to a little problem Jack had.

"Listen, Bobby. I don't want you to do it."

Riordan looked dejected. "But Jack, you just said—"

Jack held up a hand. "I said it's got to happen. I didn't say I want you to do it. Did I? Now think for a minute. You said everybody knows about it, and I agree. So you want the heat coming down on you, the minute the guy drops? No, I don't think you do. And neither do I. No, Bobby, you been working hard, maybe it's time you take a little trip. This thing gets settled in your absence, they can't even bring you in for a chat."

"I got nowhere I want to go, Jack."

Jack inhaled. "Bobby, don't piss me off. I'm doing you a favor."

Vito Romero, as a precaution, had slipped John Tuzio a little Valium with his blood-pressure medicine, just enough to take the edge off. It was Tuesday. Vito visited his wife's grave every Tuesday—the day on which she had died—rain or shine, winter, summer, spring, and fall. Tommy Magic's nephew was coming in. He had killed the sandhog, and Tuzio was in an uproar. Vito did not want to miss the cemetery because Tuzio went crazy and whacked the kid right there and then.

Vito had tried to talk Tuzio out of using the kid. If he weren't related to Tommy Magic, he would be cutting grass for six dollars an hour out on the Island. But Tuzio had some debt to Magic that Vito was unaware of, some tribal allegiance forged during their youth in East New York.

He looked up as the kid, Vinny, oblivious to his predicament, was escorted into the front room. He had no idea this might be his last day on earth. Vito almost felt sorry for him. He was dressed in one of those goofy athletic warm-up suits that so many of the guys wore. The kid had an uncanny knack for dressing like the goombahs that hung around outside, keeping an eye on things. If they had on sport coats, so did the kid; if they looked ready for a jog, so did this Vinny. It occurred to Vito that the kid must drive by the club in the morning, see what the fashion of the day was, then dress accordingly.

"Wait here."

Vito ducked into the back room. Tuzio had his feet up on the table and was obsessing over the coverage of Fat Tony's trial in the *Post*. He was picking his nose furiously. Vito cringed at the way he was digging around in there; he might cause a hemorrhage. "The kid's here."

"Who?" Tuzio pulled his finger out and looked up from the paper.

"Magic's kid."

Tuzio made a wave motion with his hand. "Bring him here."

Vito brought Vinny in and pointed to a chair. On the television, Geraldo was preening around the studio, chastising some broad for not paying enough attention to her fourteen-year-old slut daughter. Vito wanted to shut it off.

He watched Tuzio reach forward and grab Vinny by the neck and pull him close. Vito felt for the kid, Tuzio's breath in his face like that. He could see Vinny trying hard not to gag. Most people went to great lengths to avoid insulting John Tuzio, especially when he deserved it.

"Now tell me what happened. Talk to me. This job." He loosened his grip slightly, just enough so the kid could answer him, and addressed Vito. "Turn up the TV."

"Yeah?" Tuzio said to Vinny.

Vinny shifted uncomfortably. "Went up there, in Suffolk, we did the work."

"Who'd you work with?"

"The guy's brother, you know."

"No, I don't fuckin' know. That's why you are here—because you was there and I was here. Which one of them was he?" Tuzio pulled him closer each time he asked a question and then let him out again to answer. He looked like a man curling a huge dumbbell.

"Mr. Tuzio, he was the short guy, with the muscles."

"What he look like?"

"He was kind of an oddball-looking fuck, you ask me."

"You worked him over?"

"The Irish guy?"

"Yeah."

Vito kept an eye on Tuzio but watched a girl on the TV let Geraldo know that it wasn't her fault she was fat and pimply and had a screaming, shitting five-month-old baby. Then she said it: "It's the system." Vito cringed, thinking: *Marrone,* what is wrong with people, a white kid using that bullshit now, like sucking cock at fourteen had nothing to do with her predicament. He turned his attention to Vinny, thinking he'd probably make a good couple with the girl on TV.

"No, Mr. Tuzio."

"You didn't work him over? Why the fuck not?"

Vinny, confused, looked toward Vito for help. Vito shrugged.

"I thought I was supposed to work with the guy, Mr. Tuzio."

"With who?"

"The Irish guy, Terry, that's his name." Vinny smiled, like he had just passed a pop quiz with flying colors.

"Not that Irish guy—the union Irish guy. You fucking mozzarel sandwich."

Vinny smiled again. "Oh, we went to town on that guy."

"What did you use?"

"I had some knucks, the guy had this bat."

"Bat?"

"A baseball bat with a coupla nails through it."

"Nails?"

Vito watched Tuzio closely. He seemed distracted. He hoped the drug had worked. He realized Vinny did not know the guy was dead.

"The guy was whacking away like Darryl Strawberry."

"Like who?"

Vinny took Tuzio's reaction to be a racist commentary.

"Like Joe DiMaggio."

"You said he was Irish."

"He is."

"Read this." Tuzio tapped his hairy knuckles on the *Post*. "It says here—wait, you know how?"

"How what, Mr. Tuzio?"

"How the fuck to read."

"Yeah—I mean yes, Mr. Tuzio."

"That's good. 'Cause it says here the guy is dead. Now, how did he get dead when I did not want him dead?"

Vito watched Tuzio's rage struggle against the drug like a school of piranhas against aquarium glass.

"Dead?"

"Yeah, dead. Like he ain't living no more."

"Sorry. The guy was a tough guy, Mr. Tuzio. He put up a struggle. He was alive when we left him."

Tuzio attempted a glare. He looked lost in thought. He shook the nephew. "You're sorry." Tuzio started to darken but could not get there. "You want to apologize, call the widow. You wanna live, get lost before I remember something I don't like about your uncle."

The kid made for the door, looking over his shoulder. Vito was relieved.

"Hey, John. I'm gonna take off. The cemetery."

"Yeah. Okay. You know, this blood-pressure stuff, it makes me feel funny."

The day of Donelly's funeral, Billy stood behind his grandfather on the steps of Saint Brendan's. He was bone tired. He had worked a jackleg drill all the night before, then gone to breakfast, changed into his one suit, and rode the bus with JP to the church. He watched as a dozen members of the fire department's Emerald Society Pipe Band, many of them former sandhogs, decked out in full battle regalia, formed a phalanx and began to play a dirge. The keen of the bagpipes cut the Bronx morning, chasing a flock of pigeons from their nooks in the gray facade of the church. Billy felt a swell in his chest, the improbable Irish mixture of fierce pride and melancholy that the music inspired.

He glanced over the faces of the assembled sandhogs. The Irish and the West Indians were like negative and positive images of each other: the same thick shoulders and square, tough faces, the same discomfort in formal attire, the same edginess curbed by solemnity. They whispered among themselves and glanced expectantly up the block.

The funeral motorcade, a sleek black hearse followed by two limousines, rounded the corner and docked curbside. The pipers fell silent as the family was led weeping from the cars and the pallbearers carried the coffin from the hearse. A procession was formed, led by the priest and a pink-faced altar boy holding a large crucifix on high. They disappeared into the dimness of the vestibule as the band played "Amazing Grace."

Billy looked to the blue sky, then to his grandfather's stooped back. He felt numbness pushing away the sadness, obliterating any feeling. It seemed to be his only reaction to death, to loss, the numbness always triumphant over any real emotion. He wondered if there was something missing in him, something that was snuffed out unconsciously when he was three. He had no solid memory of his own father's funeral, but he was always struck by the images of JFK, Jr., saluting his father's casket. Had he, too, made some symbolic gesture? He wished he knew what JP felt, how much this ritual bore him back to the day he had buried his son, Billy's father. What hard memories did this day evoke? He felt a need for contact, so he placed a hand on his grandfather's shoulder. They walked inside the church.

It was a full mass, and Billy received communion for the first time in two years, not wanting to explain his abstinence to JP. The priest expounded on the nature of evil and the need for forgiveness, the hope of redemption. This talk did not mollify the rage of the assembled.

Afterward, they gathered at the Sligo. Standing over a generous spread of cold cuts, the men ate and discussed retribution. They undid their neckties, doffed their jackets, and rolled up their sleeves. Glasses of beer and shots were slapped on the bar. Billy sat silently, nursed a Coke, and listened.

"We let this go on, and we'll be going to one of these a week," Eamon Cudahy said. "I mean, fair play to the priest and all, but for fuck sake, they been preaching that turn-the-other-cheek shite for a thousand years, and it ain't done fuck all for us yet."

Heads nodded in agreement.

"We only got one problem," Moran said. "We can't say for sure why this happened. I mean, I know—two and two equals this piece-a-shit contractor. But we go off acting all rash, we end up jammed up by the cops, the feds. It's more trouble than we need."

The men reluctantly agreed to adopt a wait-and-see attitude. Maybe it was some random act of violence. They would keep their guard up. The beer flowed, and the talk became less focused.

"You believe the way they're going after this Bernie Goetz?" Bobby Moran said. "Guy minding his own business is about to get opened up like a sausage, now they're making him out to be the next Hitler. I mean, come on here."

JP finished the one whiskey he allowed himself on solemn occasions and turned to Billy. "Would you mind very much escorting your grandfather home, Billy? This is a young man's endeavor."

"Not at all." JP and Billy left together.

On the bus back home, JP was silent. They rolled through the north Bronx. As they approached their stop, JP grabbed Billy's wrist and looked him in the eyes. "Don't do anything foolish, Billy. You've a good head on your shoulders. Use it. I'm lonely enough as it is." He stood and walked off the bus. Billy followed, not sure what to make of his grandfather's sudden onset of seriousness.

After his grandson had gone to bed, JP took over behind the bar in Briody's. He pulled pints and poured shots for the pensioners. He spread the *Irish Echo* on the bar and sipped a club soda. The funeral had unsettled him, left him worried about Billy. He had been around long enough to know trouble was imminent. The tunnels were a hard racket in the best of times.

He took a picture from his wallet. It was of himself and the two boys and was taken just before he had sent Patrick down to live in Manhattan. For twenty years he had come up with reasons why it was necessary. First the boys' mother dying when Billy was born. They were able to pull together after that tragedy. Everyone pitched in to help with the children. Then the father was killed in the tunnel. JP knew he had never really recovered from that blow. After that he had a hard time coping. His wife was already in bad health—severe diabetes. She lost a leg to the sickness. He clung to these excuses for many years. But the cold truth was he just was not up to dealing with the two of them. Patrick was already proving to be a bit on the wild side, and sending him away was the easy way out.

He went down the bar and poured some fresh drinks. The door opened, and a man looked around the room. Not finding who or what he was searching for, he ducked back into the harsh light of the street. JP regained his perch at the end of the bar. He glanced again at the photograph. Now that his time was short, he was beginning to feel he could no longer ignore the fact that much of what Paddy had become might be a result of his being sent away. Privately, JP wondered if it was too late for a reconciliation. He was coming to the painful realization that he was so set in his attitude toward Paddy because of his own feelings of guilt. Out of sight, out of mind. He had been cowardly.

He thought of the men he had killed. For many years, he had wrapped himself in the glory of revolution, the insane pride of nationalism. It was comfort for slaughter, absolution for killing. But he knew deep down, all these years, his real motivation had been simply to avenge the murder of his own father.

He remembered the night long ago. He was thirteen years old, asleep in the family home in County Cavan. His family had coaxed a meager crop from the same hard piece of land for generations. He awoke to the sound of banging on the door, the guttural voices of the dreaded Black and Tans. They dragged the whole family—JP, his parents and grandfather, his five younger siblings—onto the front lawn under a cold autumn moon. They were drunk and out for some cruel sport. His father refused to kneel. They declared him an enemy of the crown and shot him dead in front of his family. JP charged the gunman, and his cheek and jaw were shattered by the butt of an Enfield rifle. Remembering, he touched his cheek, the indentation still visible almost seventy years later.

After his father's death he was consumed with a need for vengeance. A year later, just as he turned fifteen, he volunteered for a mission. They gave him a pistol. He walked up to a man on a crowded train platform and shot him dead. The killing earned him a reputation. They called him Duihe Fuar, the Cold One.

He was then sent to join a flying column in the Cork and Kerry mountains, harassing the Black and Tans. There the violence was worse. The one episode that stayed with him most vividly happened outside Kenmare. They ambushed an enemy patrol, and he had chased one of the soldiers down to the water. The Brit was unarmed and sobbing, panicked. He was barely older than JP himself. He pressed his pistol to the man's face and calmly pulled the trigger. They had no capacity to house prisoners. End of story. But in the hysterical teenager who knelt before him, slobbering for his life, he saw the faces of the bastards who had killed his father. With all the killing that had gone on, that was the only face he had looked into before ending a life. And for all these years, that face had haunted both his nightmares and his daytime thoughts.

"Hey, JP, I need to hydrate myself. Will you be so kind as to sell me another beer?"

JP snapped back to the present. Maybe he was not so morally superior to his grandson after all. He turned to grab a bottle of beer from the ice, thinking that perhaps he'd been a stubborn old man for far too long.

The denizens of Butcher Boy Tierney's West Side neighborhood had long ago learned to give him a wide berth. While paralyzed by fear, they prayed for his demise with the fervor of ancient villagers who prayed for the end of pestilence and famine. His exploits were neighborhood lore. By ten he was drugging and crucifying stray cats. He would float them down the Hudson, their screams echoing like those of tortured children. At twelve he was an accomplished arsonist. Two years later, he was arrested for knifing a homeless man to death, "for the fuck of it." Thereafter it just got worse. There was not a felony he would not commit. He had spent twelve of his thirty-one years in prison; only his brother's contacts and intimidation of witnesses prevented it from being much more.

The Tierney family of seven boys and two girls produced enough strife to sustain a civil war in Latin America. The father would come home and slap around Jack, the oldest boy, who in turn would slap around the next younger brother. This would continue down the line, the beatings picking up velocity until it all came down on Butcher Boy, who, being the youngest boy, would hit the streets seeking a target for his rage and humiliation.

Butcher Boy came out of his building. As he walked down the street, projecting fear like sonar in a wide arc, pedestrians sensed his mood and crossed the street or ducked into stores to avoid him—all five feet five and three-quarters inches and 171 steroid-and-cocaine-cured pounds of him. His brother Jack was pissed off because that idiot they beat up died. Like that was his fault. Now Jack was not going to pay him. He needed to come up with some cash. Fast.

He walked into the Korean grocery on the corner. There was a new guy behind the counter. The regular guy knew enough to let him take what he wanted. Butcher Boy said, "Give me the money."

When the counterman hesitated, Butcher Boy shot him in the head. He bounced off the wall, and Butcher Boy shot him again, knocking him back toward the coolers. He reached over the counter and cleaned out the cash register. He stepped outside, then, remembering something else he needed, went back in and grabbed a can of baked beans. He loved to pour them over his ice cream. He strolled down the avenue and counted the money: $119. Chump change.

Billy Adare, edgy with unburned energy, decided to take a walk. He needed to clear his head, wanted to shake the feeling that his life was closing in on him, that events were spinning out of his control. He left his newspaper on the bar at Briody's and wandered the few blocks over to Fordham University's Rose Hill campus. Passing through its gates was like stepping out of the Bronx, out of the city altogether. The grounds were lush, the paths lined with towering oak and elm trees. The sprawl and clamor of the city ceased abruptly at the walls of this place. He walked over to the library, which was housed in an old stone building that had long ago been a church. Its stained-glass windows were luminous with the cutting sunlight, the blues and greens and reds reflected on the dark stone like colored water. The air was suddenly heavy with nostalgia and remembrance. This building had served as a refuge when he was young. He would come here afternoons and lose himself in its cool recesses, secreted away with whatever book he had pulled from the shelves. The women who worked there, most of them stout Italians from the Belmont section across Fordham Road, would smile at him, amused at his fervor for books. With a wink, they would let him slide by. He had got his love of reading from his grandparents, neither of whom went past the sixth grade. They would take turns reading him to sleep when he was a child.

In high school he did poorly. The classrooms were too small to hold him, too confined. He and his friends, most often Frankie and Sean, cut school and rode the subways for hours. Downtown, they roamed the city, running wild. In the spring, trucks pulled up to the high school before classes began, belching exhaust smoke in the morning air—landscapers, masons, plumbers, general contractors, all looking for cheap muscle—the boys leaped into the trucks, delirious with escape and the chance to earn a buck. They cut the great lawns of the northern suburbs, they knocked the porches off sprawling houses, rebuilt them. Smashed sidewalks with sixteen-pound hammers, the masons too cheap, too old world, to rent a jackhammer. They felt the joy of breaking something owned by the rich. They worked in Bronxville, Pelham, Scarsdale, Riverdale, Rye. When he was sixteen, Billy dropped out of school and passed his GED. JP shook his head and told him he would live to regret it. He went to work full time for an old Italian mason. The days were long and hot, but the nights still called. Billy and his friends worked all day and partied most of the night, stopping for three or four hours of sleep before returning to the grind.

Now the library door opened, and Billy watched two young women, summer students, bounce down the steps, books held close to their chests. He turned to let his gaze follow them down the path. They wore shorts and sneakers with no socks, bright, snug T-shirts. He realized with a start that it was the anniversary of Sean's death. That was the source of his edginess. With all the preoccupations in his life, the job and Paddy and JP, he had forgotten. He felt the sharp edge of enduring guilt.

He remembered picking Sean up as if it were an hour ago. They'd put in eleven hours that day—skin burned brown, filthy from the work. But home in the shower, the fatigue rolled off Billy's young shoulders with the dirt. It promised to be a hot summer night. He pulled to the curb, tapped the horn. Sean came out of his building, his wet hair combed back, his shirt unbuttoned. He carried a dinner plate with chicken, corn, and mashed potatoes in one hand, a glass of cool milk in the other. He sidestepped a ball kicked by his little sister. Billy leaned over and pushed the car door open for him.

As Billy drove, Sean ate his dinner, chicken grease running down his chin. They laughed, cursed their cheap boss. The late-August sun slashed through the windshield from the west. In three months, they would follow that sun all the way to California and promised jobs on a fishing boat. The idea of escape, of movement and adventure, fueled them. They met Sean's cousin in a bar. They bought a case of beer in a bodega and went to Inwood Park. Night fell. They drank cold beer and listened to a boom box. Friends came and went. The air was still, charged with an oncoming storm. At one point Billy walked to the tree line to piss. When he came back, an old girlfriend of his, Lisa, was among the group.

It had ended badly for them months before. Betrayal, screaming matches, hurt feelings. They embraced, a truce. She flirted with Billy in the cottony summer night. After a while she indicated she needed a ride home. He told Sean to wait. Sean rolled his eyes. He was no fan of Lisa's. Two hours later, after secretive coupling in Lisa's stuffed-animal-lined bedroom, Billy returned to the park. It was past midnight. Sean's cousin said he had got tired of waiting and walked home. Billy shrugged. He drove home smiling, glad he had reconciled with Lisa, happy he'd gotten a piece of ass. He plunged into sleep.

The next morning JP shook him awake. His grandfather appeared older to Billy that morning. He expected a lecture on drinking, oversleeping. JP looked away at some noise coming from the street. He turned back, his face heavy. Billy worried that he was ill. "Sean's been hit by a car."

Billy shot up in bed. "What? How is he?" The sleep was gone from his brain like gasoline burning off water.

JP looked to the window again, then back. He put a hand on Billy's shoulder. "I'm sorry, Billy. I'm afraid he didn't make it."

Later, he learned the details. A hit and run. Driver going so fast Sean was knocked one hundred feet out of his boots. Dead on impact. Billy got laid, and Sean got smashed to death on Fordham Road while it was happening. They were seventeen. Five years had passed, and Billy was still crippled by the guilt. He had a recurring dream where Sean came back, not dead, but sickly. Billy would ask where he had been, and Sean would nod weakly and say he had had to go away for a while, and Billy would apologize for leaving him that night. Sean would always wave that off with an easy smile, and Billy would wake full of hope, only to bury his face in his pillow and let out a howl somewhere between rage and grief.

He stood now on this August afternoon a half decade later and wished beyond possibility that he could turn back the clock. He took out his wallet and pulled from it a picture, one of those small squares from an instant-photo booth. Four shots for two bucks. It was taken at some forgotten boardwalk down the Jersey shore a week before Sean was killed. The two of them were hamming it up for the camera, sunburned and flushed from beer, their expressions shouting that they would live forever, that nothing was capable of keeping them from joy and immortality. He rubbed his thumb gently across Sean's face, then slid the photo back into his worn wallet. He fought down a lump in his throat. He walked away from the library, back toward the brash streets, determined never again to fail anyone he loved.

Vito Romero felt foolish. He was in the B. Dalton at Green Acres Mall in Valley Stream, browsing for books on how to deal with a sociopath daughter. It was a last resort. The week before, he had gone to his sister, giving her a little bit of the problem. His sister's solution was: "Put your foot up her ass, Vito."

Vito came upon the Self-Help section and scanned the titles. There were books to solve all sorts of excesses—books for people who ate too much, drank too much, gambled too much; for people who took too many drugs; even a book for people who talked too much and one for broads who loved too much.

He saw a few books on screwed-up kids—troubled teens, they

called them. Not wanting anyone to know his business, he would take a book off the shelf, then move over to the nearby True Crime section and leaf furtively, looking for answers. There seemed to be a lot of crap about communication and sharing, stuff about finding your inner child. Who wrote this shit? Vito thought about his father coming home from the butcher shop, the stench of blood thick on him. He would sip his homemade wine and deal swift backhands to solve family problems. If only it were that easy.

An older woman, all proper and gray-haired, cast suspicious looks at him. Vito stashed the book, winked at her, and beat it out of there.

He left the mall and walked across the parking lot to the Red Lobster. The summer air was like a furnace, and by the time he stepped into the dim cool of the restaurant, sweat was rolling down his back. The place smelled of fish and stale grease. He nodded to the hostess, a young woman with pretty eyes and bad skin.

"Dining alone today, sir?"

Vito held up two fingers. She led him to a table overlooking Sunrise Highway. Vito pointed to a table in the corner, away from all windows.

"That's better."

He sat down and waited, sipping a glass of ice water. He tried to think things through, remember what he had told the person he was waiting for the last time they met. It was important to keep the pieces together—not trip over himself amid the truths and lies, the innuendo and the rumor that he passed off as fact. The whole deal had become something of a game to him. A delicate web of deceit, cat and mouse on a large scale. Give a little here, take a little there. It was one way of staying ahead of the curve, of allowing the Tuzio crew the upper hand and keeping himself out of stir. At first he had been conservative, keeping things to a minimum. Lately, though, he'd gotten adventurous, even reckless. He enjoyed watching the ripple effects of his actions, how the information given caused action and reaction in often unpredictable ways. He realized it was time to start reeling things in a bit. He also realized he did not give much of a fuck lately.

He looked up as his handler walked toward him. He thought about that winter night five years before. He was driving on the Island with a suitcase full of counterfeit credit cards. It wasn't even crew business. Stupid, doing a favor for someone, a little freelance work. They stopped him for an obstructed license plate, then got gung ho on him and popped open the luggage. They leaned on him, knowing he was stuck. Tuzio did not permit any unsanctioned business; he looked at it as if you were stealing from him. The wife had already been diagnosed; there was no way he would let her die alone. In exchange for his freedom, for the ability to be at his wife's deathbed, he agreed to supply the feds with information here and there. The agreement was he would never testify.

He noticed how the agent had gotten older and thicker since they first met. There was still that midwestern way about her—that federal-agent stiffness you never saw with city cops. Some Protestant thing, he guessed.

"Ugh. This heat, it's awful." She sat down.

"Ain't it, though."

"Reminds me of home. Except here you have the pollution mixed in. Believe me, the chemicals make it worse. I feel like I can't breathe on days like this."

Vito watched while the agent ordered a shrimp salad and a diet Coke. He passed on the food, asked for an iced coffee. The place made him a little queasy. He preferred his fish fresh. He'd eat in Brooklyn.

"My bosses are interested in construction. The flavor of the week, I guess. Maybe they're tired of fighting over credit for drug busts with other agencies."

Vito thought it funny that he spent more time alone with this woman than with any other since his wife had died. They had actually developed something that could be called friendship. Christ, his life was upside down.

"Business is booming. Everywhere you look, cranes. There ain't a kid wants to shovel concrete ain't working."

"I hear it pays well."

"Sure. You don't mind bustin' your ass. They even got women humping concrete nowadays. You want, I can get you a spot on a crew, see what you can find out from the inside." Vito liked to tease her about what he thought women should and should not do for a living. While he could understand women agents, he definitely did not think women should be hard hats. It drove her crazy.

"I have you, Vito. I don't need to be on the inside."

"Good point."

"This union official out on the Island got himself killed on his front lawn. What's the word on that?"

"The Irish guy?"

"That would be the one."

She stabbed a shrimp with her fork and considered it before putting it in her mouth. Something about her made him want to get laid. It had been ages since he had a piece of ass. The few times he had since Angie died, he had woken with an unbearable shame. It was as if she were still alive. The funny thing was, before the sickness he had fooled around plenty and never thought twice about it. Now he felt as if he had perpetrated some sacred violation. He wondered how this woman would respond if he propositioned her. She would probably give him some speech out of a government manual on dealing with pervert CIs. No. She'd laugh it off. She had confided in him over the years about the hassles she encountered being a woman on that job. He could imagine. All those hard-on agents believed they were some sort of fucking crusaders. Besides, it was not her he wanted to be with—it was someone like her but older.

"What would I know about that?"

"I figured it's more like what don't you know about that."

"I usually don't associate with those kind of people."

"Right, Vito, you told me before. What do you call them, the ethnics?" She laughed.

"Ethnics, yeah. I did, didn't I." Vito smiled.

"Well, since this is not your people, why not help me out here, Vito. Because if we get tied up looking into the ethnics, well, it makes it that much harder for us to look into Mr. Tuzio's activities in the construction field. However legitimate they might be."

"You have a point there, Mary."

She pushed aside her unfinished salad and drank the rest of her diet Coke. She motioned to the waitress for another one and said, "May I have some of your fish and chips?"

She turned her attention back to Vito. "A dead carpenter's dumped on a West Side construction site awhile back. This sandhog turns up dead. Both Irish. We know Jack Tierney is operating in areas that were once the domain of—let's just say nonethnic wise guys. That make you happy, Vito?"

Vito nodded.

"Now, I hate to say this, but you guys are old news. Irish gangsters, though, that makes my bosses happy. It might get them more ink. A nice nostalgic twist."

She popped open her briefcase and passed a photo across the table. Vito picked it up and saw himself with Jack Tierney, standing over Tierney's kid in Battery Park. He said nothing and slid the picture back across the table.

"NYPD. Thing about it is they won't say who the target is. Maybe you, maybe your ethnic friend. Maybe his kid, for all I know. I do know things are getting crazy on the West Side. These ethnics are very fond of sloppy homicides."

The picture made Vito worry. He knew Mary was stand-up and their agreement was safe. While most feds were bureaucrats with badges and seemed to exist solely for publicity, Mary was solid. NYPD was a lot scarier. Vito knew personally of at least five or six department moles who supplied various information, ranging from running license plates to tip-offs about impending busts. If Tuzio even got a whiff of his association with the government, he would nail Vito to a cross.

"What case you need to make?"

"Right now I don't know. The carpenter was a two-bit bad guy, drug problem. He was working as a scab on one of the sites. The union guy was one hundred percent legitimate. I doubt they're related, but we can't say for sure. We hear things. These days everyone looks for patterns. RICO is all the rage. Problem is, we take all the credit, so the NYPD isn't being too generous."

Vito admired the way she had hardened to the realities of her chosen profession. When they first met, she was young and just a few years out of the academy, full of that all-American idealism. He had insisted on a female handler. Chance sightings would be a lot less suspicious if he was meeting a woman. She had come to realize it was a matter not of crime being committed but of who controlled it. It was not going away. They both knew he had made her career in many ways.

They had last met three months ago. He had given her a weapons stash of a potentially rival crew. The bust was enough to keep them distracted from any plans they might have had about making a move against Tuzio. Vito thought it might be time to give Tierney something to think about: the guy was becoming brash. But he decided he needed time to think it through.

"I can ask around. Take a look-see."

"What about the other guy—Adare?"

"The fighter?" Vito shrugged.

"Ex-fighter. Unless maybe he's coming out of retirement." Mary called for the check. "I want to see you next month."

"Yeah?"

"I'm taking a leave after the summer."

Vito raised his eyebrows.

"I'm pregnant."

"Is that right? Fantastic."

She smiled. "Listen. While I'm gone, would you . . . another agent?"

"Forget about it."

"Just thought I'd check. Forget I asked. How's the daughter?"

"Okay. Better." Vito stood to leave. He was too embarrassed to tell the truth.

Saturday night, and they were sitting in Lynch's on Bainbridge Avenue—Billy, Frankie, Kevin Donohue, and Jimmy the Drooler Grogan. The place was packed with women, the beer was cold, and the night was full of promise. Elvis Costello was blasting from the jukebox when Jimmy said, "I'm gonna punch that fuck right off his barstool."

Billy felt his nerves kick up a notch. Here we go again. From the time they hit their teens, Billy and his friends had brawled all over the metropolitan area. They fought in bars and parks, at concerts and sporting events. They fought in schoolyards and movie theaters. They fought in Rockaway and down the Jersey shore and in Nathan's and White Castles and pizzerias. They once got in a donnybrook that laid waste to a McDonald's at dinnertime, terrified patrons attempting to shield their children from the melee. Billy ended up with his head slammed through the golden arches. Twenty-two stitches.

It always started the same way—over nothing at all. Bullshit posturing, rampaging testosterone, imagined slights—the ubiquitous "Hey, what the fuck are you looking at?" Win or lose, they never questioned the reasons why; they just licked their wounds and looked for the next brawl. As Billy accumulated college credits, he became less inclined to join the fray. He began to feel he had something to lose and, as a result, had last thrown a punch with bad intentions on his twentieth birthday, at a party near school. He was happy to put these incidents in the past. But the one thing you never ever did was run on your friends. Even maniacs like Jimmy the Drooler.

As he sensed Jimmy gearing up for another episode, Billy took a shot at calming him down. "Jimmy, what's your beef with him?"

"He sly-rapped me at a party in Yonkers last year, the fucking pussy. He don't remember me. I'll never forget that weasel-face fuck." Jimmy jabbed his finger toward the guy, who was oblivious at the far end of the bar, surrounded by his friends.

"Jimmy, gimme a break. You remember? You were probably stewed to the mickey. Guy could be anyone." Billy tried to inject some levity. He could see Jimmy was working himself into a froth. He was jerking his head from side to side, like he did when he was set to go off.

"Billy, don't give me that shit. You go away to college, maybe you forget how things are around here," Jimmy said in between jerks.

"What the fuck's that supposed to mean? You're the asshole that moved to Yonkers."

"You got my back or you don't, Adare." Now Jimmy was pulling his lips back away from his teeth, a more ominous signal.

"Fuck you, Jimmy." Billy was tired of his shit.

"Hey, Jimmy, you got a problem with this guy, do something about it. Don't blame Billy you got your ass kicked." Frankie signaled the bartender for a new round.

"I got my ass kicked? Fuck you, Ryan."

"Well, let's see what a tough guy you are."

Billy wished Frankie had not said that.

Jimmy the Drooler grabbed his long-neck beer, walked down the bar, tossed his chin up at the guy, said, "Remember me?" and smashed the bottle over his head. By the time the guy hit the floor, his friends had pounced on Jimmy.

Billy, pulled by the riptide of loyalty, hit the crowd swinging. His first punch landed on the top of someone's skull. Billy yelped. He grabbed his hand and was punched in the neck. The blow forced him sideways, and he tripped over a barstool and landed on his back. Through the flailing arms and legs, he watched Frankie grab two guys by the hair and smash their faces together. They both dropped bloodied to the floor.

Billy scrambled to his feet and kicked a guy in the side who was sitting astride Jimmy, punching him methodically in the face, the one-two combos sounding like small-bore rifle shots in the chaos. Billy tried to help Jimmy up and was blindsided by a guy wearing a sleeveless T-shirt. They grappled along the floor until they ended up in a mutual headlock, muttering fuck-yous to each other. The bar crashed around them until they were dragged to their feet by irate cops. The cops separated the brawlers. A sergeant said, "Let's go, assholes. Anyone gotta complaint?" Without waiting for an answer, he said, "Get the fuck out."

Later, Billy and Frankie sat in Briody's, nursing bruises and beers. It was small consolation that the other guys had looked worse.

"I can't be doing this shit, Frankie. I'll never make it to law school. Fucking Jimmy is gone. He's lost it." Billy washed down a Slim Jim with a cold beer.

"You're right. Jekyll and Hyde is becoming . . . which is the bad one?"

"Hyde."

"Dr. Hyde—"

"Mister."

"Yeah, Mr. Hyde all the time. Two sips of beer, the guy is fucking berserk. Besides, you were at college, I took the cop test. I can't afford this bullshit either."

"You took the test? No shit." Billy was surprised that Frankie had not told him sooner.

"Yeah, I don't really want to be a hog the rest of my life neither. Maybe someday we'll work together on a case or some shit. I'll arrest Jimmy the Drooler for mass murder, you put him away."

Billy laughed. "I love the guy, we grew up together, but we ain't sixteen anymore. Jimmy's still into the same shit."

"Some guys will never change, I guess. Jimmy'll be a teenage alcoholic until he's seventy." Frankie went over and dropped some quarters in the jukebox. He came back to the bar as U2 started blaring.

"Yeah." Billy finished his beer and nodded to Eddie for another round. "I still think you should go to college, part time at least. Even if you go on the cops, it'll help you."

"Billy, we been through this. I just ain't book smart."

They watched as a pair of Mexicans from the Korean grocery came in and sat at the far end of the bar. They looked grateful to be at the end of their sixteen-hour shift. They regarded the beers Eddie placed before them as if they were answers to a prayer.

"Frankie, you just never tried to be book smart. Look what you do with engines. I've seen you take apart a car engine and put it back together. You could do it blindfolded. Don't tell me that doesn't take brains."

"You ever see me use a book when I'm doing that? Billy, man, I don't even like to read. I mean, I just don't understand the big attraction, sitting around staring at words on a page. What kind of shit is that? It's been downhill with me since *Curious George.* I just ain't college material. You were born book smart."

"That's bullshit."

"Doubt it. Shit, I gotta run home and grab some more money. I'll be back in a flash."

Frankie slammed his empty beer on the bar. Billy watched him walk out. He nursed his beer, still a little jittery over the night's adventure. He had transferred out of Lehman College after his first year because it was too close to home. There were too many temptations, too many friends stopping by with six-packs. He had to leave to succeed. He thought about school. He had been home only a matter of weeks, but it seemed like a mirage. That maybe he had not left after all. He ordered another beer and thought about his time away.

He arrived upstate as a refugee. On the long train ride north from Penn Station, he was overwhelmed by a mixture of elation and dread. It was as if his life were beginning anew, that Billy Adare was being remade, that he was now afforded choices, options. He was stepping away from all that was familiar. He carried only an old army duffel bag, full of clothes. Arriving as a sophomore transfer, he stood alone on what was still a summer's day, watching as families pulled up in stylish new cars, depositing their loved ones at college. His fellow students seemed to have perfect teeth and crisp clothes. They hugged and laughed; some of the mothers wept. He felt unwashed and lonely.

There was no dorm space left, so he took a small room in a house run by an old railroad man. The eight-by-ten room was spare, containing a desk, a single bed, and a small dresser. The bathroom was down the hall. Hot water was a maybe at best. For two hundred dollars a month, it was perfect. The old man's lungs were wrecked from smoking, and whenever he was home Billy could hear him coughing. But the place was clean and the three other boarders were quiet. He took most meals at a greasy spoon down the street, ate always at the counter, a book propped up before him.

His landlord turned out to be an old trade unionist who loved to listen to Billy's tales of the tunnels. He gave Billy books about the Wobblies and Joe Hill, John L. Lewis and Michael Quill, whose picture hung on the wall of Briody's Bar. At school, he burned for knowledge. His insecurities fueled him. He maintained a sizable chip on his shoulder, which he camouflaged with an easy smile. Most of his peers were more learned. They had been shipped off to tony prep schools or reared in places where first-rate educations were easily accessible. He studied day and night, was fiercely competitive about grades: You can do it, so can I.

Billy made broad acquaintance but few fast friends. He backslapped with the jocks, brooded with the arty types, argued with the young Republicans. He developed a dislike of the few Irish he encountered there, the type that tried to out-Anglo the Wasps. These grandchildren of pig farmers and bomb throwers masqueraded as old money, ashamed of what they came from. They affected the style of John Kennedy and embraced the politics of Ronald Reagan. Billy steered clear of the beer-and-puke-soaked frat parties, where the thin stain of veneer was stripped away and they looked like fifteen-year-old kids at a Bronx keg party. Becoming part of no clique, Billy was content to sit back, a pioneer in a foreign land, observing, learning.

Money was a constant worry. He took a job with a local car service, driving graveyard. It was basically a shuttle service for drunks, but the cash was decent. After the bar rush, he'd park alongside a 7-Eleven, his books spread against the steering wheel, waiting for the trickle of late-night calls. It felt good to be working. He kept his nose burning on the grindstone. He looked at school not as an interlude before real life began but as his ticket to places that had been beyond his conception a few years before.

The first bleak winter, he met a girl from eastern Kentucky, whose grandfather had been a coal miner. They made love with a variety, intensity, and frequency that he could scarcely grasp. Afterward, he would lie spent, while she straddled him, reading from some long-dead poet. He'd laugh, imagining the guys' reaction to such a scene. An insomniac, she sometimes rode with him late at night. They would talk between fares till his shift was over. She was unlike any girl he had known in the Bronx. She railed against the bourgeoisie, cursed her parents, talked about changing the world, revolution. Billy laughed at that. At school so he could eventually get a job that did not entail breaking rocks, he found it strange that so many of these kids hated all that made their life good.

When daylight was a faint promise in the eastern sky, he would turn in the Dodge Fury, and they would nap together briefly before class. He would disentangle himself from her warm flesh, pull himself up reluctantly. She'd sleep on, not interested in what the professors had to say. When spring came, she dropped out. Said she needed to travel the world, find herself. He missed her but had known all along it was a fleeting thing. She stayed in touch. He still got postcards—India, Venice, Nairobi. She said she was writing bad poetry and fucking strangers.

College gave him perspective. Up in the mountains, ensconced in his new, leafy environs, he looked back upon his neighborhood, his family, his friends. He saw with a clarity he had not known. He also felt a dislocation. I am here, they are there. Each time he went home, he felt a shift, as if the world he was once completely aligned with was tilting away from him or, more likely, he from it. The act of leaving—not just physically, for he might have gone to work and come back and things would have been the same. He was going away to school. He had grown up thinking of college people as a different species, to be regarded with suspicion and even disdain. Now he was among them. The older generation took pride in his achievements. His friends were more skeptical. Enjoying the fact that one of their own was making it, they wondered how he could still be one of their own if he was.

At school, the separateness became magnified. He began to question his identity. He struggled to define himself. He grew to care less what the people at school thought of him and more about what they thought of him at home. He became defensive about the Irish, the Bronx, even the Catholic Church. For all his ambition, he did not want to lose what had shaped him. On some winter nights he parked the taxi on a hill high above the campus. He would gaze south and east toward home as a hard wind blew through the valley below, and he'd feel he was stuck out there in the vast dark space, caught between two worlds. There were times when he felt like a traitor.

His last year he got involved with Jennifer Drake. She was from a world he could scarcely conceive of—a world of kids who seemed to have everything. They spent their summers in Europe or doing good things in the third world. They all seemed to know each other. There was something seductive about their life. But in their midst he was always the interloper. If he did not know anyone who had gone to college, they did not know anyone who had not. They would ask about his family. He smiled and told them that his brother had gone to Auburn, and they assumed he meant the college, not the New York State correctional facility. In the end, the leap was too great for either Jennifer or Billy to make. Now, home, he was not quite sure where he fit in the scheme of things but was determined to proceed with his education.

Billy looked up as Frankie made his way back down the bar, a wad of twenties in one hand. He reclaimed his barstool.

"All right, buttercup, we's ready to rock and roll now. Let's go downtown and tackle some college girls."

"Shit, look at this knot on my forehead. I'll be lucky to get my hard hat on."

"You'll be okay."

"How come we get in these brawls? I end up looking like De Niro in *Raging Bull,* after Sugar Ray is finished with him. All your bruises are on your hands. It ain't fair."

"Maybe all those books you read make you stupid comes to barroom brawling. What amazes me is, with a brother like Paddy, you fight the way you do."

"Hey, I landed some good shots."

"You punch like a girl."

Billy laughed. "Fuck off."

"How *is* your brother?"

"I wish I could say great, but who knows with the shit he's into."

"I get the feeling he can take care of himself."

"I hope so."

Billy stared at his reflection. The knot was already discolored. His hand throbbed. Books or no books, that was still a knucklehead staring back at him.

Lenny Coyle stopped as always for breakfast before heading home through the Lincoln Tunnel. The diner sat on the western edge of Manhattan, nestled among a cluster of dilapidated warehouses. He took his usual seat, a booth toward the back, looking out over Twelfth Avenue. The waitress poured him a cup of coffee.

"Morning, Lenny."

"Sally."

She moved stiffly away from him, favoring her right foot. He knew all about her operation, her corns, her alcoholic husband and sons. He probably knew more about her than he did about anyone but his wife. He did not have to order—she knew exactly what he wanted to eat and how it should be prepared. Two eggs over easy, bacon well done, rye toast with jelly, decaffeinated coffee. His life had become a series of routines. All of which were tied directly to his job.

He looked out over the desolation of Twelfth Avenue, remembered when he was a kid nearby. The area had been alive with the commotion of rail traffic and shipping, the stench of the slaughterhouses. Now it was hard to imagine that any of that had ever taken place. He watched two transvestite prostitutes engage in a shoving match. What the hell did they have left to fight over?

Sally placed his breakfast on the table and moved away. She knew him enough to realize when she needed to give him his peace. It had been another bad night in the hole. The company was fighting them on everything, constantly riding the men without regard to safety. His brother was really being pushed to the wall. He'd been in the business almost forty years and seen all kinds of bosses come and go, but nothing like this Harkness. With him it was some kind of damn crusade. They all wanted to make money, but this guy seemed intent on bending the workforce to his will, regardless of the outcome.

Lenny watched as two guys crossed the avenue, headed for the diner. Something was odd about them. First of all, they did not fit the clientele of the diner. The place was patronized almost exclusively by truckdrivers, a few warehouse workers. These two were a real Mutt and Jeff. One tall, Italian, dressed in a guido gangster suit; the other short, Irish, in leather jacket and jeans. Something about him was off. He was smiling, but there was no mirth in it. It was more of a leer. They looked uncomfortable in the bright light of morning.

With a sinking feeling, he watched them enter the diner and make a beeline for his table. They stood over him for a minute without talking. The short one sat across from him, and the tall one went to sit next to his partner, but the Irish guy put his hand up to stop him and indicated the other side of the booth. He sat next to Lenny and picked up the cup of coffee, taking a sip.

"Help yourself."

"Thanks, Grandpa."

"It's decaf."

The guy put the cup down. "Decaf? Why the fuck bother?"

Sally came over, a look of concern on her face. Lenny went to wave her off, but the tall guy said to her, "Hold on there, sugar-butt. Gimme a cup of coffee, black, with caffeine. You want something?" he asked his partner.

"Yeah. Gimme a Coke, toss a couple of sugars, make it four, in there. And a Danish, cherry or strawberry."

Sally said, "The sugar's on the table there. Help yourself."

She walked away. The Irish guy took off his sunglasses and craned his neck around, scoping out the other patrons. He turned back to Lenny. "You know somethin'? You look like a sandhog. We hear that's a dangerous job. A guy could get hurt bad, a job like that, 's'what I hear."

"It's a living."

"Listen. We want you to deliver a message to your brother."

Sally put the coffee and the soda down. "We're outta Danish."

The short man shrugged. He picked up four packets of sugar, ripped them open all at once, and dumped them in his soda. He downed the drink before the sugar could dissolve.

The Italian cringed and said to Lenny, "You tell him he's got two weeks to come around, sign that contract thing. He don't come around, we're gonna start reducing his membership. You hear me?"

"My ears ain't what they used to be, but I think that got through."

"Good, Grandpa. Good."

They got up and walked out. Lenny stared through the window, suddenly feeling very old and very tired. For the last few years he had been looking forward to spending his retirement in the lazy Florida sunshine, him and the wife growing old together. It did not seem like much to ask for.

He thought about that night thirty-seven years before when he was with the First Marine Division in Korea. Frozen Chosun. Two hundred fifty thousand capitalist-hating Chinese troops were massed on the border, blowing bugles, screaming, beating drums, sounding like a deranged carnival, the noise eerie in the frigid air. It was zero degrees and black midnight when the Chinese army came down from the hills, raining hell on them. The air filled with blood and metal and the cold screams of the dying.

He lay with his face in the icy tundra, pulling the trigger of his M-1 rifle blindly. He prayed and screamed and cried. When dawn came, they had somehow, at terrible cost, repelled the enemy. He left some flesh and all his innocence on that frozen killing field. On the long retreat to the sea, he promised himself he would die old and in bed.

And now, after surviving that nightmare and nearly forty years as a miner, he was filled with despair at the thought of being put down like a dog by some Irish street punk. Lenny waved Sally over for the check. He wanted to get home and hold his wife.

Paddy Adare listened to Jack Tierney and knew Ray Keegan was going to die. They were in the back room of the Midnight Lounge, and the conversation was going all wrong.

"You know this kinda thing, it reflects on us in the wrong way. Gives people an idea: Hey, these guys, maybe we don't need to take them serious no more; they're getting soft." Jack held up his whiskey glass. "Now, how do you think that looks?"

Paddy just stared at him and nodded.

"This Ray Keegan, he knocks the shit outta Bobby Riordan, who just happens to be an enforcer with us. Does this right out in front of half the neighborhood, puts on a real show, takes the boot to him when the guy's down. Now Keegan, he's back inna neighborhood like nothing happened. I take this very, very personally. You might say it's been three years, people forget. That's just the thing, though, Paddy. People don't ever fuckin' forget." Tierney paused to take a casual sip of Jameson. He put the glass down in front of him and refilled it. He looked at Paddy with his flat, pale eyes.

"You know that's something we usually use to our favor. But it works against us the same way. Then how we supposed to maintain things around here? People getting away with all kinds of behavior. We look like the niggers, is what we look like, or the spics. Like we got no self-control, no tradition. It's up to us to take care of these things. 'Cause, we don't, you know what happens. It comes back to haunt us."

Paddy looked across the table at Tierney and knew the decision was made. Keegan was a dead man. Ray Keegan had been a close childhood friend. The memories hit Paddy in waves—cutting school together, playing stickball in the park, hockey, chasing girls, summer nights on the street corner. They were close until high school, when Paddy started to gravitate toward a more dangerous crowd. There was a time when Paddy considered Ray Keegan his closest friend on the planet. And though they had not been close in years, they still got along when they bumped into each other.

Tierney leaned closer to Paddy and spoke in a tone that was oily with confidence. "Listen. This one's yours."

Paddy was stunned. Tierney had not sent him on a hit in almost three years. Tierney, without putting it in words, was giving him a choice. Kill a friend or be killed yourself. This was how he exacted loyalty from those around him, by demanding that they betray everyone and everything else for him.

Paddy forced himself to smile. "There some problem, Jack? The way I see it, Riordan should get this one."

"Paddy, come on. The first guy they go to when they find the body'll be Riordan. He's gotta be in church with the Sisters of Charity when it happens, lighting candles."

Paddy could only shake his head. He felt his stomach filling with molten lava.

"I want you to take care of this. These other fuckups, who knows? I'm afraid to send them out for a six-pack anymore."

"Yeah, Jack. No problem."

Tierney shrugged and said, "Hey, just get the thing done for me."

When Billy got to his locker, Lenny was getting dressed.

"We got big trouble."

"What's up? You mean Donelly?"

Lenny nodded. He spoke quietly. "I first heard about that, I'm thinking: I know the guy, he likes the ponies. Maybe those slow horses are screwing up his cash flow. But no, I talk to his cousin Jimmy Doyle. He's going to gambling anonymous meetings like religion." Lenny took off his shirt. His chest and back bore angry shrapnel scars.

"My breakfast was interrupted the other morning. A couple of messenger boys from the assholes. What I can't figure out is, one of them was Irish."

"From the other side?"

"No, narrowback. I know plenty of Irish guys are hooked up, provide muscle."

"You want me to ask my brother?"

Lenny shrugged. "You might want to run it by him." He pulled a thermal shirt over his head.

"What about *your* brother? What's he got to say?"

"I haven't told him."

"Why not?" Billy scraped the dried muck off his rubber boots with a claw hammer.

"Not many people know this, but between you and me, my brother's heart is in bad shape. He's slated to go in for the chop this month, triple bypass. Now, with the election, no contract, he's been putting it off. He was gonna take some vacation time, sneak in and out."

"We gotta tell somebody. These guys obviously ain't fucking around."

"I'm going to spread the word. I think everybody needs to watch out for themselves, here on out. You never know."

Lenny's tone was unsettling. "What do you figure's going on?" Billy asked.

"I have a few ideas." Lenny buttoned a heavy flannel shirt.

"Like what?"

"Back in the fifties, we had a little trouble with another laborers' local. They seemed to think they should get tunnel work. They were sponsored by the international, which in them days was run by the mob out of Chicago. Things got rough. Let's just say there were bodies on both sides. More on theirs than ours." He pulled his hard hat on.

"If I learned one thing in my life, it's you got to take things into your own hands. Nobody's gonna bail us out, there ain't no cavalry gonna come charging over the hill at sunrise. I just don't know if we can do that anymore."

"Who do you think is behind it?"

"Who knows?" Lenny shrugged. "Could be just the wise guys, but I doubt it. These guys made a point of mentioning the contract. Probably the company."

"Let me run it by Paddy."

"Just be careful."

Billy was surprised. "Why?"

"You get yourself into something, might not be the right thing for a kid in your position to get involved with."

"That's bullshit, Lenny. What, am I supposed to walk away because I'm going to school? Fuck that."

"Kid, history's full of people that would have been better off if they had walked away from things that seemed important to them at the time. That's all I'm saying; don't get excited. Let's go to work. I don't want to give these assholes the satisfaction of a real reason to be pulling the shit they're pulling."

An hour into the shift, Billy Adare was scared shitless. The gang was assigned the task of cutting the steel out of a construction shaft that was no longer to be used. They worked off a round metal platform that had two levels. It was suspended by two thick cables that were raised and lowered by powerful winches at the top of the shaft. The gang dropped down forty feet, hooked the steel up to a crane, cut it with a torch. The steel was then lifted out of the hole. Each section weighed several tons.

It was Billy's turn to hook the steel to the crane. He sat straddling a six-inch-wide I beam, the metal cold on his balls. He pulled himself across gingerly, trying not to look down. If he fell to his left, it was a forty-foot drop to the platform; to his right, it was four hundred feet to oblivion. Either way, he was dead. He slid his hands out in front, grabbed the beam, and pulled himself along. He moved slowly, careful to keep his weight evenly distributed. When he got to the other side, he paused and took several deep breaths to quiet his galloping heart. He reached up and grabbed hold of the crane cable. He pulled it down and hooked it to the clamp that had been attached to the steel. His hands were shaking, but he made sure the bolt was screwed tight.

He held on to the cable, using it to lean on as he turned around. Down below, the gang hooted in derision. He ignored them and inched across the cold steel to the safety of the ladder. He climbed down on shaky legs.

"Christ, Billy, it's a good thing you're not two inches taller. You'd be scared walking around town." Lenny patted him on the back.

"Thanks, Lenny. What can I say? I hate heights, ever since I was a little kid."

"Well, it shows you got balls, climbing up there like that. It's an easy thing when you ain't scared."

The gang climbed down to the lower level of the platform while the steel was lifted out of the hole. Frankie went next. He climbed up on the steel and walked across the beam as if he were strolling down the middle of Broadway. He hooked up the steel and climbed down. "See, Billy? Piece of cake."

"Fuck you."

After coffee, as they waited for another piece to be lifted out of the tunnel, they heard a loud crash. Something was coming down. Billy looked quickly at the other men, all of them realizing that there was nothing to do, nowhere to hide. They were suspended in the shaft, four hundred feet from the top and the bottom. They stood on the platform, not daring to breathe, time frozen. Billy felt his throat tighten. It sounded like a freight train was dropping on them. The steel screamed as it fell, bouncing off the walls, shooting sparks like comets in the dark shaft. Finally it smashed into the top of the platform, tearing it open like a tin can. The cables screeched with the impact, pulled to the limit, then snapped back. The platform banged off the shaft walls, and the men were tossed around. Billy ended up on his hands and knees, his eyes closed, praying the cables would hold. He opened his eyes and stared down through the grate to the tunnel floor far below. He tasted fear like metal on his tongue.

When the platform stabilized, the men pulled themselves up until everyone was standing, shaken but unscathed. The only noise was their hoarse, scared breathing.

Eamon yelled, "Try again. You fucking coonts, you missed us!"

They laughed, relieved that no one was hurt. Since they could not be sure how badly the cables were damaged, they decided not to try to lift the platform. A bucket was lowered down, and the men were lifted out two at a time.

The gang hit Hanlon's Bar like a crew of buccaneers that had nearly been lost at sea, adrenaline still seeping into their bloodstream. The problems on the job, Donelly's murder, melted away in the pure joy of being alive. They bellied up to the bar and ordered rounds of drinks. The place had a decent crowd for so late at night. Cops and nurses, four-to-twelve workers well into their night's drinking, joking and laughing, flirting. They made way for the sandhogs.

Billy Moran held up his first beer and rubbed his considerable belly. "We made it through that, I hope everybody got their lottery tickets. Twenty-three million American dollars, and"—he stabbed himself in the chest with his thumb—"I'm gonna win it." He downed his beer in one long swallow. "First thing I'm gonna do is retire from this miserable racket. Before I get nailed for real. Day I do that, I ain't never gonna go underground again. I will not even so much as go into my fucking basement. I win, I'm gonna buy a new house, right? One of those mansions—big, huge fucking thing, six or eight bathrooms, maybe one for each day of the week. Then I'm gonna have a crew of guineas, maybe portigees, come over and fill my basement with concrete. I seen enough of the inside of this planet to last me and mine for generations."

Eamon Cudahy clutched a glass of whiskey like a life preserver. "The first thing I'm gonna do is buy me a helicopter."

"A helicopter?" Billy asked.

"That's correct. A helicopter."

"What the fuck for?" Frankie said.

"I'm gonna take a little tour of the sights—the Statue of Liberty, the Empire State, and such. Maybe I'll have the cousins along. Then when we're through, like, I'll hover over that job site and shite all over that superintendent's head."

The gang laughed. The bartender set up another round of beers and shots.

"Hey, Coyle, when's your brother gonna get us a new contract?"

"You're winning the lottery, what difference does it make? You won't need a raise."

"Moran, you show up at a union meeting, you might get the drift of what's going on."

"I got this prick new super up my ass all night, I don't need no union meeting to figure out maybe we got a problem onna job. I mean, maybe I ain't educated like Adare here, but I ain't stupid neither."

"He's a rat bastard," Cudahy said.

Johnny Cash came on the jukebox, singing about despair.

"These guys are playing hardball. You hear they've had us working when the cage was down a bunch of times."

"That's brilliant. There's one way in and out of that hole. That elevator breaks, what happens when a guy gets hurt?"

"I get the impression they don't worry about that too much. You try and get any safety equipment, forget about it. We gotta bring our own earplugs and flashlights. What kinda shit is that?"

"How they expect a man to do his job right, they don't give him the tools?"

"These guys will be a whole lot happier when they can replace us with machines."

"You can blame that asshole Reagan for that."

"Gimme a break. What does Reagan got to do with this? You guys still believe that liberal bullshit. The man has put this country back on its feet. We're standing tall again 'cause he's got the balls to—"

"He's selling us out to the highest bidder." Billy was already flushed from the beer and from the relief of the near miss.

"Ah, you go to college. What the fuck do you know, Adare?"

"Billy knows all about that crap. That's what they do in college, learn, you moron."

"Get the fuck outta here. You go to college, who you got for teachers? You got your liberals and your Commies, half of all of them are fags, cocksuckas. My kid wanted college. I says no way. I took him down myself and signed him up for the Corps—smartest move I ever made. Not a liberal or a Commie anywheres near that bunch."

Eamon turned to Billy. "Your man's half mad. Believing that movie star, for fuck sake." To the bartender he said, "Hey, Maggie Thatcher, gimme me double, or there's gonna be trouble."

The bartender, who could have passed for a bloated, booze-addled version of the Iron Lady, came over and pointed a thick finger at Billy. "You keep this little Irish prick in line, or I'll cut youse all off."

"Me?"

"Yeah. You're the one that's supposed to have a half a brain around here."

Billy shrugged as Lenny came over.

"You banking your checks?"

"Yeah, Len." He thought about Paddy and the five hundred dollars. The money was more tempting now. Life without close calls. For a brief time in the shaft tonight, he'd thought it was all over.

"Good. Last thing you want is to end up like me. I'm damn near an old man, I got shit to show for it."

Billy felt the closeness of the bar, the camaraderie. It was a feeling he never had at school. There he was an outsider; here he felt he belonged. "What's up with the contract?"

"You know, me and my brother, we don't exactly get along so great. I mean, family affairs we spend time together; outside of that we might as well be third cousins. But he's been telling me about how things are going, and it don't sound good. Just the fact he's telling me says something. There's a good chance this thing comes down to a strike. It might not be a pretty one either."

"Shit." Billy saw his tuition money fading away from him.

"Least you don't have a family to feed."

Billy felt little consolation. Although he knew Lenny was right, he felt his hold on success was tenuous. Anything that stopped him from saving enough money could easily derail his plans. He knew more than a few guys who had had great expectations, then a roadblock here or there changed everything.

Lenny called for a new round. Cudahy was kicking the jukebox. Moran was arguing with Jefferson McCoy, who was from Grenada, about the invasion of that island nation. Frankie had zeroed in on two nurses off the swing shift at the VA hospital.

The bartender came over to Billy. "You get that Irish midget off my jukebox."

"Me? I ain't his baby-sitter."

"It means she likes you, kid," Lenny said.

Cudahy turned from the jukebox. "Not a good rebel song on the whole thing."

"Since when did you need a jukebox, Eamon? Sing."

"Right you are. Hey, Maggie Thatcher, this one's for you."

Cudahy filled his lungs with air and belted out:

Well, Ireland was Ireland when England was a pup!
And Ireland shall be Ireland when England's number's up!
And I'm an Irish Cat'lic, and I go to Sunday mass,
And every Limey sonofabitch can kiss my Irish ass!
Up the Republic!

They went back to the drinking, and when the last of them, Eamon and Frankie and Billy, left near dawn, they could feel a storm gathering. They did not notice the navy-blue Chrysler parked across the street from the bar.

Billy called Paddy but did not get a call back. He began to worry. Things went from bad to worse on the job. There were no more visits by the goons, but the company was tightening up. Everybody was on edge. Rumors circulated wildly. Many of the men took to carrying weapons.

Paddy Adare watched from Murray's Gym as the rain came down hard. The afternoon sky had turned nearly black, and the wind blew the rain in howling gusts. Brilliant lightning laced the darkness, thunder rattled the windows. The winos and junkies had disappeared from the avenue, crawling into unseen crevices to avoid the torrent. It was a storm so violent it seemed intent on washing all the evil from the city streets.

As he watched the storm, Paddy thought how a series of random events shaped his life, pushing him in directions beyond his control. It started with the rock that killed his father. A few feet to either side, and he would be alive today, a hard hat in his fifties. Paddy could only guess at how different his own life might be.

He'd been two weeks away from a sure spot on the 1972 Olympic boxing team when he broke his ankle roughhousing with Mickey. A fighter he had beaten twice went on to win a silver medal and make fifty grand for a nationally televised professional debut. For his first pro bout, Paddy took home $117 for a second-round knockout in a smoke-filled Elks Club in Camden, New Jersey.

Then his hands. He held them up before the window. They brought him to the brink of the big time and failed him, just when things were coming together, when everything he ever wanted was within reach. After that it was more bad luck—even getting popped for the Johnny Scanlon hit. An off-duty rookie cop just happened to be walking past the bar and heard the shots. The guy became an instant hero. He found Paddy standing over the corpse with a gun in his hand. A gift-wrapped homicide collar. Only the fact that Scanlon was such a lowlife kept Paddy from a second-degree-murder conviction. The prosecutor seemed eager to plea it down to manslaughter, a bar fight gone ugly. Case closed. It still meant fifty months of prison time, of relentless dreariness. Prison was all the bad things from the street distilled. There was no respite on the inside, no handy means of avoiding the grinding misery.

Paddy did not blame anyone for these things. He took it as a matter of his life's course. Sometimes things roll your way, sometimes they don't. He made the best of it, dealt with it. He was a survivor who had no capacity for self-pity. He had learned early that looking to others for reasons or support was a fool's endeavor. It only made you weak.

But lately his world seemed to be closing in on him. He knew in his heart that he was losing Rosa, the one good thing he'd ever been granted. He felt a tremor of sadness, a gaping loneliness. But he had to lose her, because he did not want to drag her down with him. While he accepted the consequences of his life, he could not bear the thought of hurting those around him who were not involved. Distance would keep Rosa alive.

As he stared out the window, a realization came over him. The unease that he'd felt had coagulated into something real—fear. He was afraid of Jack Tierney.

On the street, traffic had slowed to a crawl, visibility reduced to nothingness. There might have been a time when he could have walked away from Tierney. But that time was past. In the beginning he had entertained some crazy notion that he would make a few scores, then leave, head west or south, Ireland maybe. Go somewhere away from the streets, away from fear and hurt, away from the adrenaline rush. He had aspired to a life free of violence and strife, had wanted to take Rosa and find that place where they could be together. A place where he wasn't looking over his shoulder. But ten years were gone, and it all seemed a fantasy now. He had become everything in life he had wanted to avoid. He was coming up on thirty-three, an ex-con with no discernible future. He was in so deep he felt he could barely breathe. And now he was left with the Ray Keegan hit. It was clear: Paddy hit Keegan or he got whacked himself.

He felt a hand on his shoulder and turned.

"Hey, Paddy, you here to work or what?"

Paddy looked into Murray's tired face. "No. I think I need a day off."

. . .

Mere blocks away, Jack Tierney stood looking out the window of the Midnight Lounge. He, too, watched the rain. To no one specifically he said, "This ain't shit. You shoulda seen the rain in Southeast Asia." And then it came down so hard he could not see across the street, a thick curtain of rain, a veil of water. He smiled. "This is how it was."

Jack actually missed Vietnam. It was a lot easier to run things without worrying about the law, without being held accountable for your actions. In the jungle, he had made his own rules and operated with ruthless efficiency. It was not just where he learned to kill; it was where he learned it was no big fucking deal. His government made him a killer, then he came home and it said, Oh, no, not here you don't. Jack Tierney had a hard time buying into that.

Vietnam had defined him. He served two tours, with the Special Forces and then with a special operations group. Spooks. He traveled all over the country on clandestine missions, dressed in the neutral black uniforms disavowed by the people that created them. On the second tour he'd killed or maimed nearly everyone he saw. It was his mission to inspire fear, to beat the Vietcong at their own game.

He came home a copiously decorated veteran, a week shy of his twentieth birthday. But he was a teenager in years only. He quickly put his combat skills to use on the city streets, and by twenty-five he was an up-and-coming racketeer who inspired trepidation in the criminal establishment. For nearly a decade he was content to share the spoils with the old-time bosses, but his ambition eventually got the better of him. One Christmas week, when the city was turning to peaceful and joyous celebration, he littered the streets with eight members of the old guard. By the time their corpses could be straightened up and laid out, Jack Tierney was king.

The eighties dawned, and money poured into the neighborhood. When the construction boom hit, Jack knew it was time to make a move. He started by killing a few Tuzio associates who were working the new construction sites. A bookmaker was beaten to death in a local bar, a shop steward was thrown off a roof, a leg breaker was shot full of holes. Tierney used corpses as calling cards, as entreaties. He was letting Tuzio know there was plenty of work for everyone and he was intent on getting his share. Tierney was shrewd enough not to kill any made members of the Mafia. He did not want to force Tuzio's hand. He was content to harass, to cost Tuzio time and trouble and money, to wear him down. Jack Tierney had paid close attention to his adversaries in Vietnam.

His strategy worked, and now he was settled into a comfortable working relationship with the Italians. Still, he did not trust them. Since coming home and taking over the neighborhood rackets, he'd learned that no one was to be trusted. It was the same as it had been in war. The only thing worthy of loyalty was yourself. He'd learned that lesson time and again. He also knew that fear, not profit, was the only reliable motivator.

Paddy Adare. Jack knew in some ways it was too bad. He had spent a lot of time bringing the guy along. And he was a moneymaker—no question there. But it was something that needed to be done. Things were getting sloppy. His idiot brother killing the union guy—this made Jack look bad in front of the Italians. Only good thing was they sent one of theirs along, someone to share the blame.

Until Paddy was out of the picture, he could not get anyone else involved. Maybe he should do it himself, but no. Bosses can't get involved in that crap. He needed to insulate himself better. One thing the Italians were smart about. He turned and retreated to the back room of the Midnight Lounge. He would soon know whether Paddy had carried out the contract on Keegan. Then he could make his move.

Billy came out of the shower and wrapped himself in a towel. He went into the kitchen and grabbed a bottle of Coke from the refrigerator. His grandfather sat at the table, writing a letter to a cousin in Ireland. He wrote intently, forcing his arthritic hand to make the words. His face showed frustration.

"How's it going, Gramps?"

JP looked up. "It was a lot easier last week. Live fast, Billy. You don't want to be old." He dropped the pen and stood. "You remember, now, I'm going to the country for the weekend with the Holy Rollers."

Billy laughed. JP went on the occasional church retreat weekend. He always came back with a load of good stories.

"Good. I can have some go-go girls up here while you're gone."

"You do and I'll be staying."

The phone rang, and Billy answered it. He was surprised to hear Jennifer Drake on the line. "Jen? Hold on. Let me change phones."

He handed the receiver to JP and went to his room. Taking a breath, he picked up. Wet from the shower, he listened to her speak. After their breakup, Billy had realized that their relationship meant more to him than he'd assumed. Now she was in town and inviting him to meet her and some friends for a drink. He wanted to say no, he was busy. He wanted to be macho and prideful, but every hormone in his body screamed to be ensconced in her warm flesh. And besides, he missed her. Agreeing to meet, he hung up. His hand was shaking.

JP came to his room. "Everything all right?"

Billy looked at his grandfather. "With women, who knows?"

"You've a point there, Billy."

As he dressed, he thought about the weekend they spent at her parents' house. He recognized it now as the beginning of the end for them. Already he knew that many of her friends did not think he was right for her. Billy realized this had nothing to do with how he treated her and much to do with his being a Catholic construction worker from the Bronx. He was certain her parents would regard him with trepidation.

They crossed the mountains of upstate New York and came upon a place of soft hills and open space. He had never seen a house so large. It had more windows than his apartment building and sat on two hundred acres that rolled gently as far as he could see. He could only describe it as stately.

They were met by her parents on the front porch. Her mother was blond and unnaturally trim for a woman of fifty. She had the look of someone who employed various chemicals and surgeries in an attempt to thwart time. She gave him a wide, neutral smile. Jennifer's father, his shock of white hair belying his own fifty years, seemed more at ease in his skin. Still, he looked out over his property while he shook Billy's hand, as if searching the horizon for an alternative suitor.

After a dinner of braised venison, Billy sat and enjoyed an after-dinner drink with Mr. Drake, the women away somewhere in the cool recesses of the house. The father became more expansive. Seeming to enjoy dangling the prospect of his vast holdings before Billy, he spoke of dividends, real estate tax dodges, interest rates, and sound investments. He regaled Billy with tales of his wily entrepreneurship. The talk turned to killing.

"You ever hunt dove?"

Billy had been hunting once in his life. He and Frankie had wandered into the woods a few miles north of Roscoe, carrying enough firepower to slaughter a herd of woolly mammoths. Frankie's cousin had recommended the spot, promising it was "like shootin' fuckin' fish in a barrel." They did not see a single deer, but they did shoot nine beer cans, a squirrel, two bullfrogs, and a rusted motor from a '63 Plymouth. Then they got lost for six hours. In a blind panic, they attempted to attract rescuers by firing their rifles into the air, until they were out of ammo. This proved futile. They finally staggered out onto the road after sundown, swearing each other to secrecy.

"Not dove, no. I've been hunting a bunch of times, though."

Billy wondered where you went to kill a dove.

"Ever drop anything impressive?"

Billy pictured Mr. Drake standing under a brutal African sun, his foot propped on top of an oversize carcass, a bazooka-size rifle in one hand, his pith helmet in the other. The smug look of a Saxon killer on his face.

"This and that. A deer or two. Nothing too big."

"I see." Seeming to lose interest, he stood and walked over to lean on the mantel. Billy anticipated a change of topic.

"Jennifer, well, she marches to her own beat. She doesn't always have both oars in the water."

Billy remembered, while listening to Mr. Drake describe Jennifer with these clichés, that her mother had preferred adjectives. In the six hours he had been there, she had called her only child spirited, difficult, uppity, irresponsible, insolent, sassy, and persnickety. Just letting Billy know they expected her to outgrow the silliness that produced little problems like him. Billy nodded, at his deferential best. He was trying.

"She speaks highly of you." Mr. Drake swirled his cognac and turned to lay a hand on the cheek of one of his trophies. "This moose was fourteen hundred pounds. I brought him down with one shot from a Mauser at three football fields' distance. Pulverized its heart. Nailed him while he was at rest. Yes, sir, it was the perfect kill shot. You don't want them after they've run. Meat is too damn gamy." He turned back to Billy and lowered his gaze. "I hope she's right about you."

Billy gave him his best altar-boy smile. "I hope so too, Mr. Drake."

Jennifer's father regarded him quizzically. "Call me Hank. Ever shoot skeet?"

"No, sir."

"Come on. I got a beauty of a trap out back." He put his hand on Billy's shoulder and steered him to the rear of the house.

"Out back," they were joined by the Drake women and the houseboy, Miguel. A flick of the switch threw an acre of the yard into midday. Mr. Drake dragged out his collection of shotguns, which he described as "a quarter million dollars' worth of firearms." He donned an NRA cap. They sipped vodka and lemonade and blasted many clay pigeons to smithereens. The sight of Jennifer caressing a five-thousand-dollar shotgun was strangely erotic to Billy.

Mrs. Drake, whose sport seemed to be treating the help badly, sent Miguel for another bottle of Absolut. Then, her eyes glassy from booze, she turned to Billy and blurted out, "I didn't think there were any white people left in the Bronx."

"Mother!"

"There's a few. Maybe four hundred thousand." Billy smiled.

By Saturday afternoon, Billy realized he was being tolerated. Sensing he had failed some test, he wanted to ask the Drakes exactly what his deficiency was. Was it his accent? His dead parents? Maybe his callused hands? He knew that if he and Jen had a future, it would entail elopement, maybe disinheritance. Suspecting he would never be back, he made a point of fucking their daughter in as many rooms in that vast house as possible.

The last night, as he laced into Jennifer doggy style on the lush back lawn, he looked up and noticed a silhouette in her parents' window. He was not deterred.

The next morning he was all smiles as they loaded the car and said goodbye. He was unable to detect which parent had been the voyeur. As he drove Jennifer's car back to school, Billy felt a distance grow between them. It was only a few weeks later when Jennifer said, "I think we should explore other options. I mean, we're so young." Billy guessed she was more influenced by her parents than she would ever admit.

. . .

Billy took the night off and rode the number 4 subway down to Fulton Street. As the train rocked along, he entertained many false hopes. Emerging from the sweltering IRT station, he joined the sea of yuppies pouring out of the glass towers of lower Manhattan and heading toward the South Street Seaport. There, at that vast outdoor drinking festival, revelers fresh from the trading floors hoisted oversize beers and talked loud, trying to outboast each other. The men wore trim, dark suits and bright ties, the women colored suits and running shoes. Their faces were red with merriment. The Dow-Jones industrial average had reached 2,000 that week. Everyone seemed young and in some kind of hurry.

Billy, wearing jeans and a T-shirt, felt a slight discomfort. He climbed the stairs to Pier 17, which rose above the heads of the partiers. In the coolness of the mall, the crowd was thinner. He made his way over to McQuinn's and snagged the last empty barstool. Ordering a beer, he drank it faster than he wanted to. He was anxious. Although he realized it was over between them, he still felt some need to be accepted by Jennifer and by her world.

By the time he ordered his third beer, he was having doubts about missing work. She was already forty minutes late, and he felt foolish for being there, chasing her. He began listing things he did not like about her. It was a painfully short list. Two girls, tanned and pretty, nudged to the bar beside him. Billy could smell the glory of summer on them. They ordered beers and smiled at him. He felt better.

Thinking about leaving, he looked out into the mall and caught a glimpse of Jennifer coming through the crowd toward him, her brown hair shining in the late-day sun that slanted through the atrium. Her smile seemed to light a path before her. She brought to mind blue skies and splendor. His breath caught. She was easily the most beautiful woman he had ever touched. He grabbed his beer bottle as if it alone could steady him.

"Billy." She kissed him on the cheek. She wore a white summer dress with a blue floral pattern. Around her neck was a seashell necklace that set off her stunning tan. Billy felt pallid. "This is my friend Dan, and you know Melissa."

Billy shook hands with Dan and nodded at Melissa. She had been one of his major detractors in Jennifer's inner circle. Fuck her, he thought.

They maneuvered to a table overlooking the seaport and ordered drinks. The sun was falling below the downtown skyline, and the light had turned soft and orange. The summer air was sultry and suggested untoward possibilities. Billy sipped his beer, soothed by the alcohol and her presence. He wondered if she would sleep with him tonight. That prospect made his knee twitch.

"Billy, it's really good to see you. You look bigger." She held her hands above her shoulders.

Billy shrugged. "Been working."

Jennifer turned to Dan. "Billy works building tunnels. He's a sandhog."

Dan wore a dark suit with his shirt opened at the neck, his tie loosened. Despite the encroaching darkness, a pair of Ray-Bans was pushed up onto his head. He produced a cigar with an arrogant flourish and said, "That's great." He put the cigar in his small, mean mouth.

Billy disliked him immediately. He had the slick self-assurance of the garrulous backslappers he disdained at school: the scions of success who believed that they deserved all the things that were handed to them. Dan lit the cigar, puffing mightily.

"So what do *you* do, Danny?" Billy felt his voice rise more than he wanted it to. He considered easing off on the beer. Let them catch up.

"It's *Dan*. Not Danny." He blew a thick stream of smoke past Billy's shoulder. "I'm an associate at DKJ. It's an investment bank."

"That's great."

Jennifer, sensing discord, jumped into the conversation. "Melissa and I are heading for Paris tomorrow." She needed things to be bright and sunny.

Billy was stung. He realized he was probably an afterthought; stop and see the poor slob on the way to Europe. He felt resentment simmering inside him and wanted to take it out on Dan, but he remained civil. He even said nice things about Melissa. They made small talk and drank. Billy tried to sound interested as Dan boasted about his salary and bonuses, his office high jinks.

Jennifer went to the bathroom. Dan indicated Billy's shirt with a stab of his cigar. "Yankees, ouch. Poor guy."

"You like the Mets?"

"Red Sox."

"You from Boston?"

"No. Riverdale."

"No shit. I'm from the Bronx too." Billy finally felt some common ground.

"I'm from Riverdale," Dan said evenly.

"Yeah, well, that's in the Bronx."

"Only technically."

Billy looked to Melissa. She was impassive. He took a sip of his beer. He would let it slide.

"How come the Red Sox?" Billy was proud of his light tone. He had an urge to shatter his beer bottle over Dan's fifty-dollar haircut.

"I went to school in New England."

"Whereabouts?"

"Near Boston."

"So?" Billy smiled.

"In Cambridge."

"MIT?"

Dan leaned back and drew on his cigar. He regarded Billy as if he were a cabana boy who asked to use a bathroom in the main house.

"The big H, pal."

It hurt, but Billy smiled as Jennifer walked up.

A half hour later, they were trying to decide between a party in SoHo and a bar on the East Side. Jennifer had her hand on Billy's thigh. The world was right.

Dan pulled on his cigar and said, "So I hear you're a big union man."

Billy felt his color rise. He heard Jennifer catch her breath. Leaning back, he waited while a waitress replaced their empties with a fresh round.

"You might say that." Billy smiled. He wanted the evening to work, wanted it to end with him and Jennifer naked together. This should not be too much to ask for. There had been a closeness to them once, and he refused to believe that it was gone forever.

"Guys, get real. This is no time for politics." Jennifer took her hand from his leg. Billy felt a coldness where her hand had been.

Dan laughed smugly. He removed his sunglasses and placed them in the inside pocket of his jacket.

"Relax, Jen. This is not about politics. It's about economics. Dollars and cents. Let's face it, unions are an anachronism. A thing of the past." He blew smoke past Billy. "Don't you agree, Adare? Christ, twenty bucks an hour for ditchdiggers. Get real, pal." His words hung over the table like a threat.

"Dan! You asshole."

Billy held up his hand to silence Jennifer. "Anachronism? You ever work a day in your life, Danny?" Billy stood. A craziness was coming over him. He realized that he should sit down and shut up, but he could not. He laughed. "Huh? You ever sweat for a nickel, you fucking daddy's boy? Let's see." Billy lunged across the table, grabbed Dan's left hand, and turned it palm up. Beer bottles teetered and fell; one shattered on the floor. Dan struggled to pull his plump, pale hand away, but Billy held firm. "Look. You got hands like a pussy." Billy shoved the hand back at Dan, who dropped his cigar and stood uncertainly. He backed away, saying, "You're a freak, pal." Then, to Jennifer: "You went out with this guy?" He turned and stalked away through the mall.

"Fuck you," Billy called after him. He was suddenly aware of the stares and, turning, noticed that he was the focus of everyone in the bar. He waved and sat down heavily, thinking: Christ, *I* am an asshole.

Melissa stood, her arms crossed, a knowing look on her face. A look that said she had been right about Billy all along.

Jennifer shook her head. She said, "Billy, you're so emotional."

Billy heard pity in her voice, and at this he burned with shame. He wanted to say something witty, something with a touch of sarcasm. But he was afraid that if he spoke, his voice would crack. He looked away, out over the lonely church spires of Brooklyn. He imagined the hushed, cool silence of those places, the haunting flicker of votive candles, the soft rustle as a priest made the sign of the cross. He imagined a refuge.

"Let's go, Jennifer." Melissa was insistent. She backed away from Billy as if he were contagious.

Jennifer looked as if one of her fears had just been confirmed. There was a sadness about her as she said, "I'm going."

Billy said nothing. As they walked away, he very clearly heard the word "loser." He was not sure who uttered it. He returned to the bar and ordered another beer. He felt like a stupid and mean animal, a failed human being. He attempted a few fake smiles, but it was apparent the other patrons thought he was leering: they gave him a wide berth. He drank to loosen the grip of searing regret.

The night wore on, and he spent like a sailor on shore leave. He made a host of fleeting friends as the night deepened and his cash dwindled. He kissed a sloe-eyed girl from Hackensack, who appeared to have a need for him. For this he was grateful. But then she was gone.

Later, after many more beers, he looked up as someone touched his shoulder. He turned and was surprised to see Jennifer. She swayed, then smiled and led him from that place of raised glasses and cheap laughter, down the stairs, past the last drunken stragglers, past the cleaning crews sweeping the detritus of a Wall Street party in the Age of Reagan. She led him to her family apartment on the East Side. There, in the charged plushness of that place, his resentment boiled inside him until it was as pure as hate. He wanted to make her pay. He wanted to ball his hand into a fist and smash her face, as if it were the face of every rich asshole on the planet. He wanted to break things. He wanted to hurt her for dumping him for what he failed to represent. Instead he chose his cock with which to punish her. He mounted her with fury and fucked her till they both lay spent.

After, as she slept, he lay chilled in the air-conditioned room, his rage cooled to shame. He stood and pulled the covers over her naked, sleeping form, then padded into the living room and dressed as dawn came to the city. He left, past the knowing smirk of the doorman, and started his long ride back to the Bronx.

It was raining late in the afternoon when Paddy Adare followed Ray Keegan off his job site on Tenth Avenue. Paddy watched as Keegan pulled his jacket over his head to block the hot gray rain that was slicing down and ran across the street to McMullen's. He waited a few minutes, then followed Keegan in and saw him at the far end of the bar, talking to a couple of other hard hats.

The place was filled with an after-work crowd from the site. Some sat on barstools and had coins, bills, and drinks in front of them. The rest stood three and four deep at the bar, laughing and drinking.

The jukebox bleated out an old Bob Dylan song that no one paid attention to. The bartender, a young, wiry Irishman with straight dark hair and ruddy skin, darted about, exchanging beers and shots for cash. The boisterous construction workers gave him no rest. Paddy edged his way to the bar.

A group of carpenters had formed a circle to his left and were talking shop. They all wore dungarees, work boots, and baseball hats touting their favorite sports teams. They were flushed and loud. The largest one downed a beer with a single, extended swallow, slammed it on the bar, indicated to the bartender with a circular motion of his index finger that they wanted another round, belched, and said, "I'm telling you that kid is a lunatic. You know how Scalacci is always bustin' the kid's balls, right? I mean, he rides him constantly, don't give him a break. But the kid, he smiles alla time like he don't got a care in the world?"

"Yeah, don't he, though?" said the man to his left.

"Today I see him coming back with the coffee. I ask him, Hey, why the hell you put up with that shit from him? He says, Well, he likes his coffee blond and sweet, right? I say, Yeah, so? He says comere. I follow the kid around by the shithouse. He takes the cup of coffee in one hand and holds his dick with the other, taking a leak. He's just about finished, he squirts in the guy's coffee."

"Get the fuck outta here," the second-largest one said in disbelief.

"I ain't shittin' you, Larry. God as my witness. He pissed in Scalacci's coffee. He's got this big dopey grin on his face. You know how his eyes are always going in different directions? Then he says to me, 'No matter what the guy does to me, I know I don't drink his piss. Every day, he drinks mine.' "

Larry grimaced and said, "Ah, Jesus. How do you know he don't piss in all our coffee?"

"Whatsa matter—you bust the kid's balls too?"

"Hey, as far as apprentices go, he ain't exactly what you call Flash Gordon."

"So bring your own coffee. What can I tell ya?"

Paddy ordered a beer. These poor bastards, he thought, working their lives away for a couple weeks' vacation a year and maybe a house and a car. It was worse than doing time. He was probably doing Keegan a favor giving him a quick out, saving him the headaches. Paddy sipped his beer and worried when he realized he was still trying to talk himself into this one. In the past, it was clockwork. Wham, bam, thank you, ma'm. Drop them and go. You don't look back. But they'd all been scumbags. As he watched Keegan through the blue cigarette haze, he knew it would not be easy this time.

When he was halfway through his second beer, he took a deep breath and exhaled slowly. It was time to see what Keegan was up to. He turned and shouldered his way through the crowd toward the men's room. As he went by, Keegan put out his hand, and Paddy stopped and feigned surprise.

"Paddy, how you doin', buddy?" Keegan said.

Paddy smiled and shook his hand. He recoiled inwardly at the touch, wishing the hand weren't so warm.

"Hey, long time no see, Raymo. Looks like life's been good. You're looking good." Paddy thought he did look better. The guy had gone to fat young, his handsome face and dimples disappearing under an onslaught of cheeseburgers and beer. But he had dropped some pounds and seemed to be making a comeback. Chisel away a few more layers of lard here and there, and it was the old Raymo.

"Can't complain. Been down Florida, working a couple jobs. Slow now, though."

"Yeah, no shit? There's plenty a work here."

"That's why I come back. I got married down there, Paddy." He showed Paddy his ring. "You believe that shit?" Keegan laughed. "Gets expensive, you get a wife, they like shopping so much. She's got me into clean living, though, except for the occasional beer or two. Nice girl from the South, she don't bitch and moan like these New York broads. Always wanting something you can't give them. Like they really need anything more than a stiff prick." He wiped up some ketchup with a couple of french fries, put them in his mouth and, while chewing, said, "Got a baby coming the fall, you imagine?"

Paddy stiffened. He looked over Keegan's shoulder at the liquor bottles behind the bar in an effort to avoid eye contact. He did not need this to be any harder than it already was. He'd had himself convinced that Keegan was an accident victim. Life goes on.

"You should stop by, Paddy. My ma was asking about you the other day. You always was her favorite. Why, I don't know."

Paddy hoped Keegan would not start in about the old days. He was the kind of person who lived on playground memories, relating them over and over until they grew beyond any resemblance to reality. His life had peaked in junior high school.

"Yeah, I will. Listen, I gotta go. Meet my girlfriend—you know how they get. You here for the night?" Paddy pointed to the money on the bar in front of Keegan.

"Nah. After this one I'm outta here too. Married life. You still seeing that Spanish girl from the A and P?"

"Yeah. Rosa. She ain't worked in the grocery for a long time, though, Raymo. Stay out of trouble. And oh, yeah, good luck with the kid."

"Thanks, Paddy."

Paddy was about to walk away, when Keegan grabbed him by the arm and lowered his voice. "Hey, listen, Paddy. I was hoping Jackie wasn't still pissed about that thing with Riordan. Maybe you could talk to him for me." Keegan smiled, embarrassed at having to ask the favor. "I mean, shit, Paddy, the guy started the thing. I only done what anyone from the neighborhood would of. Defend myself. I maybe hit him a few times more than I should of, but who's got control over their actions with a thing like that?"

Paddy looked at him for a moment. It really was not Keegan's fault. Riordan was an asshole, but that, unfortunately, was beside the point. He leaned closer and said, "Things have a way of working themselves out, Ray. It's been a long time. Take it easy."

"Thanks, Paddy. I really appreciate that. I was a little worried about coming home. You know, I talked to other people from the neighborhood, they said they ain't heard nothing. Still, I wanted to run it by you, seeing as how we go back so long."

At that moment Paddy hated the fact that anyone ever trusted him. He wanted to tell Keegan, Run for your life, go back to Florida, go somewhere where they can't find you and wait until Jack is fertilizer. With anyone else, Paddy might get away with scaring him off, and that would be the end of it. But if Keegan suddenly disappeared, Jack would know.

Paddy looked at that fat, sad, smiling face and thought: You asshole, you should be on some beach in Miami, watching the bikinis go by. He wondered why people had such trouble believing they could get themselves killed. They knew it happened all the time, they all knew people who had been subtracted from life as a result of crossing Jack Tierney, but they never put it together with themselves. He was suddenly angry at Keegan for his stupidity. The anger felt good, like maybe it was the juice he needed to finish the thing. He said goodbye and went into the bathroom. It stank of stale piss and wasted lives. He stood at the urinal, but could not pee.

Paddy walked back to his stool the other way around the rectangular bar. He did not want to talk to Keegan again. Downing his beer quickly, he left the bar. The wet air brought him back to focus. The rain was keeping the street empty, and a warm, wet wind was blowing up from the river. He would finish it now. Get down to business, he told himself. You don't make the rules.

He crossed Tenth Avenue and walked halfway down the block. On the north side were four abandoned railroad tenements that had housed ten noisy families each when he and Keegan were kids. Now they stood silent, waiting for the developer's bulldozer to push them under forever, like so much else in the neighborhood. Across the street was a block-long machine shop, closed for lack of business. The tenements were separated by alleys that ran through to the next block. He turned into the second alley. Keegan would pass the alleys on his way home.

Standing in the alley, he couldn't help but think back twenty years to hanging out with Keegan. If someone had told him then that this would happen, he would have laughed at the impossible suggestion. But that was a long time ago, a different lifetime, another Paddy Adare. So much had come to pass, so many nights waiting in darkness. He felt that he had fallen into a black hole and gravity had taken control, pulling him down, away from everything he once believed in.

His adrenaline started to pump, and he bounced on the balls of his feet and breathed deeply, the way he used to when he was boxing. Back then it was the screaming crowds that sent the blood pulsing in his temples and drove him on, but now the voices came from within. His senses burned with alertness. He could remember every detail of the killings he'd been involved with, what the victims' last words were and the brief, confused look of recognition when they knew it was over, when they knew that someone controlled their fate with one finger. While he waited, he could hear all his ghosts: his dead parents, his friends who died too young, his victims. They sang a chorus of death that filled him, calling to him for a resurrection he was powerless to offer. He was getting edgy and hoped Keegan would hurry.

Back in the smoky din of McMullen's, Ray Keegan finished his second beer. He had promised his wife he'd have only two. He left a ridiculously large tip on the bar, and walked outside. He was almost giddy with relief; walking to the corner, it hit him with a force. Since coming home he'd been anxious, uncertain about the mood of Jackie Tierney. He knew well the neighborhood's tradition of petty vendettas leading to bloodletting. But he'd hoped his three years of exile had been enough, and after talking to Paddy Adare, he was sure it had. He waited anxiously at the light, in a rush to get home and tell his wife that everything was going to be okay.

When Paddy saw Keegan coming toward him, he crossed to the other side of the alley and waited for him to pass. His right arm hung easily at his side, his gloved hand holding the pistol. He leaned on the cool brick wall and breathed slowly. Time compressed; every movement, every sound, became a blur of light and noise. Keegan passed so close that Paddy could hear him wheezing. He stepped out behind him, raised the gun, and squeezed off the first shot. The bullet hit Keegan in the base of the skull, and he started to fall straight down, as if he had been chopped at the knees. Paddy took two steps toward him, firing a head shot with each one. The last bullet exploded through Keegan's temple as he hit the ground.

Paddy dropped the pistol and turned right down the next alley, leaving Keegan dead on the wet sidewalk.

Joe Harkness sat back and blew a thick cloud of cigar smoke up toward the chandelier. He was one of ten businessmen occupying a prime table at a two-thousand-dollar-a-plate fund-raiser for Vice President George Herbert Walker Bush. To his left sat Charles Eliot. On the dais, not fifteen feet away, the Vice President was whispering in his wife's ear.

Harkness held forth. "I'll guarantee you this. It'll be a coon's age before the liberals see the inside of the Oval Office. 'Cept maybe to take out the trash. Maybe this Bush is no Ron Reagan, but I think he's come around nicely, last seven years. Yes, sir. He's more Texas and less Connecticut every time I listen to him. No offense, Charles." He turned to Eliot.

Eliot smiled and doffed an imaginary hat toward Harkness. None taken.

"I noticed a little item in the *Journal,* just the other day. Since 1980, that golden year in our nation's history . . . Goddamn, I still can't believe we had Jimmy Carter as our commander in chief. I realize he's a southern boy and all, but hell . . . Since 1980, the percentage of unionization in our workforce has decreased from twenty-three to eighteen percent. Now, that is what I call progress." Harkness slapped the table and sucked on his cigar.

A swarm of waiters descended on the ballroom floor. Dressed in maroon jackets and black tuxedo pants, they moved with almost mechanized speed and efficiency. One group cleared the appetizer plates, while the other deftly placed entrées in front of the well-groomed donors.

Later, as they enjoyed their desserts, a procession of white Republican men expounded the virtues of Family, Patriotism, and Trickle-Down Economics. When the Vice President was finally introduced, the crowd rose to its feet and cheered heartily for the copilot of their economic boom. Then they sat through forty-five minutes of George Bush describing his up-by-the-bootstrap rise to prominence. He never once mentioned the fact that his father was a millionaire.

At the end of the speech, Joe Harkness said, "I wish that boy did not sound like he was about to cry to his mama all the time. But shit, he'll do."

The table occupants all laughed hard. They were well fed and suntanned in their tuxedos. The 1980s had been extremely kind to them. They bespoke fortuitous investments and easily worn formality. Joe Harkness summoned a waiter and ordered another bottle of bourbon. Finally, after hearty handshakes and photo ops with the Vice President, Joe Harkness walked out into the warm July night with Charles Eliot. Harkness's driver waited curbside.

"Charles, let me drop you off."

Eliot held up his hands, palms outward. "I'll be fine. I'd like to walk off dinner." He patted his stomach.

Harkness grabbed Eliot's arm and steered him toward the waiting car. "I insist."

A state senator came out, glowing from the night's festivities. He and Eliot greeted each other with handshakes and backslaps.

"Sure, Joe."

As soon as they slid into the plush back seat, Joe Harkness said,

"Let's be blunt, Charles. What the hell is going on? I give you some work, and what has it resulted in? I got one dead sandhog, and according to the papers he is mightily dead. I appreciate thoroughness, but what good has it done me?"

Eliot gestured with his left hand. "I don't get involved in methods, particulars. It is not my area of expertise."

"Well, is that a fact?" Harkness shook his head. "No shit, Charles. I find it hard to picture you beating the tar out of anything but your John Thomas."

Eliot spoke evenly, as if trying to explain something to a recalcitrant teenager. "These men are professionals. You need to let them work on their own terms."

"Fine. They can work on their terms, but if I'm paying for their expertise, they can work on my schedule. I need results, damn you, Charles. Results." Harkness quaffed bourbon from a silver flask. "What I cannot understand is how you Yankees are supposed to be so fast, when you do everything so damn slow."

"I would not want these people upset, Joe."

"Is that so? Are you trying to intimidate me with some Mafeeah bullshit? You're an accountant, Charles. Keep that in mind. I want that contract signed. If it is not signed within two weeks, I'm going to lock the sonsabitches out on the street and bus me in some southern boys."

"I'd be careful."

"Is that right? Well, let me tell you something, Charles. You will not be the first person to make the mistake of underestimating Joe Harkness."

The limousine pulled to a stop at the corner of Park Avenue and Sixty-eighth Street.

"We'll talk in the morning," Harkness said.

Eliot got out of the car and watched as the limo slid away from the curb into traffic. He should have guessed Joe Harkness would prove a foolish man. Eliot realized it was time for him to start covering his ass.

Mary Moy picked at a salad and watched Vito Romero make his way to her table. Her craving for lard had passed like a fever breaking. Now she ate like a vegetarian, had come to loathe any food associated with dead animals. She worried she might not be getting enough iron. Vito, she noticed, looked more on edge than usual and seemed to be losing weight. They had been meeting much more frequently, and she was making great progress in her endeavor. Still, she was no closer to bringing John Tuzio down. All Vito's information was directed at players on the periphery of her intended target. Vito's appearance was cause for some concern. Besides the weight loss, his color was fading. It was as if the man himself was on his way to oblivion. He maneuvered around the hostess and sat down across from her.

"Mary. You look magnificent." He still spoke with easy charm, the dissolute actor clinging to his talent.

She blurted out, "Think so? Maybe someone should tell my husband. He hasn't touched me in three months." She felt a flush of shame, but it passed quickly. The secretive nature of her relationship with Vito Romero created a feeling of comfort. She knew that anything she said to him could never get back to anyone she knew. Lately, they had been confiding in each other on a personal level more and more. She was certain that this would not have a deleterious effect on her investigation. It was just chitchat before they got down to business.

He pursed his lips and looked at her. "You know, the first time—I told you we lost the first baby, right?—the first time, I gotta be honest, I fell into that myself. It's intimidating. This new life, guys run scared. I know ones that basically disappear—not physically, but they're really not there until the kids can walk and talk. Till they're like little people. Your husband, he's probably going through it now. I wouldn't take it so personal. Things are going to be fine."

Mary Moy nodded. "Maybe you're right. Thanks, I appreciate it. You look like you're losing some weight. You been dieting?"

Vito looked off for a moment, then turned back to her. "You might say that. It's called lack of appetite."

"Anything in particular?" She worried that his cooperation might be taking a heavy toll. She needed him.

Vito sighed, then waved his hand. "This daughter thing. She's totally out of control. Some nights she just don't come home. Most guys I know, they would be a little more forceful, they were in my shoes. Maybe one of the animals she goes out with might break his face accidentally. Messages delivered with a bat. I just don't think that would work with my Angela."

Mary sipped her water. "Vito. She's young. It's a phase. Think about it. She lost her mother, she has to read about you in the paper. These are tough times for young people, even without any of that. When I was in high school, I had a boyfriend. Arthur Brannigan was his name. He had hair halfway to his butt, a big earring, some silly tattoos. We used to stay out past curfew, drinking Boone's Farm wine and smoking grass. Drove my father insane. It's what daughters do. Then we get over it. My old boyfriend? He's a CPA. I'm with the FBI. It'll be okay." Mary had lied. She was describing her sister's escapades. She herself had been virtually angelic during her youth.

"You think so?" His voice was weak. She thought it intriguing that this man who survived in such a cruel and violent world was so vulnerable when it came to his child.

"Vito, take a look at me." Mary struck a mock fashion pose. "Business suits to work. I turned out all right. She's at that age. Believe me."

Vito nodded. "I can only hope." He looked up as the door opened, then turned back to her. "Your father, he must be nice and proud of you. I'd like to have a daughter was competent like you, a professional. My first one would be about your age now." He let it trail off. Their eyes met for a second. Mary saw there a yearning that would forever be unfulfilled.

Vito called for a glass of red wine. "So how they treating you downtown?"

"One of those days. I was a double major in college, criminal justice and art history. Days like today, I feel I should resign, move to Italy or France, get my Ph.D. Dump the husband, become a professor." She shook her head. "Sometimes I feel like I made the wrong choice. Like I made all the wrong choices."

"You go to Italy, I can help you there."

"Now, that would be a story. They'd put us on the movie of the week."

Vito sipped some wine. "You need to make sure you do what you want in this life, what's right for you, not everybody else. It's easy to get caught up in something. Then the longer you stay, the harder it is to get out. Trust me on this."

Mary nodded. "Don't get me wrong. I love my job—it's the best job in the world. Most days. It's just the politics, the bureaucracy. Someone in my position has so little control over what happens. I started this career believing I was going to end up director. But the higher you go, the more butt you have to kiss—the less honest you can be. It's frustrating. The best and the brightest don't often get rewarded."

Vito laughed. "You think it's any different in my business? It must be the same everywhere. I seen more slobs and dummies make out good than I can count. Aagh." Vito waved a hand. "What you need to do is cover your ass—do your job. That's one advantage your business has over mine—a much softer retirement plan."

"Retirement. That seems a million miles away. I just wonder, with the baby and all. I'm worried about how that's going to change things for me. If I'm going to feel torn between the Bureau and the baby." She shook her head. "What am I saying? I'm already torn. Just the way I've shortened my maternity leave."

"Oh, yeah. The choices we must make. Still, you can't walk away from the job. You're too talented for that. You just gotta find a nice balance is all. That's something I never managed for myself. Truth is, I never really tried too hard while it mattered. I wish I had it to do all over again sometimes. Something tells me you'll be all right. You're a smart kid—woman, I mean."

"I hope so."

Vito excused himself for the rest room. When he returned, all business now, he said, "What's on your mind this week?" Their personal lives were put aside. Vito had his edge back. It seemed a chemical change, as if he had swallowed some elixir while gone.

"I told you I'm going out for the baby. I'm trying to put some things together. The minute I'm gone, they'll be all over my investigation."

"You want to hear about the ethnics?"

"I'm all ears."

"What I hear is this. There's this union, the sandhogs."

"Sandhogs."

"Probably underneath us right now. Blowing up rocks. They have a problem with a contractor called Harkness and Company. The contractor is using some of those West Side guys as muscle. Guy you want to look into also is Charles Eliot. Puts people together. Arranges things, then hides up in his Westchester estate."

Mary Moy made some quick notes. "Maybe this explains the sandhog killed on Long Island?"

"I'd bet on it." Vito looked past her to the door again. He studied two men who walked in and looked around, then left. "I'd also lay odds that they might be tied in to my people."

Mary Moy was shocked speechless. She dropped her notepad and sat erect in her seat. This was the first time Vito had ever implicated his own crew in anything. Vito stood. "Listen. I need to get back to Brooklyn." He drank a glass of water and put his hand on her shoulder. "And this touching thing, with your husband? It'll pass."

Mary watched him leave. She was excited by the information, but worried. She sensed things happening, a rise in intensity. The simple statement had changed the nature of their relationship. And probably her investigation. She called for the check.

Jack watched from his front door as Butcher Boy pulled into his driveway. Look at this fucking guy, Jack thought. His baby brother got out, looked around furtively, and made his way to the door, staring at the ground as he approached. Waiting until he reached the bottom step, Jack shoved the screen door open with a bang.

Butcher Boy jumped back, stumbling a few feet down the pathway, his hand reaching inside his jacket.

Jack shook his head. "Get in here, you paranoid little asshole."

Butcher Boy pulled his hand out of his jacket and shrugged to indicate that he was not at all ruffled. Jack waited until his brother passed into his house, then slammed the door shut. He grabbed Terry by the jacket and spun him around, lifting the jacket open as he did. He looked at the pistol and said, "You're an hour and a half late, Terry. What's with the gun? How many times I tell you you don't need to carry unless you're working?"

Terry shrugged, his face a pout. "What's up?" He did not look at his brother.

"What's up? You're gonna get your ass violated, Terry, that's what the fuck is up. You do me no good if you get sent back up." Jack, seeing he was not getting a response, shook his head. "Come on, we'll take my car." He did not want to ruin this solemn occasion fighting with his brother.

They drove to Gate of Heaven cemetery in silence. Traffic was slowed by construction. Jack rolled down his window and drummed his fingers on the doorjamb. Butcher Boy stared out of his side window like a restless child on his way to visit an elderly relative. Jack switched on the radio and tuned it to an oldies station. He saw Butcher Boy squirm some more. Good. Fuck you, Jack thought.

The night before, he had learned that Paddy Adare had killed Ray Keegan. The news had come as a surprise. Maybe he had underestimated Adare. Or maybe his own power of persuasion was stronger than he realized. Either way, he needed to come up with Plan B. He had a few things in mind.

Jack pulled through the cemetery gate and proceeded to the section where their father lay buried. He shut off the engine and turned to face his brother, who was fidgeting with his seat belt and whistling some unknown tune. Jack knew Terry hated these annual visits.

"Let's go." He went around the front of the car and fell into step with Butcher Boy. When they stood over their father's grave, Jack made a sign of the cross, clasped his hands before him, and bowed his head. He was not much for prayer, or for church or religion at all. But it had meant something to his old man. Jack silently expressed his regards, told his father that their mother was okay. Butcher Boy started walking in widening circles around the tombstone, muttering to himself. Jack ignored him. He thought about how hard his father, a longshoreman, had been on them when they were kids. How he had resented, even hated, the man in his youth. But as he grew older, he came to appreciate how important that steely discipline was to his own success in life. How true the words his father drilled into him were: "Nobody's ever going to give you anything in this life. You want something, you have to go out and get it for yourself." Amen, Jack thought.

His father dropped dead of a heart attack a few weeks after Jack had returned from Vietnam and a few days after they had drunk their first beer together. Just when the relationship was changing to one of respect and friendship. Now, these many years later, his thoughts about his father were filled with warmth and pride. He made the sign of the cross and whispered, "Goodbye, Pops."

He turned to look for his brother. Butcher Boy was half a football field away. Jack called to him. "Get in the fucking car!" He turned and strode with purpose a dozen rows farther on. He stopped at the grave of Mike Flaherty and, without caring to see if anyone was watching, took out his penis and proceeded to urinate luxuriantly on Flaherty's grave.

Early in Jack's rise to power, Flaherty had been a potential rival. One night he took a few shots at Jack in an after-hours club, screaming, "I'll piss on your grave, Tierney." Flaherty missed. Jack did not.

Jack zipped up and said, "There you go, Mikey." He walked back to his car, promising himself he was not going to smack his brother in the head.

Billy followed Mrs. Ryan into her living room. She wore green slacks and a white cotton shirt. Her hair was up against the heat. Billy sat on the couch while she went to rouse Frankie. The walls of the living room were adorned with religious pictures. Billy felt uncomfortable under the baleful gazes of so many saints. In the center of the wall was the framed smiling countenance of Ronald Wilson Reagan, who several years ago had replaced John Fitzgerald Kennedy as the political icon in the Ryan household. Billy knew JP would be appalled.

He heard Mrs. Ryan yell, "Francis, get up, get up. Billy's to see you."

Frankie staggered into the living room and hit the BarcaLounger like a shotgun victim. "Oh, the pain, the pain. What the fuck time is it?"

From the kitchen: "I heard that, Francis Patrick Joseph."

Frankie mumbled, "Sorry."

"One o'clock."

"No shit. Ugh."

"Where'd you go?"

"Downtown with Maria, some guido dance club."

Mrs. Ryan burst into the room with a tray full of food for her youngest son. Turkey on white with mayo, a dozen chocolate-chip cookies, a large glass of milk, and three aspirins. Hangover food.

"Billy, what would you like?"

"I'm fine, Mrs. Ryan. I ate."

"Nonsense, you've got to eat."

"Really, I'm stuffed."

"A nice sandwich will do." She whirled out of the room.

Frankie turned on the TV and took up the remote control for the VCR. "Check this out."

They watched a series of death struggles between predator and prey. Blood lust in the animal world. Frankie replayed his favorite scene over and over—a huge prehistoric-looking crocodile exploding from a murky river to chomp a baby wildebeest in two. The crocodile appeared to be smiling.

"Look at that fucking thing! Hey, Ma, some more milk."

An hour later, after being force-fed food by Mrs. Ryan and violence by her son, Billy watched as Frankie put a new head gasket on his car.

Frankie, streaked with motor grease, said, "What the hell's going on? Paddy got any idea what's up?"

"I don't know. I can't get ahold of him."

"Maybe he went out of town or something."

"Maybe. Your mother came by the bar last night."

"The bar? Shit. Looking for my old man?"

"Yeah. He hid in the basement till she left."

"Hand me that seven-eighths. You know what scares me, Billy? She's fifty. Imagine how crazy she's gonna be at seventy. I mean, every time I leave the house, she's splashing me with holy water. Used to be only when I was going to work; now it's every time I go anywheres."

Billy sat on a milk crate. He could feel heat coming off the asphalt. A bunch of kids played stickball down the block.

"What's up with Maria—how's that going?"

"It's pretty good. You should see the nipples on that girl, Billy. Un-fucking-real. I ain't into that disco shit, though. Tricia's been asking for you. I think she's pissed off, you never called her. Broke the girl's heart."

"You're gonna lecture me on not calling girls, get the fuck outta here. Besides, I tried to call her, you remember. Her old man answered."

"Too bad." Frankie wiped a greasy hand on his pants. "I've turned over a new leaf."

"Must be all that religion you're getting from your mother."

"Could be. Or maybe it's just Maria likes to fuck so much. She's wild. We went down the shore, right? She gave me head from Point Pleasant all the way to the GW Bridge. Fucking incredible. Why don't you get us a coupla beers."

Billy walked down the block to the bar. Inside, it was dark and cool. JP was working. Billy sat down. The jukebox was turned off. Eight old-timers sat watching the Yankees game.

"Gramps, let me get a couple of beers to go."

JP opened the cooler and took out two bottles of Budweiser. He put them in a brown bag and slid them across the bar.

"Here you go, Billy."

"Thanks." Billy felt the coldness through the bag.

As Billy turned to leave, JP said, "Your brother's looking for you."

Billy stopped and turned to look at his grandfather, trying not to seem too pleased. "Yeah?"

"He left this number." JP handed him a piece of paper and, as he turned away, said over his shoulder, "Called about an hour ago."

Billy left the bar. He went back up the block and gave Frankie his beer. Then he crossed the street and dialed the number from the pay phone. Paddy answered on the second ring.

"It's Billy."

"Hey, Einstein. You want to go fishing?"

"Sure."

"I'll pick you up Sunday at two."

Paddy hung up before Billy could ask him about Lenny's visit. He figured he'd have plenty of time to tell Paddy all about it when he saw him. Billy looked forward to going upstate with his brother; it was the only place Paddy ever relaxed. A weight would lift from him, the tension easing the farther north they drove. Until he was no longer looking over his shoulder.

That night Boomer McCabe, a man with a predilection for unprovoked mayhem, shaped with the gang. He was usually paid by companies not to come to work. As the man trip hurtled toward the heading, Boomer stood at the front of the car and shot out lights strung along the tunnel walls. The other men cringed at the prospect of ricochets. He reloaded several times, dropping bullets as the train bounced along. One of them rolled against Billy's foot. He bent and retrieved it, the brass casing glowing in the tunnel light. He rubbed it thoughtlessly and placed it in his coat pocket. The rest of the miners were content to let Boomer take his target practice.

There were several Harkness men on the train. Boomer, gun still in hand, addressed these men. "I hear there's scabs working around here. I hate fucking scabs."

The Harkness men, outnumbered and outgunned, stared at their feet as if they hoped to find the secret of invisibility there.

Detraining, they shuffled off to do their work.

As Billy and Lenny set up their jacklegs, Lenny nodded in Boomer's direction. "That's one sick ticket. But he's here for a reason. These assholes want to play hardball, they're in for the game of their lives."

Paddy parked on the corner of Thirtieth Street and Eleventh Avenue. He turned the radio on low and waited for the silver van to pull up across the street. He scanned the block, looking for anything that might be law enforcement—cars that did not belong, people who stood out among the transvestite hookers and homeless winos. Everything seemed in order. Mickey had been making the pickups lately but was visiting his sister in prison; larceny ran in the family. Jack had asked Paddy to go, and he agreed without thinking.

The Keegan hit was wearing on him. He kept seeing Ray in his dreams as a fresh-faced kid with a wide smile and a quick wit. They would be standing on the corner, laughing, joking, planning the night's adventures, and then Keegan would turn to him smiling and there was a hole in his head and bright light shining from inside and his face would turn old and sad and start to gush blood. Paddy would wake up, his heart racing, and wish it were only a dream. But Keegan was dead and buried. Paddy had killed a friend.

To avoid suspicion, he had attended the wake, had sat and stared at the casket, hugged Keegan's mother. He barely made it out of there without screaming forth his duplicity. Sickened, he felt beyond despair.

Jack needed to prove to everyone that he was ruthless, that he was the one in charge. And Paddy had allowed himself to be used. It was as if he had nothing left, no will of his own. He was profoundly ashamed.

As the van pulled up slowly to the curb, Paddy grabbed the small gym bag from the floor of the passenger seat and got out of the car. Traffic was heavy on a summer Friday afternoon. He walked around the corner, and the back door of the van popped open. Climbing in, Paddy saw three men. He recognized the driver and the guy in the back seat but did not know the man in the passenger seat. His dark beard in the summer heat set off a slight alarm in Paddy. He had been buying guns from these guys for five years and had never seen a beard before.

"Where's your cousin?" Paddy asked the driver.

"He's fucked-up drunk. Been on a bender for a week now. The asshole."

"Maybe you should send him to AA. Who's the Viking?"

"This here is John. He's my old running partner; we went to high school together."

"Is that right? What high school was that, John?"

"Roosevelt."

"Oh, yeah, up on Mosholu." Paddy tested him.

"No. It's on Fordham Road. What are you, a fucking cop?" He spoke loudly.

"That's a good one." Paddy relaxed. He no longer seemed to have the energy for proper vigilance. "Whaddaya got?"

The driver threw his hands up in the air. "I thought we'd never get down to business, you fucking guys. Check this out. I got ten Rugers, twenty-two. I got some nice Glock nines. And I got a batch of them good silencers the guy makes in his basement out in Astoria. Oh, yeah, a couple thirty-eights, you want. These days nobody wants them. I was selling to some niggers the other day, they looked at me like I'm some kind of asshole. 'What the muthafuck we want with a cop's gun?' "

"They should give the cops a better gun," Paddy said.

"Fuck the cops," John said.

"What you got against cops?" Paddy asked, messing with the guy. A taxi with three passengers pulled over in front of them.

"I hate fucking cops."

"Yeah? Hate's a pretty strong word."

"Who the fuck he starting with?"

"Easy fucking does it. We gonna have the OK fucking Corral right here? This is bad for business, man. Macho shit. What are you gonna take?"

"Give me five of the Rugers and two Glocks, half a dozen silencers."

"That's it?"

"You deaf?"

"Easy, man. What's up with you today?"

Paddy wondered the same thing as he got out of the van and walked back toward his car. He was ten yards from the Monte when six cabs converged on the scene. Armed agents jumped out, weapons all pointed at his head like it was fucking D day. He calmly dropped the bag and put his hands high. No sense in fighting a lost battle. Behind him, the other agents were pulling the gun dealer out of the van. Paddy heard yelling, then the *pop, pop, pop* of a nine-millimeter pistol. He turned to see a flak-jacketed agent fall to the street screaming, blood shooting from an artery in his thigh.

The agent cuffing Paddy threw him to the ground and lay across his back, gun drawn and pointed. The bearded guy ran out of the van like Butch Cassidy down in Bolivia, a pistol blaring in each hand. Sharpshooters on the surrounding rooftops lit him up with dozens of high-powered rounds. The man danced jerkily into the middle of the street and collapsed like he'd been hit with a rocket. Puffs of smoke rose from his body. The street was silent, cordite wafting over it. Paddy cursed softly.

He was surprised that they were ATF agents. They picked him up and read him his Miranda while dragging him to a waiting van. Inside the van, they cursed and punched him. He doubled over to shield himself from the blows. Lying on the metal floor, he remembered leaving the gun from the Keegan hit. He had bought it from those guys. His stomach burned.

Paddy sat in the conference room at ATF's downtown HQ, handcuffed to a table. A thousand paranoid scenarios ran through his mind. Did Jack set him up? Would they link him to the Keegan hit? Was that shot agent dead? Forcing himself to be calm, he breathed deep and slow. He would not say shit to them, just recited his lawyer's phone number over and over like a mantra. On the table before him were cigarettes, which he pushed away, and a diet Coke, which he sipped slowly. He'd been waiting an hour. The suspense was ruining his stomach. He could not believe that asshole came out of the van like that. What gets into people? It was a routine gun bust until that cowboy started firing.

After another twenty minutes, a man came into the room. He was not a federal agent. Paddy recognized him. It was Detective Patrick Cullen of the NYPD. He picked up the cigarettes, said, "Mind if I do?" and lit one. "That's right, you were the fighter. Probably never smoked."

He pulled a chair out and sat directly across from Paddy. "Guns," he said. " 'The proliferation of high-tech handguns is the single greatest danger facing America.' Do you believe that? I don't. Comes from some bullshit brochure I was reading while I was waiting to see you. Written by some college boy, no doubt. Guy will end up being director of this Mickey Mouse outfit. You watch. We all know the problem is not guns per se. It's mutts like your buddy Jack Tierney."

Cullen pulled hard on the cigarette. Paddy sat silent.

"You know why I don't like guns?"

"Lawyer."

"Yeah, we'll get around to that. I got—what I got in you is a captive audience. It's been a long time since we had a chance to chat. No one listens to my theories anymore. They call me names, think I'm a liberal. *You* don't have a choice." He stubbed out the cigarette. "Bear with me. Let's start over. You know why I don't like guns?"

Paddy shook his head.

"There you go; that's better. We keep this up, we'll end up on *Nightline* together, that dopey-looking Koppel guy with the orange hair trying to interrupt us, go to a commercial break. Anyway, they're unnatural, that's why I don't care for them."

"Unnatural?" Paddy decided to humor him.

"Exactly. It screws up the fight-or-flight response. You familiar with that?

"No."

"It's simple. All advanced organisms, including us, *Homo sapiens*, react to danger in one of two ways in a natural setting. They either run for it or start swinging. Now, this changes based on stimuli—that's reasons. I mean, a guy like yourself, you being a fighter and all, guy puts up his dukes, roughly your size and shape, my guess is you smack him one. Now, maybe we get one of these guys seven feet tall, three hundred pounds, good with his mitts—you might think better of it and hotfoot it. You follow me?"

Paddy finished the soda. "Sure."

"Okay. You remember the first time we met?"

Paddy looked at him. "PAL?"

"Yep. Shit, that's what—twenty years now? Time flies."

"It's not moving too fast right now."

"Right. So anyway, we introduce guns to the scene. Factor in this variable has nothing to do with what God or Mother Nature intended.

All of a sudden we got assholes should be running, they're squeezing the trigger instead. Other guys, maybe they'd stand and fight—now they want nothing to do with it. Something bad has to result. It ain't natural."

"Good point. Can I see my lawyer?"

"Oh, that. That agent got shot, he's gonna be fine. You ask me, it might be a good thing. He'll learn. Nowadays all the agents come out of college, raised on *Starsky and Hutch, Dirty Harry,* that crap. Get to think they're invincible. Still, they're going to squeeze you guys because of it."

Cullen left without ever saying why the NYPD was involved. Paddy knew better than to ask, but it worried him. Two federal agents came in. They leaned on him for an hour and a half, cursing, yelling, trying all their bad-cop bullshit. Paddy sat and asked repeatedly for his lawyer. They finally relented, promising retribution. Paddy was not impressed. He made his phone call, and they drove him over to the Manhattan Correctional Center, where he was pedigreed. He slept restlessly in a holding cell. He awoke to his lawyer.

Vito looked up as his daughter came bounding down the stairs. For a moment, before she noticed him, there was a sweetness about her. She looked like the innocent girl she was supposed to be at her age. His throat tightened. Then she turned and spotted him idling by the curb, and it was as if a mask had been pulled down over her face. She aged instantly, the sweetness replaced by a bitterness and resentment. He felt powerless.

Pulling in her shoulders, she rolled her eyes at her companion, then broke away and sauntered toward him, all insolence and hard edges. She wore a miniskirt with black fishnet stockings, ripped in many places. Her hair was piled high on top of her head, and she was chewing on a wad of bubble gum that looked to be the size of his fist. The usual assortment of pins and rings and appendages adorned her head. She got in the car, slammed the door, and sat, rigid, staring straight ahead.

His hands thick and clumsy on the steering wheel, Vito cleared his throat. He, too, looked straight ahead, out onto a street lined with thick, sturdy elms. It was the kind of block he'd moved them to when she was born. The kind of block he thought would shield her from the evils in the world. That dream had soured long ago. He sat, a man too far into middle age, a man utterly incapable of understanding his own flesh and blood.

"How are you?" he asked.

Silence, sigh. "Fine."

As of late, her outright hostility had been supplanted by this haughty indifference. As if he was a slight irritant to be endured. He felt somehow that she believed she had outsmarted him. They drove on, the silence between them like razor wire.

This little trip was being undertaken on the advice of Mary Moy. He was taking her to a therapist. A shrink, of all things. He'd had to double her allowance to get her to agree. Christ, he was bribing his own daughter. An allowance had been a foreign concept in his youth. You want something? Go out and earn it.

He pulled onto the Cross Island and was struck again by the belief that his life was catching up with him. That all his sins were being visited on his offspring. This girl, this only child of his, was so full of hate. Perhaps this was God's way of paying him back. Mary Moy spoke of phases and things passing. Vito feared it was something much worse. He felt he was infecting his daughter, that long after he was gone, she would carry this baggage and pass it down. That his bloodline was poisoned.

Angela sat next to him, blowing huge pink bubbles. He tried to pinpoint the place and time in his life when it all began to slip away from him. Vito did not consider himself evil. He felt that in most respects he was a good man. Though his family had been poor, his father had been honest, hardworking. He was not brought up to be an animal, like Tuzio and some of the others. He simply took the lure of easy money. It galled him to realize that laziness was the root of all this shit in his life. He felt pathetic and lonely.

One of the bubbles popped and the gum was all over her face. She pulled it off her hair.

He turned into a small strip mall and parked the car. "Angela, honey, you're, ah, not gonna go in there with that, are you?"

She regarded him as if he were roadkill. "No, Daddy." She took the wad out and stuck it firmly on his dashboard. He felt his fist clench and anger well up in him. His field of vision darkened. Exhaling, he followed her out of the car to the storefront clinic. He looked around quickly, embarrassed, then ducked into the office behind his daughter.

Inside, a small waiting room contained two imitation-leather couches, a coffee table between them. Four other people sat there, two women and two men. They all read magazines intently, no one looked up at his entrance, no eye contact was offered. It reminded him of going on collections in the old days to the porno shops around Times Square. Feeling uncomfortable, he approached the little window where the receptionist sat.

She looked over the tops of her glasses.

"May I help you?"

Vito spoke softly. "Romero. Three o'clock."

The woman turned her head. "What was that?"

Vito cringed at the loudness of her voice. "Romero," he said, a little more forcefully.

She looked down at something before her and said, "Oh, Romero. Three o'clock. Have a seat."

He sat on the edge of one of the couches. Angela, pacing the room, turned on her heel and came toward him. He prayed she would not make a scene. She sat next to him and crossed her legs demurely. Picking up a magazine from the coffee table, she began leafing through it. He felt relief. She turned to him and said for all in the room to hear, "Daddy, are these people all lunatics?"

Vito coughed and shifted in his seat. "Shh."

"It's really nothing to be ashamed of. Lots of people are crazy."

Vito looked quickly around the room. The others were sneaking glances over the tops of their magazines. He shrugged in apology.

Ten minutes later, a young man with long hair came out and said, "Angela?"

The man had on khakis and a blue button-down shirt with a tie. He wore a small gold hoop in his right ear. Jesus, Vito thought.

He shook the guy's hand; it was soft and effeminate. "I was, ah, my friend said there was gonna be a woman, ah, counselor."

"Oh, there will be. This is just preliminary. An evaluation. The regular sessions start next week."

"Oh. I see."

"Here are some forms for you to fill out concerning payment schedules. Angela, please follow me."

Vito turned and regarded his daughter. She looked like some demon child from one of those horror movies he used to see on Flatbush Avenue when he was young. She followed the guy through a door. Vito suddenly felt sorry for the young man. He sat down and perused the forms. Yeah, right. He *might* put his name on this crap. He had a thick roll of bills in his pocket. He planned to pay in cash.

Picking up a magazine, Vito wondered how long this was going to take. Not long, evidently. He heard Angela scream, "You fucking pervert!" Then he heard a slap, loud and clear in the waiting room. There was a crash, and the door through which his daughter had disappeared flew open. Angela ran out through the waiting room, toward the parking lot. Vito turned back as the young man came out, speechless, a red handprint on his face. The patients were all looking at Vito now. Eye contact no longer seemed a problem. Vito got up and followed his daughter out to the street, thinking: Now what the hell do I do?

When Jack Tierney first got the call, he was wary. It was not from Vito Romero but from another Italian, a man he had met once or twice. He had been tempted to call Romero and check it out, but the guy insisted they meet first and that it was coming down from the old man, Tuzio. Jack wondered if maybe it was a hit. Although he liked working with them, he could not figure the Italians out. They seemed to operate in a bizarre fashion, and the logic of their actions, or lack of actions, often escaped him.

The Italian suggested a couple of restaurants for their meeting, one in Brooklyn, the other in Manhattan, but Jack demurred. He knew well the Italian fondness for mixing lead and linguine. Jack counterproposed a couple of West Side Irish bars, as much to bust the guy's chops as anything else. They finally settled on, of all places, a Japanese joint in midtown.

The meeting had been very enlightening. He had cringed watching Tommy Magic eat that raw fish crap. Jack had gone with a thick Kobe steak and a couple of beers, then enjoyed sticking him with the bill. He knew the reason they called him Magic. The guy was good at making people disappear. He looked just like the singer Roy Orbison. Except he smiled more.

Tommy Magic had spoken in what Jack thought of as typical wiseguy circles. Nothing was said explicitly, things were hinted at, alluded to, specters were raised, fortunes promised. You needed to fill in a lot of blanks to figure those guys out sometimes. Vito Romero had been that way in the beginning, but after they got used to each other, the conversations were much more straightforward.

It was too bad about Vito, though. Because if Jack read the situation right, Vito Romero was not long for this world. Jack smiled. Romero was a smug prick after all. This Magic guy had been much more deferential, hinted at opportunities opening up, a new era of co-operation, like they were the fucking Russians or something.

Jack realized that just the fact of their taking him into their confidence over a matter of such grave concern demonstrated the position to which he had ascended. As he listened, he felt a great sense of importance. He believed this was another step toward his goal. The arrests, killings, and betrayals were taking a toll on the once mighty Mafia. These factors would enable him to assert himself. He envisioned a day when he would lord it over all crime in New York City. He knew he was smarter and more ruthless than his competition. He had been to war—not the petty bullshit of these mob executions, but the real hell of full-blown battle—and he had returned unscathed. None of the Italians like Tommy Magic or John Tuzio had ever seen so much as a skirmish. Jack Tierney believed it was his destiny to become warrior king of New York. Now if only he could get rid of that fucking Paddy Adare.

Paddy walked out of the MCC into the bright midafternoon sunshine. His lawyer, Barry Geller, said, "Patrick, you look well for the wear. I hope you were treated with dignity."

"Not bad, Barry, considering."

"Good. Come see me in a few days, and we'll go over things, straighten you out."

They shook hands, and Paddy snagged a cab. Picking up his car, he went to get Billy. He did not want to deal with Jack yet. Three hours later, they sat on the deck of his lawyer's lake house in the Catskills, a bottle of Jameson on a table between them.

Paddy was reflective. The specter of a return trip to prison did not sit well with him. "You know when I knew you were okay? When I knew you knew about the blood?"

Billy shook his head no.

"That time you ran away to visit me at Clinton. What were you, fifteen maybe? You run away from home in the Bronx and hitchhike to the Canadian border to visit me in the middle of the winter. Blood. You know what it means, Billy."

"How did you know about that? The guards told me I couldn't come in because I was too young. JP went nuts. They drove all the way up to get me," Billy said.

"Yeah. Drove all the way to get you. Didn't bother to see me." His face flushed. "One of the guards I got along with told me all about it. Told me my kid brother had balls. But he wasn't getting it. It's not just balls, Billy—any dumb fuck can have balls. It's the blood. That's where courage and smarts and everything worthwhile comes from."

Paddy drank another shot. The whiskey was loosening him up. He was surprised at how good it felt to talk to Billy. It had been a long time since he had opened up to anyone. He always had to watch what he said, keep his stories straight. In the course of his daily life he had to perpetuate a thousand lies. His life was a series of falsehoods aimed at deflecting enemies, the authorities, his own conscience at times. Everything needed to be calculated, because words were part of the game and they could be just as fatal as bullets. He could tell Rosa how he felt about things, but he couldn't talk about his business. She'd told him right from the beginning that she was concerned only with how he treated her and she didn't care what he did for money. As he thought of her, loneliness came over him like a fever.

His stomach burned from the whiskey, so he took a shot of Maalox. He looked over at his brother and thought it was strange how they'd turned out, how two brothers could be such different creatures. But different or not, he was realizing that Billy was one of the few human beings on the planet he could trust. This college kid that he used to chase around. He was proud of him the way a father would be proud of a successful son because the kid was smart and took advantage of it. Paddy respected that. Especially in someone who didn't have it all laid out in front of him nice and easy, like so many others.

"Blood, Billy. Don't you ever forget it, brother."

"Why don't you just get out, do something else?"

Paddy was surprised. Was it that obvious? He needed to pull himself together. He sipped more whiskey.

"That seems to be the question of the week." He attempted nonchalance but failed. "Look at these." He held his hands up to Billy. Paddy felt an abiding need to explain himself, to gain absolution from his brother. "This was it. I had my way out. There wasn't a man out there could beat me, you know that. When these went on me, it was like someone robbed me, Billy, took my life from me. I was twenty-two, and my picture was in the paper, my face was on television. Me, just a punk kid from the West Side. The last few fights, remember, were on network TV. They drove me around in a limo wherever I wanted to go. I'd sit back in those soft seats and watch the city go by, everyone trying to peek in and see who was in there. It was me."

He poured another shot and drank it down.

"I was happy then, you know. For the first time since I went to live downtown." He shrugged. "I was doing what I loved and making money at it. Shit, I was not only making money at it—I was practically being worshiped for it. Everybody wanted to know Paddy Adare, because I was a white kid that was actually winning in the ring. People went nuts. They wanted to know me, be my friend. Wherever I went, people were always touching me, putting their hands on me, like I was a good luck charm or something. They offered me money, cars, their fucking wives and daughters. You wouldn't believe it, Billy. Then these fucking hands." He held them up again.

"They weren't too bad at first, but once I started getting in with guys that took a punch, they would bust up on me, especially the right. The last fight, remember, went seven rounds before I finished the guy—tough fuck he was. I busted my right in the second round but kept going like a maniac. There was blood dripping down my arm when they went to take the gloves off. My hand was mangled—it looked like a pit bull just spent an hour with it. I was two fights away from a million-dollar paycheck.

"After that it was the operations. Doctors said it was all over, so I figure, Okay, I got a little dough, I'll just have to face it, no self-pity shit. Besides, my manager hooked me up with one of the network guys, says he'd hire me to do some announcing. I got excited about that—the guy takes me to lunch, tells me I'm their man and that he'll fix me up with his bosses. So I go to the big meeting, and then they tell me wait for the call. Two weeks go by—no call. I call him. He takes my call, says, No problem, Paddy, old buddy, we just need you to take some diction lessons. Means they didn't like the way I talked. I tell him I'll do whatever it takes. Well, I never took no lessons, and he never took no more of my calls."

Paddy poured two more shots, and they tossed them back. Billy winced. Paddy went on, feeling lighter from the whiskey and the talk.

"I had fifty grand, couple nice cars, right, I'm still doing good. It was just about then Tierney comes up and tells me there are six guys—we whack them, we own the West Side. I told him to count me out. He says no problem, but he gives me a look that bothered me. Like somehow he knew I'd end up with him."

Paddy leaned back and looked out over the lake. Billy sat still, waiting for him to go on. On the lake a powerboat sped by, pulling a water skier behind it. It was getting late, and the light was shifting, getting softer. Paddy waved off a mosquito.

"Sure as shit, a fucking year goes by, and I'm down to about five hundred and one car. Instead of being smart, maybe investing some money, I went nuts. I couldn't help it, you know. I got a taste of that life—the women, the money, the good times—and it was like an addiction. I wanted more." Paddy stopped talking. He stood, said, "I gotta piss," and went to the bathroom.

As Billy awaited his brother's return, he listened to the sounds of darkness settle over the lake. The treble sound of insects grew in intensity, the rustling of nocturnal animals emanated from the underbrush. Somewhere across the lake a party was commencing. Laughter and faint music echoed over the dark water. Paddy's story weighed upon him. He wanted to offer assistance, sanctuary. The knowledge that this was beyond him saddened him.

He watched as Paddy came back, buttoning his pants, and sat down heavily. He continued where he had left off. "And there was only one way to get it. This time I went to Tierney, he didn't have to find me."

Billy shook his head. "I just don't see how you could be involved in killing people."

Paddy was silent for a minute. He figured, Fuck it. Tell what happened. He was not looking for forgiveness. Having made up his mind, he said, "You know, the first time, I was a kid, sixteen. I was hanging out in a gin mill down Forty-fourth Street, this guy calls me out. Now, in those days I loved to fight, I was angry all the fucking time. Anybody give me the least bit of an excuse, I'd be dropping fives like there was no tomorrow. I mean, I really enjoyed hurting people, they give me the slightest excuse. I kept my mouth shut, unnerstand, but I also took no shit. Anyway, this fucking guy musta seen *Midnight Cowboy* and moved to Manhattan from some hick place. Shit-kicker boots, talking with a drawl—you pretty much needed an interpreter, understand the guy. We go out front the bar, guy pulls a knife out his back pocket. The time he got the thing out, I nail him one. It was weird, but I knew, the way the punch felt, something was wrong. He goes down like a sack of cow shit, slams his head on the curb. That's it. He don't move. He don't even bleed. Nothing.

"Tommy Tierney, Jack's brother, was tending bar. He comes outta the joint. Checks the guy out. Looks up at me and says, 'Paddy, you killed the fucking guy.' But I knew already. Now we got this guy, he's a problem. 'Cause he's dead on the sidewalk there. Well, Tommy had a pretty cool head. We get the guy in the trunk of Bob Drury's car. Took him down and tossed him off one of the piers." Paddy poured himself a glass of whiskey. He felt like a fist was unclenching in his chest.

"I remember he went off the end into the water. He lands feetfirst, right, and as he's sinking his eyes pop open. I could swear the guy was looking right at me. I mean, a dead guy, he's dead as a fucking Friday night in the diamond district, and he's looking right at me. Then he was gone, that's it, history. I got real shit-faced that night, and then I waited. I waited for them to find the body and somehow it would lead right back to me. I was positive they'd get me. Six months, every time I saw a cop I froze. But nothing happened. It was like the guy just vanished or he didn't even exist. It wasn't in none of the papers, the cops never brought it up. I almost had myself convinced it was just a bad dream.

"Later, when I had to do it on purpose, when I knew the reason why I was doing the thing and what was going to happen, it was easier because of that time. I don't think I coulda ever done it if it wasn't an accident the first one. Because it happened, right, and then it was over and nothing ever came of it. And that's the weirdest feeling in the world. Realizing you could just kill someone, stop them from fucking living, and nothing ever come of it."

They sat in silence, then Billy said, "I don't know, Paddy. I mean, it's against everything we were taught. The Church, nuns—thou shall not kill. How do you put that, you know, aside?"

"Billy, we don't kill old ladies, citizens." Just old friends, Paddy thought.

"Still. Even scumbags. How do you stop thinking it's wrong?"

Paddy breathed out heavily. A look like shame came over his face. "You don't."

Billy wondered what carrying that around felt like. He imagined nightmares and the debilitating fear of apprehension. A Catholic terror of the afterlife. What if all that Satan stuff was real? If eternal misery, the fires of hell, awaited the killer? Even the threat of prison, a concrete reality of this world, was enough to deter *him.* He remembered his visits to see Paddy. The prison had loomed as stark and indomitable as death itself. At times Billy wondered what circumstances might prompt him to kill. He wondered if Paddy's move to the West Side was the cause. If their histories were reversed, would he be sitting explaining his murderous past to Paddy? He would never know.

He remembered first hearing about Paddy's arrest. He was shooting baskets behind the school, when Frankie ran into the playground, shouting, "Hey, Billy, your brother killed a guy, your brother killed a guy." Billy stopped mid-dribble and turned to Frankie in disbelief. But the look on Frankie's face told Billy it was true. The ball bounced away from him. He felt his world close around him, felt a stillness he had never known. The screams of the playground faded to white noise. He ran home to his grandparents. When he burst into the apartment, his grandfather turned and reached out to him, embracing him wordlessly.

"What are you gonna do?" Billy asked now.

Paddy propped himself up in his chair. He clutched his whiskey. Billy watched him pull away, shut himself down. His eyes hardened. "I'll make out."

Billy wanted to embrace him. Tell him everything was going to end happily. That they would stand together. That he might not be able to save him but he would always accept him. He stood and went to the bathroom. When he came back he told Paddy about Donelly and about Lenny's encounter.

"He said the Irish guy was short, with muscles?"

"Yeah. Blondish hair. Real weird fuck, he said."

Butcher Boy. Paddy wondered if Jack was involved. He doubted Terry would work with the Italians on his own.

"I'll look into it. And hey, things go bad, strike or whatever, I'll get you on a job."

"Okay," Billy said. "Good, I'll need it."

"Come on, let's catch some fucking fish."

Billy followed Paddy onto the dock behind the house. He decided to address the issue of his grandfather. "Maybe you should call Gramps. I know he's stubborn, but he's family, Paddy. He told me the other day to give you his regards. Maybe you should reach out, put all the shit behind you. I think he's ready."

Paddy took a breath. "Family? There's my family right there." He pointed his finger at Billy.

Billy was in no mood to work. The weekend partying with Paddy had taken a heavier toll than usual. He felt listless and toxic and swore that he would never drink again. He pledged allegiance to a life of fresh vegetables and sit-ups, of avoiding gin mills and adopting the sleep habits of a Methodist minister. He drank a gallon and a half of ice water. He watched talk shows and considered taking the night off. At ten o'clock he forced himself to head for the tunnel site.

Deep beneath the streets of the city, Mule McIntyre's men were fixing a derailment. A concrete train weighing forty tons had jumped the tracks.

"These guys, they run the thing off the tracks, think it matters? They get to sit and watch us bust a nut, trying to fix it." Lenny indicated the operating engineer, a kid about Billy's age. He had long, greasy hair hanging out from beneath his hard hat. He sat on a bucket, reading the latest issue of *Easy Rider.* On one fist was tattooed the word *FUCK,* on the other the word *YOOZ.*

"It means another coffee break for him."

Bobby Moran, the brakeman, came over to them. "I tol' the kid five, six times, cut the hot-rod bullshit. He laughs at me." He shook his head and said, "Wiseass punk," as he walked away. Eamon Cudahy looked at the operator with rabid interest.

They turned their attention back to the train. The gang put four heavy metal jacks along the lower side of the car that had left the rail. While four men jacked in unison, another four used long metal bars to get leverage. Billy was on one of the bars. When the jacks were fully extended, the men with bars threw their shoulders into the work and tried to shift the car back onto the tracks. On the first three attempts a jack slipped and the car settled back down with a bang. They took a short break and on the fourth try managed to shove the car back onto the rails. Breathing hard and sweating from the effort, they leaned on the train.

Cudahy took off his hard hat and wiped the sweat from his forehead. Putting the hat back on, he walked over to the operator, still reading. Cudahy grabbed the magazine and threw it to his left, where it landed in a mud puddle. The operator looked up, but before he could say anything, Cudahy knocked his hard hat off his head and said, "The next fucking time you come round that bend, you're going slower than you can crawl, or crawling is how you'll be leaving in the morning."

The operator looked toward the rest of the gang as if he wanted to register a complaint. Finding a hostile audience, he silently shook his head and went to retrieve his hat.

The gang went back to blowing bottom. Though not the hardest of jobs in the tunnel, blowing bottom was probably the dirtiest. The tunnel rock had to be cleaned to ensure a proper bind when the concrete was poured. A team of three men was assigned to each air cannon. They wrestled the cannons back and forth, forcing the muck along into piles so it could be picked up by mucking machines. When the heavy stuff was moved, they made additional passes, mixing water in with the air until the rock glistened. The air was almost solid. The men dripped muck and cold ground-table water. When they were finished, they sat to eat lunch. The talk was about a sandhog killed the day before on another job.

"I get home today, the wife is sitting in the kitchen, crying," Moran said as he unwrapped a sandwich. "I says, 'What the hell's the matter?' You know? I mean, she cries over a sad movie now and again, but she usually don't cry for no reason. She points to the paper, had the headline about McBride getting killed in Welfare Island. Says she don't wanna hafta read about me like that."

"You sure she wasn't crying 'cause it wasn't you?" Cudahy said.

"Now that you mention it, I ain't too sure. You prick."

The mention of the accident turned the talk to somber history.

"Yeah, we had that battleship bucket loaded with muck settin' top a flatcar." Bobby Washington spoke softly. "That sonofabitch broke loose, there was hell to pay down the line.

"I can still hear that train coming down on us. By the time we realized what it was, there was nothing we coulda done. I tried to figure if it would be safer to get behind the platform or on top of it. But by that time it hit us." He shook his head. "I was just lucky, I guess. It was like the war all over again. The ones that was okay, we went around trying to get the others. A few had lost their arm or leg. I picked up a hand, Buddy Kean's." Washington stopped talking then.

After a moment of silence, Lenny said, "It was a miracle only one man was killed."

They all nodded.

"Not like that cave-in back in '79. I had some kinda luck that day. I was taking a piss when that rock came down. Maybe thirty seconds in either direction, I would have been under it with those guys." Moran shuddered, still awed by the stroke of fortune.

The talk went on until it was time to go back to work. They recounted near misses and brushes with fate. They lamented those less fortunate, who were caught at the wrong place at the wrong time. It was always the same way when someone was hurt. Men showed scars and told tales. It was a communal experience for anyone who spent any time underground. For every casualty, there were a hundred close calls that left men grateful to be going home that night to friends and family. Every day contained the possibility that when the shift was done they would be unable to wash the muck off and go home. But it was that very possibility that created bonds which did not exist in other workplaces. The person you disliked most on the job might be the first to come to your aid in an accident.

The Mule looked at his watch. "All right, lads." Even he lacked the usual belligerent edge. Their faces streaked with muck, their clothes soaked, they went back to work in the thick air.

During late break, a Harkness man named Harris joined the conversation, spitting tobacco juice into a Styrofoam cup. He was tall, wiry, and toothless, with bad acne scars. He had the lumpy, scarred knuckles of a barroom brawler. He shook his head and went on about how easy he felt the sandhogs had it. He was all bluster and provocation. "Y'all come down work a salt mine, maybe a mercury mine, you see what minin's all 'bout. I tell you, and I shit you not neither, you get down under there, takes a man do that work. I never seen two men on a jackleg drill in no mercury mine, and that's the truth of it. Yessir, you see what minin's all about then." He spit more juice into the cup and swished it around, staring at it as if trying to glean some truth from the bilious mixture. "None of these candy-ass work rules you boys got enacted up here."

The Mule's gang exchanged glances. They were tiring of the man's mouth but recognized it as a company ploy. Since the Donelly murder, the company was placing more and more of its own men in open spots in gangs. Many of them were surly ex-cons. The union was urging the men not to get dragged into fights, not to give the company legal ammunition, but patience was waning.

Lenny looked at Billy and nodded in Boomer McCabe's direction. Billy turned to see Boomer sitting behind the rebel, nodding to himself, a look of quietude on his face. He had a half-eaten apple in his hand, which he began to toss in the air and catch softly.

"Yep. You guys ain't about much, comes to minin'," Harris said.

"Where you from?" Frankie asked.

"Texas." Harris's tone said, Is there anywhere else to be from? "Matter a fact, I cain't wait to get back to those miles and miles of Texas. A man cain't hardly breathe, place like New York."

"Shut up," Boomer said as he bounced his apple core off the man's hard hat.

Harris stopped in midsentence, his eyes narrowed. Then he smiled, as if he had located something he'd been searching for. He turned slowly to face Boomer, who remained seated. Nobody spoke.

"We got us a problem here, boy? You lose your apple?" He spit a long stream of tobacco juice onto Boomer's boot. "Huh, Mr. Badass?"

As Boomer stood, Harris produced a hunting knife from his belt. Billy saw the halogen light dance off the blade and made an instinctive move for Harris, but Lenny grabbed his arm, holding him back. Boomer, coming up, grabbed a spud wrench from Cudahy's hand and brought it hard across the rebel's face. Boomer moved so quickly that Billy was not sure it had happened except for the sound of tempered steel on skull bone.

Harris staggered two steps to his right and spun toward Billy and Lenny, out on his feet. As he went down, Billy saw that Boomer's blow had knocked the man's left eye out of its socket. It was still attached by the optic nerve and hung down on his cheek. Harris made a soft, womanly sound and fell on his face in the muck, crushing the eye like an overripe plum.

"Show you what miiinin's all about." Boomer gave him a swift kick in the side with his steel-tip boot, then walked away, disappearing into the tunnel mist. His expression had never changed during the incident. Billy thought it was the same look he might wear for a routine task, like stirring milk into his morning coffee.

Lenny walked over to Harris's prostrate form, knelt, and felt his neck. "He's alive. Call for a stretcher."

Cudahy picked up his spud wrench and wiped the splatter of blood on his muddy pants. "Ye reap what ye sow."

Paddy, his stomach on fire, drove over to the Midnight Lounge to confront Tierney about the sandhogs. The sky was turning dark. Angry, bruised clouds were rolling in from New Jersey. Pedestrians scurried along the streets, trying to outpace the coming deluge. He double-parked on the avenue and ducked into the bar. The place was empty except for Sully the bartender and two retired longshoremen. The television blared.

"Jack?" Paddy asked the bartender.

Sully nodded his head toward the back room. "He's meeting with Ugly Jesus and his pistolero."

Ugly Jesus was a local drug dealer who paid tribute to Jack for the privilege of selling narcotics in the neighborhood. Something Jack was smart about, Paddy thought. He never dealt directly in drugs but took sizable cuts from everyone who did.

Paddy ducked into the back room. Jack looked up in midsentence and nodded at him. Ugly Jesus, who was aptly named, sat across from Tierney at the lone table, trying to remain calm. His skin was badly marked with pustules. His hair was slicked back and gathered into a small ponytail with a red rubber band. He wore a tank top that displayed arms covered with tattoos, many of which portrayed his namesake in varying degrees of distress. Against the wall Bobby Riordan and Miguel Fernandez, Ugly Jesus's bodyguard, stood with their arms crossed. They both looked like they had drunk sour milk.

"Mr. Jacks, I truly and sincerely will deal with this. Some of the fellas got themselves a little overambitious maybe. This I will correct. Everything is cool. I'll put in a little extra, make the thing right between us."

Ugly Jesus's tongue darted out to lick his lips. Jack Tierney sat stony-faced. Someone had been selling cocaine in the neighborhood supplied by Dominicans from Washington Heights. Jack could not tolerate this. The longer Tierney remained silent, the more Ugly Jesus squirmed. He looked as if he expected a trapdoor to open beneath him.

He licked his lips again. "Alls I'm sayin', Mr. Jacks, is that this was not . . . not something I was aware of it's happening . . . it's going down. You see, my peoples are solid. But some others . . . " He shrugged to indicate helplessness.

Jack stood and walked over and stared the bodyguard in the face, then he turned back to the table and leaned over, his hands splayed. He spoke quietly. "You got twenty-four hours. I want those responsible dead, and I want them dead publicly. I want a message—a very clear and simple message—sent. If this don't happen fast, you better find a new fucking line a work, and a new address to go with it. 'Cause you don't fix this and I find your skinny ass, I'll chain you to a fucking jukebox and drop you off a bridge."

Ugly Jesus pulled back and looked up at Jack. Paddy could tell the guy was struggling between fear and his sense of machismo. Fear won. "For sure, Mr. Jacks. For sure."

Jack waved them out solemnly. Paddy noticed Riordan had a deep suntan, for the first time he could remember. He must have gone to the beach during the Keegan hit.

"Hey, Paddy, nice job, you dropping that dirtbag Keegan."

"Yeah, Bobby, great." Paddy fought the urge to crush his windpipe. "Jack, I gotta talk to you."

"Bobby, give us a minute. Paddy here has something on his mind." He put his hand on Riordan's shoulder and steered him to the door.

Paddy watched him go, knowing he would be waiting for any sign that his master was in distress.

Tierney indicated a chair. "You want a beer? Something?"

Paddy sat down. "No."

"How'd you get popped?"

"Bullshit. Wrong place, wrong time. That's not what I want to see you about." He tried for a neutral tone. Paddy did not want the conversation to be about his arrest.

"So what's on your mind, Adare?"

"I just talked to some people I know up in the Bronx. They tell me someone's making a move on the sandhogs. I was wondering if you know anything about it." Paddy watched Tierney's face, trying to read it. But despite knowing him for years, he could find nothing. Tierney was inscrutable.

"How would I know?"

"You talk to your Brooklyn friends, I thought maybe you might of heard."

Jack shrugged. "I'll ask around, you want."

"Jack, these guys are our friends. I got family involved."

"What, that college kid?"

"That college kid is my brother."

"Yeah? So what would a college kid have to do with something like that?"

"I'm gonna look into it."

"I would not do that, I were you." Tierney's voice hardened.

"Why not?" Paddy felt himself getting angry.

"Let me poke around, see what I see. We don't want to rock the boat." Jack smiled.

"Fuck rocking the boat, Jack. You gonna stop me from taking care of this?" Paddy was almost certain Jack was involved. The knowledge weighed him down.

Tierney stood, his face reddening, his aloof crime boss act going to pieces. "Listen, I'm calling the shots around here, Paddy, that's just how the fuck it is. Now, I said I'll do you a favor and look into it."

Riordan, ever the obliging subordinate, stuck his head in.

"Everything all right here, Jack?"

Tierney shot him a withering look.

"Sorry." Riordan actually bowed his head before closing the door.

"Come on, Paddy—we gonna let something don't have anything to do with us come between us?" Jack switched tactics, turning on his buddy-buddy bullshit, the greasy charisma. Paddy was sickened that he had ever fallen victim to such false charm.

"It's got plenty to do with me." Paddy struggled to keep his voice even, his fear and anger at bay.

"All right, I'll look into it. Gimme a coupla days on it. I mean, if someone's made it their business, who knows what the hell's going on. You just gotta give me a break here. Let me sort through things. It ain't like I just ask those guys a question and can expect a straight answer."

"Keep me posted." Paddy stood.

"Of course." Jack produced a match and lit a fat Cuban cigar. "Come by tonight. We're gonna get a card game going."

"Yeah, sure." Paddy looked Jack in the eyes. He could see the black silent challenge in those pale eyes: What the fuck are you gonna do about it? He turned to leave.

"Send that fucking oaf back in here."

Paddy met Mickey Lawless on the way out. They went over to the Blarney Stone and nursed some beers. "You hear anything about a move on the sandhogs?"

"I ain't heard anything like that. Why?"

"I talked to my brother the other day. Somebody laid a bad beating on the secretary-treasurer, he ends up dead. A few other guys been paid visits. The thing that gets me is one of the guys was Irish. Sounds like Butcher Boy."

"The guy does plenty of freelancing to support that coke habit. You read awhile back about that drug hit out in Jersey, the motel?"

"The yuppie guy?"

"He's been bragging all over the place about that one."

"Maybe I should go talk to my old friend Terry."

"I'd be careful with the guy. That cocaine is making him crazy."

"The cocaine? He was crazy long before that." Paddy shook his head. He knew he had a fight coming on, and he did not know if he was up to it. The bar, Mickey, faded into the background. He could choose to go along—submit to Jack, become his whipping boy—or he could stand and fight what would certainly be a futile, foolhardy battle. A suicide mission.

"You hear about me and Keegan?"

Mickey rolled his eyes skyward. "That just ain't fucking right. He's really lost it. Fuckin' Jack thinks he's Al Capone, the fucking nut."

Rosa heard the knock on the door, picked up the remote control, and hit the Mute button. She got off the couch, figuring it was a neighbor or a maintenance man. There had been no call from the doorman. As she walked, she pulled her hair into a ponytail and secured it with a rubber band. She looked through the peephole and pulled back when she saw Paddy. Grabbing the dead bolt, she briefly considered not answering the door. She laid her forehead against the cool plaster of the wall and took a breath. It felt as if she were being torn in two directions. She trembled, and her palms began to sweat. She willed him away, because she knew it would just make everything that much harder for her. Her choice had been tough, and it was all she could do to stick to it. She said no softly to herself, but flipped the lock and let Paddy Adare back into her life for what she knew was the last time.

He stood uncertainly in the doorway and did not speak. Rosa was shocked by his appearance. Something seemed to have been taken out of him, as if a part of him were already dead. Smelling the whiskey heavy on him, she grabbed his arm and led him to the couch. A great chasm of pity opened inside her as she sat him down. She embraced him, pulled him to her, held his head close.

They sat without speaking. Holding him, she thought back over their time together, considered all the promise it had held. She had believed for a long time that he would be able to break away, to escape before his world consumed him, that they could have a life. She knew him to be good, knew that with other circumstances his life could have led to something far different. She'd seen so many of them pulled down and battered by the life they led, crushed by their blind devotion to a dying way of life, the old codes, the machismo. The bullshit.

In Paddy she had sensed something unique. That despite his toughness there was life inside him, a spark that would save him. But now it seemed to have flickered out.

He pulled away and sat up straight. "I just wanted to see you before you left," he said softly.

"I know. I wanted to call, but . . ." She was embarrassed at the deception. She had been forcing herself not to make contact. It seemed the only way to persevere.

He waved it off. "You don't hafta. I know a clean break—it's best for both of us." He looked blankly around the room. "We had some good times, though, right?"

She nodded. There was no bitterness in his voice, just, it seemed, a plea for assurance, for confirmation that something in his life had been good. "We did," she agreed.

"Can I stay?"

She squeezed his arm and said, simply, "Yes."

In the morning she lay alone and watched as the sun cast light through her window. Turning on her stomach, the sheet wrapped around her naked form, she could smell Paddy on her pillow. Their lovemaking had been gentle and earnest. She had expected the intensity of a grudge fuck, something punishing and final from him, but it turned out to be something else entirely. It was as if he was savoring her, trying to milk some last bit of closeness out of their relationship. Wrenching guilt washing over her, she pulled the sheets off and stood, trying to steel herself, to maintain the course she had chosen. Confused, she sat back on the bed and cried softly. She cried for what might have been.

After a while, she got up and made coffee. In the living room, a stack of flattened boxes awaited packing. She showered and dressed, then went about the business of moving her life to another place, another level. She set about it with firmness, knowing there was no one in this world who could do it for her.

Billy awoke after a day of hot, tortured sleep and stumbled into the shower. He used only cold water, trying to dull the feverish ache induced by the heat. It was scant relief. He finished, put on a pair of shorts, and went into the kitchen. Pouring himself a glass of fresh-squeezed orange juice, he sat down. JP left the papers for him each day. He checked the Yankees' box score and grimaced. They had lost badly again. This depressed him, so he pushed the papers away and picked up the day's mail. He leafed through junk mail and bills and stopped abruptly at a letter from Columbia's law school. The blue school seal seemed to rise off the paper like a 3-D postcard. He held the letter to the light from the windows, felt its heft. He put it back on the table and paced the room. His stomach jumped and fluttered. This was it.

He went over to the window and saw JP out front, talking to Frank

Lopez, the Cuban from the fourth floor. Billy surmised they were trading stories of revolutions won and lost. JP pointed up the block. A sanitation truck screeched to a halt. A child ran out to greet the workers as they leaped from the back of the truck. Billy turned, picked up the letter and brought it to his room. He sat on the bed, closed his eyes, took a deep breath and opened it carefully. He read the first paragraph: "Congratulations! Your application for Columbia Law School Class of 1990 has been approved." Billy put the letter on his desk, shouted, "Yes!" and pumped his fist in the air. He called Frankie.

On his way out, he told JP the news. His grandfather smiled and embraced him, in a rare display of public emotion. "The Ivy League, is it, Billy? It's about time the Adares took their place among the elite." JP laughed. "Good work."

Billy, Frankie, and Jimmy the Drooler drove to Terrence McCracken's apartment just over the city line in Yonkers. They sat in the living room and watched the Yankees game. A battered air conditioner struggled to drop the temperature a few degrees. The walls were adorned with posters of hyperbreasted young women hawking various alcoholic beverages. The furniture, worn castoffs from various relatives, had a somewhat hazardous look to it. A large bong with a skull-shaped base sat on a coffee table made of two empty cable spools spanned by a cracked four-by-two sheet of smoked glass. The apartment had a certain murky odor that Billy could not identify. They toasted Billy's academic achievement with cold Buds. Terrence, anxious to play a gracious host, brought out a tray of sloppy joes, causing Frankie to say, "Sloppy fuckin' joes? This is like being back in grammar school." Frankie then ate four, conceding that Terrence's secret sauce set them apart from the Catholic-school version.

Jimmy the Drooler, alternating between hits off the bong and mouthfuls of beer and sloppy joes, said, "Columbia—this mean we get free tickets to Baker Field?"

"Jimmy, you're an asshole," Frankie said. "Columbia's big time. Billy gets in there, and alls you can think of is yourself. Typical."

"College is college. Besides, they got the worst football team in the history of the sport. I'd be embarrassed. Pass me some more hot sauce."

"Sure you'd be embarrassed—you can't even read, you fucking moron." Frankie made an aggressive grab for the last sloppy joe.

"What? I can fucking so too read." Jimmy sputtered, and bits of marinated meat sprayed his T-shirt.

"Guys, cut the shit," Billy said. He was elated and did not care what Jimmy thought. Jimmy had always been a ball breaker. He was the only kid from the neighborhood who did not like the Yankees. He in fact did not root for a single home team. His teams in the four major sports were the Houston Astros, the Vancouver Canucks, the Phoenix Suns, and the Miami Dolphins, not because he had any affinity for those locales or teams, but because he knew it would piss everyone off.

Terrence went into the kitchen and came back with a huge bowl of potato salad. He wore cut-off shorts and a T-shirt that read FRIENDS DON'T LET FRIENDS BEER GOGGLE. "Here, check it out. My mom made this. It's excellent."

"Bullshit. Your mother can't cook for shit, Terrence. You get better potato salad at a soup kitchen, made by some homeless gorilla." Jimmy turned to Frankie and Billy. "Her potato salad sucks. Remember his sister's wedding?"

Terrence stopped in midstride, the bowl in one hand, a large wooden spoon in the other, a dangerous look on his face. Terrence and Jimmy routinely argued and fought with each other. Their mothers' respective cooking abilities were a persistent source of strife. Terrence was about to retaliate with a comment about Mrs. Grogan's meat loaf, when something long and green scampered out from beneath the couch, darted along the living floor, raced an arc across the wall behind the television, and disappeared toward the bedroom.

"Holy shit. You see how big that thing's gotten?" Terrence stood wide-eyed.

"Looks like a gila monster."

When Terrence moved into his apartment, it was besieged by cockroaches. He read somewhere that geckos were a natural enemy of the insects, so he purchased one and let it roam the apartment. He saw it only every few weeks, and each time it seemed to have doubled in size. Cockroaches had become a rarity. Billy now knew the source of the mysterious smell.

"Someday that thing's gonna swallow your dick when you're sleeping," Frankie said.

"That would be just a snack."

"Fuck you guys. I'm putting the potato salad away."

"Ouch, don't be so fucking mean, Terrence."

"I'm gonna kill you, asshole."

"Come on. Let's go smack some balls around, shag some flies," Billy said.

They gathered themselves and went to Van Cortlandt Park. Terrence and Jimmy took to the outfield. Billy stood by as Frankie blasted fly balls deep into the Bronx sky. Billy caught the balls as they were thrown home.

"Billy, man, that's fucking great," Frankie said. "Columbia. I remember you always said you were gonna go there. Fuck Jimmy, he's jealous."

Billy tossed him a hard ball and Frankie caught it, pitched it softly before him, and smashed it deep, over the heads of Terrence and Jimmy. They scrambled toward the tree line after the ball, trying to trip each other on the way.

"You hear what happened at Jimmy's trial?" Frankie lit a cigarette.

"The one for beating up his girlfriend's family? He pleaded down, right?"

"Yeah, well, he had the case beat, you know? I mean, Karen Murphy's family, they look like something out of *Deliverance,* they kept contradicting each other. The brothers almost came to blows right in front of the jury. So then Terrence—he's supposed to be Jimmy's star witness—he gets on the stand."

Terrence emerged from the woods running, ball in hand, threw it back to Billy and Frankie, and was tackled by Jimmy. Frankie took the ball, hit it and two others in quick succession. They rained down on Jimmy and Terrence like mortar shells.

"So the lawyer, Jimmy's lawyer, starts running Terrence through the paces—where they were, what they were doing, right? So Terrence is like, first we went to this bar, then that party, then this bar, then back to that party, like he's talking about Mardi Gras or some shit."

Billy caught the balls and served them up to Frankie, who let them rip. "The judge is listening to this and he says, 'Excuse me, Counselor. Mr. McCracken, by this time approximately how many alcoholic beverages had you consumed?' So the whole courtroom's quiet, you know? Waiting. Terrence is deep in thought. He actually—I swear to

God, Billy—scratches his head. Finally he turns to the judge, all serious, and says, 'Your Honor, I guess about twenty-five.' The judge looks like he just got a bat stuck up his ass. He yells, 'Witness dismissed.' I'm sitting with Mr. Grogan, and he slumps in his seat, poor guy. So after that they cut some deal. He caught five years probation, piss tests. Later, Jimmy's all mad, says, 'Terrence, how could you?' Terrence says, 'Hey, I was under oath, and besides, twenty-five ain't that many drinks.' "

Frankie hit two balls sky-high. Jimmy went after the first one, Terrence the second. The balls came down within a foot of each other, and the two erstwhile PAL outfielders converged on the same spot. Frankie and Billy winced at the sound of the collision.

"Will you look at those morons. Fucking Columbia, Billy, that's excellent."

Billy nodded in agreement. It was all he could do to keep from jumping up and down with joy.

Paddy Adare slept the translucent sleep of the combat soldier. Images, aborted dreams, flashed through his mind as he teetered on the brink of unconsciousness. Finally a dream took hold, pulled him under. He watched as a dozen coffins were carried along on a dark current of water, some black river raging. His vantage point was from on high. As the coffins passed beneath him, he saw that they had glass tops. He watched as his parents and his friends floated past toward eternity. Then he watched as Ray Keegan came past, his wounds still fresh. There was one last coffin, trailing far behind the others. As it came by he could see Billy inside, clawing at the glass. Paddy awoke with a scream.

His days were full of torpor and unease. He went through the motions, making the rounds, but it was a lethargic mime of his activities. He took to drinking whiskey late in the afternoons and drank until he could not stand. He found it harder to keep himself together. He stopped going to the gym altogether. Paddy knew with a cold certainty that he was lost.

When Jack sent him on collections with Butcher Boy, he did not resist.

They drove to a deadbeat's house in Queens, Paddy only half aware of Butcher Boy's rambling.

Butcher Boy rolled up his window and said, "Thing about Jack, he's got one a those photogenic memories, you know what I'm saying? I mean, shit, things I forgot about, from when we was just kids, you know? Don't forget nothing. What makes him the big man, you know? Like the other day, he's telling me about the time I poured ammonia in my second-grade teacher, Sister Agnes of the Ascension, in her fucking ginger ale. Shit like that. I ain't got a clue till he reminds me. She deserved it anyways. Made me write 'I will not slap girls' thirty, forty thousand times or something.

"I could eat a fucking horse. You hungry, Paddy? Whaddaya say we stop McDonald,s, Burger King, some joint like that. My treat. McDonald's." Butcher Boy giggled.

Paddy popped the cassette out of the stereo and flipped it. Tom Petty and the Heartbreakers.

"Remember I shot that nigger behind the counter, McDonald's down Times Square? Only a pellet gun, it was. But I walk in there—all right, I'm stoned, just watched *The Mechanic,* with Charles Bronson. I'm a kid, stoned outta my mind, like I'm fucking him. Like I'm The Mechanic. All I do, I ask the nigger, some extra ketchup, know what I'm saying? No big deal, right? Shouldn't a been anyways. I mean, it's his job." Butcher took out a Handi Wipe and scrubbed his face hard. Than he cleaned off his hands and threw the wipe out the window.

"I ask the shine for some ketchup, right away he starts with that slavery-went-out-a-long-time-ago shit. I can't fucking believe what I'm hearing. So I say, I says, Hey, Nigger, shut up, all I want is my ketchup. Next thing you know, he whips this thing outta his hair. Paddy, this is fifteen years ago, they still had them fucking Afros, three, four feet high, right? He takes this rake outta his hair—I swear, they musta been using it to whack the cows for the Big Macs, the size a the thing. Now he's waving it, looking like a Zulu motherfucker warrior, like he wants to shrink my head or some shit. The only thing he's missing is a bone through the nose.

"Me? I'm calm. I'm steel. I'm the iceman. I pull out the pellet gun, was using it to plug rats downa railyards. I mean, Bronson couldn't a done it any better, Paddy. I start squeezing away. First one gets him right in the forehead. Bink. He drops the murder weapon and starts running for the back—I mean, this buffalo is setting some world records, I ain't shittin' you. I nail him in the ass a few times for good measure. By now the place is empty. I reach over the counter for my ketchup, take my Quarter Pounders with cheese, two large fries, whatever, and stroll out like nothing went down.

"Shit, I remember things pretty good myself, come to think about it. Maybe them photo-fucking-genic memories run in the family. Think that's possible or what?"

"Yeah Terry, sure. Anything's possible, you think about it. Let's get this done first, though. You can eat later."

"Yeah, I guess I ain't so hungry after all."

Paddy turned to Butcher Boy and said, "You fuck up that sandhog, out in Suffolk?"

Butcher Boy turned away sharply from Paddy's gaze. "I-I—what's a sandhog, Paddy? What would I know about any sandhog getting killed? Fuck that. I got no idea."

Paddy sighed. He was now convinced that Butcher Boy was involved. Jack too. This depressed him even more. Paddy turned the stereo up loud enough to prevent Butcher Boy from talking.

Mary Moy walked to the SAC's office with the file for Operation Wrecking Ball in her hand. She was apprehensive. She had put in for maternity leave to start in September, maybe early October, and worried her superiors were about to move her aside. She'd hear a pep talk and a lecture on teamwork, and then all her work would be offered up for some ass-kisser to take credit for. Her fears were confirmed when she entered the office and saw Deputy Director Martin Leary with the SAC, Frank Marella. She and Leary had worked together briefly in Washington. She knew him to be a smug bastard and an opportunist. His presence could only be bad. It meant the suits in Washington were about to alter the course of her investigation.

Leary reached out to her, shaking her hand. "It's good to see you, Mary. You look fantastic." He went to pat her stomach. She pulled back, thinking, This jerk is unbelievable.

"I'm told your work on Wrecking Ball has been outstanding. You're making quite a name for yourself."

Mary nodded. With Leary you never knew if he was issuing a compliment or a thinly disguised rebuke.

"Please have a seat." He made a show of helping her. "Someone in your condition can never be too careful."

"My condition is fine." She tried not to sound too tough. It gave guys like Leary free rein to brand her as a bitch. As Leary switched into his self-important bullshit mode, she had a vision of herself shooting him through the window into the Manhattan sky. She fought a smile.

"We've been reviewing your files on Wrecking Ball and, well, it's good stuff, excellent. It does, however, seem that if we are going to have any real impact, we need to make this case, ah, come to fruition soon. Sooner than later. It—and Frank will agree with me—it all seems to hinge, at this point at least, on your CI, one Vito Romero. Excellent memo writing, by the way." Leary turned his back and stared out the window, then twirled back toward her. "Well, let's get to it here." The fake smile. "We go back a long way, Mary. I believe I can speak honestly with you." He looked at Marella, who shrugged. "We need you to get Romero to testify."

"He won't." Mary shot Marella an angry look. Leary was about to ruin her whole case. It was bad enough she needed to take time off. She had reduced her maternity leave and planned to do some work at home. Now this bureaucrat wanted to sink everything for a bogus election-year trial. She was putting together a case that would decimate mob influence in New York construction, and she needed time. Romero might eventually take the stand. But not if pushed.

"I can understand your trepidation here, but we're catching all kinds of heat on this. We need to make a case."

"Election year's coming up, Leary. Maybe it will get you that soft Justice Department job."

"That's a cheap shot, Moy."

"Something you know all about. I'll tell you what *I* know all about." She stood up and leaned on the desk. Frank Marella took a breath. "I know about this case. I know about fourteen-hour days in shit conditions, and I know *all* about Vito Romero. He will *not* testify." She sat down, already regretting her outburst. Leary would be around for a long time.

"Thanks for sharing, Mary." Leary smiled smugly. "We need him, and you're going to produce him. You come back from maternity leave"—he said it as if it were something obscene—"you just might find yourself off the case and out"—he waved behind him, over the flat, rolling expanse of the continent—"there someplace."

"You're killing him, just like you're pulling the trigger yourself."

"We're not talking about Joe Citizen here."

"Martin." Marella stopped him.

"I need another six months."

"You're taking off time already, Moy. The Bureau can't operate on the whims of its investigators."

"Whims?"

"What's that song? I remember it from college. 'You can't always get what you want.' "

Mary stared at him. "That's right, Leary. I forgot you were such a hipster."

His face went wan. "What's that supposed to mean?"

"You're the aging boy genius; you figure it out."

"I think maybe you're becoming too involved with your CI. It happens with agents like you."

"Agents like me? You mean ones without tiny little testicles, like you?"

Leary, for once, was speechless.

She left, feeling a depression coming on. She had grown to like Vito Romero. She knew his options were about to be severely limited. She wanted to be the one to tell him. God, if only she could have a drink.

In the quiet of break time, Billy moved up the tunnel, away from the gang. He pissed against newly blasted rock. Soon they would be holing through. Work crews were tunneling toward them from the south. The idea was to meet flawlessly in the middle. Everything was on target. He knew that meant they were beneath Columbia University. If he could drill straight up, nine hundred feet through bedrock, he would be sitting in a classroom. So damn close.

He walked back to the gang. As Billy approached, he saw the Mule stand up straight, a look on his face like he had just received horrible news. He held one hand up like a traffic cop and clutched his chest with the other. Then he staggered backward and fell hard in a puddle of muck.

The gang stared at the Mule in confusion for a moment, stunned by the very idea that the man was down. They ran to him as he lay convulsing on the tunnel floor.

Lenny leaned over him and said, "Back off, give the man some room." He leaned over, felt for a pulse. The Mule's breath was shallow and uneven. Lenny pulled up and turned to the other men. "Heart attack. Get the man car in here."

Cudahy grabbed the phone and called back to the shaft. They took turns trying to revive the Mule. They pounded on his chest and breathed gulps of air into him. Five minutes later, the train pulled up to them, carrying a stretcher. They put the Mule on the stretcher and hoisted him onto the man car. Lenny had torn open the Mule's shirt to perform CPR. His chest was so pale it seemed to glow in the dimness of the earth.

The train sped for the shaft. The Mule was hanging on, the hugeness of his life fighting to the end. When they got to the cage, they saw that the bellman, a Harkness worker, was drunk. Lenny ran to him.

"Get the goddamn cage. We got a man down."

The bellman looked up, his eyes blurry. "Cage is broke."

"What? How come no one told us?"

The bellman, sensing a bad situation, started to slide away. "They said to keep you working." He turned and ran.

"Let him go," Lenny said.

There was no other way out. They sat and waited while the Mule died. Cudahy closed the Mule's eyes and draped a yellow rain jacket over him. Ninety minutes later, the cage came and took them out of the hole. On the surface, emergency crews waited, their faces solemn in the swirl of red light. Bernie Coyle, the business manager, was waiting for his members. He walked over and pulled the rain slicker off the Mule's head, then covered him again. "That's it," he said. "We're all going out."

They looked over to the company trailers, dark and silent. With no target for their rage, they cleaned out their lockers and walked off the site. The strike was on.

Joe Harkness assembled a task force to deal with the strike. They sat around his office. It was himself, Chris Devine, Eliot, John Webb, his director of security—a former FBI and army intelligence man—and what looked to Harkness to be about a bargeload of lawyers. They listened politely as a representative from the Contractors Association voiced his organization's objection to the way Harkness and Company was conducting itself. The man spoke in businesslike terms about how things were done in New York. How relationships between contractors and the trades were mostly positive and how this was mutually beneficial. Harkness cut him off in midsentence and had him escorted to the door.

When the man was gone, Harkness listened as the lawyers discussed various legal strategies. They spoke of replacement workers and injunctions, of media campaigns and public relations, political pressure. Accountants projected the cost of the strike to the company, the union, and each worker. One man revealed what was in the union strike fund and how long it could last. After three hours of this, Harkness waved them all out except for Devine, Webb, and Eliot.

"What a load of horseshit. Now we can get down to business." He stood at his desk and leaned forward, resting on his balled fists. His knuckles were white from the pressure. "I'll not mollycoddle these bastards. I want escalation, damn it. I want these bastards' feet to the fire. Devine, I want you to draw up contingency plans for strikebreakers. In the meantime, one of those jackass lawyers is supposed to come back in the morning with an injunction, so we can keep pumping out the tunnel. That way we'll be ready to roll. Webb here is lining up the talent. He tells me he can have five hundred men here on a day's notice."

He turned and strode back to his liqour cabinet. He broke the seal on a new bottle of bourbon and poured himself a large glass of whiskey. "Thank you, Mr. Devine."

The superintendent stood and left. When he was gone, Harkness sat and leaned toward Eliot and Webb. "Charles, this man here is the genuine article. He's dealt with all designs of hardasses around the planet. He has been to the brink and back. Santo Domingo, Vietnam, Cambodia, Nicaragua. When he shows up, it's all about bad things happening. I want you to put him in touch with your people. I'm confident he can handle them. He's dealt with far worse."

Webb leaned in, giving Eliot a hard stare. His eyes were small, too close together. Eliot could sense something amiss in the genetic code.

"I'll be glad to, Joe. I think they'll get along just fine. Just fine."

"I want these fuckers to know they picked the wrong man to tussle with. They will bear the brunt of my wrath, by God."

Eliot shuddered on his way out of the office. There was no way he was going to introduce that nut to anyone.

Billy called Paddy the minute the picket line went up, and his brother came through with a job, as he'd promised. Billy planned to walk the sandhogs' picket line during the evenings. Getting to the new job site early, he saw a handful of hard hats milling around, drinking coffee and talking sports and pussy. Billy asked for the laborers' foreman. A fat carpenter turned and pointed toward the trailers. "He's over there, the blue trailer. Big, tall, ugly fuck. Watch out—he usually takes a liking to young guys like you."

The others laughed. Billy found the foreman.

"What do you want." It was a statement, not a question.

"I'm Billy Adare. I'm here to work. My brother sent me."

The guy stood up and nodded toward the door. They went outside in the harsh early-morning light. The day threatened to be blistering.

"Sorry, I didn't know who you was." He called to a group of men. "Hey, Jimmy, comere." A thin, darkly tanned man of about fifty came over to them. He was wearing a cut-off T-shirt, and his arms were covered with faded tattoos.

"This is Adare's kid brother. Put him with those guys on the stone crew."

Billy followed the man into the building. It was cooler and smelled of wet cement and sawdust.

"You a sandhog?" The shop steward looked him over.

"Yeah."

"Better you than me. I ain't cut out for that crap. Underground. I need the fresh air. Look, here's a list. You go up on three, four, five, all the way up to seven. There's a bunch of crates laying around up there. You find the stones listed on these sheets." The guy ripped the top two pages off and handed them to Billy.

"And kid." The steward winked at him. "Don't knock yourself out."

Billy shook his head and walked up to the seventh floor, which was the top of the block-long portion of the building. A narrower tower started on the eighth floor and rose forty-two stories above the city. Billy made a circle of the floor, checking the crates, each of which held half a dozen stones that were to be used as the skin of the building. He found one of the stones he was searching for.

He was on the sixth floor, an hour after he had started, when the shop steward came up.

"What do you want for coffee?"

Billy thought about having a coffee, then changed his mind. Even in the shade of the building he was already sweating. He ordered an iced tea.

"How you making out?"

"I only found one so far." Billy was apologetic.

"One? That puts you way ahead of schedule. Slow it down. You don't want to make any enemies for yourself. Come down to the third floor in about ten minutes for coffee break."

Billy watched him go down the stairway. He made another circle and walked down to the third floor. The entire crew was sitting around on crates and buckets, talking and laughing. The shop steward had returned with the order. He took numbers and bets for the night's sporting events, paid off winners, and collected from the losers.

"Where's Dragone?"

"I think he was headed to Florida, last I heard."

"He better, that prick. He's digging a hole for himself." The shop steward counted money, a pencil behind his ear. He held a small notebook pressed between his elbow and his side.

Billy finished his iced tea and was ready to go back to work, but nobody made a move.

"Hey, Itchy, what's the temperature you got?"

The man called Itchy leaned over and peered at a thermometer nailed to the railing.

"Lookit here, ninety-two in the shade."

"All right, you guys back to work, or whatever. It hits ninety-six, we're shutting down. I don't give a rat's fuck what that superintendent says."

Billy looked at his watch. A forty-minute coffee break. This was more like a vacation. He put five dollars down on the number with the shop steward, who gave him change of a twenty. They walked back toward the stairway.

"How's this job ever going to get done?" Billy asked.

"Hey, who cares? The quicker it's done, the quicker we're outta work. Listen, everybody's making money. Two months ago we were three months ahead a schedule, so we're making up for it. This job will finish on time, don't worry about that. You just show up. Nobody's gonna fuck with you, you being Paddy's brother and all. Just take it easy, you got it made."

"I'm used to working a lot harder. It's weird."

The shop steward stopped and looked at him. "No offense or nothing, but you must be—and I'm doing this damn near thirty years—you gotta be the first guy I ever come across complains about not doing enough work. Besides, these days everybody's making money. Like I said." He counted off on his fingers. "The contractors, the developers, the sub-fucking-contractors, the bankers, the laborers, carpenters, bookies, 'lectricians, the guy runs the friggin' coffee shop. I mean, on and on and fucking on. Don't worry about that—money is being made hand over fist. Ain't nobody losing out here. Relax, kid, you're a white man in America. Take advantage of it."

Billy went back to looking for the stones, and when this proved futile he climbed up to the roof out of boredom. He stood and watched the city shimmer below in the heat rising from the streets. The air was still and had weight to it. He took off his shirt and sat down, getting some sun for the first time all summer.

At lunch, Billy walked over to a Blarney Stone on Eighth Avenue. To the right inside the door was a lunch counter. Great hunks of gray marbled meat waited for the cook's knife. Potatoes, cabbage, and mixed vegetables sat in trays of tepid cloudy water. A fat man with a face as red and thick as a boiled ham lorded over the steam table. He was sweating so profusely he appeared to be melting into the station. He regarded Billy with dull eyes. Billy ordered a corned beef on rye with a pickle, paid, and took his plate to the end of the bar. A short, white-haired Irishman looked up, and Billy ordered a Bud draft. Thankfully, the bartender used an iced mug.

The bar began to fill with hard hats off the local sites. A group of UPS drivers took a booth in the back. A rare day game was on the television, the sound turned down. Everything in the place had a sheen of sweat on it and looked green in the weak fluorescent light. A few overhead fans failed to get the air moving. Billy shooed a fly off his plate and ate slowly. He was grateful to be working, yet he felt things were going to get worse before they got better. The problems with the sandhogs and his visit with Paddy had left him unsettled. He believed he was about to be confronted with choices he did not want to face, choices that would reverberate far into his future. A deep, consuming anxiety seemed to be growing inside him.

He knew there were plenty of times, when he was out drinking with the guys, that he professed some limitless romantic loyalty to friends, family, and union. How he would dive on the sword for his brother or friends, stop the bullets. He just did not know what price he would really pay for that loyalty. He wondered how much school had devalued those things, or if it had at all. Maybe it was just a handy excuse, a cloak for cowardice. He pushed half his sandwich away and ordered another beer.

He remembered how at school he tried to explain to the few people he was close to what it meant to be from the neighborhood, the claims it had on you, but it fell on uncomprehending ears. They just assumed it was easy to walk away, to rise above your station. In fact, they took his presence as proof of that, as validation of the system that had worked so well for them, left them ensconced in the safety of privilege, a rarefied place in the history of their nation, their species. Billy knew it ran much deeper, that he would always be rooted in the world that had shaped him. And it was more true with Paddy. He'd been shocked at how vulnerable his brother had seemed. It was nothing in particular, just that the aura of invincibility had evaporated, the confidence been reduced. That scared Billy. He wanted to help Paddy, but it left him feeling useless. Billy knew he was out of his league when it came to dealing in Paddy's world. He hoped things would work out with his brother, and with the union. He had little choice but to pray they would. He finished his beer, feeling small solace in its cool depths.

"Hey, Adare, what are you dreaming about?" The shop steward appeared, slapped him on the back. "Come on, we got work to avoid."

As they walked back onto the job site, the shop steward said, "I ever tell you, when we're done here they're gonna put a big bronze plaque above the entrance? Yeah, it's gonna say, 'Never have so many been paid so much to do so little.' "

After work, Billy went home and showered. At dinner, JP was silent, but Billy knew there was much being expressed in that silence. It hung between them like an unbreachable void. He considered trying to explain things but decided not to bother. If nothing else, his grandfather knew Billy had to work. Even if it meant taking a job that Paddy had set up. He hailed a gypsy cab for the ride to the picket line. As he rolled up on the site, he was surprised at the size of the crowd. Walking the line, besides the sandhogs, were operating engineers, carpenters, top laborers, and teamsters employed on the site. Two large barbecue grills, crafted from a halved fifty-five-gallon drum, were set up on either side of a long table. The smell of seared meat filled the air.

The men were dressed for a day in the park—shorts, T-shirts, baseball hats. Garbage cans filled with iced-down beer and soda were spaced along the tree line. Cops leaned against the fence, gratefully accepting cold soft drinks from the strikers. Picket signs, their messages ranging from the mundane to the creatively obscene, were in abundance.

Billy found Lenny flipping burgers.

"Hey, Billy, you want a burger?"

"No, thanks, Lenny. I just ate."

Lenny deftly removed a half-dozen burgers with a spatula, placing them on buns laid out on a large plate. Frankie, dressed in sweatpants and sneakers, a Yankees hat on backward, sidled over and grabbed the plate.

"I'll distribute these, Lenny." He bathed them in ketchup and walked off toward his car.

Lenny removed his hat and wiped the sweat from his forehead with the back of his arm. Billy stood a few feet from the heat of the grill. Men pushed their way to the table where the hot dogs, burgers, and condiments were laid out.

"How's the new job?"

"Good. I mean, easy. It's not like working here—it's kind of boring. Job's winding down."

"Hey, just go along with it. You got a month is all. Bring your pillow. Last thing you want to do is step on somebody's toes down there."

"I hear you."

They heard a commotion and turned to see Bobby Moran, his ponderous belly clearing a path before him, bearing down on the grill, carrying enough flank steaks to rebuild a slaughtered steer.

"Clear way," he bellowed. "We got real meat now. We'll eat like men, not some fucking Cub Scout troop." The men cheered. Moran dropped the meat on the table, and the weight of it buckled the table's legs.

Someone yelled, "What'd you do, Moran, butcher your twin brother?"

"Yeah, but that was last Labor Day. This here is USDA Uncle Sam–approved grade A." Moran used his gut to inch Lenny away from the grill and grabbed the spatula. "Allow me, Brother Coyle."

"My guest, Brother Moran."

Moran began hacking off pieces of beef and tossing them on the grill. Flames jumped and smoke rose, swirling into the coming twilight.

Jefferson McCoy tried to put some fish fillets on the grill next to Moran's beef. "Get them fish entrails outta here, you West Indian degenerate." They compromised, each taking over a grill.

Bernie Coyle came by and gave a pep talk. He promised things would soon be settled; talked about strike funds and unemployment; urged the men to avoid violence at all costs. He shook hands, listened to complaints, and ate bloody steak.

The mood was almost festive, the camaraderie and spirit running high. The strike was something of a relief after the months of antagonism. At least now the battle lines were clear. The union had not endured a difficult strike in almost forty years. No one dared cross construction union picket lines in New York.

"No," Butcher Boy said. "You drive, I shoot." He had a brand-new MAC 10 machine pistol and was anxious to use it for real. Vinny said, "Fuck, you get to have all the fun."

"Just drive."

They were cruising up the Major Deegan Expressway in a stolen Dodge minivan. Butcher Boy was determined to do this one right. Jack had still not gotten over the sandhog idiot dying, when he heard about the Korean grocer. Butcher Boy had not seen him that angry in a long time. Not since Terry had dropped the cinder block on that mailman.

He was ready for this one. He had made two dry runs. Knew where the place was. Knew how to get out of there quickly. They had a second car waiting in the Metro North parking lot. They'd make the switch and drive home. No problem.

"So, Sammy junior, how was your weekend?"

"The fuck you calling Sammy junior?" It was the third time so far Vinny had called him that. At first he thought it was a mistake.

"Shit, ain't you seen that movie about Son of Sam, serial killer? It's wack. That's you." Vinny laughed.

Butcher Boy was not remotely amused. He gripped the MAC 10 and had an urge to shoot the wiseass. Vinny was lucky he was driving. "Don't call me that."

"Fucking A, Terry. It's a joke. Don't be so serious, man."

"Don't call me that."

"Wow. Mr. Sensitive all a sudden."

They turned off the Deegan at East 233rd Street and drove past Woodlawn Cemetery. Butcher Boy instructed Vinny to turn left onto Katonah Avenue. They drove north on Katonah, rolling closer to their destination. It was two o'clock in the afternoon. The street was busy with pedestrian traffic. Young mothers walked children in and out of the stores. Groups of teenagers congregated on corners. The unemployed and the retired ducked into the coolness of bars to catch a game on television.

"Pull up right here."

Vinny pulled alongside a parked car. Butcher Boy climbed into the minivan's back seat. "Don't drive away till I say so."

Butcher Boy pushed the safety to Off. He grabbed the door handle and slid the side door of the van open. Passersby did not turn to look at such a common occurrence. Butcher Boy raised the pistol to a point above the people's heads and opened fire at the storefront union office. The sheet glass exploded into a million glistening shards. People screamed and dove for the sidewalk. Butcher Boy emptied the first clip. As he was changing clips, Vinny hit the gas and made a hard right on the corner. Butcher Boy tumbled out of the van and bounced face-first off a car parked on the narrow street. Vinny was halfway up the block before he realized he'd lost his partner.

Butcher Boy got up bleeding and shot the pistol into the air to discourage pursuit. He ran down the street and dove in the van's side door, yelling, "Drive, you asshole."

Butcher Boy did not say a word. Vinny was actually laughing. Ha ha. "You shoulda seen your face, Sammy. Fucking running up that street. I'm sorry, maybe you don't think it was so funny, but your face—holy shit, you should of seen it." Vinny laughed and laughed.

They parked the van on Webster Avenue. They walked into the parking lot. Butcher Boy went to the trunk of the car. He popped it open and said, "Hey, Vinny, check this out."

Vinny came over, and Butcher Boy reached up with his left hand, grabbed him by the hair, and pulled him down. With his right hand he drove a nine-inch hunting knife up between Vinny's throat and chin, straight into his brain. He threw him in the trunk and said, "You shoulda seen your fucking face. Ha ha," then slammed the door shut.

Tuesday morning, 6:40 A.M. Billy waited outside the job site, sipping an iced tea, his hard hat tucked under his arm. Something thick and warm that resembled a fog lay over the city. Rivulets of sweat trickled down his sides. He had barely slept during the offensively hot night. He watched as a sky-blue Trans Am pulled up a few feet from him.

The driver, a beefy young man in gym shorts and a tank top, got out, looked around, and went over to the passenger seat. Billy watched as he opened the door and helped a laborer from the site out of the car. The laborer put his arm around the driver's neck and hopped onto the ground. The driver, outweighed by some fifty pounds, lowered the man as gently as he could, said, "The friggin' village idiot I got here," and left.

The Trans Am tore up the street and screeched to a stop. The reverse lights came on, and the car came back, rocking to a stop in front of Billy. The driver rolled down the window, said, "Here. Give 'im these," and tossed out a hard hat and a work boot. He hit the gas and was gone. Billy picked them up and turned to the laborer, who was lying on his back, muttering, "Ah fuck, ah fuck," over and over. Billy squatted down and looked at his bare foot. It was bloated and purple.

"When'd it happen?"

"Ah fuck, ah fuck. Yesterday, playing softball." He sat up and looked at the foot. "Ow. Fuck."

"They're gonna know it didn't happen here, today."

The laborer winced. His body was deeply tanned, but his face was wan. He shook his head. "I got the right doctor. Take care of everything. You gotta be my witness, man. I did it right here, okay? I'll toss you something, get my settlement."

Billy looked off down the street and shrugged. "Yeah, whatever."

"I'm serious, guy. I'll put a fuckin' pool in your backyard."

At lunch, the men gathered near the street and sat on planks supported by buckets. They ate sandwiches and ogled the parade of secretaries and aspiring actresses. In between bites they shouted and cajoled. The men seemed to fall into two distinct camps when it came to this activity. There was a loud minority like the fat man who stood a few feet from Billy and shouted gems like, "Hey, sweetheart, I'll fuck you till your kidneys quiver." He looked to Billy like a man who might enjoy doing bad things to twelve-year-olds. Others took a more diplomatic approach, making futile attempts to charm passersby with lines like, "Wow, you hafta fill out an application, get that pretty?" Most of the men shook their heads and asked the harassers if they had sisters, mothers, daughters, wives. For this they became targets of abuse. The women reacted variously. Most pulled down within themselves and passed silently, some glowered, some tossed off smiles, not taking the comments for anything more than they were.

Billy finished his fourth iced tea of the day as the men stood and started making their way back to their work stations. Everything was slowed by the heat. Even the ubiquitous construction dust failed to rise in the hot, wet air.

Billy returned to the eighteenth floor, where he was chipping out some concrete that had been formed wrong. He was changing the bit on his chipping gun when a man approached. By his tool belt, Billy recognized him as an electrician. He was lanky and had the florid good looks of an aging high-school power forward.

"You the sandhog?"

"Yep."

The man extended his hand. "Johnny Finnegan. I'm with the 'lectricians."

Billy shook his hand. "Name's Billy Adare."

The man looked like he was going to speak but paused and stared out past Billy over the city skyline, as if he recognized something there. He looked back to Billy and said, "Hope you don't mind my asking, but, ah, they tell me your father was killed down there."

"Yeah. He was."

A chipping gun started across the floor. "I lost my father too. Not in the tunnels; he was with the 'lectricians, like me." Finnegan pointed out past Billy. "See that? World Trade Center."

Billy turned and took in the twin towers, which were partly obscured by the poisonous haze. He nodded. Finnegan went on. "All around the world people know that place. It's world famous, like the Statue of Liberty, right? It's a symbol of New York, of America. I see it, you know what I see?"

Billy shook his head. He heard an argument break out behind them.

"I see my father's tombstone. He went down an elevator shaft. Forty stories. I was thirteen. Goes without saying, it was a closed casket."

Billy turned back to face him. Though he did not recall the event, he knew his father's casket was closed as well. There were not many open ones for construction workers. Finnegan turned his head away as if he was embarrassed by his revelation. Billy said, "I know, I know. It sucks."

Finnegan turned back to him. "Yeah, well, I guess that's how the ball bounces." He caught himself, winced. "Oh, Christ, no pun intended. Listen, I got a hook with the local. You want, I can get you in the apprentice program. You don't want to be a laborer—no future in that."

"Thanks, I appreciate it. I'm going to law school, though. September."

"No shit? Smart guy, huh? Good for you, good for you. Still, I made eighty grand last year with OT—ain't bad for a high-school diploma. Lemme know, things don't work out."

He walked away, and Billy put his goggles on and went back to chipping.

It was just before afternoon break when Billy noticed a bunch of men clustered together, looking out the far side of the building. Curious, he went and joined them. Down below on the street there was commotion—a circled crowd, police cars, an ambulance. The bull's-eye of the circle was a human form, a body. A puddle of bright-red blood was visible. From two hundred feet up, Billy was not sure, but it appeared the body was headless.

The men went to the ground floor and learned what had happened. A four-by-six oak beam had fallen from an undetermined floor. An exchange student from France was decapitated. He'd been in the country for two days. The job was closed down. All workers were to be interviewed by detectives the next day. Billy left, walking around the block to avoid the carnage. He'd seen enough of it lately.

When Billy got to the tunnel site, he learned about the drive-by shooting. The festive mood on the picket line had turned to one of outrage and frustration. The men huddled out of earshot of the cops guarding the picket line. They discussed retribution.

"We don't hit back, these bastards will destroy us."

"I say we drag Harkness out of his house and fuck him up."

"The minute we do, they win," Lenny said.

"What are we supposed to do, wait for the cops? They can't do a thing about this. I say we beat the shit out of those assholes for starters." Frankie indicated the two dozen company guards who stood around inside the gates. They carried clubs and exuded recidivism and poor education. They were all bad teeth and Confederate-flag tattoos. Harkness and Company had bused them in from out of state.

Anger was as distinct as the humidity.

Frankie walked toward his car and motioned for Billy to follow. Eamon Cudahy accompanied Billy. Frankie opened the car door and sat in the rear seat. Reaching down, he said, "Billy, check this out."

Billy bent to look in the car. Frankie held a large shoe box. When he took the lid off, Billy saw two bombs. Each consisted of a fuse and three sticks of Tovex explosive wrapped in electrical tape. Billy felt a knot in his stomach.

"Frankie, what's up with that?"

"Eamon made us a little Belfast special here. It's time we send a message back."

Billy did not want to appear scared.

"What are they for?"

"We go over the fence tonight. Toss them in the trailers. No one's going to be there. Just make a little noise." Frankie covered the bombs and slid them back under the seat.

"This come from the union hall?"

"Nah. No way. They can't get involved in this shit. This is a little freelance work. Me and Boomer are gonna handle it."

"Frankie, this is a job for someone like Boomer. Why do you need to do it? What about the PD? They don't take convicted felons."

"Billy, come off it. You think I'd do this, we could get caught?"

"We'll be distracting them down this end, Billy. There's not a thing to worry about." Eamon seemed gleeful at the prospect of destruction.

"Not a thing," Billy repeated.

"Billy, this has got to be done. I'm a sandhog. I'll worry about being a cop when I become a cop."

Billy heard the rebuke in Frankie's tone.

They drank beer and barbecued hamburgers and hot dogs, waiting for darkness. Someone pulled his car close to the gate and had the doors open, with the radio playing loudly. The cops and guards stood listlessly in the heat. Night came slowly. The sun seemed reluctant to fall. Billy drank faster than he should have done, trying to take the edge off, using the beer as a shield. He was nervous about Frankie's involvement. He briefly considered leaving, putting some distance between himself and the impending violence, but he could not. It might be seen as a betrayal. Cicadas sang in the depleted patch of woods surrounding the site.

When it was finally dark, Eamon came up behind them and motioned Billy and Frankie aside.

"All right, lads." He seemed a ghostly presence. Billy thought there must have been many damp Belfast nights when Eamon huddled like this to right some ancient wrong with a bullet or a bomb. "We've a problem. Your man Boomer's been on the vodka all night. He's too pissed to be of use to us."

"Shit." Frankie turned to Billy. "Billy, come around back with me. I just need someone to cover my ass, okay?"

Billy looked up, surprised. He wanted to say no but, under the imploring gaze of Eamon Cudahy, simply said, "Sure." He felt his balls crawl up against his body.

"Good lad. There's no need for precision now, just get it close. Be sure to wait fifteen minutes."

Frankie and Billy drove around to the back of the site. They parked on a dead-end street and waited. On their left was a hurricane fence, surrounding the job site.

"You all right?" Frankie asked. Billy heard a tremble in his voice. He'd known Frankie long enough to know the excitement outweighed the fear.

Billy felt a numbness. The adrenaline made his arms and legs feel heavy, his heart race.

"Yeah. Let's get it over with."

"Ten more minutes."

Billy was surprised. It felt as if an hour had gone by.

Frankie looked at his watch. "I hope there's nobody in the fucking things."

Billy did not even want to think along those lines. He could deal with blowing up a trailer or two; people were a whole different matter.

"Let's go," Frankie announced.

They got out of the car. Frankie grabbed the box from under the seat and handed it to Billy. Then he reached into the back seat for a pair of bolt cutters. Billy looked up the dark block and saw no one. They walked the twenty feet through the woods to the fence. The night closed in on them as they peered through the small stand of trees on the inside of the fence. No one was watching the back. Frankie quickly cut a square hole in the fence and dropped the bolt cutters. Billy followed him through the hole. They crept up to the tree line. At that point they were fifteen yards from the trailers. To their right the main work shaft sat, silent and abandoned.

Sounds of commotion from the front gate drifted up toward them. Billy could feel the sweat rolling down his back and chest. He and Frankie exchanged looks. Billy opened the box, and Frankie grabbed one of the bombs. They turned the timers to fifteen seconds. They counted five, and Billy threw his in a high arc. It landed on the roof of the super's trailer. Frankie tossed a line-drive strike through the trailer window.

They turned and ran, and just as they reached the fence, the bombs went off in quick succession, like a one-two punch. Billy felt the heat and force of the blast on his back. Frankie scooped up the bolt cutters, and they hit the car at a dead run.

Later, in the bar, secure in the knowledge that no one had been hurt, Billy felt good about what he had done. Message delivered. The sandhogs who knew about it bought him drinks and slapped his back. The college kid would make his old man proud, they said. Billy smiled through the booze, happy to bask in the glow of brotherhood—the bond of men who fought for something: to keep food on their tables, roofs over their heads. It was a timeless fight. But somewhere deep inside him, a regret was echoing.

. . .

Butcher Boy finished his Twinkie and waited for the knock on the door. He knew exactly why Jack was on his way over. That bigmouthed Italian asshole. Why should it be his fault the guy could not shut up, that he got what he deserved? He'd love to see what Jack would've done if it was him the guy was talking shit to.

Butcher Boy got up and paced back and forth. He was dressed only in gym shorts. He had just finished lifting, chest and arms, sixteen sets for each muscle group. He felt good, pumped.

There was only one thing to do, one way to handle Jack. Lie. He felt he could pull it off. He wasn't hungover or crashing off a coke binge. His nerves were strong, steady. Just look Jack in the eye and say, "I got no idea, really, Jackie." Simple as that. Then Jack would have to pay him. He had plans. Pick up a little blow, grab that girl from the video store was always eyeing him, and head down the shore, Atlantic City maybe. Everything was cool.

When the knock finally came, he sauntered over to the door and pulled it open wide, offering his apartment to his brother. There was big brother Jack, the war hero, all stony-faced like he expected. Jack came into the room and waited for him to close the door.

"Where's the guinea kid?"

Butcher Boy gave him his innocent-boy look. "How should I know?"

Jack stared at him, then said, "Is that right? According to those guys, he ain't been seen since he worked with you, Terry. How'd you leave off?"

"I dropped him off by his car, down Fifty-ninth Street."

"Is that right? Look at me, Terry. Look me in the eyes."

Butcher Boy was in control. Jack had something about looking people in the eyes, that was his problem. He brought his eyes up.

Jack slapped him hard across the face. "You lying piece of shit."

Butcher Boy tasted blood. His ear rang with shame and rage.

"You're taking money out of my fucking pocket now, Terry."

"I didn't do nothing."

"I didn't do nothing," Jack mimicked him.

Butcher Boy felt like he was going to cry. He struggled to keep the tears in.

"Terry, you're becoming a major-league liability, you hear me? Hah?" Jack shoved him, then slapped him in the head, lighter than before. "Now tell me what happened to the guinea kid."

"I don't know."

"Where'd you leave off?"

"I tol' you. I left him at his car."

Jack shook his head. He was calmer. "You know whose ass you put on the line here, Terry? Do you even give a fuck? You lowlife fucking junkie."

"I ain't no junkie. I didn't do nothing."

"You fucking disappoint me, Terry. You really fucking truly and deeply disappoint me. My own flesh and blood, my own brother. You treat me like a nigger off the street."

"Jack," Butcher Boy whined.

Jack walked a few steps farther into the living room. He turned around and took a pistol from his waistband.

"Jack?"

Jack took a silencer from his jacket pocket. As he was marrying it to the pistol he said, "You of all people know what I do to people that fuck me, Terry."

"Jack, come on."

"How many more times are you gonna fuck me, Terry? How many more times are you gonna bite the hand that feeds you?" He cleared the pistol. "Tell me."

Jack raised the pistol and pointed it at Butcher Boy's face. "Tell me, Terry, why I shouldn't do you right here and now."

Butcher Boy could not speak.

"You think you deserve another chance, Terry? Do you?"

Butcher Boy nodded.

Jack turned the pistol to his own head. "You want me to do it for you, Terry? You know the way you fuck up, you're killing me the same as if you shot me—do you realize that?"

Jack lowered the pistol. "Siddown."

Butcher Boy sat on his couch. Jack sat in front of him on the coffee table, so their knees nearly touched. Jack grabbed Butcher Boy's hand and put the pistol in it. He covered the hand with both of his own.

"Terry, I swear to you, you fuck this up, you better leave town. You better run to the fucking ends of the earth. You hear me?" He squeezed Butcher Boy's hands for emphasis. "I'm at the end of my rope with you, Terry. So you better make sure, this one time, there really ain't no fuckups. This is the most important thing you'll ever do. Let me know, Terry, right here and now if you ain't up to it. 'Cause we can end it right here. I'll give you a one-way ticket anywhere you want the fuck to go. Just as long as you promise not to come back."

Jack stood up, holding the pistol. He looked down at his brother.

"Jack, I'll handle it." Butcher Boy was grateful for the chance at redemption in his brother's eyes.

Jack wiped down the pistol and dropped it on the couch.

"Paddy Adare."

Butcher Boy looked from the pistol back to Jack. Wow. Those were the last two words he ever expected to hear.

The next day, full of poison and remorse, Billy Adare showed up for work. For once he was glad that it was such a soft job. He climbed to the roof and surveyed the city, wondering how it had come to this. He looked north to the Bronx, which appeared bucolic from this height and distance, a sleepy domain on the horizon. He hoped last night's little adventure was the end of it. He did not have the balls for this crazy shit, even if he believed it was the right thing to do.

Billy peered over the edge of the roof. Far below, the life of the city surged through the streets like the blood of a great snarling beast, unimpeded by his concerns. He was just one more fool in its hard history who'd gotten in over his head. Vertigo pulled him away from the concrete chasm. He felt the need to take a step back from his life and hunker down, to escape as unscathed as possible.

Out on the Hudson, pleasure boats roared playfully, their hulls gleaming in the summer sun. Billy wondered if there was anything he could do to shake the dread that had descended on his world. Last night in the bar, he had felt his actions were cathartic, that he had exorcised something. But now, in the hard light of morning, he felt confusion and trepidation, the booze-induced euphoria laid low by the shock of a new day and the weight of a deed done and irreversible. He turned to search out some work, lose himself in toil for a while, escape into mindless drudgery. He wanted to work until he was numb.

As he neared the staircase, a helicopter raced overhead. It seemed close enough to grab. He watched its trajectory across the skyline. When he turned back to the door, his brother was standing there.

"Einstein, what's up?"

Billy recognized it as a weak attempt at levity: Paddy wasn't there to shoot the shit. He watched as Paddy walked to the edge of the roof and looked down. Billy stood a few feet behind him.

"Shit, I can see my apartment from here." Paddy turned his back to the neighborhood and sat on the parapet.

Billy thought his brother looked drawn and distant in the sunshine. He seemed entirely something of the night, caught unwillingly in daylight.

"Nice view." Paddy smiled weakly.

Billy nodded. "What's going on?" A question to which he did not want the answer.

"Things are getting a little out of hand." Paddy looked over his shoulder as if for confirmation of this belief. He turned back to Billy and leaned forward. Spitting between his feet, he started to talk again but stopped to let the helicopter hammer past overhead. When it was quiet, he said, "I want you to change job sites. I got a problem. Might be nothing, but it's a good idea you ain't so visible for a while. I got you a spot on a crew up in Harlem, onna West Side. Lots of OT."

"What kind of problem?" Billy asked. His hangover seemed to grow in intensity. Someone was screwing a metal plate into his skull. He was queasy.

"It's no big deal. It's just things ain't what they used to be." Paddy stood up. "That's all."

Billy said, "What can I do to help?"

Paddy looked at him for a minute. "Not much. Don't worry about it. I mean, the one thing you can do is take care of yourself, any problems come up."

Paddy looked out over the city again. Billy was not used to this. Paddy had always been the type of person who focused all his attention on you when he spoke to you. Even when he was being pleasant, his intensity had a withering effect. He turned back to Billy, smiling, but the smile projected more sadness than mirth, a smile for what might have been.

"Here—I want you to have this." Paddy reached behind his back and pulled a small silver pistol from his belt. He held the gun before him.

"Paddy, what the fuck?"

"Just insurance, Billy. I want you to take it just in case things—in case someone tries to get me through you."

Billy said nothing. He looked at the pistol in Paddy's hand. It gleamed like evil in the sun. Standing twenty feet from the roof's edge, he felt vertigo hit him like a sucker punch.

"Paddy, someone would just take it away from me."

"Bullshit. You know how to handle it. It's a thirty-two, like we used to shoot upstate." Paddy, for the first time that morning, seemed fully alive.

Billy shook his head and looked north to the Bronx again. In one short day he'd gone from college boy to pistol-packing mad bomber. He no longer felt in control of his life.

Paddy lifted his arm and pointed the pistol west, past the roofs of Hell's Kitchen, and fired, emptying the eleven-shot clip into the void over the Hudson. The spent shells danced across the rooftop, forming a half-moon at his feet. He turned to Billy. The cordite hung in the air, and Billy thought of the tunnel. He longed for the refuge of a midnight shift in the cool earth.

Paddy popped out the empty clip and slapped in a new one. Turning the barrel toward himself, he handed the pistol to Billy. "You'll never make a lawyer if you get don't get to law school."

Billy took the pistol and felt its weight like doom.

"These guys are psychos. I just don't know how it's gonna play out."

Billy went down on one knee and slid the pistol along his ankle. He stood up.

"I think Tierney's behind the move on the hogs."

"Serious?" Billy felt detached.

"Wish I wasn't. Come on. That shop steward's getting your money."

Billy followed Paddy toward the stairway. There was nothing much left to say.

Rosa sat Indian-style, her legs folded underneath her, on the floor of her empty bedroom. She was dressed casually, jeans and a T-shirt, her hair pulled back in a single thick braid. She could hear the moving men in the next room, taking the last of her belongings to the truck parked curbside. Before her were two shoe boxes full of photographs—one of old family photos and the other filled with snapshots of her life with Paddy Adare.

She grabbed a stack from her family box and leafed through them. There were many shots—holidays, day trips to Orchard Beach, the Jersey shore, family picnics in Riverside Park. In all of them people were smiling, seemingly happy, the sun always bright. She laid them out on the parquet floor before her, the way her brothers used to lay out baseball cards when they were kids. Beams of late-afternoon light shone through her window. The room, duly scrubbed to ensure the return of her security deposit, smelled of Murphy's Oil and lemon.

The pictures portrayed togetherness and love. Rosa knew the truth to be a different matter altogether, so many of those idyllic outings shattered by anger and booze, her parents going at each other with the particular frenzied hatred reserved for loved ones, she and her brothers terrified and confused. She thought it odd that those moments had totally eluded the permanence of the camera, yet she knew the images were seared into her consciousness, as indelible as glacial scars on a mountain face.

She stared at the pictures of her mother, a fierce and stubborn woman, dead at fifty-five. Dead young from heart failure, an overload of all those blunted feelings, all that rage, all that struggle with the man she loved, the man she had married at sixteen, the two of them young, hungry immigrants from similar poor places, separated by geography only. Rosa guessed there had been a pleasantness to them once, a sweetness that would be soured by the demands of child rearing and toil, immolated by alcohol and disappointment. She'd learned too many hard lessons about love from them. She never thought she'd be able to give herself to a man, to let her life become entwined with another. She swore she would avoid her mother's fate at all costs, even her father's fate, because her mother dished out as much as she took, her spouse's equal in cruelty when need be.

Paddy had surprised her, had brought out something in her she thought no one would ever reach. He'd placed no claim on her, exacted no price for her love and affection, and as a result they had effortlessly grown close, their love strong. She knew from the beginning that his vocation would be their downfall, yet things moved along so well and easily that she put that inevitability aside. Her love for Paddy was thorough and true, yet she refused to lose herself, to surrender her life, her aspirations. For weeks she had fought off the notion that she was abandoning him, because she knew that if she did not forsake him she must abandon herself. That she could not do.

She lifted the lid from the box with photos of Paddy and picked up the first one. It was of a six-year-old at a family gathering. He stood, his gazed fixed on the photographer, his hands, though they hung at his sides, clenched into fists as if he was ready to fight, was seeking the battle joined. As she held the picture her hand started to shake, and she put it down and closed the box, shoving it away from her. She took the box with her family pictures and stood. Her head was light, and she felt tears welling. She left the room and pulled the door firmly shut behind her.

John Tuzio turned on his stool and said to Vito, "What's this I hear, the guy's a fucking rat?"

Vito tried to figure out how this bit of information on Paddy Adare had gotten back to Tuzio. The Irish gang was Vito's operation. That Tuzio was receiving intelligence on them from someone else, solicited or not, was a very bad sign. It meant Tuzio was probably checking up on him on the sly. The veracity of the claim was suspect. Vito, an engineer of many a false story, knew how the game was played.

"I met the guy—what?—twice? First time was maybe ten years or more ago. When he was fighting. Last time was maybe six months back. Not to worry, John." Vito remembered being impressed by Paddy Adare both times. He also remembered Tierney's indication that he was having problems with him.

"Everybody tells me not to worry, not to fucking worry. That's the same thing they told Tony Salerno." Tuzio slammed his fist on a copy of the *Post*.

"There's only one guy can tie anything together, that's Tierney." Vito sought to assuage his boss's paranoia before it mushroomed into something sloppy. He knew Tuzio had a grudging admiration for Tierney.

"One guy? What about that cocksucka?"

Vito realized he meant Eliot. Tuzio had taken what Vito viewed as an unhealthy interest in the pictures they had of Eliot in flagrante.

"He's not a stupid man, John."

"Is that right? Well first of all he got a picture like that with a cock in his mouth. That makes him stupid, in my book. Next, you said one guy ties me in. Now I got two. Maybe you meant one guy and one faggot?"

Vito remained silent. Tuzio looked around the room absently. He looked to Vito like a man befuddled by the present, searching the dark corners of the social club for a simpler past. Vito wondered what ghosts he saw there. He'd noticed a gradual unease settle on the old man over the years, a shift in demeanor so subtle he was sure no one else noticed. John Tuzio, in the eyes of his competition and crew, was still the bloodthirsty mafioso who had bludgeoned his way out of the gutters of East New York.

"I was wondering maybe this cocksucka might cause us a problem." Tuzio's focus rebounded audibly. "I see this thing with the Irishers"—he slapped the *Post* again—"it's getting too fucking loud for me. I'm telling you, Tony Salerno—we can't trust our own, never mind some cocksucker or a bunch of fuckin' Irish." Tuzio stood up. He almost never stood up once he was inside the club. Vito was slightly alarmed. "You see this Eliot, and you straighten him out. These Irish—I don't want this coming back to us, Vito."

Vito had not heard Tuzio use that tone of voice with him in years. He looked at his boss, a man he was bound to by blood, and waited to hear what was next. For once he was totally unsure of what to do. But Tuzio sat back down hard and stared off into the corner again, chasing phantoms in the dark recesses of a past he was utterly chained to. Vito turned and walked out. He had an appointment to keep with Agent Moy. He expected to hear bad news.

Billy got off the IRT train at 125th Street and walked toward the river. The sky was high and clear for the first time in two weeks, and as he neared the water, a stiff, cleansing breeze swept over him. He jounced down the hill, feeling the gun in his boot, the weight of it oddly reassuring. Billy had resigned himself to the weapon's presence.

The job site stretched for a half-dozen blocks, the street torn up, backhoes interspersed along the way. The air smelled of wet dirt and diesel smoke. Billy walked toward what he assumed were the bosses' trailers. Workers were pulling up in cars and getting out with hard hats in one hand and styrofoam cups of coffee in the other. Billy found the super, a tall man in his mid-fifties, leaning against a trailer, smoking a cigarette. He was watching two groups of workers prepare for the shift. One group consisted of a dozen burly black men, the other was a group of equally stout men that Billy believed to be Italian.

The super flicked his cigarette away and raised an eyebrow at Billy, inviting him to speak. He had a hard face softened by deep smile lines.

Billy said what Paddy had told him to. "I'm with the coalition. I'm supposed to start today." The absurdity of this was not lost on Billy. But he was still surprised by the man's response.

"You"—he pointed a thick finger at Billy—"are with the coalition?" He laughed heartily, then struggled to catch his breath. Years of smoking echoed in his battered lungs. When he regained his breath, he said, "Just what the fuck coalition is that? The Coalition for a Free Ireland?"

Billy noticed that all the men were watching them now. "New City Empowerment."

Again the laugh, like wet gravel mixing with sand and cement. "Now I can retire, 'cause I seen everything. The coalition, he says." He looked over to the black men by the generator truck. "Hey, Idi Amin, comere. I got one of your oppressed bro-shines over here. Whitest fucking black man I ever seen."

One of the black men put down a jackhammer and walked over to them. He was a large man dressed in denim work clothes and worn boots. Around his waist was an apron made of two canvas mailbags stitched together. He bore an uncanny resemblance to the deposed strongman.

"You Adare?" Billy nodded his head, and the man said, "Follow me." As they walked away, the superintendent laughed again.

They came to a hole in the ground that was roughly eight feet square and only a couple of feet deep. Inside, two jackhammers with short drill steels lay among broken rock. The man pointed over to the generator truck and said, "Get yourself one of them masks and some earplugs, 'less you want to breathe shit and bleed out your ears all day."

When Billy came back, the man said, "My name's Roberts. Here." He tossed Billy a hard hat. "You gonna need a apron too. I'll give you one of mines, you bring me a new one tomorrow. Stop any post office, they give you some bags. Have your woman sew them together. Otherwise the jackhammer wear through your pants in half a day. Grab an air hose, hook up your drill."

Billy did as he was instructed. The project was a sewer excavation, replacing hundred-year-old copper pipe with new high-tech plastic. Billy was to help drill new catch basins, which entailed cutting ten-foot-deep holes in solid rock; No blasting was allowed. Drill, split, chip, and dig. The kind of chain-gang labor Billy could relate to.

Roberts did not have much to say, so Billy just worked alongside him quietly, wondering what to do about Paddy and about the pistol in his boot. They stopped for a water break midmorning, and Roberts pointed out one of the Italians. "That scrawny Eyetalian, he the foreman, don't know but three four words of English. Just ignore the muthafucka. You work, nobody gonna say shit to you."

At lunch, Roberts left Billy and went to join the other blacks who ate sitting along an old rusted guardrail. The Italians, all of whom appeared to be from the old country, sat in a line opposite their black coworkers. They drank homemade wine out of mason jars and ate loaves of bread laden with cold cuts and olive oil. They spoke only Italian. As Billy walked past them they stopped talking, as if they thought he could understand them. They stared at him until one said, "Hey, Irish, whadda you, with the effe bee eye?" and they broke into laughter, some splashing wine like blood on their soiled shirts.

Since he had not brought a lunch, Billy walked up to the McDonald's on Broadway and ordered a single cheeseburger and a Coke, his appetite dulled by the mounting heat and the toil. The morning breeze had ceased, and the air had thickened in its absence. Billy had sweated through his dungarees. He finished his meal and bought a gallon of spring water at a bodega, something to slake his ravenous thirst. When he had set up his drill that morning, he was surprised to find there were no water lines for the jackhammers. When he asked about this, Roberts laughed scornfully. "Sheet. Take that potato sack and soak it, then wrap it around your drill steel. That's what they consider wet drilling around this company. You ain't with the sandhogs now, baby." Though this surely helped, it by no means was the way to eliminate rock dust. His throat was raw from sucking it all day.

By the afternoon break, Billy felt he had truly experienced the full range of the foreman's English skills. As far as he could tell, it was, "cock-a-suck," "muth-a-fuck," "work-a-some-more," and "no-a-way," in a thousand different combinations.

After listening to one of these harangues, Roberts poured some water over his head and, watching the foreman walk away, said, "That there is the missing fucking link, I shit you not."

Billy rode the train home looking like a man of forty-five. Every pore, every crease in his skin, was filled with the poisonous white rock dust, and every time he moved, a cloud of it would rise from him and chase another subway rider away. When he got home, he showered for a full half hour, as if the volume of water could cleanse him to the core of his being. That night, for the first time in a long while, he slept the dreamless, peaceful sleep of the innocent.

Vito Romero watched Mary Moy enter the coffee shop on Forty-third Street and make her way to his booth. She was now noticeably with child and walked with the slight side to side motion of the overweight. A seriousness on her face heralded bad news. She sat down heavily and drank his untouched glass of water. A thin sheen of sweat covered her face.

Mary Moy said, "Vito, they want me to get you to testify. I can't win this one. I've tried to stop it. I went to the wall on this."

Vito was calm. "I've been expecting it. Mary, I know how the game is played. You can't feel bad over this. I knew the first time we met that this day would come. Don't beat yourself up. It's just the kind of thing you are gonna see. Job you got, you should get used to it." Vito looked at her and knew for certain that it had not been her idea. "Still, this is a major problem for me. I know you understand."

"Vito, maybe—I mean, the Witness Protection Program. You can start a new life. It's—it's not the worst thing in the world."

Vito waved in dismissal. "Mary, this is my life. I won't run and hide somewhere, trying to forget my past. Spend the rest of my time looking over my shoulder, waiting for a bullet to strike. I want to thank you for the warning. Now I need to do what's best for me. You understand this?"

Mary nodded her head. "I can't help but feel like I let you down. Like maybe I could have stopped it somehow."

"Come on, now. You been around long enough to know *I* put myself in a lose-lose situation here, not you. I made my bed. You're just doing your job. You got to keep on going. Remember, you're supposed to be the good guys. I'm with the bad guys."

"I wonder sometimes."

"That's nonsense. You did the right thing here. Always remember that." Vito stood. He had much to take care of.

After he left, Mary Moy sat there, feeling lousy. She knew that the minute the word got out, even if he refused to testify, Vito was as good as dead. She thought of that asshole Leary. Vito Romero had been a valuable asset for a long time, and now, to make himself look good, Leary was willing to subvert everything and to endanger a man's life for the sake of a promotion. She wondered how long she could deal with such bullshit.

Paddy Adare watched as Mickey Lawless stacked computer boxes. His living room looked more like an electronics warehouse than a human habitation. Mickey, dressed in a pair of cut-off shorts, wore brand-new basketball shoes that, like everything else in his place, from the furniture to the toiletries, were stolen.

Since Paddy had known him, Mickey had been a pathological thief who stole not for profit but for the pure joy of taking things that did not belong to him. Watching him exult over his new plunder, Paddy thought about a summer day when they were twelve years old. They were in a sporting-goods store in the Village, when a clerk left a knife case unattended for a moment. Mickey reached over the counter and snatched a half-dozen fine, imported hunting knives. They fled to the piers, and Paddy watched, astonished, as Mickey gave a knife to him, then tossed the others into the murky Hudson. When Paddy asked him why he had so plainly wasted his efforts, Mickey shrugged and said, "I don't need them." Simple as that.

Paddy once heard a neighborhood bartender compare Mickey's views on possession to the Indians'. To them the air is free, the land is free, the water, the sky—it all belongs to everyone. Mickey was the same way, but he extended that philosophy to everything man-made. Ironically, though Mickey had stolen millions of dollars' worth of everything, paintings to show dogs, jewelry to guns, he was always broke.

Mickey pointed to the computers. "Hey, Paddy, your brother's a college guy—think he knows how to use these friggin' things?"

"You gonna keep track of your loot or something?"

Mickey looked at him as if he did not understand the question. "Nah. It's just the wave of the future, the Information Age, I was reading. Why should just the yuppies be in on it, you know?"

"You tell me." Paddy stepped over a disassembled stereo and sat on Mickey's new couch. It was soft leather. Paddy figured it must be worth a few grand. "Nice couch."

"Yeah, it's cool. I got it off a showroom floor. Me and Steven Reilly, we dressed like delivery guys and walked right out of the place. I laughed my balls off. The manager held the door open for us." Mickey was pleased with himself.

"Listen, you want, I got something big coming up soon. I've been working on it for months."

"How big?" Paddy asked.

"Diamond district big."

Paddy would usually be intrigued. Mickey had brought him in on some sweet scores over the years, none of which had ever led to questioning by the police, but Paddy was too preoccupied with Jack. And his brother. The last thing he wanted to do was bring Billy into his messy world. And although he believed giving his brother the gun had been the right thing to do, he felt helpless, as though he had set Billy up for a bad fall. The kid had worked too hard to get fucked over because of his brother's bullshit, Paddy thought. Yet he was not a baby, and working in the trades sometimes brought you into the wrong circles. Paddy was angry at himself for making excuses: he had dragged Billy into this—no one or nothing else had. But he was even angrier at his own paralysis. He had always found his salvation, his validation, in action. Even on those occasions when he knew the odds were not in his favor, he was able to be decisive. He felt sickened. In the worst of times, doubt had been only on the edges of his consciousness. Now it consumed him.

"Hey, Paddy. Yo! What's up with you these days?"

Paddy looked up at Mickey, who was staring at him like he was looking at an accident victim. "That Keegan thing still bugging you?"

Paddy stood up. "For one, yeah." He walked over to the kitchen and poured a glass of water. "It's Jack—I don't know." He sat back down. "He's turned on me. I can't figure it out."

Mickey shook his head. "You ain't that stupid. I gotta spell it out for you? Fine, here goes: *m-o-n-e-y*, cold cash, plain and simple, cut and fucking dried."

"Yeah, maybe."

"Attila the Hun."

"What?"

"Attila the Hun. Guy was like Hitler, way back."

"Yeah, I heard about him."

"I told Jack about the guy once. You know how he was always busting my balls about reading books, probably 'cause the guy can't read past Dick and Jane. He wanted to know what I was learning, all that reading. So I figure I'll give him something he can relate to. I tell him how Attila took over most of the world, how he used to fuck with the Romans. They were scared shitless of the guy. I mean, every now and again he'd send a half million of these fucking gorillas on horseback down on them. So anytime he farted in their direction, they'd hand over mountains of gold.

"Guy becomes Jack's idol. Remember from school, that story? *Mice and Men*? 'Tell me about the rabbit, George'? That's how it was with Jack for a while. 'Tell me about Attila, Mickey.' "

Paddy knew how Jack could latch onto something. "Why'd he stop?"

"I told him how the guy died."

Paddy put a hand palm up. Mickey let loose with one of his altar-boy grins. "He got shit-faced and choked on his own puke."

"I should be so lucky." Paddy wished Jack were as stupid as Mickey made him out to be.

Lunchtime. Billy climbed out of the hole and dusted himself off as best he could. He told Roberts he might be a little late coming back from lunch. Roberts agreed to cover for him. Billy went over to the water truck, filled a gallon bottle with cold water, bent and poured it over his head. He took a towel from his gym bag and dried his hair, then wiped his face as clean as it was going to get. He walked up the hill to Broadway, flagged a gypsy cab, and, getting in, said, "Columbia. One sixteenth and Broadway."

At the gate, he was stopped by a security guard. Billy produced his acceptance letter, and the man looked him up and down, then waved him through. He breathed in the air of the campus. The buildings looked indomitable, as if they would last a thousand years. Billy felt pride and wonder, and great fortune. He walked around the perimeter of the common. Hearing the quiet echo of success and power, he smiled broadly, a bounce coming to his step. This was his school now. The place seemed to scream knowledge at him. His struggle, his discipline, were adding up to something. It had all seemed a vague possibility just months before.

The law school registrar's office was chilled by air-conditioning and operating with a quiet hum. There were three short lines. Billy took his place on one and observed the clerks behind the counter, seated at a dozen desks, all bent to their tasks. The line moved slowly. Everyone seemed to be working out a complex financial deal. In front of him, a woman, with a young man by her side, began to lace into a clerk at the counter.

"Maybe I'll call the Better Business Bureau. See what they say about this lousy treatment." The young man, presumably her son, looked sheepishly at his feet. Billy wondered if the woman thought she was buying life insurance. He glanced at his watch. He did not want to push it at work. There was rumor of a layoff coming up. As the only Irish on the job, he'd probably go first. That's just how the business was.

The woman was finally straightened out. Billy put his letter on the counter and smiled. "How you doing? Crazy lady, huh?" The clerk smiled and rolled her eyes. "I have my down payment." Billy placed his bag on the counter and took out ten stacks of hundred-dollar bills.

The clerk raised her eyebrows and looked uncertainly at Billy. "I—we don't usually take payment in that form."

"What? Cash? Look, they're good bills. I mean, it's not like it's counterfeit."

"I'm not saying that. I just—I need to get my supervisor."

Billy sighed as she disappeared into an office across the room. Several minutes later, she returned, trailed by a man in a blue suit and a maroon tie. He looked impatient. He came up to the counter and looked at the money, then back at Billy.

"I'm John Kurten, assistant registrar. Where'd you get so much cash?"

Billy was puzzled. He looked at Kurten, then down at his filthy, greased-streaked clothes. Wasn't it obvious? "I made it. I mean, I earned it."

"Well, it's just irregular."

"Irregular? It's cash money." Billy suppressed his urge to add "asshole."

"Would you mind very much returning with a cashier's check?"

"Listen, I work every day. I'm already late coming back from lunch—I can't take any more time off or I'll get shit-canned. With this and what I'm going to make the next few weeks, and with student loans, I'll just barely make it. Just take the cash, all right? I can't afford to come back."

Kurten gave him the superior look of an uptight bureaucrat. "I wish I could help. But we have—and if you come to school here you'll see—we have a certain way of doing things. It's really best for everyone."

Billy followed the guy's glance. Another suit appeared at a side door.

"Who's that?"

"That's our registrar. He doesn't get in—"

"Hey, excuse me." Billy waved to the man, who stopped and looked at him. "Can you help me out here? Your guy's not taking my money."

The man walked over to Billy and looked at Kurten, who averted his gaze. He turned back to Billy and said, "Laborers'?"

Billy was impressed. "Yeah. I'm a sandhog, but we're on strike so I'm working with Local Twenty-nine to earn my tuition money."

"I used to have a book."

"What local?"

"Eighteen A. Helped me through school too. Saint John's."

"Concrete local."

He nodded. "That's right. What's the problem?"

"Your guy won't take my money, says cash is no good here."

He looked at Kurten. "He has a thing about rules. What can I say? Take his money, John, write him a receipt. Good luck." He shook Billy's hand and disappeared into his office. Kurten did as instructed, muttering something about irregularity.

Outside, Billy did not see a cab, so he jogged back to the site purposefully, his boots slapping the hot sidewalk.

. . .

Vito left the social club and drove toward his sister's house in Bay Ridge, careful to make sure he wasn't being tailed. His sister had a strong aversion to Vito's business, and he did not wish to risk her ire by having an agent watching her house while he stopped in.

He caught the light on Fifth Avenue and tried to figure what Tuzio had meant about straightening Eliot out. In the years he had worked for Tuzio, Vito had heard his boss use that expression to order everything from paying off beat-cops to force-feeding a turncoat battery acid. The light turned green, but a sanitation truck blocked the intersection. Vito waited patiently as a cacophony of angry horn blasts shattered the tranquillity of residential Brooklyn. In all those cases, Vito knew precisely what "straighten out" had meant. But now Tuzio's mood swings and increasing instability made Vito uncertain.

The sanitation truck driver, apparently pissed off at the honking motorists, stepped out of his vehicle and made a show of inspecting for imaginary damage. When the light changed again, he jumped back in and roared off, leaving his antagonists stranded for another red. Vito shrugged. Waiting for a light was the least of his worries.

On the green, he punched the accelerator and made a hard left turn from the right lane, shot the wrong way down a narrow side street, made another left, and pulled into an empty driveway. He waited several minutes, then, certain he was not being followed, drove the half mile of Brooklyn back streets to his sister's house. He parked a block away and walked down the leafy street, trying to pin down who was cutting into his action with the Irish gang. Who had access, who would know? He felt his world closing in on him, felt Tuzio's allegiance waning, his boss's suspicions taking root.

As Vito walked along, a Con Ed truck passed him slowly, the driver eating a sandwich as he examined the tightly packed houses in search of the right address. For years, Vito had accepted the high probability of his early demise. When Angie was still alive, it sometimes worried him greatly. But now it was a fact he dealt with easily. He almost looked forward to his death, especially when, on Tuesdays, he laid flowers before her cold tombstone. He sometimes thought this made him a fool or, worse, weak. He was no psychiatrist, but he felt it took some kind of courage to face death with such aplomb. During his time in the business, he had seen many examples of how men he considered tough guys turned blubbery and wept for their mothers when faced with the Great Beyond. Then again, Vito thought, don't kid yourself. He might not be immune to hysterics when his own time came.

His ruminations were interrupted when his sister's screen door flew open and his three-year-old nephew, Anthony, moving with alarming agility and swiftness for a toddler, came tearing naked down the front steps. Before the door could snap shut, Vito's sister, bearing the excess girth conferred by six pregnancies, descended into her front yard with all the grace of a landlocked sea lion. She made for her son. Anthony stopped halfway to the street, squatted, and proceeded to shit on the sidewalk.

"You little sonofabitch!" Vito's sister grabbed the kid by the arm, hoisted him into the air, and laced his backside with her free hand, the slaps like firecrackers. "You sonofabitch," she said again.

Vito doubted his sister was aware of the acumen with which she described herself. He thought she had not noticed him, but she yelled over her shoulder, "Vito, come in," as she dragged Anthony up the steps. Vito sidestepped his nephew's statement and followed his relations into the house.

"Sit down, Vito. Let me get this animal in the tub."

Vito nodded and sat on the couch, which was encased, like the matching love seat and two chairs, in clear plastic. His sister still went big for the dago decor, Vito thought. If his parents had made more than a meager living, he was certain his mother would have had the same living room. The thick gold shag carpet on the floor, his sister had told him, set off the gold trim on the red living room set. In one corner of the room was a working fountain with a Virgin Mary rising above two angels who dispensed water from stubby penises. Vito, who had not been to church in years, would have laid five to one that the fountain was blasphemous. His sister called it artistic.

She came back to the room in a huff, a line of sweat on her brow despite the arctic blast of the central air. Vito wished he had a sweater.

"You hungry, Vito?"

He looked at her, wondering where his little sister had disappeared to. In the fifteen years of her marriage, she had gone from a slender, dark beauty with an easy smile to an obese, bitter complainer. He could picture her on *Oprah,* probably with his daughter, both of them blaming the world at large and everyone and everything in it for their troubles. Maybe there *was* something to blame for the way people turned out. Her husband, Joe, was an unlikely source. The guy was no superstar, but he ran a small teamster local out of Queens and ran it legit. Vito had never trifled with that. Joe was an easygoing guy who would give you the shirt off his back, literally. A decent working stiff. Vito, who consorted with men of all kinds who were united in a single desire to get over easy, to make a score no matter who or what they had to fuck to do so, was impressed by his brother-in-law's devotion to family and union. Still, Vito thought, maybe he's a good guy, but who knows what transpires between two people alone, out of view of the world, of family and friends.

"No, Donna, I'm fine. I'm good." Vito patted his stomach, unsure of how to proceed.

"You believe that little bastard Anthony? I tell him it's bathtime—the kid hates to bathe, for chrissake—he pulls that crap all over my goddamn sidewalk."

Vito suppressed a smile. The kid was innovative, that you had to give him. "He's a kid. They don't know, Donna."

"Oh, Vito, all due respect, you had—what?—one daughter, and Angie to carry the load too. Let's be honest here. After six, then you get to know the way these little animals think."

Vito ignored the dig at his parenting skills. He knew better than to engage his sister in this type of verbal warfare.

But her tone softened. "He knows. This one—the five others, maybe when they were his age, no—but this one. He's Satan's child, this one."

Vito was surprised to hear his sister talk in such a way about her son. Donna had been the product of a late and unexpected pregnancy. Vito was fifteen when she was born, and this was long after the doctors had assured his mother that she was unable to bear any more children. There had been complications with Vito, so Donna's conception had shocked everyone. His mother, steeped in Sicilian tribalism, had deemed her the miracle baby. From the time Donna could crawl, she was treated differently, revered by their mother and relatives, the neighbors even. She had grown up drowning in the old superstitions, handicapped by them.

Vito looked around. Some fucking miracle. He felt pity for his brother-in-law, imagined the man being ground into nothingness by his sister's unrelenting materialism.

"Coffee, Vito?"

"No. I can't stay. Donna, I need to tell you something." He stood up.

His sister must have sensed that this was not his occasional stop-and-chat. She became quiet. "Vito, tell me. What's wrong?" Concern leaning to panic. When she stopped thinking about herself, his sister was a perceptive person.

Vito held up his hand. "I need you to be calm. I might be going away soon, and I—"

"You been arrested?"

"Donna, please, siddown." Vito forced her gently to the couch. "You know what I do. This life. I might be going away. I'm arranging things so you, the kids, Angela—you'll be okay."

"Vito?" It was almost a keen.

"You'll hear from a lawyer. He's a very good friend, the best. He'll give you details. Do not—Donna, listen to me—do not trust anyone else. Do not talk to anyone else. The lawyer's name is Farelli."

His sister started to sob, and Vito felt a great love for her. Like all of us, he thought as he walked out the door, she was a creature of forces beyond her control.

Billy ordered a cheeseburger deluxe to go and waited for it at the counter. He watched the Greek owner stand and drum his fingers on the cash register. Billy had been coming to the diner since he was five and had never seen the man move more than twelve inches from the till. The only time he talked was to bark orders at his immigrant staff, which, once entirely Greek, was now fully cheaper Mexican. The place was experiencing a late-afternoon lull, just a few postal employees on break, so the owner was quiet. Billy was dirty and tired from work. His arms and neck were burned by the sun. He paid for his meal, took it to Briody's, and perched on a barstool, ordering a beer to down the food.

The news was on television, the sound turned up to accommodate the dulled senses of the pensioners who sipped idly at beers and whiskeys. Billy watched as some yuppies, all about his age, were dragged out of an office in handcuffs. They were tearful. He wondered if they would end up in Rikers; they would fare poorly in that environment.

Frankie came in and, taking the next stool, scooped up half of Billy's french fries. He shoved the handful in his mouth and spoke as he chewed. "That fucking cunt Maria."

"Yeah?"

"She's fucked up big time."

"I see it hasn't ruined your appetite." Billy moved the container to his right, away from Frankie's grasp.

"I eat a lot when I'm upset. It's like an eating disorder. You cold-hearted fuck."

"Yeah, right. Your whole life is an eating disorder. So what happened, did she go back to her own kind?"

Frankie ordered a beer, a bag of potato chips, and a pickled egg, which he popped into his mouth like a breath mint.

Billy grimaced. "I know for a fact that that egg has been sitting in that jar of piss since we made first communion."

Frankie shrugged, wiping a drop of brine off his chin with his T-shirt. "Big deal. I'm in pain, Billy. Have some sympathy." He washed down the egg with half his beer, then split the bag of chips down the middle and set it on the bar like an offering. "She went to Miami with some guy, Dominic, used to fuck her. Says they're just friends now, though."

Billy laughed. "Yeah, and the dog don't bite. What are you going to do? Swear off pussy?"

"Nah." Frankie finished his beer.

"I thought it was true love."

"Shit, you know, she says she still loves me but she's—"

"Just not in love with you," Billy finished for him.

"Yeah, is that a twat thing or what? 'Cause I ain't never heard a guy say that."

"So what are you gonna do about it?" Billy finished his cheeseburger.

"It's time for Plan B."

"What's that?"

Frankie looked at his watch. "I got a date with her kid sister at eight o'clock tonight. She's just out of high school, hates Maria. Some jealous-sister shit."

Down the end of the bar, Danny Duddy, a local drunk, awoke from a stupor, surveyed the bar through one wandering eye, and yelled, "I'll kill each and every one of you." He concluded with a noxious belch before slipping back into a restless slumber.

Billy said, "See that? It all started with a woman too."

Frankie shuddered theatrically, then dismissed Duddy with a wave. "Ain't a twat alive could do that to me."

They went to the pool table and proceeded to play eight ball. Billy was on a roll and won the first three games easily.

"What'd you step in?" Frankie asked after the third trouncing.

"Maybe my luck is changing. Comere, check this out." Billy backed away from the pool table, out of sight from the bar. He crouched and retrieved the pistol from his boot, wiped the rock dust off, and handed it to Frankie. "Paddy gave it to me. He's got a beef with Jack Tierney. Says he's behind Donelly, the drive-by, all that."

Frankie caressed the pistol. "Nice. Beretta. My old man's got the same one, I think." He handed it back to Billy. "But fucking Jack Tierney. Billy, man, that's like worse than the Mafia. You should head for the hills—that gun ain't gonna help much."

Billy slid the gun into his boot. Frankie's reaction was unnerving. Despite Paddy's visit and the gun, he had not considered Jack Tierney or his minions an imminent threat. Maybe Frankie was right. Maybe Tierney would settle a score any way he could. He suddenly felt a tightness in his chest. A fear.

They reclaimed their barstools. Billy ordered another round.

"I don't know, Billy. My cousin's a cop down there—I mean, the stories about those guys."

"All right, Frankie, you made your point," Billy snapped, trying to hide his displeasure from the bartender.

"Billy, I'm just worried for you. I mean, stories about heads chopped off, body parts—gruesome shit."

Billy heard concern in Frankie's voice and was grateful, but he knew that his friend, who had stood up for him on countless occasions, could not save him now.

"Lenny still at the picket line?"

"Nah, he left. I don't know, Billy. Lenny and them might of had their day, but it's another world now."

Billy realized that. But he knew he could still count on Lenny for sage advice. Besides, he needed to let Lenny know about Tierney's involvement. He finished his beer and left the bar, passing Danny Duddy on the way out. He begrudged the man his oblivion.

"That's right—a fucking rat." Jack Tierney punctuated this pronouncement by tossing back a glass of whiskey and slamming the empty on the table. He was holding court in the back room of the Midnight Lounge and passing on a piece of information with grave implications for the gang. Or so he wanted them to believe. He looked over the faces of the men gathered in the room. They were all here, all except Paddy Adare, that shoplifter Mickey Lawless, and Jack's brother Terry. Jack Tierney saw doubt and confusion in the eyes of those before him. He knew they would not accept easily this news that his tried-and-true right-hand man, Paddy Adare, had turned on them. Except for Bobby Riordan, the one who never questioned Jack Tierney. Jack wished he had a legion like him.

In response to their uncertain expressions, Jack said, "I got it from a guy down the courts. He's with the marshals."

The group stirred uneasily. The back room was nearly airless. Bobby O'Neil said, "You gonna take the word of some cop over Paddy? I mean, gimme a break." He laughed uneasily and looked side to side, trying to elicit some support.

Jack held his gaze. "We was in Nam together. I trust the guy like a brother. Now, this hurts me more than any of youse. I brought this guy along, made him what he is. How do you think I feel?"

No one answered Jack. He paced back and forth behind his table. "Each of you is facing twenty-five years, except maybe that degenerate shoplifter Mickey. That's a quarter-century easy on what he can say, what maybe he's said already. That's without RICO, and these are feds involved, which means RICO is most likely." Jack refilled his glass and sat down. He let his gaze pass over each of them. "Now, maybe you don't believe me. Take a look for yourselves." Jack opened a drawer in the table and, with a flourish, produced an official-looking document. He slid it across the table. "Take a look, pass it around."

He waited while the gang perused the papers in disbelief. They muttered among themselves. He knew there would still be doubt; there always would be. But as long as fear kept that doubt from turning to any action against him, he could live with it. He looked at his watch. The problem should be taken care of by now, if his brother could just do this one thing right.

He gathered the forged grand jury testimony and put it away. He stood, feeling good about things, about the reaction of the gang. Except maybe Bobby O'Neil. But Jack had a solution for him too, guy wanted to bitch and moan. Jack would seal him in a fucking oil drum full of lye. He smiled at the thought and patted O'Neil on the back. "We just gotta hang together on this, everything will pass. Everything will be okay."

Vito began to notice the little signs, subtleties that even their perpetrators were probably unaware of. When he arrived at the social club, the lummoxes sitting out front no longer gawked in awe of John Tuzio's right-hand man. Tommy Magic was around more often, and though he never blamed Vito outright for his nephew's death, a tangible threat hung between them, unconsummated only because Tuzio was not yet convinced that it was the thing to do.

Vito knew enough about Tommy Magic to know the guy did not give a crap about his dead nephew. He saw simply a golden opportunity to whack Vito and move up, a way to make more money. Because with Vito gone, Magic would certainly step up in the organization, would ascend from the ranks to become the number-two man. In fact, Vito knew Tuzio had elevated him over Tommy Magic for a reason—to keep a potential rival in check. But now Tuzio, stewing in paranoia, was closing ranks, going back to his roots, surrounding himself with a praetorian guard from his youth. He was a man totally prepared to cut his losses to save his own skin.

Vito paused outside the club. Four of the human watchdogs, dressed in those silly athletic outfits, sat idle, looking up at him. He recognized one as Tommy Magic's driver. Vito said, "Hey, you training for the Olympics?"

"Huh?" Dull stares. Horns sounded on the avenue. A siren hiccuped and was silent.

"That outfit." He pointed at the guy. "Alla you." He sprayed them with his forefinger. "You look like some fucking yam track team. Here." Vito produced a roll of bills and peeled off a twenty so crisp and new it could be used to slice mozzarella. "You're dressed for it, run down the deli and get me a sandwich—prosciutto, provolone, some olive oil." Vito made an upward motion with the bill. "Let's move it, Jesse Owens."

The driver looked at his pals, all of whom looked away. Vito might be down, but he was not out, and they knew it. The driver stood, sullen-faced, took the money, and started walking toward the deli.

"Jog, you fat fuck," Vito called after him. "Get yourself some Gatorade with the change." Vito smiled as the guy started shuffling along the avenue, like a hippopotamus evading a pack of pesky hyenas. He knew he would pay for this insult, but he no longer cared. He ducked into the club to await his meal.

Broad daylight. That was big brother Jack for you, Butcher Boy thought as he waited with the gun in his belt. Guy always wanted to make an impression, let people know they could be got anytime anywhere. He ordered another strawberry shake and kept his eye trained on the gin mill across the street. According to Jack's information, Paddy Adare would be stopping in to make a pickup sometime soon. He was to jump him, empty the pistol into him, was what Jack wanted. No room for error.

He still had a hard time believing this one, though. Jack seemed to be getting a little crazy, killing his own guys now. Butcher Boy had always liked Paddy. The guy never talked down to him or tried to make him feel stupid, like some of the other assholes in the gang. Or like Jack. Butcher Boy drank deeply of the milk shake, a nice thick one. He'd had to send the first one back three times before they thickened it up right. He'd fought the urge to shoot the fag waiter for rolling his eyes at him, making a show of being disgusted by what Butcher Boy considered a simple request. Maybe the guy would not get shot, but he sure as fuck was not getting no tip.

There was another new construction site next to the bar across the way. Butcher Boy watched a gaggle of people dressed in suits and hard hats walk around the perimeter, trying to look important. He wondered why some assholes wore a hard hat with a suit—it wasn't like they might grab a shovel and start working. He figured maybe it was to protect against the real workers dropping tools and shit off the building on them. But there wasn't even a building yet; it was just an empty lot.

He polished off his third shake and was about to order another, when he saw a black Monte Carlo pull up to the curb, Paddy Adare visible inside. Butcher Boy signaled for the waiter, caught his eye, and yelled, "Hey, fruitcake, gimme a check." Sure enough, the fag throws his arms in the air and starts bitching and moaning. He stalked over to Butcher Boy's table. "You talking to me like that, pal?" Like he fancied himself some tough-guy superhero with his big arms.

Butcher Boy wanted to do this right. "Just gimme the bill, will ya." Trying, really trying, not to get involved. He was a professional. He could not imagine Charles Bronson letting some asshole actor waiter come between him and a job. But here was Arnold Schwantzanecker, ripping his check out of the book.

"Just be lucky you're a short little dick, or I'd teach you some manners." He slapped the check on the table and stood over Butcher Boy.

Butcher Boy stiffened. He was not going to let that comment about his height piss him off. He needed to focus on the job at hand. He stood. The waiter was almost a foot taller than him. He drew his pistol and stuck it in the guy's nose. The actor backed up, his hands raised, not so tough now. Butcher Boy thought hard, trying to come up with something cool to say, something along the lines of Dirty Harry: "Feel lucky, punk?" But nothing came, so he raised the pistol and brought it down on the point where the muscleman-actor-waiter's nose met his forehead. His face split like a tomato, blood everywhere. Down he went.

Then someone screamed, they were all screaming. "Call 911! Somebody call 911!"

Butcher Boy made for the door.

Paddy turned off the ignition. Tossing a police parking permit on the dash, he stepped out of the air-conditioned Monte and slammed the door shut behind him. Another day as Jack's delivery boy, this one hot and sunny, the streets busy, kids on their way to play in the park, old ladies sitting out and reminiscing, yuppies on lunch break coming over for the cheap food on the avenue. Even a few tourists walking uncertainly, beyond the boundaries of the chamber of commerce maps.

This was to be his last stop for the day, chump change from one of Jack's bookies. It was a job they usually sent a neighborhood kid to do. He had thought long and hard about his predicament and started to believe he should sue for peace. The sandhog action complicated things. If he had stayed more involved, maybe he could have staved off the situation, convinced Jack it was not worth it. He knew he could not continue. His stomach was shot, and he was constantly looking over his shoulder, spending each night in a different place. Yet Jack refused even to acknowledge a problem. He just kept dumping shit work on him, taking digs whenever he could.

The bar was thick with the sickly-sweet smell of beer spilled and left to rot. There were three old men inside, all huddled at the end farthest from the door and the light of day, like they were afraid they might somehow spill out into the street and melt in the sunshine. Their concentration focused on the booze before them, none of them even looked up at his entrance. The shelf behind the bar was filled with bottles offering four choices: rotgut gin, vodka, sour mash, and rum, crap they made in wasted cities like Akron, Ohio, or Gary, Indiana. The dive was an alcoholic way station, the last stop before the loony bin or the street. It did nothing to brighten his dark mood. He walked down to the end of the bar, and the myopic old barman looked up at him. "I feel important somehow. You dropping by and all."

"Come on, Murph. The smell is gonna kill me, so hurry up."

"Well, next time call ahead. I'll get a crew of Guatemalans in here, make it nice for you."

Paddy held out his hand, and the old man put his racing form on the bar, leaned over, and produced an envelope. Paddy took it and slid it into his back pocket. Wasting no time with pleasantries, he made for the door and the air, fighting down bile. He pushed the door open and noticed a commotion across the way, some waiters from the trendy diner craning their necks to look up and down the street. Paddy figured someone had done the old dine and dash.

Butcher Boy ducked into a doorway two stores down, cursing the asshole waiter. He was trying to decide what to do, when he looked up at the bar. Perfect. Paddy came out and made for his car. Butcher Boy, his gun held straight out, sprinted, firing the first shot when he hit the middle of the street. People ducking, screaming, diving behind cars, light poles, each other. Butcher Boy shooting until Paddy was down, shooting until the noise was gone, shooting until he had done what Jack wanted him to do.

. . .

Paddy Adare tasted gunpowder before he heard the shots or felt the bullets. The first bullet grazed his skull and spun him around. The second caught him in the meat of the shoulder and knocked him off his feet. Three more shots were fired. One of these hit him in the leg. He landed on top of a pile of garbage bags. As darkness came over him, he realized that it was Butcher Boy who had shot him.

Billy sat at a table in the smoky afternoon quiet of a gin mill on Castle Hill Avenue. With him at the table were Lenny Coyle, Eamon Cudahy, and a man named John Brick. The man looked to Billy to be about sixty. He had white hair, greased back hard, and the type of severe Irish face that could have been carved from pink quartz. His thick glasses, the kind that made most men look stupid, did not have that effect on John Brick.

The muscular, weather-beaten arms that extended from his short-sleeved button-down shirt were laced with faded green tattoos, mementos of long-ago battles and an angry youth. His large, battered knuckles seemed to be pushed up around his wrists.

At Lenny's urging, Billy told John Brick everything he had learned from Paddy about Tierney's activities. Brick smoked Camels and listened with such intensity that he appeared to burn Billy's words into his brain. He interrupted rarely, to clarify a name, a description.

He seemed to Billy an utterly humorless man. Billy had heard of him. His name was whispered on job sites and at union meetings. He was the union enforcer. The man called in when things were beyond civil solutions.

As they got up to leave, Brick grabbed Billy by the wrist. "They tell you you look a lot like your father? He was a good man."

Billy followed Lenny and Eamon out of the bar. He felt privileged somehow.

"You're one lucky fuck, Adare."

Paddy was not pleased to see Detective Patrick Cullen. But he figured it was a small price to pay for being alive. He did not know where he was. He looked to his arm and saw the IV. He felt doped up and numb.

"I figured I'd see you in hell."

"You will. But we ain't there yet. You came close, though. The doctors are pretty amused. You always could take a punch. You get shot in the head, bullet goes around your head instead of through it. Teach me that trick, you get a chance. You take one in the shoulder, misses your jugular by a couple of inches. They're going in after that one in a while—make a nice souvenir. The third was a leg shot, clean through your calf. You can probably run the marathon tomorrow."

"How long have I been here?"

Cullen looked at his watch. "About seventy-two minutes."

"I needed a little rest. How's the nurses?"

"All big fat broads. I know better than to ask this question, but it's kind of my job. You gonna help me out here, Adare, let me know who the lousy shot is, maybe I can give him some marksmanship lessons?"

"I wish I knew. I ain't fucked any married women lately, but some guys got long memories."

"Listen. Going back a long ways, I always thought you were okay despite your friends. A call came in fifteen minutes after you got here. Alls the guy said was, and I quote, 'Don't bother fixing him up—we're just gonna kill him when he gets out.' I warned you about your friends a long time ago. I hate to tell you I told you so. No, actually I enjoy the fuck out of telling people that. When you're ready, I'd go out the back way." Cullen stood up.

He turned at the door and said, "For old times' sake, I'm leaving a uniform by the door till you get out. Your memory clears up, you know where to find me. 'Cause, you against most of those mutts, my money's on you. With Jack Tierney, I might just have to go the other way. Good luck."

After Cullen left, Paddy tried to figure out what he was going to do, but he could not focus. Instead he drifted off to a soft, deep place of bliss and no pain.

Paddy Adare awoke at 4 A.M. and for a moment forgot where he was. He had dreamed vividly: dreamed of Rosa and sun-drenched days of happiness and peace, of immortality. Now, awake and conscious of his predicament, aware of his wounds, he wanted to flee. He did not feel safe from Jack Tierney in this room. He stood, weakened by bullets and barbiturates. Woozy, he felt he would topple over, so he leaned back on the bed. The floor tiles were cold on his feet. The place smelled to him of death, the antiseptic smell of hospitals and morgues. He rested for a moment, breathing slow and deep, only vaguely aware of pain, pain he knew would spread later when the drugs were flushed from his body.

He stood again and padded on shaky legs to the closet, where he hoped his clothes would be. In the weak light from the street, he saw that only his pants and shoes were there. He grabbed them and shuffled back to the bed, where he sat down and pulled the pants on with great difficulty. He had scant use of his left arm and felt like he was working against some invisible tide that held his limbs at bay. Finally he stood and, unable to button his pants, slipped his feet into his blood-splattered sneakers. Outside, a siren raced through the neighborhood streets.

When he opened the door to his room, the light of the hallway pained his eyes, and he pulled back from it as if it were an inferno. He squinted to shield his constricting pupils and caught a glimpse of himself in a wall mirror. His head was swathed in white gauze, and his skin was drained, the color of the dead. He turned from it, preferring the flare light of the hallway to his own ghostly countenance.

A patrolman, clean-cut and uniformed, came out of his sentinel chair as if ejected. He seemed only mildly surprised that Paddy was ambulatory.

"I gotta get out." Paddy's voice sounded to him as if it were coming from a great distance.

The patrolman nodded. "The DT said you'd wanna go. It's okay—we got a car downstairs."

Paddy decided he had no choice but to trust Cullen.

"You want I should get a wheelchair or something? You don't look so hot."

Paddy shook his head no. His only chance at survival was a quick willful recovery.

The patrolman said, "Suit yourself, guy. Follow me."

Paddy forced himself along the pale-green hallway, focusing all his attention on a six-inch square of the cop's back. His calf started to ache with each step; a sharp pain ran like fire up the back of his leg when it left or met the floor. His head began to throb. He took this as a good sign. The cop led him onto a freight elevator. The doors opened on a basement garage. Two beefy detectives emerged from an unmarked car at their approach, one black and huge, dressed in slacks and an ill-fitting sport coat, the other white and nearly as big, in an Adidas T-shirt and surfer shorts, garish in the subterranean light.

The white detective stepped forward and directed Paddy to the rear of the sedan. He helped Paddy in and shut the door after him, then reclaimed his front passenger seat, saying, "Let's hit it." The black man drove.

The white detective turned and looked at Paddy. "Listen. You probably should lie flat, seein' as how you got a lot of enemies and all." Paddy took the detective's advice. He slid down on his good shoulder and tried to steady himself as the car pulled out of the garage. For the first few minutes, all Paddy heard was a series of staccato directions—left, right, left, right—and with each order the car jerked in that direction. After maybe a dozen turns, Paddy felt the car accelerate sharply; a red light began to swirl around the interior of the car, which in a matter of seconds had reached a considerable speed. The detective turned again to Paddy. "Cullen says to take you where you want to go. You got something special in mind? Maybe South America? Shanghai? I don't think we got time for that, but the tristate area is within reason."

Paddy had been thinking hard on a destination since he first awoke. His instincts initially said lake house, put some miles between himself and the island of Manhattan, but he ruled it out. Jack might not know its precise location, but he knew it existed, and Paddy doubted Barry Geller could withhold the location from Jack Tierney. He ruled out the Bronx because he had burdened his brother enough and was not certain his grandfather would provide him haven even in his present condition. He briefly considered Julius King in Brooklyn, and while he trusted the leader of New City Empowerment, Jack knew of that connection. The same could be said of Murray's Gym. Paddy decided the one place he could lie low and regroup without risking anyone else was an apartment he kept down in Alphabet City, on Avenue A.

The gang had a dozen or so safe houses scattered around the city—

places to stash guns and drugs, contraband and fugitives. Paddy had kept this one for himself, knowing that someday he might have need of it.

He pulled himself upright. "Union Square."

The cop looked at him. "You sure?"

"Yeah, I'm sure."

Paddy did not want them to know where he was going. He'd call Cullen and thank him, but while he realized the cop wanted Tierney badly, Paddy had something else entirely in mind for him.

The detectives exchanged looks, but they dropped him off across from the park. The predawn air was surprisingly chill. Paddy limped to the corner and hailed a cab. The driver surveyed him warily before stopping in the middle of the street. Paddy got in and winced. The drugs were fading, the pain rising, coming on strong now. He gave the man the address.

As they pulled up to the building, light was spreading in the east, the black sky dissolving to color like ink bleeding from the page. Paddy paid the cabbie and stood in the doorway, fumbling for the right key. The door opened from within, and Paddy was relieved to see Mario, the superintendent, regarding him with concern.

"What hap?"

"Car crash."

"I see. Want help?"

Paddy accepted gladly; the five flights of stairs had loomed as insurmountable. He took Mario's arm, the old man surprisingly strong, and they ascended together, pausing on each landing so Paddy could gather strength.

Billy picked a shady spot for lunch. His back against the fence, he stretched out his legs. Since meeting with John Brick, he had felt a palpable sense of relief: things were going to sort themselves out. He had even considered leaving the gun at home that morning. Balancing a sandwich on his lap, he flipped through the *Daily News*. He almost passed right by the article. Roberts had come over and sat next to him, and Billy absently turned the page. After Roberts settled in, Billy turned back, and the headline stopped him cold: HELL'S KITCHEN GANG SHOOTING. Billy saw his brother's name on line three and raced through the article. He could not believe it. He flipped the paper over to look at the date. He thought maybe it was a joke. He stood.

Roberts was saying something, but the words echoed away from him. Billy dropped the paper, went over to the trailer, grabbed his dungaree jacket. He yelled to Roberts, "I gotta go." Roberts sensed something was wrong and started to move to him, a question on his face. Billy ran toward Broadway. Roberts could only watch him disappear up the hill.

The hospital staff assured Billy his brother was alive and had checked out. As he walked to the Midnight Lounge, a calm came over him. He felt sharp, lucid. He had purpose. All those things he longed for and aspired to—the degrees and the comfort, the social ascendancy, the good life—fell away from him like false promises to a lover. He was almost giddy with the pureness of blind devotion to his brother. He stalked down the avenue, aware only of the warm gun metal in his hand and the desire to save Paddy.

He gripped the pistol in his jacket pocket and wove his way through the crowded summer streets of Hell's Kitchen. He fell in behind three Asian men who strolled as if they had no destination at all. He went to pass them and collided with a middle-aged man who was dressed far too warmly for the summer day. The man pulled back angrily and said, "You better watch yourself, kid."

Billy smiled. He knew this was something he had to do. He walked on, and when he came to the Midnight Lounge, he squared himself with the door and pulled the pistol out of his pocket. He entered the bar and raised the gun like a threat before him. The half-dozen patrons looked up with alarm. Billy, backlit and as of yet faceless from their perspective, demanded the whereabouts of his brother. No one moved. No one spoke. The bartender's eyes jumped, scared, between Billy and the back door. Billy, his pistol trained now on the bartender, moved for the back room.

His calm was going fast. His gun hand started to shake. What was behind that door? Was Paddy there? Was it death? He was five feet from the back room when the front door opened and the sounds of the street rushed in. Billy turned only his head, to look behind him. His body was still committed forward. He recognized Mickey Lawless.

"Billy! No!" Mickey closed the distance between them and took Billy's arm, lowering the gun. "Let's get the fuck out of here. Paddy ain't here."

Billy did not resist. He let Mickey lead him out of the bar. On the street, Mickey pushed him toward a waiting car.

Back inside the bar, Jack Tierney, holding a .357 in one hand and a half-eaten slice of pizza in the other, emerged from his sanctuary. He raised an eyebrow at the bartender.

"The kid, Adare's brother, it looked like."

"The college kid?"

"Yeah."

Tierney considered this in silence for a moment. "What, he come down here to gimme his lunch money?" When no one answered him, he said, "Buy the house a round," and returned to his room.

Federal Agent Mary Moy, seven months pregnant and just a few weeks away from her maternity leave, was shocked and concerned by Vito Romero's phone call. She suspected the worst, although he had not been very forthcoming. Having decided to meet him without notifying her office, as he had requested, she pulled to the corner of Seventy-fifth and Broadway and watched as Vito emerged from a bagel shop, carrying a briefcase. Moving toward her car, he looked remarkably composed.

She reached over and unlocked the door to her family sedan. Vito slid in.

"Let's drive. It's a nice day for a drive, no?"

Mary Moy nodded, and they pulled out into traffic, headed uptown. Mary took the Henry Hudson Parkway, the Hudson River calm and glasslike on their left. They crossed the George Washington Bridge and drove north through the late-summer lushness. When they neared New Jersey's state line, Vito pointed out an exit labeled Scenic Lookout.

Mary parked alongside a picnic area. They sat at a stone table facing the Hudson Valley. The air was clear; great birds rose and swirled above them. Sightseers and young couples walking hand in hand took in the vista. To the south, New York City lay harmless.

"I always loved it up here. Me and Angie used to come up here when we were young. We'd look out over the city and talk about our dreams—things we were gonna do, places we were gonna see." He turned to Mary. "I appreciate you coming, all you've done. I want you to have this." Vito put the briefcase in front of her on the table. "In it you'll find enough to remove John Tuzio and others from the streets, put them away forever. It will go a long way toward making you a legend in your, ah, field of endeavor, Agent."

"Why?" It was all she could manage.

Vito shrugged. "I don't know. There comes a time when a man has to rise to the occasion. I read that somewhere once; I can't remember where, but I like the sound of it. When a man's gotta look back over his life, he's gotta look at the big picture, Mary, figure what he wants to leave behind. I done a lot of things, lived a life I wasn't always proud of." Vito paused to watch a girl ride by on a bicycle. "Maybe I want—well, I know there ain't no going back, so maybe if I can make a small amends, maybe that's all I can do at this point. It just feels right."

The girl came past again, her hair golden in the summer sun.

"Now promise me—and I need this—you'll wait on this till I'm gone."

"You going somewhere?"

"Don't be naive."

"Vito, it doesn't have to be this way."

"That's where you're wrong, Mary. You come from a different place, Agent. Please keep that in mind."

"Your daughter."

Vito was quiet for a minute. "Let's be honest with ourselves. It's something I'm trying to do lately, hard as it is. She'll be better off. Maybe you could look in on her occasionally. She'll be staying with my sister." Vito stood and walked to the edge of the palisade. He looked over the valley and raised his arms as if he were about to explode into a graceful final swan dive. Lowering them, he turned back to Mary Moy. She watched him approach and wished there were something she could do to change his mind. But he was right. She was from a different place.

On the drive back, he was expansive. It was as if he relished his predicament, had made his peace. She dropped him off in Manhattan, and as he walked away she felt certain she would miss him. She drove off, trying to keep her feelings in check.

For four days, Paddy Adare did not leave the apartment on Avenue A. By the fourth day, the pain no longer sickened him, and he actually slept through the night. Mario's wife, Antonia, had made the trip up the five flights several times a day. She brought him thick vegetable soups she made in her kitchen, soups that seemed to breathe strength into him; she brought fresh bread and dark wine, ripe fruits, these foods like medicine. Antonia spoke little English, and as she dressed his wounds with the sureness of a medic, she spoke softly to herself in Italian. He realized that she was praying over him.

On the fifth day, she brought him a burning mug of syrupy coffee and an old wooden cane. After he finished the coffee, she handed him the cane and nodded toward the windows and the street. He dressed with her help and made his way down the stairs to the daylight.

The day was warm, the streets were surprisingly still. A few stout young Latino mothers pushed baby strollers, and a gaggle of pale, sickly punks in black, earrings and nose rings in abundance, made their way up the street. He limped toward Tompkins Square Park, his calf stronger than he had expected. He was lucky to have Antonia and Mario. At first he had wondered what prompted their sympathy, then he remembered how, a couple of years before, when he first rented the place, he had helped arrange a transfer from an upstate prison to one just outside the city for one of their sons, who was dying of cancer. The move saved them the brutal journey to the Canadian border. It was a simple favor that Paddy had forgotten until he noticed the holy card she carried for the kid. He marveled at that small token returning to possibly save his life. It gave him hope.

In the park, there was much more activity. He sat on a bench and watched a group of neighborhood kids play street hockey, their shouts and exertions bringing back his own playground days. He thought of the time after he was done with fighting and headed west. Sitting on the beach in California, watching the sun drop slowly into the Pacific, he had felt promise, thought maybe he could make a life there. The promise quickly faded. The place was full of two-bit hustlers and wannabe stars. Everyone was playing an angle. But behind shellacked smiles was a sickening desperation. Hell's Kitchen, with all its insanity, suddenly seemed stable, a base where you knew what people were about, what their motives were. As he sat now, his wounds healing, he wished he had stayed in California. You can never be betrayed by someone you don't trust.

He would build his strength. And then he would settle things with

Jack Tierney. He leaned his head back on the bench and soaked up the bright sun.

Vito Romero, confident that his affairs were in order, that those he loved would be cared for, went, as always on Tuesday, to his wife's grave. Dressed in a conservative black suit, his hair newly trimmed, he bore fresh-cut flowers. As he strode along the pathway past the rows of tombstones, he ignored the inscriptions chiseled in the cold stone. In past visits he would calculate the ages of the dead, seeking lives shorter than that lived by his wife. He knew it to be a petty thing, covetous even, yet it served to ease his heartache, to soften the cruelty of his loss.

He left the path when he reached the gnarled old oak that served as a signpost to his wife's row. The cut blades of grass clung to his shoes as he walked on. He thought it strange that the newly dead grass smelled so lush, so alive. The day had turned somber, the morning sun yielding to thick clouds, the sky now several shades of gray, like gunships on a darkening sea. Coming upon his wife's resting place, he read, for the thousandth time, "Angela Romero, 1938–1982, Beloved Wife, Beloved Mother."

Bobby Riordan looked up as the Italian guy said, "There." He was pointing at a man Riordan knew to be Vito Romero. Riordan said, "Okay," and took out his gun. The man drove closer, and Riordan emerged from the car. His left hand held a bunch of flowers they had bought at a bodega in the city. The cheap, scentless flowers provided camouflage for the pistol in his other hand.

"Angie." Vito said her name aloud, as if his dead wife were listening. He bent and placed the flowers gently before her grave. Standing up, he heard a car approach, crunching on the gravel, sensed its engine throbbing as it idled along. He did not turn. Instead he focused on a huge black bird—a crow, he imagined—that had lighted on a mausoleum several rows farther on, a thick warbling coming from its chest. He considered it a portent, a hard one at that. Feeling someone's approach, he made the sign of the cross and began to pray. It was a simple prayer from his boyhood in Saint Anthony's parish in Brooklyn, from the days when he ran through those streets dreaming of one day being another Joe DiMaggio, when he was a boy who could not have foretold the man he was now. He offered up the prayer and closed his eyes. He asked only for forgiveness. He considered kneeling, but no. For this, he would stand.

The bullet knocked him forward, and he fell, draped over his wife's tombstone. He slid down to the ground, his blood bright on the dark granite. Although the first bullet killed him, he was struck three more times.

Bobby Riordan dropped his flowers and made tracks for the car, not quite running, but walking so fast he was in danger of falling forward. Cemeteries gave him the creeps.

With one phone call to his old friend Julius King, Paddy Adair induced chaos on construction sites controlled by Jack Tierney. Busloads of supposed coalition members descended on the West Side from Brooklyn and the Bronx. They carried placards and chanted, blocked streets and shut down millions of dollars' worth of construction work. Tempers flared, blows were exchanged. Angry hard hats pelted the protesters with wood and chunks of concrete. On one of the sites there was gunplay, a bystander was grazed. Police responded with riot gear, mounted units, and tear gas. Arrests were made. The story led the evening news, and the tabloids readied sensational headlines.

Jack Tierney was not amused. He watched from the back room of the Midnight Lounge. The reception on his fuzzy, battered twelve-inch black-and-white television may have been poor, but Jack Tierney understood very clearly. He knew who was behind the assault on his domain. He also knew it was time to act with finality. He called Bobby Riordan into the room.

"Get Terry. I got something needs to be done."

Paddy surveyed the block from Eliot's front porch. Sturdy old houses that seemed to hold the secrets of privilege, thick trees, sleek expensive cars, circular driveways. He imagined smart, bright-eyed kids and trust funds. It was the kind of place where bad things are never allowed to be seen in the light of day. He rang the bell and heard it echo throughout the house. After a minute, a woman dressed in a French maid's outfit opened the door and gave him a curious look.

"Are you here for the party?"

Paddy pushed past her. "Business. I'm here on business. Be a sweetheart and get Eliot for me." The woman started to protest, but she saw his eyes and turned to the back of the house. Paddy followed her as far as the kitchen. He watched from the window. Eliot, standing on the lush back lawn, halfway between the tennis courts and the swimming pool, was entertaining a party of men and women who could have passed as relations. They were tan and mostly thin. He finished a story, and his listeners pulled their heads back and roared with laughter. Paddy had no time to waste. He banged the screen door, and the crowd turned. A shadow passed briefly over Eliot's face, but he caught himself before his guests could sense anything was amiss. The maid whispered something to him. He excused himself and made his way over to the door, which Paddy opened for him.

"Paddy, this is quite a surprise." Eliot was going for light and breezy, but Paddy could feel the tension in him. Good. He had him off guard, vulnerable. He'd comply; Paddy was going to make sure of that.

"Office?"

"This way." Eliot indicated the interior of the house with his tanned left hand. "Drink? Maybe a bite to eat?"

Paddy shook his head no and urged Eliot forward with a hand to his back. They went down a long hallway, passing several rooms on each side. Pictures—landscape scenes, country fields suffused in soft, friendly light—lined the walls. Paddy thought they might have been painted nearby. At the end of the hallway was a closed door. Eliot entered and Paddy followed. He shut the door behind them and pulled down all the shades. He pointed to a seat in front of a computer table. "Sit." He took out a pistol, a Glock 9-millimeter, and said, "We need to do some business. I know you know by now the problems I got. You got two choices. You do what I want, or I leave you dead on the floor here. Understand?"

Eliot said yes, the word barely audible. Beads of sweat appeared on his forehead.

"You wanted to get yourself involved. Now you pay the price. What's in that Cayman account?"

Eliot turned to the keyboard. He spent several moments punching keys. He motioned Paddy to take a look.

"Tell me."

"Four hundred twenty thousand dollars."

"Here." Paddy handed him a piece of paper. "Break it up even and wire it into these banks. Half to each one. Leave the twenty grand in there. That will piss him off even more. No—on second thought, fuck him."

After a few minutes, Eliot turned to him. "Done."

"All right, let's go."

"What?"

"We're gonna go get it. Come on." Paddy grabbed him by the collar and pulled him from the seat. "You do the right thing, you won't have Jack to worry about."

"I've guests—I can't just . . ." Eliot was pointing back through the walls, indicating his gathering.

"Let your wife handle that. And just keep in mind one thing—I'm the one with nothing to lose."

Paddy waited for Eliot by the front door. He had exchanged his polo shirt for a white button-down and a tie. He was visibly nervous. Paddy opened the door and indicated his Monte Carlo. "You know, you better calm the fuck down. These bank people might get suspicious." He got behind the wheel and said, "Chuckie, you should have figured out you wasn't such a tough guy before you decided to be moneyman for the bad guys." Eliot nodded. He seemed to have lost his color.

They drove away from Eliot's house, down a broad shaded street. Paddy maneuvered the car to the business district of the village. The buildings were of red brick; there were no large signs. Everything was understated. All the people visible were white and bore a look of casual affluence. They brought to Paddy's mind one of the fashion catalogs Rosa used to leaf through.

He pulled to the curb a few car lengths from the first bank. Eliot had begun to tremble. Paddy reached over and slapped his face. "Get your fucking act together. Take a quick trip to Paris. Visit your kids.

Before you get back, Jack will be finished, one way or the other. Now don't piss me off. Let's go."

The procedure was the same in both banks. The branch managers knew Eliot well. They were escorted to a secure back room, where the money, in crisp hundred-dollar bills, was counted out and placed in the bag Paddy was carrying. He was surprised at how little space the money took up. Eliot introduced him simply as a client, and no one raised any questions. Paddy dropped Eliot off at home and drove away. The weasel was probably already on the phone to Jack. He'd make the call, then, with his wife, head for the airport. It was just what Paddy wanted. Jack in a fury, acting rashly. He was almost starting to enjoy himself again.

Mickey Lawless entered the bar and sat, his back to the wall, eyes trained on the front door, while aware of the open back exit, down past the bathrooms. An escape if needed. He ordered a beer and tried to sort things out. Since Paddy's shooting, Mickey had been on edge, uncertain as to how it would impact on him.

He grabbed the cold bottle of Bud and drank. The bar was empty and cool, the air-conditioning going full blast. The barman nodded, leaving Mickey's twenty on the bar. Mickey believed he should run, head for safety in obscurity. He had never been in Jack's good graces, was a bit player on the fringes of Jack's criminal enterprises, close with Paddy only. Now that Paddy was on the outs, hunted by Jack and his goons, Mickey knew he was on shaky ground indeed.

Problem was, he really had no idea where to go. Besides doing time upstate, he had been to the Jersey shore a few times and the Poconos once, period. And to make it worse, he was short on cash for now, and his only hope for fast money was the score he had planned for the next week, a score he could not move up. He had five days to kill. He would lie low, score, then flee, maybe go through a travel agent. Somewhere sunny, with hula girls, suntan oil, piña coladas poolside—what he understood the good life to be.

He ordered another Bud and paid little attention when the bartender made a phone call down at the other end of the bar. The alcohol began to soothe him. He decided he would stay with his sister in Woodside, play with his nieces and nephew. He'd stop on the way out and buy them some toys.

Halfway through his third beer he watched as the bartender turned from the window and, with the remote control pointed at the TV, made the sound unbearably loud. Mickey raised his head to complain and gasped as he saw Bobby Riordan enter the bar and make his way toward him. He pivoted on his stool, poised for flight, knowing he could outrun the lumbering Riordan, but he turned right into Butcher Boy's twisted, grinning face. Trapped, he struggled to maintain himself, but failed. He began to sob.

Jack Tierney strode to the black sedan parked in the abandoned railyard and said to his brother, "Open it."

Butcher Boy obliged, and as the trunk of the stolen Mercury popped open, he stepped back and smiled, like a cat that had just deposited a wounded, flightless bird at its master's feet.

"What he say?" Jack looked dispassionately at Mickey Lawless, who was hogtied and gagged, his eyes wide with pain and terror, his face beaten beyond repair. Jack took notice of the angry cigarette burns along his arms, neck, and face. They had been thorough, of that he could be certain.

It was Bobby Riordan who answered. "He don't know much of nothing, you ask me, Jack." Riordan looked away from the trunk. Cars and trucks rumbled past on what was left of the old West Side Highway.

Jack leaned over and placed his hands on the lip of the trunk. He spoke as he might to a lover, his voice low and reassuring, the substance of his words at odds with the tone. "We'd get prisoners in Nam, gooks out in the field. When we were done with them, we'd tie them like this, leave the rope between their necks and feet. You know what happens when they can't hold their feet up? Hah, Mickey? They choke to death. That's what. Oh, sometimes it took a day, sometimes a week. You fucking shoplifter." Jack turned to his brother and Riordan. "Take him over to Newark, put him in long-term parking. I want this fuck to die slow."

Riordan made an uncertain face. "Jack, what if—you know—he kicks, makes noise or something? I mean, maybe we should put him someplace else."

Jack fought down his anger. "You got any bright ideas, genius?" He had no one else to depend on now. There were only his psychotic brother, who was being hounded by the police, and Riordan, perhaps the dumbest man he had ever known. Still, Jack had always been at his best when things looked bleakest. He thought about the time in Nam when his patrol was ambushed. Out of six men, three were killed instantly. He was not harmed. His other two men were badly maimed. One with a sucking chest wound. It was plain that they would not survive. He slit both their throats to save them from being tortured to death by the VC. He then crawled on his belly through the rank jungle night to safety.

Riordan, his brow wrinkled, kicked some gravel around, staring at his feet, his brow wrinkled, as if trying to find some solution there. "I was thinking—"

Jack cut him off. "That's fucking great. *You* was thinking, huh, Bobby? You're a fucking drone, Bobby, and drones don't think, they just do what the fuck they're told." Jack reached forward and yanked a pistol from Riordan's belt. He turned and fired two quick shots into Mickey Lawless, wiped the pistol down with his shirt, and dropped it at Riordan's feet. "Now take this piece of shit to long-term parking. And hurry the fuck up, so you're back in time for that other thing."

At two forty-five, the foreman shut down the generator. The day's work was done. The drill runners let the air out of their lines, broke down their equipment, and rolled up the air hoses. By three o'clock they had loaded the trucks. Billy walked up the hill toward Broadway, tired and dusty from a day of breaking rocks in the summer heat. As he neared the elevated line, he noticed a dark-blue Chevy parked alongside the McDonald's. The three white guys who sat inside were as conspicuous in West Harlem as midwestern tourists. Billy felt the pistol in his boot, its presence reassuring.

He slowed down and looked around. There were not too many places to run to, and he doubted his plight would arouse sympathy in any of the neighborhood residents. He wondered if they were cops. He stopped and could feel a line of sweat trickle down his side. It felt like ice water. The car doors opened, and all three guys got out and started toward him, the driver calling out, "Hey, Billy, comere a second. Paddy wants to see you." Now he knew they were not cops.

He started to back away, looking quickly to his left, then his right. They were thirty feet from him and moving in. The driver turned back to the car, and Billy dropped his hard hat and ran toward the river, the men shouting after him. He heard the car screech and the doors open and close. Billy cut left and sprinted up a side street, toward two five-story tenements. He ran to the rear of the buildings, saw a fence closing off the alley between them. Billy scaled the fence as the car pulled to the curb ten feet away. He dropped down the other side and ran through the back door of the building. Stopping for a moment to let his eyes adjust to the darkness, he saw he was in a basement laundry room. A woman stared at him as she folded a sheet. Two kids sat on the floor, playing with a toy fire truck. Billy nodded at the woman. "Stairs?"

She pointed with her head back over her shoulder. "Through that door."

"Thanks." Billy pushed through the door and hurried up the stairs. He came out into the lobby. Three residents were checking their mail. Billy ran past them into the bright light of the street. His legs were heavy, and his lungs burned with the rock dust he had been sucking all day. To his left, neighborhood women stared at him from their lawn chairs. He saw the car coming down the hill from his right. As he turned to go back into the building, the car door opened and one of the guys came lunging at him. Billy sidestepped him and shoved. The guy was off balance and landed hard on his hands and knees, cursing.

Billy heard the Chevy race toward him. He ran down the block, into the side door of the McDonald's, shoving people out of the way. He yelled, "Call the cops!" and crashed through the front door, running for the el. The downtown train was screeching into the station. Up the stairs three at a time, he hurdled the turnstile. The token clerk yelled, "Pay your fare!" and banged on the bulletproof glass. Billy fought his way up another staircase through the tide of detraining passengers, who cursed him as he ascended. He hit the platform as the doors closed. Billy ran alongside the accelerating train, slapping the windows and screaming. He ran to the end of the platform and bent over, hands on his knees, gasping for air. The train roared away, leaving him alone on the platform. But not for long.

He stood straight and turned. Two of his pursuers were on the platform now, walking toward him. No longer in a hurry, they were actually smiling as they closed the distance. Both held pistols at their sides. Another train glinted far uptown, like a false promise on the horizon. Billy looked over the railing to the street. It was too high to jump, and the blue Chevy sat patiently below. The driver looked up at him from the window and pointed his finger like a gun, grinning. Billy was glad everyone was having such a good time. He gave the guy the finger, then turned and jumped onto the tracks and scurried to the uptown platform, carefully avoiding the third rail. He pulled himself onto the deck and turned to see the two guys cursing and lowering themselves awkwardly to the tracks. He bolted into the station, through the turnstile, and down the stairs.

At the bottom, he turned right into the driver, who punched him hard in the face. Stunned, Billy fell into a sitting position on the street. Stationary objects danced in his vision. He heard laughter and curses. They dragged him to the car and threw him into the back seat.

As they pulled away from the curb, the guy sitting to Billy's right punched him hard in the ribs. Billy doubled over and felt a blow to his spine.

"That was a real pain in the ass," said the driver. They were all still breathing heavily. "What are you, some kind of fucking track star?"

Billy, dazed, could feel panic coming over him. He tried to tell himself that if they were going to kill him he would be lying under the el. This gave him little solace. He looked out the windows as they drove down Broadway past Columbia University. It was a bright, sunny day—the kind of day for kids and lovers. The sidewalks were teeming with pedestrians. Billy tried to settle down and focus. Come up with some plan. One of his abductors was wearing a syrupy cologne. It was hot in the car, the windows rolled up.

The man to his left shifted uncomfortably. "Turn on the AC at least, will ya? I'm suffocating."

"It's on full blast. I guess I need Freon."

"Yeah, you guess." He elbowed Billy. "We crack these windows, you scream, I'll dump your body right here, fucko."

Billy nodded, thinking he would scream his head off at the first stoplight. He watched a group of college kids walking up Broadway, laughing. They looked full of promise and privilege, and Billy felt that world, which he had moved in briefly, falling away from him. He was suddenly aware of the pistol in his boot; it felt like a branding iron on his leg. An eerie calm came over him. He knew what he had to do. He leaned back against his seat and waited.

At Ninety-sixth Street, the driver turned right, and Billy realized he had to act before they hit the West Side Highway. The light ahead turned red, and the car slowed. Billy bent over and said, "I think I'm gonna be sick," and retched. His guards pulled back away from him. Billy grabbed the pistol and cleared it on the way up. The driver looked in the rearview mirror just in time to see Billy raise the gun. The driver jerked his head away as Billy squeezed off the shot. The report was deafening, as the bullet tore through the driver's cheek, taking out three of his teeth, before it cracked the windshield and dropped on the dashboard. Cordite and warm blood mist hung in the air. Billy turned the pistol to his left but was punched into unconsciousness before he could fire a second time.

The driver stared at the bullet and moved his tongue around in his mouth. He looked lost. "He shot me," he said to no one in particular. Bobby Riordan leaned over and looked at the wound.

"Yeah, no shit. You talk, you can drive. Let's get the fuck out of here."

A week after being ambushed, Paddy Adare sat in his apartment on Avenue A and cleaned his pistols. Only his shoulder wound still troubled him. He did not have full range of movement but was confident that it would not prevent him from carrying out his mission. Disassembling his Glock 9-millimeter, he cleaned it, and snapped it together. He strapped an ankle holster to his leg and slid a .32-caliber Beretta into it, then lowered his pant leg. He stood, rolling his hurt shoulder—the left, luckily. Unless he got into a serious hand-to-hand struggle, it would serve him fine.

He walked to the window and looked out over the tenements across the way. The sky was darkening. Music from the neighborhood bodega blared into the twilight. Paddy switched off the air conditioner, pulled on a lightweight jacket, and left the apartment.

On the street, he felt good, alert. He would go to the diner, eat a nice meal, and relax. Then, in the dead of the night, he would pay a visit to his old friend Butcher Boy.

He walked toward Tompkins Square Park. The streets were filled with punk-rock types, an urban sideshow, kids from the Midwest and New England who, mad at their parents, hung around the East Village for a summer before going home to front lawns and stability.

It was a pleasant evening. A perfect night for payback.

. . .

"Where's Paddy?"

"I don't know."

"No?"

"No."

"He's your brother, you don't know?"

Billy looked up and saw that Riordan held a butane blowtorch. It came to him that this was the worst thing he had ever looked upon. Riordan lit it and smiled. The torch came alive with a whoosh. Billy smelled the burning gas and wanted to vomit, but there was nothing left inside him. The blowtorch seemed to burn all the oxygen around him. His breaths were short and pained. Riordan raked the flame across his face. Billy screamed. He smelled burned hair, flesh.

"Where is he?"

"I . . . don't know." Billy wept. He was beyond all caring.

Riordan waved the torch in front of Billy's face again and laughed. Billy pulled away. Riordan let his arm drop casually to his side. The flame burned the back of Billy's hand, seared him to the bone. He yelled and jumped in his seat. Tears ran down his face. Jack Tierney stepped forward and punched him in the nose. Billy felt a tendon rip in his neck, and his head went numb. Through the pain, he knew with great shame that he would have told them his brother's whereabouts if he could.

Paddy stood across from Butcher Boy's apartment in the dark hour before dawn. The block was empty and quiet, save for the buzz of the streetlights. Paddy had been there two hours before, when Butcher Boy, fresh from a bout of power drinking at the Midnight Lounge, staggered up the block and disappeared into his tenement after twice dropping the front door key.

Paddy looked the length of the block once more, then, with his baseball hat pulled low over his eyes, walked down to Tenth Avenue and let himself into one of the buildings with a jimmy bar. He ascended to the top floor, treading as lightly as possible. Pausing at the bottom of the roof stairs to catch his breath, he shifted the pistol in his waistband, pulled out a pair of thin gloves, and put them on.

He climbed the last flight and saw the emergency bar across the door, its sign proclaiming that an alarm would sound when it was opened. Paddy cursed softly. Deciding to chance it, he pushed at the door and closed his eyes, expecting a siren to signal the neighborhood that someone was up to no good. There was only silence and the rush of air.

Stepping quickly onto the roof, he let the door close most of the way, then inserted a chunk of wood to block the door from clicking shut. He turned and crab-walked across the roof to the edge. The buildings were connected, so he simply stepped over the two-foot rim separating the buildings. Several blocks away, a tugboat horn sounded mournfully on the river. He made his way to the rooftop directly adjacent to Butcher Boy's. It was littered with empty beer cans, and several crack vials sparkled in the weak city light.

Paddy took the pistol out and attached the silencer, then cleared the gun, putting a round in the chamber. He crossed to Butcher Boy's building and, holding the pistol, leaned over the edge of the roof to locate the fire escape. The pistol he put down the back of his pants, the waistband holding it snug. He lay down, parallel to the edge of the roof, then swung his legs over the fire escape and, putting most of his weight on his healthy right arm, lowered himself till the arm could not hold him and let himself drop. He landed with his weight too far back and fell against the fire escape railing. Scrambling to right himself, he kicked a plant off the landing. He gritted his teeth as the clay pot hit bottom with a crash. A dog several floors below started barking.

Paddy moved quickly down the one flight and pressed himself against the wall between the two windows to Butcher Boy's apartment. On his right was the kitchen, on his left the back bedroom, where Paddy assumed his target was sleeping. Sliding the pistol out, he held it, barrel up, by his ear, and waited, trying not to breathe. The dog stopped barking.

Paddy listened hard for sounds from the apartment. A blue television glow emanated from the bedroom window, but he heard no sound of late-night TV dribble. The sound was probably turned off. He thought he heard someone breathing, the deep breaths of slumber, but maybe his mind was just playing tricks on him. The sky was just beginning to lose some of its blackness. He had to get the job done.

He dropped to his right knee and turned, peering into the kitchen window. Only shapes were visible, everything blurred by night. The window was open six inches, a closed screen before it. He put his ear to the screen and listened. Nothing.

Paddy pulled back and took a deep breath, then, transferring the pistol to his left hand, with his right he reached over and forced the screen upward. He stopped and listened again. Still silence.

After a minute, he opened the window and ducked into the kitchen. The gun before him, he lay flat for a moment on the kitchen floor, so as not to be outlined in the window. When no one stirred, he rose to a crouch and made his way to the door and swung into the hallway, staying low. The apartment smelled of ammonia, of hard cleanliness. Pausing against the wall, Paddy felt his heart pound in his chest. He could hear Butcher Boy snoring, and he padded toward the sound. It led him to the living room, and there, flat on his back, one arm hanging off the couch, Butcher Boy, fully clothed, twitched in a deep slumber.

Paddy watched for a moment, almost feeling sad for him. The guy had been cursed from birth, but Paddy pushed that aside. He wanted to kill Butcher Boy, wanted him to die. And he wanted him to know he was going to die. He stepped forward and kicked the sleeping man hard in the side, then moved back, pistol aimed for the kill shot.

Butcher Boy jerked awake and sat up. "Who's there?"

"It ain't your mama, Terry."

"Paddy?"

Paddy fired three shots to Butcher Boy's head, the *thwump, thwump, thwump* of the silenced explosions sounding unexpectedly loud in the tidy apartment. But he knew that to be an illusion. He stepped close and examined the gore, then, pressing the muzzle to Butcher Boy's perforated skull, fired twice more for certainty.

Billy came to and immediately wished he could escape back into the comfort of dreams. He was facedown on a concrete floor, his hands and feet bound, duct tape over his mouth. The room was dark and hot. It smelled of piss and mildew, of things furtive. He was aware of intense pain, pain that took a few moments to sort out, to specify. He distinguished the various hurts one at a time: his jaw ached badly, he assumed it was fractured; the left side of his ribs burned; his left hand was scorched, swollen and numb; his testicles felt pulverized; there were a dozen other pains, places where blows had found their mark. He tried to roll over but failed to gather enough strength.

He sensed he was alone in this place. He had no idea how long it had been since he was grabbed off the street. He struggled to fight off despair. The separate hurts began to blend again, his consciousness reduced to a world of hurt.

Mary Moy worked with a team of prosecutors as they readied a series of arrests. Romero's information had proved a gold mine. Connections that were only suspected were verified. Rumors translated to hard facts. A case built on innuendo became something solid. Besides the tapes, there were financial records with sweeping implications. The list of suspects was impressive. The first arrests would include John Tuzio, Charles Eliot, and Joe Harkness. A big media event was planned. There would be no polite surrenders at FBI headquarters.

When she finished with the prosecutors, Mary Moy returned to her office. She typed her report on Vito Romero. Then she went over to her shelf and pulled down a Nynex yellow pages and flipped until she found a local florist. She sent flowers to the funeral home in Brooklyn where Vito was being laid out.

The salesman asked, "Who do you want it to be from?"

Mary Moy said, "From a friend." She hung up, wishing there were more she could do. No one close to her had ever died before. Even her grandparents were still all alive. Then again, she had never been close to anyone who had come from as hard a place as Vito Romero. She felt the sting of loss, confusion. Mary felt that she had truly lost a friend. She left the office and went home for some rest. The next few days promised to be frenzied.

Paddy went back to Avenue A and slept an untroubled eight hours, waking up just after noon. He rolled out of bed, his shoulder stiff from the night's endeavors. He stood naked and grabbed a towel. In the shower, as he ran down the previous night's work, his conscience was clear, his will strong. The only thing that stood between him and freedom from Jack's tyranny was one more killing. This one he would relish.

He toweled off and dressed, dungarees and a T-shirt. After a series of stretches, to coax more mobility from his injured arm, he picked up the phone. He rang his machine and listened to a week's worth of messages as he paced the living room. Hearing Jack's voice, he stopped. "Scumbag, don't expect any help from your petty-thief buddy. Let's just say he's had an accident." Paddy squeezed the receiver till his hand ached. Jack laughed. "Oh, yeah, you punchy fuck, somebody here wants to say hello." He heard Jack say, "Drag him here." Shuffling noises, a groan, and then a hoarse whisper. "Paddy?"

Paddy was stunned. It was Billy.

"Yeah, a family affair. I'm gonna introduce him to Terry. It's too bad, but one of you is a dead man—you or the college kid. The choice is yours. Think about it. You know where to find me, asshole. Bring my fucking money." The laugh. The machine went off. Paddy slumped down in a chair and dropped the phone.

Jack let himself into his brother's apartment and immediately smelled death. Holding up his hand to silence Bobby Riordan, he drew his pistol. He moved stealthily toward the living room, though he knew it was too late for caution. As he came into the room, he saw his brother, half lying, half sitting, his skull ruined, blood thick on him. Jack let out a sound somewhere between anguish and rage. He moved to his brother, bent, and cradled his head. Then he stood and turned to Riordan, his voice even. "Call the cops, get this cleaned up. Meet me back at the bar as fast as you fucking can."

"Jack, I don't wanna—"

"Shut the fuck up. I don't want him left alone. You call them and wait, nobody's gonna think you're the shooter, asshole."

"All right, I'll wait, I'll wait."

Jack sped back to the Midnight Lounge. He was calm, his rage focused and burning pure. He muttered to himself. For once he did not care about money. He cared only for the cold comfort of vengeance.

Paddy knew he needed help and that there was only one place left to turn. He called the man named John Brick, the union enforcer. They had worked together on a contractor problem several years before. Paddy told him about Billy, and Brick agreed they should meet right away. Paddy drove north with abandon. He parked on Katonah Avenue in Woodlawn and ducked into Hanlon's Bar. He hesitated, letting his eyes adjust to the cool darkness. Lenny Coyle waved to him from a back table, where he sat with three men. As he approached, Paddy realized with a start that one of the men with his back to the door was his grandfather. He stopped cold and looked at John Brick, a hand indicating JP's back. Brick looked up at him and said, "Sit down. He's got a right to be here. I called him. He knows everything."

As JP stood and walked to him, Paddy stiffened, unsure of how to react. His throat tightened. He expected recrimination, blame. It was their first face-to-face encounter since his grandmother's funeral, four years before. Instead of harshness, his grandfather merely grabbed him by the shoulder and said, "Come, sit with us."

Paddy nodded and followed him to the table.

John Brick leaned toward Paddy. "The Italians have dropped it. It's just Jack Tierney. We set the record straight. Convinced them that this was our problem." Brick spoke in hushed tones. They huddled over cold beers.

Paddy considered his grandfather and hesitated. But there was no time to waste. He said, "I gotta take him out. The other guys in our crew, I know for sure there is no way they'll keep this up if Jack is gone. I was hoping you can help me. I need some explosives. I want to start with his club, flush him out."

Brick looked at Paddy, then turned to Eamon Cudahy, the fifth man at the table. "You put something together on this?"

"I don't want anything messy, anyone else hurt," Paddy said.

Cudahy said nothing; he simply nodded in affirmation.

Brick said, "When?"

Paddy looked at them. "Tonight? I don't think we have much time."

A group of strikers came in and stacked their picket signs in the corner by the jukebox. They sat heavily at the bar.

Cudahy glanced at them, then returned his focus to Paddy. "I need to make a call, but it shouldn't be a problem. We had something in the works already. Only thing is, someone's got to get close now. Might be a bit risky."

"I'll handle that," Paddy said.

"This doesn't have to be a suicide mission. I mean, a little time, maybe we can work something out," Brick said.

Paddy shook his head. "You don't know Jack like I do. He's not like the Italians—they'll listen to reason. Jack doesn't work that way." Paddy paused for a minute and looked at the men gathered around. He turned to his grandfather, surprised at the fierceness in his eyes. "I just whacked his brother. He won't stop till he gets me. Or I get him. There won't be any compromise this time."

"Jesus," JP said.

"All right," Lenny said. "Let's meet at seven—the diner down on Eleventh Avenue?"

Paddy turned and looked JP in the face. He was about to apologize, offer some explanation, mitigation, but JP grabbed him by the wrist and said, "What's done is done. Just bring your brother home, Patrick."

Paddy put his arms around his grandfather and said, "I will."

He shook hands with Eamon, Lenny, and John Brick. He turned back to his grandfather and said, "Need a lift?"

"Yes, I do."

They walked out of the bar, into the bright sunshine of Katonah Avenue. Paddy stopped to let an old woman pass and ducked into his car. It struck him that tomorrow the world would go on much the same as today. The sun would shine and old women would make their way home from the grocery. Only, he might not be around to see it. This did not matter much to him, as long as his brother was. He started his car and pulled away from the curb.

They turned down Webster Avenue in silence. Paddy felt a level of comfort with his grandfather that he had not expected. He went to turn on the radio, but JP said, "It's been far too long for us not to be talking to each other, Patrick."

Paddy nodded his head, unsure of how to respond.

"There were some things in my life, things I've done. Maybe we're not so different after all."

Paddy looked across the front seat at JP, who sat staring straight ahead. He wondered how much it had taken his grandfather to say as much as that. He pulled to the curb at Briody's. JP put his hand on the door handle and said, "Call me as soon as you get Billy." Paddy watched as he walked away and disappeared into the bar. He put the car in gear and drove directly back to Hell's Kitchen.

. . .

Billy did not realize he had drifted off again. Now he was awake, heard them coming, then suddenly the room was bright, the light like a blow. Hands grabbed him from behind and pulled him upright. He knew if they let him go he would surely topple. They turned him. It was Jack Tierney again and the big one, the one who had hit him in the car. The one who smelled of cheap cologne.

Tierney reached up and ripped the tape from Billy's mouth. Billy drank the air deeply, trying to clear his mind. "Untie him." Riordan went behind Billy with a knife and released his hands. Billy raised them. The left hand was burned swollen and purple, but the right seemed to be in working order, the blood coming back into it now.

"I gotta piss."

Tierney looked at him. "Take him over the corner, help him out."

Billy, his feet still bound, was led, hopping, over to the wall by Riordan. At first he could not release the stream, but finally it came. Billy held his head back. When he looked down, he saw that blood had darkened his urine. It looked like he was pissing grape juice. He groaned and was suddenly chilled. Riordan took him back to Tierney.

"You're outta luck, schoolboy. I was really thinking about cutting you loose, I got ahold of your fucking brother. But I just find out he paid my little brother a visit last night, shot him full of holes. That makes me very unhappy. So this is it—you're still bait, that ain't changed. But when I'm done with that fucking punch-drunk piece-a-shit brother of yours, I'm gonna strangle you, nice and slow." Tierney tightened his hands around Billy's throat, then he let go and stepped back. Billy gasped for air. Tierney turned to Riordan. "Tie him to the chair, put some more of that tape on his mouth. We'll finish him later. Maybe I'll make his scumbag brother watch it happen."

They left him and closed the door. Billy found it difficult to care anymore.

Joe Harkness felt his world collapsing around him. He sat in his office, flushed from nervousness and bourbon, his small hand wrapped around the neck of a Jack Daniel's bottle. He was hot in the chilled room. Two NYPD detectives had just left him. They'd spent half an hour in his office, toying with him in that wiseass New York way they all seemed to have, alluding to things, hinting that they knew more than they did, trying to get him to blunder his way toward self-incrimination. Like a fool, he had let them in in the first place. From now on he would heed his attorneys.

The union dogged his every step, the Italians no longer wanted to deal with him, Eliot was not returning his calls. There were picket lines everywhere he turned—his apartment, his office, even his house in Ossining. The militant sonsabitches even had coal miners protesting at the family farm in Virginia, cursing his wife and kids.

Now, as he sat, three hundred replacement miners were on buses rolling toward New York. He had to decide on that pronto. Was he ready to escalate this thing? Could he fold and save any face at all?

"Joanne, get my lawyers in here."

"Which ones, Mr. Harkness?"

"Every damn one of them."

He poured another bourbon, thinking maybe it was time for a trip to the islands, let this thing sort itself out in his absence. He was trying to decide between Antigua and Saint Martin, when the door flew open. A horde of G-men, yelling about a racketeering indictment, handcuffed him and led him through the outer office. Cameras, movie and still, lined the hallway to the elevators. Bright lights washed him in an angry glow. He stared at the floor and felt a powerful need to urinate.

Paddy slid out of the booth. Leaning over the table, he said, "Whatever happens, thanks." Lenny watched as Paddy walked away. He had seen that look before. In Korea. The look said, I know I might not come back, but it doesn't matter. He saw Paddy roll his shoulders once, like a fighter after bouncing into the ring, and disappear out onto the streets of Hell's Kitchen, carrying a gym bag full of explosives. Lenny shook his head. It all seemed such a waste.

Paddy circled the block twice. Jack's car was not to be found. He parked halfway up the block and watched the Midnight Lounge. Night was coming over the neighborhood. The streets were experiencing a dinnertime lull. A cool wind was sweeping down from Canada. People bent into this unexpected breeze.

Paddy kept his eye on the bar while he readied his weapons. He took his U.S. Army issue .45 from under the front seat, chambered a round, and slid it into his shoulder holster. The gun weighed almost three pounds. He took the Beretta .32, flipped the safety off, and slid it between his belt and his stomach. Beside him on the seat was the gym bag containing the explosive device he got from the sandhogs. He had turned down their offer for further assistance. This fight was all his now.

He watched a black Chrysler pull to the curb. Bobby Riordan got out, looked around, and ducked into the bar. Paddy gave him five minutes to get settled in the back room, then he took the bag and left the car, crossing the street. As he pulled open the bar door, he drew the .32 from his waistband. Before the door closed behind him he shot Sully high in the chest. The bartender fell backward and then to the floor, a cascade of liquor bottles raining down upon him. The half-dozen patrons, all old men, sat stunned, motionless.

Paddy put the bag down by the wall. He motioned the drinkers out the door. He replaced the .32 and withdrew the .45. He positioned himself by the door to the back room. Riordan emerged, gun in hand, as the patrons scurried out the front door. Paddy wanted to laugh. Those departing had probably not moved so swiftly since a pier brawl in the fifties.

He smacked the .45 across the side of Riordan's skull. This did not have the desired effect. Riordan yelled and staggered to his left, but he stayed on his feet. He turned as blood started to spill from the wound. He went to raise his gun, and Paddy shot him in the knee. The blast from the .45 was thunderous in the confines of the Midnight Lounge. Paddy's ears rang. Riordan went down in a sitting position, a look of angry surprise on his face. Paddy kicked the gun out of his hand, then went and locked the front door.

He looked over the bar. Sully lay helpless, still alive. Paddy ripped the phone off the wall, turned his attention to Riordan. He bent over the lumbering enforcer, lifting his chin with the barrel of the .45.

"That looks bad, Bobby. Looks like I hit an artery." Paddy watched the rapidly accumulating pool of blood as it spread out from beneath Riordan. He shifted to his side to avoid it. "Where's my brother?"

Riordan managed a smirk. "Fuck you."

"No, Bobby. This is where you got it all backward, you stupid fuck. It's fuck *you*, Bobby." Paddy rammed the pistol into Riordan's mouth, shearing off the enforcer's front teeth. He pushed the barrel to the back of Riordan's throat. "Where's my brother, you piece of shit? You better tell me, Bobby. I ain't fucking around with you." He pulled the gun out and rapped Riordan across the head, too hard. He slumped over, unconscious. Shit.

Paddy went behind the bar. He grabbed the first-aid kit and slapped it on the bar. He pulled out Band-Aids, gauze, peroxide, threw it all aside. He found the smelling salts. Reaching beneath the bar, he took out the machete hidden there. Sully whimpered. "Paddy, please. Help me."

"Help you? You know where my brother is?" He kicked him savagely in the ribs. "That help?"

He went back to Riordan. He took the enforcer's belt off and tightened it, tourniquet fashion, above his wound. He broke open the smelling salts and waved the vial under Riordan's nose. His head snapped back, his eyes popped open, a stunned look on his face.

"There you go, Bobby. Last chance. Where is he?"

Riordan stared at him. Nothing. The loyal foot soldier till the end. We'll see, Paddy thought. He spread Riordan's left hand on the floor, raised the machete, and hacked off the tops of his four fingers. Riordan let out a bellow and grabbed Paddy with his good hand. He tried to pull him close and bite him with what were left of his teeth. Paddy smashed him in the throat with his elbow. Riordan let go. Paddy stood.

"I'm gonna whittle you down to nothing, you fuck. Where is he?" Paddy kicked him hard three times. He bent down and grabbed a handful of Riordan's hair. For the first time in his life, he saw something human in Riordan's eyes. He saw fear.

Riordan nodded his head. Paddy leaned a little closer.

"Forty-first," he managed to say.

"There, Bobby. That didn't need to be so hard."

Riordan nodded. Paddy pulled the machete blade across Riordan's throat, giving him the wide smile in death that he never had in life.

He took the C-4 out of his bag and set the device on the bar. Sully moaned. "Oh, shit. I forgot about you, Sully. I'm sorry." Paddy leaned over the bar and shot him in the balls.

"See you in hell, asshole."

He took out the remote and walked into the night air. He hit the switch. It would give him thirty seconds. He crossed to his car. There was a *whomph,* and the two small windows collapsed, almost politely, their glass tinkling to the concrete. Smoke erupted from the door. Paddy drove off as sirens began to wail.

Jack drove. He had the college boy, or what was left of him, in the trunk. When Riordan did not show up on time, he had dragged the kid out by himself and loaded him in the car. Now, as he drove down the avenue, he wondered what had happened to Riordan. There was no answer at the Lounge. He sensed something had gone badly. When he came upon the smoldering ruins of his headquarters, he hunkered down in the seat and drove by. There was a horde of cops, reporters, the yellow blare of crime scene tape. He saw body bags being loaded into coroner's vans. Law enforcement types stood idle. It appeared there were no survivors.

He cursed. That fucking Paddy Adare was laying Jack's empire to waste. He drove several blocks and pulled over. He got out and opened the trunk. Now he might need the college kid alive. He reached in and felt for a pulse. It was stronger than he'd expected. Jack punched Billy twice and slammed the lid.

He needed to come up with a plan, bait the trap. He felt as he had on patrol in Nam. It was always in those moments when things were darkest, when he was beyond fear, beyond the weak constraints of physical discomfort, that he was at his best. His survival was on the line. It was time to reel Paddy Adare in, put an end to his assault—to fuck him where he breathed.

He thought of his own dead brother. He had not yet told his mother. There would be keening, hysterics, blame slapped squarely on his shoulders. Her hot, rotten breath in his face. There would not be easy forgiveness. With all his brother's troubles, all his shortcomings, Terry was still their mother's favorite. The baby, her baby. Jack got back in the car. He started the motor and sat, enjoying the smell of new leather. The car was a class act. The best Detroit had to offer, sleek weightiness and power. A beast built for the open highway. An American car. Plenty of trunk room, he thought, and laughed.

Paddy turned onto Forty-first Street and made his way down the block, pulling up the car several buildings before the tenement. The place held special dark meaning for the Tierney crew. It was where Jack had performed some of his most twisted acts. He jokingly referred to it as the "ball-peen basement," his favorite instrument of mayhem and hurt being that style of hammer, which he wielded with precision, always leaving the kill shot to the head for when it was far too late to have much meaning: when his victims had been reduced to blobs of pulverized meat. Paddy got out of the car. A homeless man mumbled across the street. The wind was stronger here, close to the river. It was an autumn gust, sweeping down across the chilled expanse of the Great Lakes to announce the death of a season.

He made his way toward the abandoned building, the heavy .45 in his hand. He pressed the gun to his thigh. Riordan's blood had thickened on him, its smell sharp. Paddy was focused, alert. He knew his brother had little time left.

Mary Moy stood to the side as the stretcher was wheeled past her. The attendant cursed as it snagged on the threshold of the Midnight Lounge. He shoved, and the body bag slid partly off the gurney. His partner said, "Yo. Easy does it, man. I don't like the stink no better than you." The first attendant retched and righted the corpse, tightening the straps. Mary walked a few feet away and watched as Patrick Cullen came upon the scene. He wore his gold detective shield around his neck and sipped a diet Coke. Despite the chill, he was dressed in shirtsleeves and seemed flushed. The expanse of his belly tested the construction of his shirt. Two uniformed cops stepped aside to let him pass.

He looked past Mary to the smoking husk of the Midnight Lounge. He nodded as if impressed. "Looks like somebody is cutting into your collars, Agent."

Mary Moy shrugged. She was tired and chilled. It had been a long day, and she wanted to get home and rest. Wrap herself around her husband, imbibe some hot tea, anticipate her maternity leave. Instead she was surveying the detritus of an internecine mob war. She wondered for a moment if her investigation had precipitated this. She sighed. It was not something she wanted to consider.

"So I see. Any suggestions, bright ideas, how we put an end to this?" She indicated the ruins behind her.

The crowd that had gathered, with great expectations of witnessing slaughter, began to disperse. No one seemed to be dressed for the change in the weather. They bobbed up and down to keep warm. Beyond the police line, someone said, "It ain't about shit, 'cept some fuckin' body bags."

Cullen said, "It's down to Adare and Tierney, by my accounting. It'll play itself out. One of them left standing for us, the other"—he pointed at a body bag—"gift-wrapped in plastic. A great savings to the taxpayer." He took Mary by the arm and led her toward the street.

"Any idea who we'll have the pleasure of putting on trial?"

"Agent, it's hard to say. After seeing this, I might lean toward Adare. This ain't his style, though. Means he's gone over the edge, for whatever reason. It's been a long time since Tierney had to fight his own battles. Alla same, he don't lack for cunning."

They stood and watched as the firefighters reopened the street to traffic. There was much honking and cursing. The firemen retaliated with obscene gestures. Mary Moy watched this commotion. The smell of burned flesh was making her queasy. She worried that all this violence was bad for her unborn child. "Any way we can head it off? Before someone innocent gets caught in the crossfire?"

Cullen took in a deep breath. He almost seemed to be enjoying the smell. He exhaled and said, "We gotta try, right? But between you and me, why bother? Let them do it for us. It's a lot easier that way. Besides"—Cullen nodded toward her swollen midsection—"ain't it about time to take care of some real business? Maybe we should leave these mutts to sort themselves out." Cullen looked off down the block. " 'Cause you keep it up, and crap like this"—he jabbed a thumb over his shoulder—"it gets to where it has the same effect on you as a family barbecue."

Mary Moy watched him. It seemed as if he was trying to revisit a time when scenes like this had still been horrific to him. He turned back to her and waved in dismissal. "Ah, what the Christ. Come on, I'll walk you to your car. The neighborhood's gone to shit."

Jack Tierney, aware he was being routed by a lone, washed-up fighter, considered dispatching a variety of ethnic hit squads. He could send Italians, Dominicans, Puerto Ricans, Chinese even. A bounty might be placed. Bring me the head of that douchebag. But no, this one he wanted himself. Besides, the kid in the trunk was his ace in the hole. Adare would come after him hard and sloppy. Jack would be waiting. He dropped a quarter in a pay phone and let Adare know exactly where he was going to be. And when.

Paddy decided to forsake caution and go for a frontal assault. Time was crucial, and he doubted Jack had any backup. He walked back to the corner and called the number Cullen had given him. He told the switchboard operator his name and gave the address. If anyone was left alive, he wanted Cullen to be there to pull Billy out.

Back down the block, there was no sign of Jack's car. Paddy snuck down the alley between the two buildings, picking his way through the rubbish: broken bottles and bricks, a soggy busted-out mattress, used condoms, the glitter of crack vials. The alley smelled of piss and the shit of the stray dogs that roamed up from the railyards. Somewhere, back on the block, a man cursed loudly in Spanish. When Paddy came upon the back door, it was ajar. Though sensing no one was there, Paddy held the pistol out before him. He sneaked down the stairs and crouched. Swinging into the basement, staying low, he pressed his back against the wall. His heart beat in his ears, the sound seeming to drown out all others. But then he heard a shuffling, a curse. He was blind in the dimness of the basement.

"Billy, that you?"

Someone grunted. A shape, barely discernible, moved toward him through the blackness.

Knowing it was not Billy, he did not hesitate. He aimed at the form approaching him and squeezed off a round. There was muzzle flash, and the shadow jumped backward and collapsed in a heap. Paddy scurried toward him and produced a lighter. Its flame lit up the staring eyes of a dead homeless man. The place had a thick stench. It smelled of rot. He surveyed the room and found the .32 Beretta he had given Billy. He backed out quickly and hit his car, running.

Jack pulled his new Caddy onto a darkened job site on the bank of the Hudson River. He had tried unsuccessfully to contact some of his remaining crew members and arrange a posse to ambush Adare. They had become scarce. After he finished off Adare, there would be the little matter of housecleaning. Swift and bloody lessons taught.

The site was fenced in. Beyond the fence, the skeleton of a seventeen-story condominium rose starkly against the night sky. The first three concrete floors had been poured when a scandal broke and all work was halted. There were allegations of bribes, shady dealings, fraudulent environmental impact statements. A commissioner committed suicide on the eve of his testimony. A stable Long Island family was shattered. Rumors suggested the man was heavily indebted to Jack Tierney's gambling operation. The building was dubbed Rivergate by the tabloids. Litigation ensued. The project was in legal limbo.

Jack flashed his headlights, and the night watchman roused himself from his guard shack. He came to the fence with a nightstick in his hand and annoyance on his face. He shielded his eyes from the glare of the headlights.

"What the fuck?"

Jack shut off his lights and stepped from the car, letting the guard see him. Like most people employed on neighborhood sites, he owed his job to Jack Tierney.

"Oh, sorry, Mr. Tierney. I had no idea." He fumbled for his keys and undid the padlock holding the gate shut. He pulled it open wide and placed a stone against it to hold it open. "Can I do something for you, Mr. Tierney?"

Jack regarded him. He knew the kid from somewhere but could not place him. What he was sure of was that he feared the Tierney name enough to do what he was told. "Yeah. Let me pull in. I need a hand with something."

Jack swung the car through the gate and parked behind the plywood guard shack. He popped a breath mint in his mouth and climbed out of his vehicle. The watchman pulled the gate closed behind him. Jack said, "Leave it unlocked. Comere."

The guard came over and met Jack at the rear of the Caddy. Jack put the key in the trunk lock and said, "You keep your mouth shut?"

The watchman took a breath. He appeared nervous, yet eager to please. "Yeah, Mr. Tierney. I ain't no rat. Whatever you need."

Jack smiled. He wanted the kid to trust him. "Good. I need someone—you"—Jack patted him on the back, his buddy now—"to help me out. What's your name?"

"John. John McDermott. Friends call me Johnny Mac."

"Good, Johnny Mac. Let's go." Jack turned the key and popped the trunk. He grabbed the guard by the arm and pulled him in for a look at his captive. The guard winced but did not avert his gaze. He simply said, "Ouch."

"You do the right thing here, I'll take care of you. Here, get his legs. I'll take his arms."

Paddy ran up the stairs to his apartment. He changed quickly and put his bloodstained clothes in a Hefty bag. He had wiped down the .45 and dumped it in a sewer. He checked the .32 he had found in the basement. One bullet was missing. He wondered what end of it Billy had been on. Paddy had decided to drive to Westchester and visit some hell on Jack's family. Maybe come to a trade-off. He washed his face and looked in the bathroom mirror. He barely recognized himself. His hair was wild, his pupils were wide with crazed energy. He turned the water to cold and ran handfuls of it through his hair. His mouth tasted like burning metal. He swigged some Listerine and made for the door. On the way out, he noticed the answering machine light blinking. It seemed to glow like another sun. He punched the Play button. "Rivergate. Tonight, asshole. Bring my fucking money."

Paddy took his jacket and the .32. This time he did not leave Cullen a message.

"You believe this crap?" Patrick Cullen asked Mary Moy. They were walking back to their cars when his beeper went off. "Never a dull goddamn moment." He reached beneath his belly and pulled the offending gadget off his belt. In his meaty hand, it looked like a toy version of the real thing. He hit the button and squinted. "Christ. Hang on a second, Agent. We might have something here." He walked to a pay phone. A poorly dressed man in his twenties was leaning into the phone, talking intently. He gestured wildly with his hands, as if the person he was talking to might be able to read his body language, glean some import not evident in his words. Cullen reached over his head and pushed the receiver hook down. The man turned to confront him and stared into Cullen's chest, the badge hanging before his eyes. "Police business. Beat it, you fucking mutt." The man was about to register a complaint, but Cullen brushed him aside with a swift backhand. Mary Moy rolled her eyes. Cullen made a quick phone call and came back.

"Bingo. Adare left a location. Let's swing by?"

Mary put a hand on her stomach, shrugged, and said, "Why not?"

When they rolled up on the scene, several patrol cars were parked at angles to the curb. Cullen turned to Mary Moy. "Lemme take a quick look."

He waved over a uniform. "What's up?"

"One DOA. Some homeless guy."

"Homeless?"

"Yeah, some old piss bum. Looks like he got a heavy round in the chest, blew out half his back."

"One guy?"

"You got it."

Cullen ducked back in the car. "That's weird."

"Hey, Mr. Tierney. That wasn't too bad." The guard was breathing heavily from the effort of carrying the unconscious Billy Adare up two flights of broken stairs. There was blood on his face from where he had wiped the sweat off. Jack Tierney waited till he could speak without gasping. Christ, he was getting out of shape. After this he'd hit the weights, some jogging. Get his edge back.

Jack tried to figure this McDermott out. Where did he know the kid from? He was somebody's brother or son. He considered using him against Paddy, then thought better of it. The kid could turn out utterly useless, cause a problem. Carrying a body was one thing, doing battle against a worthy foe something else entirely. "Do me a favor? Grab my jacket out of the car."

"Sure. No problem, Mr. T."

Mr. T? What, all of a sudden they're pals? That settled it. Jack figured McDermott had served his purpose. As soon as he turned his back, Jack raised the pistol and shot him behind the ear. The bullet took off the top of his head but caught him at a glancing angle. The watchman did a little jig and fell to the concrete slab, moaning. Jack Tierney entertained the idea that this was just not one of his better days. He cursed and pressed the muzzle to the watchman's head. He pulled the trigger. *Click.* Nothing. Yet it was the loudest sound Jack Tierney had ever heard. "Fucking cock fucking sucker." He grabbed the dying McDermott by his sweatshirt and dragged him to the edge of the floor. He stood straight and used his right foot to nudge him into the abyss. The watchman fell soundlessly into the Hudson and was borne away by the cruel tide.

Jack walked back to the middle of the floor. He realized where he knew the kid from. Jack had worked for his father once after coming home from the war. Joe McDermott, a teamster boss. Nice guy, if Jack remembered right.

He crouched and squeezed the trigger again. *Click.* Shit. He took out his handkerchief and draped it on the floor. Adare's brother moaned behind him. He disassembled his pistol by feel. It was something you learned to do every day in Nam. He had seen men die because they were too lazy to clean their weapons regularly. He wondered how that might have felt. A squad of black-toothed gooks charging from the tree line, and you pull the trigger and—nothing. To know you were dying because you were a lazy, undisciplined goatfucker. He put the pistol back together, his hands steady as steel. He pointed it toward the high-rises of midtown. *Click.*

He considered running, taking the time to regroup. But he knew he could not leave the bait behind. He contemplated tossing the kid in after the watchman. It was then that he saw the sweep of Paddy's headlights. He bent and dragged Billy Adare to the middle of the floor. The kid began to stir. Jack hoisted a piece of rebar and climbed atop a packing crate. He tightened his grip on the steel like a power hitter and waited. He'd been outgunned before and survived.

Paddy screeched to a halt at the fence enclosing Rivergate. He took the pistol from the passenger seat and slid out of his car. Pausing for a minute, he shielded himself behind the fender. The building's silent steel frame loomed above him. Behind it, a tugboat pushed a bulky string of barges up the Hudson. Lights played on the water. The river was all dark turbulence.

Paddy knew the layout of the structure. He had visited the site several times before work was halted. There were stairways at all four corners. Until he closed the ground between his car and the base of the building, he would be exposed.

He ran on an angle to the gate, expecting the scream of bullets. But there was only the lost howl of the river wind. He slid through the narrow opening in the gate and dashed under the protection of the floor, proceeding on instinct now, his thought processes shut down. He made directly for the northwest stairway. He moved with both speed and caution, picking his way through the construction debris scattered about the site.

Pausing briefly at the bottom of the stairs, he listened, then he climbed past two landings to the next floor. The second floor was wide open, clear of any material. His breaths were short and sharp. He sensed that Jack Tierney and Billy were just above him.

He ascended to one landing, then, at the next, lowered himself to the stairs. He crawled up on his elbows and knees and peered at the concrete floor at eye level. There were some crates, a pair of upended wheelbarrows, a scattering of concrete chunks and sawed-off rebar. Twenty feet from his face, his brother lay.

Jack kept as still as he could, his weapon at the ready. He detected movement on the stairway behind him. Aware he had only one opportunity, he waited to pounce.

Paddy knew there was no time to waste. He moved, swinging the gun in a wide arc, closing the gap to his brother. As he knelt over Billy, for a moment he forgot about Jack. He saw Billy's condition and a great scream of remorse rose from his belly. Feeling anguish and guilt, he wanted Jack Tierney's blood. He heard a movement, and as he turned, Jack Tierney came down upon him. The blow from the rebar drove him to the ground, his collarbone snapped. The gun flopped from his hand, skipped across the floor, and discharged. He looked up and saw Jack raise the rebar over his head like a battle-ax. Paddy rolled to his good shoulder and bounced to his feet. Jack came by him, missing with a wild swing. Paddy delivered three short, sharp left hooks to Jack's side, snapping each punch. Tierney groaned and struck out with the rebar as he toppled. The metal caught Paddy in the temple, chipping bone and ripping open a bloody gash. He staggered after Tierney and kicked at him wildly, landing glancing blows. Tierney rolled on his side and absorbed the last kick. He grabbed Paddy's leg and yanked him off his feet. He sank his teeth into the meat of Paddy's newly healed calf.

Billy heard a scream and opened his eyes. He watched what at first to him was merely a dream, some dark vision from his unconscious. His dreams had been feverish, twisted images of places devoid of hope. This scene was more vivid: his brother and Jack Tierney engaged in an epic battle. They rolled and thrashed on the floor like two beasts intent on destruction. Billy, his head against the floor, could not tell from the tangle of blows what leg or fist belonged to whom. The fight possessed a fury that seemed born in the fires of hell. He wondered for a moment why they were fighting. Then, feeling a deep chill, he realized that he was awake. The two adversaries were on their feet again, backlit by the lights of the city. Through the haze, Billy noticed something in the near distance. It was a pistol.

Paddy Adare knew he was beaten. He lay, broken, on his back, as Jack Tierney stood above him, poised for the kill. He willed himself to move, but it was beyond him. He was dead. This knowledge did not trouble him. But the thought that he could not save his brother opened a deep and terrible chasm within him. He moaned with despair and awaited the last blow. He saw the leer of triumph in Tierney's eyes. Paddy Adare knew that the one fight in his life he truly needed to win was lost.

Billy pulled himself unnoticed across the floor to the gun. He blocked out the violence and poured his concentration onto the pistol. It was the only way he could go on. After what seemed a very long time, he had the gun in his hand. It felt cold but familiar. He could no longer see his brother. He saw only Jack Tierney, standing against the backdrop of the city, a weapon on high. Billy steadied himself and squeezed.

The first bullet caught Jack Tierney high in the chest. He was just starting the final downswing with the piece of bloody rebar. The bullet stopped his momentum, and instead of a vicious final stroke, he stumbled into a lazy swing that came down wide around his own body. The rebar clanked harmlessly to the floor beside him. He looked puzzled for a moment, and then came a fusillade. He danced away from his victims as a torrent of lead ripped the life from his body. He retreated until his feet ran out of concrete and he pitched backward into space.

"Go figure," Cullen said. He drove away from the murder scene on Forty-first Street. He caught a light on Twelfth Avenue and cursed. He looked casually to his left. "Holy shit."

"What's up?" Mary Moy snapped to attention. She had been dozing off.

"That, if I ain't mistaken, is Paddy Adare's car." Cullen pointed out an empty black car pulled up to a construction site at the river. Its door was open, the headlights were still on. Cullen made a hard left, cutting across traffic. He pulled to a stop alongside the Monte Carlo.

They got out of Cullen's car and heard the tinny, small-caliber shots, almost lost in the wind. They ducked and looked up, to see Jack Tierney descending, to land impaled on rebar, two pieces of steel sticking up through his dead hulk. Mary winced. The sound had not been pleasant. She walked over to Tierney's corpse, pressed his eyes closed.

"Come on." Cullen, behind her, holstered his pistol. "Let's see what we got here."

They made their way to the third floor.

"Adare?"

There was silence. The two forms lay motionless. Cullen checked them both for signs of life. He took the pistol from Billy's hand. "I ain't mistaken, this might be the fighter's brother. Jesus, we better get a meat wagon in here, get these two to Saint Clare's. They ain't looking too good."

That autumn the stock market fell with the leaves, and just as suddenly as they had appeared, the cranes were gone.

ACKNOWLEDGMENTS

Anyone who attempts to write a book, be it fact or fiction, will find that while you may sit down alone, you need lots of help to get it done. I am blessed with many friends.

First I want to thank Chickie Donohue, a master storyteller and the best of friends.

There are too many sandhogs to list. But I need to point out Buddy Krausa, who got me my first shifts. Without him this book would not have been possible. I'd also like to thank the past and present leadership of Tunnel Workers and Miners (Sandhogs) Local 147: Richie E. Fitzsimmons, Richie T. Fitzsimmons, and Ed McGuinness. There were a host of foremen who put me to work, including Joe McCloud, the Daly brothers, Pete Ward, the Duffy brothers, George Gluzak, Bobby Platt, Billy Selkirk, and Connie Mahoney. John Crean, Timmy Hickey, and Tony C. were always supportive. Donny of the Blasters, Drillrunners and Miners LIUNA Local 29 and Pat and Martin Walsh of LIUNA Boston sent me to work. Barry Feinstein and Joseph McDermott at the Teamsters union helped keep the wolf from the door.

Many people read this manuscript in various stages. Lis Guiney suffered the horrible mood swings of a writer and read passages four or five hundred times. Gigi Georges spent many hours turning it into something coherent. Their insight, dedication, and editorial assistance were invaluable. Jake McDermott, Diane Torres, Sean Reilly, Bill Clemens, Kirk Kelly, Nick Brown, Blanche Fallon O'Neil, Patty Kelly, Bill Mulrow, Mike Fernandez, Frank Shattuck, and Jim Phelps all offered suggestions and encouragement.

Veryln Klinkenborg made me believe I could write. Paul Elie seconded that. Shannon Ravenel pointed me to the door of my agent, Nat Sobel. He and his partner, Judith Weber, did not call the cops when I showed up and have become my friends as well as partners. They are blessed with a great staff: David Chestnut, Laura Nolan, and Sarah Jackson.

At Knopf I'd like to thank my editor, Sonny Mehta; his talented assistant, Janet Cameron; and Paul Bogaards, my publicist, as well as all the great people at Knopf. All writers should be so lucky.

Finally, I'd like to thank my family. Especially my brothers, Dennis and Kevin, and my mother, Catherine Lopez, née O'Connor—a girl from Alexander Avenue in the South Bronx who taught me to read and I guess started all this.

A NOTE ON THE TYPE

This book was set in Caledonia, a face designed by William Addison Dwiggins (1880–1956) for the Mergenthaler Linotype Company in 1939. It belongs to the family of types referred to by printers as "modern," a term used to mark the change in type styles that occurred around 1800. Caledonia was inspired by the Scotch types cast by the Glasgow typefounders Alexander Wilson & Sons circa 1833. However, there is a calligraphic quality about Caledonia that is completely lacking in the Wilson types.

Dwiggins referred to an even earlier typeface for this "liveliness of action"—one cut around 1790 by William Martin for the printer William Bulmer. Caledonia has more weight than the Martin letters, and the bottom finishing strokes of the letters are cut straight across, without brackets, to make sharp angles with the upright stems, thus giving a modern-face appearance.

W. A. Dwiggins began his association with the Mergenthaler Linotype Company in 1929, and over the next twenty-seven years he designed a number of book types, the most interesting of which are Metro, Electra, Caledonia, Eldorado, and Falcon.

Composed by ComCom, an R. R. Donnelley & Sons Company,
Allentown, Pennsylvania
Printed and bound by Berryville Graphics,
Berryville, Virginia
Designed by Virginia Tan